IN THE ENCHANTER'S CASTLE

To win through to the inner chamber where the jewel lay, Jill needed the guard's key. And there was only one way to get it. She drew her dagger and struck swiftly.

The guard cried out and collapsed. She was sickened. She had killed an innocent man to save her world . . .

She stooped for the key. The body twisted and began to turn black; the eyes glowed a deep red; the face distorted into something evil and inhuman . . .

The creature grabbed her, screaming horribly. She brought the sword down on the arm that clutched her, and it was neatly severed—but its grip tightened all the more.

It was a gargoyle, she realized. And it could not be killed . . . except in a very special way . . .

And the Devil Will Drag You Under

A novel by

Jack L. Chalker

A Del Rey Book

BALLANTINE BOOKS • NEW YORK

For my father, Lloyd Allen Chalker, Sr., who will never read it, and probably wouldn't like it anyway, and for my mother, Nancy Hopkins Chalker, who will but might not like it, in minor payment for letting a crazy kid like me have such weird habits and coming out a writer. No one who enjoys my books will ever know the contributions we all owe these two people.

Contents

And the Devil Will
Drag You Under

Main Line +2076

WHEN THE END OF THE WORLD IS NEAR, SPEND THE
remaining time in a bar.

The little man looked out the slightly frosted windows of the bar and scowled. Although it was closer
to noon than to evening time, it was dark out there,
and there was a reddish color that made the scene
more ominous. The frosting twisted, distorted, and bent
the coloration, making it a deep, sparkling red wine.

That reminded the little man of what he had started
out to do, and he turned back to the bar itself. "Another double," he ordered, his voice high and raspy,
with a trace of accent that seemed to belong vaguely
to Europe but to no particular language.

The double arrived and he surveyed it critically,
sniffed at it, then started to sip. He looked around at
the others in the bar.

Not many. The bar was near the University, but
there were no classes now, hadn't been since The
Accident. The only people still around these days
were the ones working on research projects, trying
desperately to find some way to stop or reverse what
was happening, or, in the worst case, to cope with the
terror that was rapidly approaching—too rapidly, the
little man knew. Some might survive, at least for a
time. Some, but only a very few.

And only for a time.

Those others here—these few. He looked at them
carefully. A couple of old drunks; several tired-looking
middle-aged men and women, some in lab whites, sitting, not talking, trying to take some sort of break
from nonstop work before they dropped. They'd be

sleeping now, he knew, but for the fact that they were too tired to do even that.

Who could sleep now, anyway? he reflected.

None of them fit, though. None were what he wanted, what he had to have. That disturbed him; he had been sending the summons out for days now, and there had been little or no response. People who would do, who would fulfill his needs, *were* about here, somewhere. He could feel them, sense their auras—not perfect, of course, but adequate.

He sighed, drained the double, and fumbled in his pocket. From it he brought a small object that seemed to blaze with a life of its own, a large precious jewel of absolute precision.

He put it in front of him on the bar and stared at it hard, stroking it with his right hand as if caressing a loved pet. The barman glanced over, looked curiously at the thing and the equally odd little man, and started to go over to him.

The man felt it, felt the disturbance. He slowly took his eyes off the gleaming jewel and stared at the bartender. The curious man suddenly had an odd expression on his face, then turned to continue wiping the glasses. The little man returned to concentrating on the jewel.

His mind went out. Yes, he could feel them, Yin and Yang, male and female. Close by, so close, yet not here, not in proximity. He concentrated hard on them, locked in on them, called them hither.

Not perfect, no, but they would do. They would do —if they would just come to him.

A terrible, cold wind was sweeping through the streets of Reno, Nevada. The woman shivered and pulled her coat closer, trying to ward off some of the icy effects. It didn't help much.

She shouldn't be out in this, she knew. She shouldn't be anywhere near this place—and she didn't know why she was here now, or where she was going, either, yet she kept walking, kept fighting the wind and the cold, barely looking where she was going.

Her mind seemed fogged, slightly confused. She had

resolved to end it by the sea, with the Pacific now lapping at the Sierra Nevada, and had prepared for it— yet she was here, in Reno, a mountainous desert that no longer had much of a purpose. Most of the people were gone, or huddling inside, or praying in churches for some sort of deliverance. Although she'd never been religious, she had considered joining them at the last. With all other hope gone, the church was the only thing left to cling to.

That was what she had started out to do, out from the fairly comfortable room in a now-deserted motel, out to find a nearby church.

And yet, now the church didn't seem so important any more. Only walking, making her way through the byways and back alleys of this low and spread-out city, going somewhere, it seemed, but she had no idea where. Her legs seemed to have a mind of their own.

The only traffic left now was some military vehicles making their way along streets where only the howls of lonely and deserted animals were heard and an occasional rat would scamper.

She rounded a corner and suddenly felt the full force of the strong wind; it bit into her, and she lowered her head to try to protect her face from the new blast.

She wished she knew where she was going, and why.

He was a strong, strikingly handsome man dressed much like a lumberjack. He, too, had no idea why he was here. He had been going to New Zealand, he recalled. That was where they said the best chance would be. He had been ready to go, had gotten a corporate jet authorized, and gotten into his fancy sports car in Denver for a ride out to the airport.

But he hadn't gone to the airport, a short distance away. He had continued, as if in a dream, driving all-out like a maniac for this place a day ago.

And now he found himself wandering the cold, wind-blown streets strewn with litter and garbage and the remains of civilization in which nobody cares any more. Wandering, still not knowing why.

Wind whipped and buffeted him, and he pulled up

his collar and wished idly that he'd thought to pack a ski mask. It was getting hard to see, like skiing without goggles.

He bumped into the woman before he saw her. It was a hard bump, and they both tumbled over and gave out oaths which, once composure returned, turned into mutual apologies.

Both were back on their feet so quickly that neither could offer the other assistance.

"Hey, look, I'm sorry," they both said at once, stopped, and laughed at their synchronisticity.

The woman suddenly stopped laughing and a strange look replaced that of mirth.

"You know," she said wonderingly, "that's the first time I've heard laughter since The Accident."

He was suddenly serious, too, and nodded for a moment. "I'm Mac Walters," he told her.

"Jill McCulloch," she responded.

He looked around. "Hey! It looks like that little bar is open over there! Let's get out of this crap and relax," he suggested, then added, "That is, unless you have something more important to do."

She chuckled dryly. "Does anybody these days? Lead on."

They quickly crossed and walked past the few abandoned storefronts down to the place. THE LIGHTHOUSE, the small sign announced.

A blast of warmth greeted them as they entered and shut the door behind them. Electricity was getting to be an intermittent rarity; to find a place such as this, with everything working and all looking so normal, was like finding the pot of gold at the end of the rainbow. It couldn't exist, not in these times, but it did. They didn't question it, just found an empty booth and sat down, exhausted, across from each other.

The barman spotted them. "What'll it be, folks?" he called.

"Double bourbon and water," Walters called back, then looked over at the woman just now getting out of her heavy fur-lined coat. *She is damned good-looking,* he thought.

"Scotch and water," she told him, and he relayed

the order to the barman. The drinks were there in less than two minutes; in the meantime they just sat there, more or less looking at each other.

She was small—no more than one hundred and sixty centimeters, maybe shorter—but she seemed exceptionally—solid? He struggled for a word. *Athletic,* he decided. Like a gymnast or a dancer. Her hair was cut short and seemed just right for her face, a sexy oval that seemed somehow almost perfectly childlike. *She has green eyes,* he thought suddenly.

While surveying, he was being surveyed. He was a *big* man, not much under two meters in height, but there was no fat. He was in excellent condition, and his ruggedly handsome face was complemented by a rich, full red beard and long but professionally styled matching hair.

And while they looked at each other, they were in turn being looked over by a strange-looking little man sitting on a bar stool.

The woman seemed to sense his intrusion and turned to look at him for a moment. He averted her gaze and turned back to his drink, but he had caught the look in her eyes. *Haunted eyes. Both of them. They know the score. They've given up hope.*

The song on the radio was over, and an announcer's voice was on.

"The massive flooding has pretty well wiped out the Midwest; the Great Plains are once again covered by a sea, as in prehistoric days," he told his rapidly dwindling listening audience. "Refugee shelters were established but the panic in recent days blocked the highways, and the massive distances involved were too great for most. Like those in most lowland plains areas, the people were trapped with no place to go."

Chalk one up for Reno, the little man thought smugly. No ocean was going to get between the Cascades and the Rockies, certainly not to this elevation.

He reached into his pocket for a cigarette, found an empty pack, and cursed under his breath. *Funny, these people,* he thought. Money was still important to them even when the world ended. He sighed, got up, and went over to the slot machine, then fumbled in his pockets. Finally his hand seized on a quarter, his last. He put it in the machine, pulled the handle, and didn't even bother to look at the spinning wheels. There was a *chunk, chunk, chunk* of tumblers falling into locked places; it came up three bars and clinked ten quarters into the little tray. He scooped them up mechanically, went over to the cigarette machine, and fed four of them in.

It suddenly occurred to him that he could have done that with the cigarette machine and nobody would have cared or noticed. *Protective reaction,* he decided. *Never do the obvious.*

". . . estimate the asteroid will strike within the next seventy-two to eighty-four hours," the radio was saying. "It is believed that some will survive the impact, even those not at a tangent to the strike area or its opposite position. Your local Civil Defense units will be giving instructions on impact and post-impact procedures. Please pick up these instructions and associated equipment at local-disaster relief stations as soon as possible."

The little man chuckled. He knew the rules. The thing was being attracted to Earth like a bee to honey; it was on a dead-straight collision course, and it was picking up speed. There had been some talk that it might hit the Moon, but calculations quickly showed that a vain hope. Wouldn't have mattered, anyway, he knew. The rogue asteroid that was now looming in the sky, blocking heat and light and causing massive upheavals in the Earth, wasn't any bigger than the Moon, anyway. A direct hit on the satellite, forcing it into the Earth, would have the same effect as the asteroid's strike.

The worst part of it was that they'd done it to themselves. A little glitch, that was all. A huge, juicy, fat rogue asteroid, coming very close to Earth. What a nice chance! Go up, discover that it has tremendous mineral resources on it—a treasure house, they called it. Headed toward the sun in an ill-fated parabolic orbit that would bring it too close to the burning orb. It would have been incinerated, all that wealth a waste. How nice instead to take the challenge to make it a new satellite of Earth, far enough out so. that it didn't do much harm, of course, but close enough to be easily and cheaply worked by the plundered Earth.

Just a few special kinds of superbombs planted here, a few others there, on the asteroid, a nicely timed and coordinated detonation, and it would miss the sun, whip around, and come back. More bombs to brake it and park it. Just so.

Just so.

Only all the bombs hadn't gone off. The special things had to be individually and carefully built, but there had been no way to field-test an individual bomb, only a design. And the values were too critical—no redundancy. They had shot their wad on it in their stupid optimism, and it hadn't worked. It wouldn't work. The initial explosions had gone fine, and the asteroid had whipped around the sun and was now on its way back at tremendous speed. Time to put on the brakes. Oops! No brakes? And the dumb bastards had actually gone into those bombs, to try to fire them manually!

Some of them *did* fire. Some, not all. Enough to point the damned thing straight at the Earth.

From an orbit a few million kilometers out, the gravitational effects would have been annoying but not serious—and slow. More than made up for by the riches of the place.

But now the thing was a bullet, and even though it raced at thousands of kilometers per hour to its target, it seemed to move in slow motion, like a bullet creeping toward someone in front of a firing squad.

It didn't matter now. Three, four days, the radio had said. Not true, he knew—and he knew that the people still around, the people in this bar even, didn't believe it, either. Hours. A day or two at most. The Earth had already started to wobble, to crack. There would be little left when the thing hit, anyway.

The barman wanted two bucks before he'd give him any more doubles. He sighed, got up, and went back over to the three lonely slot machines. He had six quarters, but he didn't need them. He put a quarter in the first one, and before it came up three oranges he had already put a quarter in the second one. By the time the third one was spinning, the second had come up three bells, and now the third one had three cherries.

He returned to the bar with a handful of quarters and plopped them down on top the bar. The barman had an almost stricken expression on his face; he shook his head incredulously and poured a double for the little man and one for himself.

Even the young couple seemed distracted by his little display. The machines rang an electric bell whenever a jackpot came up, and the din from all three going off within seconds of one another had been impossible to ignore.

He turned on his stool, looked straight at them, and smiled. Picking up his drink, he hopped off the stool and wandered over to their booth. "Might I join you for a moment?" he asked pleasantly.

They seemed to hesitate for a second, glancing first at him and then at each other, but both were also fascinated, and it was something that took their minds off the reality outside.

Jill McCulloch and Mac Walters shrugged at each other, and Mac said, "Why not? Have a seat?" He scooted over to allow the little man to sit next to him, opposite Jill.

The man looked something like a skid-row bum— tiny, frail, with an unkempt growth of gray beard and a stained suit that might really have been brown but was definitely slept in. He reeked of whiskey and stale cigarettes.

"You áre from the University?" he asked them pleasantly in his slightly accented tones, his voice unslurred by the prodigious amounts of alcohol he'd been consuming.

Jill shook her head negatively. "Not me. I don't even know why I'm in this crazy city."

Mac nodded. "Same here." They introduced themselves by name.

The little man seemed pleased. "I am Asmodeus Mogart," he responded, then paused and pulled out a cigarette, ignoring Jill's obvious distaste for both the smoke and him. He looked at them seriously.

"You know we only have one more day," he said softly, matter-of-factly. "And you know that no one in the end can survive."

They both gave involuntary starts, not only from the assurance and authority with which he spoke, but also because his words brought their attention back to the one thing that they had, for a brief moment, managed to put at the back of their minds.

Walters looked anew at the strange little man. "Are you from the University yourself?" he asked, thinking that the stranger's condition could easily be explained by current events.

The little man smiled. "Yes, in a way I am. Not in the same way as some of the others around, though. A different one."

Jill's eyebrows rose. "Oh? Which? I didn't know any of them were still going."

He grinned now, revealing nasty, yellow-stained teeth that seemed somehow inhuman. They all came to a point. She decided that, overall, he was the most repulsive-looking man she had ever seen.

"Not any one that you would have heard of, I assure you," Mogart told them. "And not one that you could pronounce in any event." His expression grew grave. "Look, would you save this world if you could? Particularly if it meant the only way to save your own lives?"

They looked at him strangely. "What kind of question is that?" Walters wanted to know.

The little man looked thoughtful for a moment, then drained his double and crushed the glass beneath his foot. The barman didn't see this. They watched as Mogart reached down and picked up a long splinter of glass and unhesitatingly pricked his thumb with it. He squeezed on the thumb, in no apparent pain, until a drop of blood appeared.

The other two gasped.

"A true blueblood, as you can see," Mogart said lightly. And it was true. Unless there were some kind of trick involved, his blood *was* blue—and not a dark blue, either. A nice, pretty sky-blue.

He reached up and pushed back his long gray hair, revealing his ears. They were small, and back flush against the side of his head. They were basically rectangular, except that the outer edge of the top of the rectangle had a sort of S-shaped curve. They were not human ears, anyway—more like those seen on gargoyles and demons.

Mac Walters edged a little away from the strange man, almost pressing himself against the wall of the booth. Jill could only stare at the little man, or whatever he was, in horrid fascination.

"I have a tail, too," the little man told them. "But pardon me if I do not disrobe. It is enough to show you that I am not human. I trust you are convinced of that?"

"Who—what—are you, then?" Jill demanded.

The little man sucked on the thumb he'd penetrated. "I told you—Asmodeus Mogart. At least this week, anyway." He looked sadly at the crushed glass. "I am, as you might have guessed, an alcoholic. Things tend to blur a bit when you have that problem." He sighed, considered calling for another double, discarded the idea for the moment, and continued.

"As to what I am, well, you might think of me as a University professor on leave. A behavioral scientist, you might say, studying the charming little civilization you have—ah, had here."

"But not from any University on this world," Walters responded. "Are you here to study us at the end or something?" That thought suddenly became the most important thing to both of the humans, far more so than what the little fellow was.

Mogart shrugged, a wistful look on his face. "No, no. I was—ah, terminated, you see. Drinking. There was a scandal. Since I was on the project that created this research run, they decided to stick me here."

"Research run?" Jill prodded.

He nodded. "Oh, yes. Probabilities Department, you know. Get yourself a nice hypothesis, and they construct a working model. This universe of yours, for example. One of hundreds they've done. Maybe still do. I'm out of touch after so long, you see."

Mac Walters was horrified. *"Construct? Universe?"*

"Oh, yes," Mogart replied casually. "Easy to do, they tell me. Lots of machines and data and all that, but not really difficult. Just expensive." He gave a mournful sigh. "That's the problem, you see. It's the whole universe they've built, not just this little planet. I actually took pride in hand and tried to talk them into saving it. Actually made the trip—first time in I can't remember how many centuries. They didn't care." He looked at each of their faces in turn. "Face it. If you had a rat colony, observing how it worked, and one of the rats died, wouldn't that be *part* of the experiment?"

Jill McCulloch shook her head disbelievingly. "I can't accept all this. Here it is the end of the world and I'm sitting in a bar talking to a madman."

The little man heard her comment but ignored it. "You see, this thing has caused me a problem. Stay here and die with you all, or go home."

"That's a *problem?*" Mac asked him, thinking there'd be no choice.

He nodded sadly. "They'll put me out to pasture in some nice little place, but it's a cold little world and there's no booze. None." His tone was sad and tinged with self-pity, and there seemed to be tears in his dark, slanted eyes. "I couldn't stand it. So, you see, I must go for the third alternative, try it, anyway."

They looked at him curiously, expectantly. In other circumstances they would have beaten hasty exits, dismissing him as an imaginative drunk or a drunken madman—which, in fact, they still really thought he was, deep down. But in other circumstances they wouldn't be there, not now, and they certainly would not have invited him to sit down with them. When the end of the world was nigh, and you had exhausted all hope, you sat in a bar and listened to a drunken madman and took him seriously. It didn't hurt in the least, and they were getting more than slightly tipsy themselves.

"What alternative?" Jill McCulloch wanted to know.

The little man seemed to forget himself for a moment, then suddenly animation gripped him again.

"Oh, yes, yes," he mumbled apologetically. "But, you see, that's why I didn't do this sooner. Too many drinks, too much lost time. Now I can no longer pick and choose the best people to send. Now I must feed the broadest possible requirements into my, ah, computer, let's call it, and take what I can get. I sent out the call, and here you both are. See?"

They didn't see at all.

He looked at Jill McCulloch. "How old are you? Tell me a little about yourself." His hand went into his pocket, and he seemed to be touching or rubbing something inside that pocket. Neither Jill nor Mac could see him doing it.

Jill suddenly found herself wanting to talk. "I'm twenty-five. I was born in Encino, California, and lived most of my life in Los Angeles. My father was a former Olympic team member, and from the start he decided I was going to be a star, too. Bigger than he was, since he never won a medal. I was put into gymnastics training before I can even remember. When Mom died—I was only seven—that only increased my father's determination. I got special treatment, special schools, coaches, all that. I barely missed the Olympic team when I was fourteen, but made the U.S. meet. I did it at eighteen and won a bronze medal. But shortly after that, the drive started to go. I just didn't seem as sure of myself as I was. I knew I'd had it, and Dad seemed to accept it. I went to USC, taking a phys. ed. major—after all, it was all I knew how to do. Maybe become a coach, find the next gold medalist. I got bored, though. After all, I'd *had* all that stuff since I was born. I dropped out when I was twenty and got a job doing some disco dancing, got a little place near the ocean, and spent my time swimming, surfing, hang-gliding, and generally drifting."

Mogart nodded. "But you have kept yourself in excellent physical condition, I see."

She nodded back. "Oh, yes. When you do it for your whole life, it just becomes second nature to you."

Mogart sat back in the booth for a moment, thinking. The pattern had been youth, athletics, bright mind, and guts. This one looked all right. He turned to Mac, his hand still in his pocket. "You?"

Now it was Walters' turn to feel talkative.

"Ever since I was small, I wanted to be a football player," he told them. "I worked at it, trained for it, did everything I could to make the grade. Hell, my father was a West Virginia coal miner—I saw what that life did to him and Ma. No way. And I did it, I really did. Big high-school play got me scouted by Nebraska, and they signed me as a running back. I was good—real good. But after a friend of mine was hurt on the field and they told him he'd never play again, I got smart in other ways, too. I took my degree in business. I was signed by the Eagles and played almost five years with them and the Broncos, until my knee really started in on me. They told me there was a risk of permanent damage if I kept playing, and I started looking around. Kerricott Corp.—the big restaurant and-hotel chain—made me an offer. I'd been working with them in the off season after I got my M.B.A. from Colorado. I took it. Junior executive. I was on the way up when this stuff happened. Me and a few of the others were going to take a plane to New Zealand, but somehow I wound up here."

Mogart seemed extraordinarily pleased. Another good fit. "You would never have made it to New Zealand," he consoled. "No fuel stops, most of the islands gone or the volcanoes erupting. Same with New Zealand. It's gone." He shifted. "How's your knee now?"

"Fine," Walters responded unhesitatingly. "I think I got out in time."

"Either of you married?" Mogart prodded. "Family?"

"I was married once," Walters told him. "We busted up a year and a half ago. I guess she's dead now. I don't know about West Virginia—I haven't been able to get a line east of the Rockies. I guess they're all gone, too."

Mogart turned his head to look at Jill McCulloch. "You?"

She shook her head slowly from side to side. "Dad

wouldn't move out. We tried, but by the time he decided to do anything it was too late. The tidal waves, you know. He was all I had—close, anyway. Gone now." That last was said so softly it could hardly be heard, as if for the first time she was suddenly facing up to what "gone" really meant.

"Do either of you have any experience with weapons?" Mogart continued his questioning.

"I'm pretty good with a rifle and did some deer hunting with a bow and arrow when I was a teen-ager, but nothing else," Walters told him.

"I—this might seem silly," Jill said hesitantly. "I'm a pretty good fencer. It was one of the secondary sports I took up that helped build up my reflexes and timing."

"Ever kill anyone, either of you?" Mogart pressed.

They both looked startled. "Of course not!" Jill huffed. Mac treated it like a joke; he smiled and shook his head negatively.

"Do you think you could do so? Could you kill if, by doing so, you could stop that thing up there from hitting the Earth, maybe even reverse a lot of what has happened here?" Mogart's tone grew serious, almost anxious, and there was no doubt in either of the others' minds that the question was not being asked from a purely theoretical point of view.

"I—I'm not sure," the woman replied.

"Depends," was Walters' response. "If somebody was trying to kill me, maybe I could."

The little man sighed and lit another cigarette. He needed a drink, but didn't dare right now. "Well, that's not exactly what we have here. But some killing might be necessary—and, in fact, you might be killed instead." He paused, lapsing again into that daze, but only for a moment.

"Look," he continued earnestly. "Here's the situation. I told you how the University sets up these universes. The processes used and the equipment required would seem like black magic to you. I should know— I think I'm the model for most of the devils and demons on this world. So let's think of it as magic, complete magic. Your science is devoted to finding the laws by which things work, and it's a comfortable way to do things—but all of it, necessarily, is simply defining the laws established artificially for this universe by the Department of Probabilities. Those laws don't apply everywhere. So let's take nothing for granted, and just accept it as magic. It works about the same way, anyway."

He reached into his tattered coat pocket and pulled out something, placing it on the vinyl tabletop for them to see. It was a huge stone, like a perfect giant ruby, multifaceted and shining, almost as if it were on fire with a life source of its own.

"A device—an amplifier—no, check that, a magic stone," Mogart explained. "A link with my own world, and with all the others, too. A vessel of great power during the setup stages, drawing power from outside your universe. With it I have enormous power by your standards. I make people do things against their will, change minds, put on funny shows, transport myself where I will. It's still not very powerful comparatively speaking. Its limits are too great—it cannot handle enough power to do a big job."

"It does pretty well against the laws of probabilities," Walters noted, nodding toward the slot machines.

Mogart smiled. "Oh, dear me! No! You presuppose that the machines are random. Most people do. Actually, they have a system of weights and pins in them, governed mechanically by the coins put in. That's how they set the payoffs. The more coins in, the more weights depressed, the more pins go out longer to catch the elusive payoffs. I merely increase the weight so that the pins come out all the way. I win nine out of ten times that way."

"Psychokinesis," Jill guessed. "I saw a TV show on it once."

Mogart nodded. "If you will. I've been using the power to try and slow our unfriendly asteroid out there. There has been some effect, but it's very slight on an object of such mass."

"Perhaps you could add more mind power by adding more people," Walters suggested, not even considering the fact that he was taking all that the little man had said at face value.

Mogart shook his head from side to side. "No, no. The number of inputs actually decreases the output power. More drain. You'd need matched minds, and that would be impossible unless there were more exact duplicates of me—and one of me is too much for most people. No, it's not more input, but more *amplification* that's needed. The stone just doesn't have sufficient power to do what it's being asked to do."

"Then you need more stones," Jill put in, thinking aloud. "How many?"

"Five," Mogart replied. "Five more, that is. The progression is exponential. Two stones joined together have ten times the power of one; three, ten times two, and so on. It's a neat solution. Nobody in the field has enough power to change the rules of the world, let alone the universe, he or she is in—but a lot of us can get together if something monstrous goes wrong and fix it."

"And the end of the world isn't monstrous?" Walters asked incredulously.

The little man sighed. "The end of your world, of this planet, yes. One world in a vast universe, and only one of many universes. Planets and suns die all the time. No, you wouldn't comprehend the nature of a catastrophe enormous enough to cause a bunch of us getting together. So we have a problem. How do we get enough of the stones and get them into my hands in time to stop this crash? I can't get them from the University; Probabilities has them too well guarded for that. That means we have to get them from others of my own kind in the field."

"Steal them, you mean," Jill put in.

He nodded. "If you will."

"Any more of your kind on Earth?" Mac asked.

"No, there's usually only one per civilization, and this one in particular is not highly thought of, which is why they chose me for the job. And we can't get the stones from legitimate research personnel, either. They would be more than willing to destroy their little worlds rather than give up their stones, and may have University security helping them. No, we'll have to pluck them from the rogues like me."

"Rogues?" Jill echoed questioningly.

He nodded. "Ones who, like myself, got into trouble and were exiled to various little-used and unimportant places where they could cause no real harm outside their own prison. Most choose it, like myself, rather than face the alternatives of an eternally dull retirement or a mindwipe." He looked at them both seriously. "We can't die, you see. We reached that point and passed it eons ago. We neither die nor reproduce. And that, of course, brings up the other problem—the ones you must steal the stones from, they are immortal, too. *They* can kill you, but you can't kill them."

"Then how . . . ?" both of the humans asked together, letting the question trail off.

"We must find the agent, then somehow steal the magic jewel. Not once, which is hard enough, but five times. And we haven't any room for failure, either. Time isn't consistent on the various levels—some run at this time rate, some run much faster than we, some run much slower. Which is good, for otherwise we'd never have the time to do the job. So, with time pressing, we are limited to universes running at a much faster clip than here—say an hour here equals a day there, or even faster rates. That narrows us down to only a couple of dozen. Now, add to that problem the fact that we must use only rogues, not anyplace with a project going on where security could be around. When I put all those requirements together, I come up with only five possibilities. Five! Thus, we must enter each of those worlds and steal the magic jewel—and we cannot fail even once, or we won't have enough power to knock that damned rock out of reality. And, with time so short here, we alone must do it. I can help, but the two of you must do the real work. There is no one else, nor is there likely to be."

Mac Walters gulped, and Jill McCulloch again experienced that sense of total unreality about the conversation.

"Do you both agree to try?" Mogart pressed.

Walters nodded dully.

McCulloch sighed, not believing a word of what she was hearing. "Why not?"

The little man nodded. "Now, indulge me here. I know you both think this is end-of-the-world madness, so this little bit extra will not hurt, either. Just believe me that, for various reasons, it's necessary."

He reached out and picked up the jewel, holding it in his outstretched right hand, palm open and up in the center of the table.

"You first, young woman. Just place your hand over mine and the jewel—no, palm down, on top of mine. That's it." His tone grew strange; even his voice started to take on a hollow, echoey quality.

"Repeat after me," he instructed. She nodded, and he said, "I, Jill McCulloch, freely and of my own will, accept the *geas* and all others which shall be placed upon me." Then he stopped. She repeated it, forgetting the word "geas" until prompted. "And I accept this one as my liege lord in service, and accept his mark and bondage."

She frowned slightly. The language sounded like something out of *Dracula;* she had the odd feeling that she was selling her soul. Still, she repeated the man's strange words.

"What is done is done and cannot be undone," Mogart intoned, "under the Seal of Blood."

Suddenly there was a burning feeling in the center of her palm, as if someone had just stuck a lot of needles in it. She started in surprise and tried to pull her hand away, but it seemed frozen there.

"It is finished," Mogart proclaimed, and her hand came free. She withdrew it and stared at her palm. On it, like some sort of tattoo, was a small pentagram inside of which were two stylized strokes, like goat's horns. There were little flecks of blood around it, inside the pentagram, but they soon dried and the pain quickly faded.

"Now you, Mr. Walters," Mogart said, turning to the man, who was staring at the woman's palm in mixed wonder and apprehension.

"What's happening there?" he asked nervously.

"A necessary process," Mogart responded coolly. "Binds you to the jewel, and so will allow you to pass into other planes at my direction and also will always keep you in touch with me. Come! Come! What have you to lose? And time is of the essence!"

Walters put his hand over the jewel in Mogart's palm a little hesitantly. But he did it, going through the same ritual, and, despite forewarning, experiencing the same burning and etched design on his palm as the woman had.

Mogart smiled, let out a deep sigh, and put the jewel back in his pocket. "I am the sole input," he intoned lightly under his breath. "The two are bound as my vassals, and so it shall remain as long as I have need of them." He lapsed into thought for a moment, then said, "All right, let's get things straight. We have five jewels to get and we have very little time. The best way is to dispatch each of you to a different plane—a one-person operation. As soon as you have the jewel in your physical possession, just wish yourself back to me and you will come. That should simplify matters a bit—you won't have to worry about a getaway. Without their jewels, the rogues can't even give chase. If one of you has more success than the other, well, we'll continue with the operation with the other, and if we're lucky, both of you will combine for the last two quests."

"You mean we'll be alone?" Jill gasped. "Not even a team? I thought the two of us—"

"No time," Mogart cut her off. "But you won't be alone. *I* cannot go anywhere physically from this plane except back home—the Main Line, as it's called. But I can be summoned when needed, and I can also prepare the way. You will be matched to the plane—time rate, language, whatever will be needed for you to be both unobtrusive and safe from death through ignorance of local conditions. Also, it's possible for anyone with a jewel to find the whereabouts of any other jewel-bearer, just in case. Since you are bound to me, it's just about the same, so you won't have to comb a whole world." He slid out from the booth and stood. "Come on! Let's be away!"

They also slid out and stood, and as they did, Mogart walked in back of the bar, took a glass, and poured himself a straight double shot of Scotch.

The young couple looked nervously at the barman. He seemed still, as if frozen in position, eyes wide open but unseeing. Mac went up to him and examined him closely.

The barman seemed to be alive, but a living statue.

"No, nothing's wrong with him, or with anybody else in the bar," Mogart told Mac, anticipating the question. "It's us. As soon as you both entered my service, I started speeding us up. We won't be able to put you in the proper planes until you are physically, temporally, matched to their rates." He downed the contents of the glass, coughed, belched, and then came back around the bar.

"All right. Just a second." He took a piece of chalk from the blackboard behind the bar announcing special drink prices, cleared a place in front of the bar of furniture, and motioned them both to come to him.

"Stand close together," he instructed, "while I draw this thing. Don't touch or cross the line," he warned.

Quickly he bent and sketched out a chalk pentagram around them, with the three of them in the middle, then stood up and turned to face them.

"Ready?" he asked, and before they could reply things started to happen.

The entire bar and its people and contents seemed to fade slowly out of existence. It was replaced with a grayness, a nothingness that nonetheless seemed to be substantial, to be something or some place. They had no bearings; even the floor was gone, and they felt as if they were floating. Now and then images would flicker by for an instant, but never long enough to tell what shapes and scenes they held.

"It is now six-fifteen, in your world, on the evening of August twelfth." Mogart's voice came to them, not as if he were speaking but as if he were somehow projecting his thoughts into their minds. "Remember, time is of the essence, and one failure means we all fail. Even though the worlds in which you will exist run much faster, time will not stop on Earth. The quicker each jewel is procured, the better."

"Where are we going first?" Jill asked, still feeling that she was in some sort of strange dream.

"We will choose the lines temporally closest to ours and close in as we go," Mogart explained, at the same time explaining nothing.

"I'm not sure I want—" Mac Walters began, but it was too late. One of those flickering images came up and he felt himself being pushed out into it by a force too strong to resist.

A few seconds later Jill McCulloch felt the same shove.

What they wanted was strictly beside the point, Mogart thought with satisfaction. Time *was* of the essence, and the sooner they got started the sooner he could get back to that damned bar and get himself another drink.

Main Line +1130
Zolkar

1

SHE FELL AS IF FROM A GREAT HEIGHT, YET SHE HIT cool grass with little impact and rolled comfortably. Then she picked herself up and looked around.

She was on the edge of a forest, near a main road paved with hand-hewn bricks leading off to a town in the distance that seemed to be out of the Arabian Nights minus the desert. Spires and minarets abounded, the only tall structures in a village otherwise without any real multistory buildings. Everything seemed made of brick or of some sort of adobe.

It was a quiet place, though; some birds flew and whistled in the winds above the trees, and occasionally an insect would buzz by, but beyond this there was a stillness.

It is really a pretty scene, she thought.

She heard someone move near her and turned with a start to see Mogart. At least she hoped it was Mogart —he was now nude, and, she discovered irritably, so was she.

Mogart was much more alien and fearsome when unclothed. From his forehead now sprang two tiny horns which, she realized, had probably been there all along but were masked by the thick head of hair, and his face looked much more demonic and inhuman. His upper torso was squat and surprisingly muscular, and, she saw, he had no navel.

From the waist down he was covered in a deep blue fur tinged here and there with gray, leading down to two powerful animal-like feet terminating in cloven hooves. His tail, tied somehow in his suit, was now revealed to be long and serpentine, ending in an arrow-shaped membrane. Even his hands seemed more fearsome, more menacing, his long fingers terminating in what might better be described as claws than hands.

"Please don't be alarmed," he said gently to her. "First of all, I can't translate the artifacts of a world without more power, and that, alas, includes clothing. But this should serve a good purpose as well. Now you see me as I really am, and you have your memory of me as a disguised human of your line. This should give you more clues as to what to look for in my brother here. We all would look identical to your eyes, I assure you—so you're looking for another like me."

She accepted that much, still having some of that dreamlike feeling. "But what about me?" she asked him, concerned. "Surely I can't go nude into a new society." She stopped for a second, thoughts diverted. "You are transparent," she noted. "I can see very slightly through you."

He nodded. "And you, too. We are slightly out of phase with this world as yet, deliberately. We can perceive its reality but are not yet a part of it. I cannot be—this is about as much as you can get of me. We are ghosts here; they cannot see or hear us. Come, let us go toward the city while I brief you on this rather strange place. Do not be worried if we encounter anyone; I assure you and your modesty that we can't be seen, heard, or felt."

She had no choice; she started walking with him over to and then down the road.

"The city is called Zolkar; we are still on the Earth and within your own standards of what is human, so we don't have that problem."

"And the jewel—the other one of you—is in this Zolkar?" she quizzed.

He nodded. "Yes, indeed. I dare not get too close to him or he will become aware of my presence—and that would be disastrous. But it is definitely in Zolkar— the jewels draw each other together like magnets. It is here. I know this because we are here, and we could therefore be nowhere else."

"What sort of place is this, then?" she prodded.

"A very nice one, really," he responded. "As I remember it, the Philosophy Department got into a big dispute over whether or not there was an innate moral sense, or whether or not people could be trained to have a totally ethical behavior set. This world is one of the attempts at finding out. Do you know anything about the Islamic faith?"

She shrugged. "Not much. I *thought* this place looked kind of Middle Eastern, despite the trees."

"This is approximately the location of San José, California, in your world," he told her. "And the faith here is more like Islam than others, about in the same way that Judaism and Pentecostal Christianity are more like each other than either is to, say, Zen Buddhism. The rules are fairly simple and basic—sin is defined by the rules as anything you think of as a sin, within certain limits, of course. Insanity is compensated for, and conscience is established by social rules taught from the cradle. The difference is that if you commit a sin in our little corner you might feel guilty, but here sin is divinely punished. It makes for a wonderful experiment in Pavlovian conditioning—divine justice is meted out equally to all. It works pretty well, at that— drop a gold coin here, and they will rush to return it to you. There is none of the fear and tension plaguing your civilization. It's pretty dull, actually, which is why the experiment was abandoned."

She stopped short. "Do you mean that anything I do that either I or this society considers wrong is punished? A bolt from the blue?"

He nodded. "Oh, yes. Just so. The University uses this place now only for the most serious miscreants of my own people."

Jill was sure she wasn't going to like this at all. He caught her reluctance and said, "Look, we need the jewel and we have no slip-ups allowed us. You *must* do it."

She shook her head in bewilderment. "But how do you steal a jewel—or *anything,* for that matter—when you can't get away with anything?"

He shrugged. "Hopefully you'll figure that out. As you will see, particularly among the younger ones here, there *is* sin, but it doesn't last long. Excessive pride might make you incapable of lying; vanity is a sure guarantee of ugliness. Severity increases with repetition, so a first-time thief might lose only a couple of fingers."

She shuddered. "Is there any way to reverse this divine verdict?"

"Oh, yes," he replied lightly. "If it's a sin with victims, you must confess to your victims and beg their forgiveness, which will wipe away the sin. They have to forgive, you know. Otherwise they'd have no charity or compassion, and that would mean *they* would have divine retribution in kind. If you commit a victimless crime, you bear the punishment until true repentance and contrition is within you, and you beg God for forgiveness. Commit the same offense three times and you're stuck with it for life."

They were approaching a robed and bearded peasant walking alongside a cart being pulled by an enormous bison. They approached from his rear, and Jill became conscious once again of her nudity.

"I told you we aren't of this world as yet," Mogart chided, and walked around the cart. When she hesitated, she felt a strong taloned hand grab her arm and pull it forward.

It was true. The peasant paid them no notice whatsoever. Once she accepted the situation, she went over and walked beside the peasant, even putting her hands in front of his eyes. Neither man nor animal took any notice at all.

She felt better, relaxed, and they entered the city.

Still, she began to have a different sense of unease as she looked at the alien buildings and exotic dress of the inhabitants. This was not her world nor her people; even if time were not a factor, it would be almost impossible to feel at home here, to operate inconspicuously and, yes, daringly.

For the first time she grasped the reality of the situation, and it unsettled her. She felt like a spy in a strange land, an amateur spy totally ill-equipped for a dangerous mission.

"I don't think I can manage this," she muttered.

Mogart seemed less bothered. "Don't worry so much. I wouldn't just plop you here alone. Ho! See? The street we're looking for!"

They turned a corner and she saw a nearly deserted street composed of cracked one- and two-story adobe houses.

Mogart seemed to know where he was going, and she had to trust him. At the ninth door he stopped, turned, grinned, showing those sharp, stained teeth, and said, "Come on. Follow me." With that he walked right through the door without opening it.

The action was so startling that she just stood there a moment, amazed; suddenly a hand emerged, grabbed her arm, and pulled her through. There was no sensation; she just passed through the door as if it were not there and then she was inside.

The house was covered with a straw floor; at the back of the single room was a crude fireplace, and hung on hooks around the room were flickering lanterns that smelled of some kind of foul oil. Near the back of the room were two beds of matted straw stuffed inside wood frames. A low wooden table flanked by thick woven straw mats were the only other furnishing.

Sitting on the mats were two children. The boy,

wearing the same loose-fitting robe she'd seen on the peasant, was munching some kind of confection that looked like peanuts imbedded in hardened molasses. He looked no older than ten or eleven, and he was filthy and disheveled. A couple of flies buzzed around him, although he took no notice. The girl looked perhaps a year older; she showed signs of being close to turning into a woman, and her hair, like his, was very long. She appeared to take a little better care of herself than the boy did, but it was only a matter of degree. Both of them could stand several hours in a hot tub, Jill decided.

"Who are they?" she asked.

Mogart smiled. "The boy is called Gaha'auna, which means 'Shadow of the City'; the girl is Ma'houdea, which means 'Bright Star of the Night Skies.' Both are orphans—street urchins, really—who make their living by begging. Charity is a virtue, so they never starve, although these are a poor people and you'll not get rich on it. This can be a cruel culture for those without family, no matter what the cause. They have great value, though, since children have a freer hand in this society than adults, whose roles are pretty much predetermined, and street urchins are worldly-wise far beyond their years."

She looked them over. "They are brother and sister?"

Mogart chuckled. "Oh, my, no. Just partners, you might say. This place has been vacant for a while, so they moved in. In a society where sin is divinely punished there's no need for locks and such, so they'll be all right until the place is rented again. The landlord knows about them, but until he has a renter it would be uncharitable to throw them out, a minor sin in its own right."

She nodded thoughtfully. "And they—ah, they *know* what I'm here to do?"

"More or less," Mogart told her. "I've used them on occasion before. You see, I can't actually enter this level of existence myself—my brother's jewel prevents me. So when I want something—they make a simply *incredible* wine here, for example—I need help. I can make myself known, with difficulty, in the other levels."

Jill sighed. "All right, then. I guess it's mostly a matter of doing it. There isn't much choice, is there?"

He shook his head sadly from side to side. "Not if we are to save our own lovely world. Act quickly here —the time frame is much, much faster than ours, but it is still the slowest of the five in relation to us. A full day here equals more than an hour back home—and every second counts."

The boy shifted uncomfortably. *"Sama'har du ting zwong,"* he said matter-of-factly to the girl.

She nodded, looking a little nervous, and shifted position slightly. *"Frum du tossiang, jir zwa,"* she responded uneasily.

"I can't understand a word they're saying," Jill noted. "How will this ever work?"

Mogart smiled again. "Integration. I cannot drop your physical form here—it would, well, interfere with the physics of the thing, let's say. Nor, of course, could you learn the language and all else in so short a time. So the arrangement is to integrate you with someone here, in this case that girl. I'm going to slip you in, so to speak, so you'll be inside her head, in full control of her mind and body."

That thought was unsettling. "Then what becomes of her?" Jill asked.

"Oh, she'll be there, just pushed way back into the unconscious. Her personality, that is. You'll have limited access to her memory, which will include the basics like language. Occasional flashes of her past might come to you, along with certain knowledge, but it's not controllable. The moment you have the jewel in your hand, just wish yourself back to me. Saying my name would do it. That will restore her to normal, and, I assure you, both of them will be well rewarded for it." He paused a moment. "But time is pressing. Our Mr. Walters is on a slightly different time frame, but I better get to him soon or he could have some problems where he is."

With that Mogart left her side and walked to the area between the boy and girl, on the table, in fact. As he did so, she noticed for the first time a series of small cubes of onyx on the table—two dozen at least. Mogart stared down at the randomly scattered cubes and seemed to concentrate.

The low fire in the back suddenly flared up, and a sudden gust of wind seemed to rush through the room. Both the boy and the girl suddenly looked at each other. The girl seemed scared.

Then the cubes started moving, each appearing to take on a life of its own and to slide and form a pattern on the table. One end remained open, but Jill could already tell what the small cubes had formed.

A pentagram.

"Du grimp zworken ka mugu," the boy told his female partner.

She remained frozen, staring into the center of the pentagram, the small opening in it right in front of her now. She didn't, couldn't, move.

Jill McCulloch sympathized. This ritual was eerie enough when she could see Mogart, know who was doing it, and know at least a little of the man behind the magic. They couldn't—they saw only the flare and the wind and the cubes form the shape. It would scare the hell out of anybody.

"The wind and fire flare are caused by the interaction of our existence, out of phase with theirs, coming in a bit," the wizard or demon or exiled professor or whatever he was told Jill matter-of-factly. He turned and faced the stricken girl and sighed. "Hmmm . . . Well, I hate to do this, but . . ."

With that he reached into that body-pouch of his and brought out the jewel itself. He held it out in front of him, stooped down, and placed it right in front of the girl's frightened eyes.

"Rise!" he commanded. *"Dugou!"*

The girl got up. She stood limply, blankly, as if she were an animated corpse, her eyes on the jewel Jill was sure she could not see. It was unsettling to watch such power being wielded, yet there was some reassurance as well. Each jewel amplified the ones before by a factor of ten, Mogart had said. Six might well deflect an asteroid.

"Enter the pentagram!" Mogart ordered, stepping

back to the far limit of its small border to accommodate her. The girl stepped forward, up onto the table, close to him and inside the figure. The cubes did not close behind her.

Mogart turned to Jill. "Your turn," he called softly. "Enter by the opening. I think we'll all fit."

She found herself walking to the table, walking up onto the hard surface, as if she had no will of her own.

The onyx cubes closed behind her, forming a tight fit. Jill felt a little more herself now, although she found, just by trying to step back a bit, that she could not escape the pentagram. It was like a brick wall.

She looked down and saw that the boy still sat, watching the whole thing with interest but no fear.

Then Mogart stepped literally into the girl, so that both were occupying the same space. It was a weird sight, to say the least, to see the two together, yet not merging, as if they were some strange three-dimensional double exposure.

The girl's mouth opened and uttered a stream of gibberish that sounded very much like the language the two young people had spoken. It was not her voice, nor Mogart's, but her voice trying to be his. The effect was ghastly, like a voice from the dead, but it didn't seem to bother the boy at all. Instead, he nodded and responded to the girl. For over three minutes Mogart, through the girl, and the boy, who sat outside the pentagram, engaged in a dialogue Jill could not follow. Finally it ended, and Mogart stepped outside the girl's body and turned.

"Go up to the girl and touch her," he ordered softly.

Jill suddenly became hesitant. "I'm not sure I like—" she started, but found herself doing as ordered, anyway.

"Remember—only the jewel can return you to me," she heard Mogart's voice warn her. "Fail, and you are here as long as you live."

With that she felt an enormous shock, as if suddenly colliding with a wall at high speed, her head seemed to explode in pain, and she sank into unconsciousness.

Inside the room the boy watched as the fire and wind

diminished; there was a sharp but not loud cracking sound, and the cubes suddenly and violently shot out in all directions across the room, banging against the adobe walls. He had to raise his hands to fend off one, and it stung.

On the table the body of the girl collapsed into an unmoving heap.

2

They were strange dreams, and yet somehow familiar. She had dreamed a part of these dreams before, long ago, in the twilight of childhood and on the threshold of adolescence. True, some of the settings were odd, even bizarre, yet others were not, and there were human universals involved.

Some of the dreams were pleasant, some nightmarish; many were erotic in one way or another. She tossed and turned through them, barely aware that they were dreams.

Then one began to dominate: a world where bison roamed and the people looked like American Indians and a funny little devil named Mogart, who told her to go steal some jewels to help prevent the end of her world.

"You awake?" came a voice, that of a young boy whose prepubescent soprano was slightly tinged with the promise of forthcoming manhood.

Jill McCulloch awoke and opened her eyes. Her body ached; she felt as if she'd been sleeping for hours on a bed of concrete.

This is the room, that straw-filled adobe room, she thought wonderingly. And over there, reclining on a woven mat and munching something, was a boy—no, *the* boy.

This isn't a dream, she realized with growing horror. *This is real!*

She sat up unsteadily and shook her head to clear the remaining cobwebs. She was still on the table! *No wonder I feel so black-and-blue,* she thought. She looked down at herself as if to confirm the impossible that she already knew, somehow, would be there.

Small, bony limbs with almost no body development, covered by a skin of deep reddish brown like the boy's. She was inside the girl's body! She *was* the girl!

"How—how long have I been out?" she managed, feeling awkward and ill at ease.

The boy shrugged. "Hour maybe, maybe two. I wasn't sure if the whole thing had come off or not."

He was talking very differently than she'd expected. Then she realized he was talking in his own language, as was she. It came easy, as if native to her, and it sounded natural. Only traces, nouns mostly, of English remained in her mind—words like "airplane" and "electricity" and countless others that had no counterpart here.

"You know I'm not—ah, not the girl," she stammered, trying to open an impossible conversation.

He nodded. "Oh, sure. I knew that the moment you opened your mouth. Your manner's different, too."

"You're not—ah—surprised?" she ventured, amazed at his matter-of-fact attitude.

He shook his head. "Naw. This is—lemme see— about this many times this year alone." He held up three fingers, and she realized that he couldn't count. With a start she realized she couldn't, either. The ability was there, sort of, but she didn't seem to be able to get to it, pull it out, use it.

She understood that she was dealing with the limits of the beggar girl; whatever the girl knew, so did she. The rest was locked away, perhaps in the same mental closet as the girl herself.

"The others," she prompted. "They also used the girl's body?"

Again he shook his head from side to side. "Naw. Different folks'. She's only been with me a little bit, since the short days. But you got to remember that you *are* her now, to everybody but you and me, so get used to it."

His attitude astonished her, and she pursued it. "These others—what did they come for?"

He shrugged. "Different things. One for wine, I remember that. One for some kinda seeds. I dunno what the third was after. They was all trouble, though."

Her eyebrows rose. "Problems?"

He nodded. "Dumb. Didn't know how to behave or anything like that. Lots of trouble. I think you're gonna be the worst."

That got to her. "Me? Why?"

"You got to get a jewel from the Holy Elder, and I never heard of nobody in religion ever givin' anything. They always want you to give. And I understand the Holy Elder don't know you're here and wouldn't give you this jewel, anyway, right?"

She nodded. "Something like that."

He sighed. "Well, you might as well relax, then. You're gonna hav'ta learn the ropes around here pretty quick, and I kinda think that once you do, you'll see you're gonna be here an awful long time."

Jill didn't like that at all. "What do you mean?"

The boy chuckled. "The Holy Covenant states that none may take what belongs to another without the consent of the one it belongs to," he explained patiently. "In other words, if the Holy Elder don't wanna give it to you, there's just no way you can get it."

She exhaled slightly and murmured under her breath, "We'll see about that." She glanced about. "Where are my clothes? I'd like to look around outside just to see what sort of place this is."

The boy howled with laughter. "I knew it! Boy! You girls is dumb!"

"What do you mean?" she snapped angrily.

He was still laughing. "The Holy Covenant," he responded. "I guess in the spirit world or wherever you all come from it's different, but this is Zolkar. You got to obey the Holy Covenant. You *got* to, whether you like it or not. Had one of you a while back who was a grown-up—married, too, although her husband was out of town so she didn't hav'ta worry about that part. Wouldn't wear the veil. Stepped outside into public, Holy Spirit struck her, *zam!* She don't have no nose or mouth or anything! Started chokin' to death, of course. I got the veil on her all right, but she wouldn't repent. Dumb, you see?"

Jill was aware of a queasy feeling in her stomach. "What happened to her?"

"Died, of course," the boy replied, still chuckling slightly. "How long can anybody live without breathing?"

She sighed. "All right, you made your point with your little story. I'll do what you tell me. But I only asked for some clothes . . ."

He nodded. "That's it exactly. You're a *girl!* Girls don't wear clothes. When you change into a woman, then some man'll claim you for a wife. *Then* you put on clothes and veil and all, and nobody but he and his family see you any other way again. That's the system, see? That's the way things work."

She was appalled. Clearly females weren't people here, they were objects. It was like a Middle Eastern harem, only worse.

She wanted out of this world as quickly as possible.

"So what happens if it's cold?" she asked, trying to keep her outrage under control.

He shrugged. "Then you don't go out, of course. Don't happen often around these parts anyhow, and not now for sure, not with the long days here. Cools down at night, sure—that's why the fire's here. But it's mostly wetness. Tomorrow will be warm, even hot. You won't have no trouble."

Except being naked in public, she thought sourly. Aloud she said, "Then I can just go out now, like this?"

He nodded. "If you want. Dumb, though. After dark, this much, the air'll go right through you. Gonna rain, too. Heard some thunder a little bit ago. Besides, all you got are dark streets and a bunch of grown-ups with night jobs. Wouldn't help you see anything or find anything you couldn't do better in the morning, and you'd probably get at least a cold. Might as well relax, try to sleep—bed's over there. Tomorrow morning I'll take you on a tour." He yawned.

She sighed, got up, and went over to the bed. It was only a slight improvement over the table and she didn't feel all that sleepy, but there was not much else she could do. The boy was right.

Medieval sexism and divine punishment, she thought, and shook her head in helplessness. Nothing had ever looked so hopeless.

As she lay there, trying to sleep, her thoughts went back curiously to her father. "Never quit," he'd told her. "Quitters are losers."

But this is a little bit different from getting a ten on the floor exercise, Daddy, she answered him, but he was still there, still staring down at her, urging her on, insisting she was the best, that she could do anything.

And it was with those memories of a dead man and an alien world that she finally drifted off into sleep.

"Wake up!" the boy's voice called through a fog.

She groaned slightly and came a little bit awake, just enough to assure her mind and body that she'd rather go back to sleep. "What time is it?" she mumbled.

"After dawn," the boy replied. "The streets are sunlit and soon townsmen and traders will be about. It is the start of the day."

"I think I'd rather start the day a little later," she managed, and started to drift back into sleep.

Suddenly within her mind came a voice, a vast and ancient voice that was at once fatherly and chiding but nonetheless quite inhuman.

"SLOTH!" it charged, and then was gone. Suddenly she felt a force, a current, run through her entire mind and body. It wasn't painful, but it was certainly powerful, as powerful a stimulant as she'd ever known or received.

She was wide awake now and virtually leaped from her bed. She felt like a coiled spring, supercharged, and somewhat frustrated at not really knowing just what it was she was supposed to do. It frightened her a little, too, and she said, more to herself than to the boy, "What's *happening* to me?"

The boy smiled. "Welcome to Zolkar," he replied playfully. "I don't know how it is beyond the world where you come from, but here you *will* act in the manner that the Holy Covenant says—whether you want to or not. Don't worry, you'll calm down in a little bit. That was only your first reminder. It gets worse the more times you do it."

His words held little comfort for her, now or for the future, but this little taste of Divine Will had a sobering and frightening effect on her. What kind of a place *was* this, anyway? And what kind of a life?

"Let's go get something to eat," the boy suggested, and moved toward the door. She followed, glad to be doing something.

Although it was probably not a half hour after sunrise, a lot of people were up and moving about. The air was filled with a curious mixture of odors, those of excrement and drying mud and garbage mixing with exotic smells of freshly baking bread and other active kitchen odors.

The temperature was already warm; there *had* been a thunderstorm during the night and the signs of it in mud puddles and drying walls were everywhere, but now, with the sun starting to bear down and evaporation well under way, the air was almost like a steambath. If in fact her nudity presented no barrier or threat except to her modesty, then she was better off than the boy, who obviously was expected to wear the heavy if ragged robe.

Her shyness quickly wore off as they turned a corner and walked down a main street crowded with numerous robed and long-haired men and women dressed in colorful but baggy cloth dresses wearing "veils"—actually pieces of cloth tied in such a way that they were not so much veils as kerchiefs over nose and mouth. All the women looked like a gang of female bank robbers in some western drama. None of them paid her the slightest attention, and the final barrier dropped when she saw many female infants and girls as naked as she.

The supercharging that had gotten her up was wearing off, and she could think more clearly now. "Where are we going?" she asked the boy.

"Just up ahead," he replied, gesturing but not breaking stride. "A small cantina that sells to the merchants and people in town from the farms. Just relax and keep quiet and let me do all the talking. You don't want to make any more mistakes, 'specially out in public," he warned. She didn't mind this in the least. If she could help it, she wasn't going to hear that weird voice again.

A number of kids were gathering near the cantina—perhaps a dozen or so, all of whom seemed to be in boy-girl pairs. They ranged in age from about five or six to eleven, which, she guessed, was close to her own age. She found the numbers difficult to dredge up; when she thought, *Five* or *six,* her mind said, *About the age of her friend Cathy's daughter.* The concept of age was there, but not the figures.

The other children seemed to recognize them.

"Just don't say anything you don't have to," the boy cautioned her.

"These others—they are all orphan beggars, too?" she whispered.

He nodded. "It happens. There is no dishonor in it."

"I—I didn't mean that there was," she shot back, a bit startled by his reaction.

They joined the crowd of children, and she shut up as he made no further comments. She felt a little awkward and there was a creeping depression growing inside her. Nothing was going right; nothing she said or did was right. The objective looked more and more hopeless every passing moment.

The boy greeted several other boys by name; they were regulars and friendly. The girls, she saw, generally kept quiet and deferred to the males, which was culturally irritating but, considering her situation, provided a comfortable blanket in which she had no obligations to screw up.

One problem surfaced immediately, and it was almost comic. The Zolkarian language was most compact; a number of sounds went together to form different words depending on the mere arrangement of this syllable or that. As a result, names tended to be single long terms that, nonetheless, meant graphic things to the listener. It was awkward—the language went in for elaborate names, yet provided no simple way for nicknames or shortenings. It made for long-winded talks.

"Hey! Shadow of the City! I hear you did real good in the Street of the Nine Thousand Buffaloes yesterday!" a chubby eight-year old called.

"Not bad, Whisperer of the Long Marsh Grasses," Shadow of the City responded. He looked around. "Flower of the Long, Dark Hills is no longer with you, I see."

The pudgy Whisperer of the Long Marsh Grasses nodded. "You know how it is. Man came along a couple days ago and offered her Solace. Said she looked like his dead daughter or something. I dunno. Who can ever understand 'em?"

"Women?" Shadow of the City responded quizzically.

"Naw. Grown-ups," the pudgy one replied. "I may have something working with Flower of the Deep Orange Sunset, though. We'll see. Free Wind of the Black Earth is turnin' grown-up fast, and he may just decide to give up the life and turn shareholder."

And so it went, with the massively complex names coming quickly and the conversation, while very human, running on an alien cultural level. The words were there, but not the meanings.

The children were all there because of the cantina, run by an elderly man named Winged Dancer of the Buffalo Stampede. He dealt mostly in confections and bite-sized, open-faced sandwiches. The culture had no refrigeration, and therefore storage of such things was impossible. Rather than just throw the stuff out, the next morning he gave it to the poor kids, showing kindness and charity at absolutely no cost. Sometimes he had nothing, of course, but the beggar children's subculture had a way of knowing just how much was available.

The sandwiches smelled really rancid, and Jill passed when they were offered to her. The trouble was, she didn't know whether they were truly rancid or if that was the way they were supposed to smell. It didn't matter; the other kids wolfed them down happily, and she got a good share of the sweet pastries and rolls, which tasted excellent despite being hard and more than a little stale. When you're hungry that doesn't matter much, and if she were starving, even the sandwiches would look attractive, she knew.

The appetite of Bright Star of the Night Skies, whose body she now wore, was almost birdlike, and Jill was soon full. It took a bit longer to satisfy Shadow of the City, and there was little left by the time he, too, was filled. Finally he turned and said, "All right, now let's go see if we can find your jewel."

They got up, although it took about another fifteen minutes of saying goodbye to all those long-named types and wishing them good days and good fortunes before they were able to break loose. Finally on their way someplace, Jill felt free again to talk and question her young guide.

"I notice that everybody seemed to be in boy-girl pairs," she noted as they walked back to the main street. "Why is that?"

Shadow of the City looked a little bemused. "It's not seemly for a male to beg unless he is crippled," the boy explained. "That means a girl must do the begging. But girls can't touch or spend money, so the system always results in that kind of partnership."

Another bit of craziness, she thought.

"And what if you can't find a partner, or you outgrow yours, like your friend back there?" she continued with the same line of thought, suddenly realizing the meaning in some of the odd commentary. "Do you starve?"

The boy chuckled. "Did Whisperer of the Long Marsh Grasses look like he was starving?" he asked.

She had to admit that, if anything, the chubby boy could have stood a diet, and said as much.

"Sometimes the girls outnumber the boys, which is fine, since more than one can beg for a boy. So if a boy gets without a partner, then an extra girl moves in with the boy who needs one. That's how I got you— that is, how I got Bright Star of the Night Skies—aw, you know what I mean."

She nodded, sympathizing with his confusion. Had the boy not already had experience with others from outside his world, he could never have handled this conversation at all, she realized.

"But you don't have that now, do you?" she asked him. "What happens when there are more boys than girls?"

He shrugged. "If things are going good, we all chip in to help him, and there are always places like the cantina. If times are real bad and he faces starvation, say, he might die or he might take The Risk."

They were walking along the wide central street now, and she realized that the town was truly a city with perhaps ten thousand or more people in it. They were heading toward the tallest building in town, that was for sure—she could see the odd pyramidal tower's top ahead.

"The Risk?" she prompted, glad to get whatever added insight into this new culture she could.

He nodded grimly. "Appealing and praying to the Holy Spirit for divine charity."

"You get it?" she asked, fascinated.

His smile turned sardonic. "Oh, you get it, all right. It just might not be what you think. You come to judgment right then and there, really, and if you're found completely worthy, then you'll get what you need. If not, well, I've known guys struck dead on the spot or turned into buffaloes or even girls!"

She didn't like the obvious distaste of that last, and said so. He just grinned and shrugged it off.

She sighed, reminding herself that she was, after all, talking to a small boy—hard as it was to remember that sometimes, with his older-than-his-years manner—and changed the subject.

"What happens when you grow up?" she asked. "I understood you to say that you can't beg any more."

He nodded ruefully. "Manhood means you must act honorably always, and that means an honorable job. If you can't find one or somehow learn a trade—which is hard to do if you're an orphan—then you become a shareholder and go out and work on the land of a Lord for a share of the crop."

She recognized that part, anyway, from her history classes. Feudalism pure and simple. The poor sold themselves to the rich for food, clothing, shelter, and protection. This would be the fate of most of the boys, and it was sad to think of such bright and free spirits voluntarily chaining themselves for life. It was a depressing if certain future, one obviously not talked about much, as she could feel from his manner. Still, once aired, the subject remained in the mind and had to be discussed.

"You girls have it easy," he said irritably. "Some guy will come along and take you in and give you everything you want, and all you have to give him are babies. Even if you don't, there's always church service. Not boys. We're stuck with the responsibility."

To her that sounded like a no-win situation.

They had by then reached the temple square. It was enormous, a grassy park with four paths forming a plus shape and intersecting at the temple itself, a huge pyramid made out of massive stone blocks whose only entrances were atop hundreds of stairs.

They stopped across from it. "The main temple of the Holy Spirit," he told her in tones hushed and reverent.

"The strange-looking man with the jewel—he works there?" she asked him, a little awed herself. She tried to imagine building such a massive structure by muscle power alone and couldn't.

The boy nodded. "Works there and lives there, as do the church leaders and Women of the Spirit."

She stared anew at the structure. "Hard to believe anybody actually could live inside there."

"It's not as bad as you think," he replied. "I've never been inside, but the whole park here, grass and all, forms a roof over a big castle that maybe goes down as far as the temple goes up. Enormous number of rooms and lots of twisty passageways. I think it's part of a big cave or something. Leastwise all I heard is that it's cool down there but always breezy so the smoke doesn't bother you."

She sighed. On top of everything else, the man she sought lived inside a virtual fort of unknown dimensions and honeycombed with labyrinthine passageways. She began to think she would never even *find* the demon with the jewel. Suddenly a thought came to her.

"You said something about girls giving themselves to the church," she recalled. "And just now you said some people called Women of the Spirit lived there. Just what does that mean?"

He shrugged. "Beats me. All I know is that any girl who's passed blood but is unclaimed could show up at one of the four doors there and give herself to the church and get taken in. What happens after that nobody knows, since I don't think anybody ever sees them again."

That was not cheering news for several reasons. For a brief moment she had an idea to volunteer herself—at least that would get her inside and perhaps give her some familiarity with who and what was where—but puberty was required, and this body was still months, perhaps even a year, away from that. How long had Mogart said? One day here equaled more than an hour back home. Certainly not enough time. It didn't matter, though; she was certain she couldn't stand a year in this society. Of course, if she didn't solve this problem she'd spend more than that here, she realized suddenly, and new urgency came over her. Her mind raced.

"Look, you know the one I'm looking for?" she asked almost desperately.

He nodded. "The Holy Elder himself, the ruler of the temple. Of course. No one else has hair on his face of any amount, and he has lots of it, plus a lot more. He is not human; that is how we know he is the Holy Elder. He is only half man, and half something else."

That description fit Mogart pretty well, and Mogart had said that to humans his kind would all look basically alike. This line of questioning was becoming interesting now.

"And how do you know this about the Holy Elder? Have you seen him?" she pressed almost desperately.

The boy nodded. "Oh, yes. He comes out for services and prayers, of course, at midday." The boy suddenly saw where she was heading with this line of questioning. "No services scheduled for a week," he told her. "Prayers, of course, every day at midday, but that won't do you any good."

"Why not?" she asked, not wishing further disappointment.

"Because you're praying, of course," he responded in that condescending tone that told her she had asked something dumb.

She let it pass, and considered ways of approaching the demon at the midday ceremony.

"He *does* have audiences, though," the boy said suddenly.

Hope soared. "Audiences? With common people?"

He nodded. "I've never been to one, 'cause the only reason you're supposed to go is if you have a problem too big to solve. Almost everybody does, so it's crowded, and he usually only gets to talk to a few."

Obstacles, she thought. *Always obstacles.* But these were lesser obstacles, ones that could be surmounted. She just wished she had more time.

"I'd still like to be here for the midday prayer," she told him.

He shrugged. "All right, but it's only gonna mean trouble. We can set up here and beg until it's time. Might as well get *something* done."

Begging, it turned out, was a universal sort of thing for any culture. Jill was filthy and her hair was, too, but that didn't stop Shadow of the City from finding a remaining mud puddle and applying even more mess to her, almost getting her to wallow in it.

"It washes off," he assured her. "But the worse you look the better the pitch."

"I thought charity was a must," she responded, recoiling from the muck.

"It is," he agreed, "but not to the point of going broke. You give what you can afford, and then usually only once a day. Do you know how many begging teams there are in a city of this size?" He paused and added special emphasis to his next sentence. "Especially right around the Holy Temple?"

She got his meaning. If she wanted to be here at midday, she would be working in the most competitive of neighborhoods. It was hard to ignore a beggar child when you were within sight of the temple, so competition would be fierce.

Surprisingly, even to her, with a little coaching she proved pretty good at it. Begging was particularly difficult in this sort of society, where you couldn't tell a good lie without immediately getting tripped up. The boy told her that even a small lie would result in having to tell the absolute truth for a pretty long while, and no fudging.

Still, it was easy. The mud, the sun, and a little time made her a truly pitiful-looking sight. Even worse was when she had to go to the bathroom and discovered that buildings had lime-filled pit toilets in the back most of the time and that toilet paper hadn't been invented. The working and well-to-do had their special cloths, but you brought them and took them back for washing out. The poor just endured the smell and sometimes more until they could get to a river or other water source.

Looking pitiful, you then spotted a mark—a likely giver—and went to work, running out to him, pleading with him, telling him that you were dependent on his kind generosity for the smallest things and lacked everything, all in the most pitiful, miserable voice and with the most desperate expression you could muster. Most of the time they'd just say something like, "I am sorry, but I have nothing I can give you but the blessings of me and my house to the Holy Spirit," which was easily the Zolkarian equivalent of "I gave at the office." Still, she got coins—more than she expected, much more, obviously, than the boy had expected.

Shadow of the City would stay in the background, watching her follow and beg and plead with a mark. If the mark was inclined to give, then he would toss one or more coins on the ground—never hand them to the girl. That was the cue for Shadow of the City to emerge, slowly, walk over and pick them up and stuff them into his robe as if he had just been walking down the street minding his own business and happened to see them.

It was a cultural charade, true, one of those social

rituals of an alien society, but the system worked and preserved the boy's dignity. Women, of course, were assumed not to have any dignity to begin with.

And then it was midday.

She had just finished with a mark and gotten a small coin when she heard, behind her, the blast of what sounded like an enormous combo of air horns. She jumped, turned, and looked up. From where she stood she could see two of the doorways high up. Inside men were blowing on what looked like giant shells of some kind, making the tones that carried over the whole city.

The boy was immediately at her side. "Enough business," he told her. "We have a day's worth plus here, anyway. Now we must pray." He looked at her, a serious expression on his face. "Now, at the first horn, you must stop. In a moment a second will sound, and with that you fall completely down on your stomach, face to the ground. Then just repeat what everybody says and do what they do. Don't do anything else—this is required by Holy Covenant!"

The last was a real warning here, she knew.

Then came a second set of blasts, and she was aware of everyone around her, in the street and in the square, dropping down, lying on the ground face down. Shadow of the City went down in front of her, facing her, so she could both see and hear him.

A new voice took over, obviously with a great deal of amplification. She couldn't imagine the source of that amplification, though; it sounded almost electronic.

"I praise the Holy Spirit, who is with me always," the voice chanted, and the crowd repeated it. She followed along. The phrase was repeated several more times.

"I am the property of the Holy Spirit, who is my Lord and master, be I Lord or slave," came the voice.

Again the litany was repeated, not once but several times.

"I exist only to do His will," came the next line, and so it went. Basically the whole chant was a total pledge of submission. Its only saving grace was that it was rhythmically quite beautiful; in Zolkarian it rhymed and was perfectly metered poetry.

"Praise be to the Holy Spirit, whose will is my will," came the chant.

She started to repeat it, then stopped and gasped. She recognized that voice now, even if it was reverberating unnaturally all over the town. Of course!

It sounded like Asmodeus Mogart!

"Complete the chant!" the boy murmured. "Hurry! Before the next line! You must catch up!"

"But you don't understand," she whispered back. "That's—"

"Too late," sighed the boy, and a new line came.

3

It was over now, over for everyone else, anyway. She was still excited and started to get up, but couldn't. Instead, inside her head, that unearthly, inhuman voice intoned, "CONTRITION!"

She couldn't move out of the prayer position. "Shadow of the City! What's wrong? What must I do?" she called, her voice slightly panicky.

The boy, who had already gotten up, squatted down in front of her. "Your people sure are dumb," he sighed. "The simplest little thing there is and you can't repeat a few words without fouling up."

"Never mind the insults," she shot back. "What do I do now?"

He sighed again. "I don't know. The general rule is that you keep saying the prayers over and over until you believe them, obey them, and are genuinely repentant. Even for one of us that could take days; I'm not sure it'd ever work for you. Could you ever believe in and fully accept the Holy Covenant?"

She collapsed and sighed as tears of frustration rose within her. No, she had to admit—to herself, she couldn't. This God or Holy Spirit or whatever was as inflexible as a computer—it probably *was* some kind of cosmic computer. It would accept nothing less than total submission because it could do nothing else, and it could see into her mind.

"Then I'm stuck here, in the middle of the street, in the praying position?" she moaned.

The boy thought it over. "Well, there's one way. Every once in a while people run into problems like yours—not for being this dumb, though. Sometimes you just get caught in the system whether you want to or not, and it's hard to feel guilty when the whole thing wasn't your fault. Then we take them to somebody with the power."

"The power?"

He nodded, although she couldn't see. "Yeah. We sit you there and they look at you and give you a potion to drink that makes you kinda sleepy, and then they tell you how you gotta feel and you do."

A hypnotist, she thought. Maybe that would work long enough to get her out of this!

"Look," she said. "Maybe that's the way. Then it'll be all right, it'll wear off, and we'll—"

"No good," he responded, cutting her off. "It doesn't wear off. If it did you'd be back on the ground. Oh, sure, if he just looks at you, to get rid of a headache or something, the effect wears off—but this problem would take the potion, and that doesn't wear off."

And that wouldn't do at all, she understood. If the hypnotist made her believe not only in the system but in its rightness and naturalness, she'd accept it, even want to live in it. She'd be a good Zolkarian girl and wait anxiously to be taken into a household and have babies.

No way.

"There's no other way?" she moaned.

He thought for a moment. "You gotta understand, this wouldn't even be a problem if you was one of us. No, I guess the only thing you can do is take The Risk."

"The Risk?" she repeated, then recalled that that meant petitioning the Holy Spirit directly—but not knowing what would be done about your problem. "What would I tell Him?" she asked, a little frightened.

The boy shrugged. "Tell Him the truth. He might excuse your ignorance. Then again, His ways are not for folks to understand. He might just make you Zolkarian, and that would solve the problem."

This problem, and this world's problem, she thought glumly. Not hers. "There is no other way?"

"Nope. That's about it. You can think on it a little."

She did, and grew increasingly uncomfortable, while drawing the same blank as he.

"There's really no choice, is there?" she said at last, and he admitted ruefully that there wasn't.

Ever since she was a little girl, religion had played little or no role in her life. A nominal Catholic, her less-than-pious father seldom got her to church or catechism classes—too much time out from gymnastics practice. Later there were the meets themselves, and the training. She went to church, usually, at Easter and Christmas time, and the most religious she had been in recent years was a few blasphemous oaths and little prayers before a meet. And now here she was, stuck, having to pray to a God she knew was there but somehow couldn't take seriously.

She waited a little, composing in her own mind what she must say, then took a deep breath and decided she was as ready as she'd ever be. She felt the same way she had before big and important meets, standing there at the starting line, only a good deal more helpless since the result here did not depend on her effort alone. "Here goes," she thought aloud, and plunged in.

"Oh, Holy Spirit, hear my prayer," she began, closing her eyes. "Please—I need your help. I am a stranger here, a spirit from another world, inside this body from your world. My name is Jill McCulloch, and my world is close to its end from a great moon that is going to hit it." She paused a second, hoping that flattery would work. "We cannot stop the Moon alone. We need the aid of your Holy Elder to save us. I was sent here to get that aid, and I have not been able to figure out how to reach him. It was this desperation that caused me to miss the ending of the prayers, for when I heard his voice I could think only of my own home in terrible danger and that this was the man who could save my people. Can you excuse a poor foreigner whose desperation to save the lives of her people is foremost in her mind? Only you, Holy Spirit, can excuse and help me now. I seek and plead for your help."

She stopped, anxiously waiting for something—movement, the voice, anything—to happen; but nothing did and she began to worry. In a closed system like this one, might anything from outside that system be accepted, let alone understood?

Suddenly she became conscious that all was different. She felt a burning sensation across her back and saw that the area immediately around her was lit up in an almost intolerably bright golden glow, while beyond was darkness.

"JUDGMENT!" came the voice—only now it seemed a real, if no less powerful and inhuman, sound. "WOMAN, I HAVE HEARD YOUR PLEA!" the voice told her. Now she felt tension rising in her; from what the boy had said, anything was possible.

"I HAVE LOOKED INTO YOUR MIND AND FOUND IT INDEED STRANGE," the Holy Spirit told her. "YOU ARE NOT COMPATIBLE WITH MY UNIVERSE! THIS MUST CHANGE!"

She experienced a sinking feeling. *I've lost,* she thought, *but I'll never know.*

"SO HEAR THE JUDGMENT. YOU ARE FREED OF PENANCE. YOU MAY ALSO SEEK HIM WHOM YOU NEED. BUT WHILE YOU ARE IN THIS PLANE, YOU MUST OBEY ALL THE MANDATES OF THE HOLY COVENANT! ALL! YOU WILL NOT BE ABLE TO DO OTHERWISE. ALSO, IT IS A WRONGNESS FOR YOU TO INHABIT THE BODY OF MY SERVANT. YOU SHALL HAVE A SIMULACRUM OF YOUR OWN! I HAVE SPOKEN!"

The experience was kind of awesome and frightening in spite of her rationalism. "Please!" she pleaded. "Will you help me in my mission? The Holy Elder might not go along, and I cannot take what is not freely given." She considered her own statement briefly; it didn't sound like her.

"THERE IS A WAY TO ACCOMPLISH ALL GOOD WORKS,"

the Holy Spirit told her. "THAT WAY, HOWEVER, IS TO BE FOUND IN STUDY OF THE HOLY COVENANT."

And, suddenly, it was over. Jill felt normal space and light return, and knew that she could move again. She looked up to see the boy gaping in surprise. She looked to one side where she saw movement, then at herself.

The girl, Bright Star of the Night Skies, was getting dizzily to her feet. Jill was in her own familiar twenty-five-year-old body, still naked.

The boy recovered fast and looked at her. "You're the woman who was in the body?" he guessed.

She nodded. He glanced around almost fearfully. "Come on!" he said urgently. "We have to get you off the streets quick!"

"What do you . . . ?" she began, then suddenly realized what he meant. She was nude, reasonably attractive, and out in an open square during peak hours, and she was now bound by the Holy Covenant. Any man could come up to her, tell her to go with him, and she'd be stuck.

"Where?" she asked anxiously.

He looked around. "In back of the buildings over there. There's an alleyway mostly blocked with trash. Follow me!"

He took off on a run; the still-dazed girl followed him, and the new/old Jill McCulloch kept up.

Her black hair had always been cut short; now, she discovered, it hung down almost to the ground and she had to struggle against the almost two-kilogram weight —nothing for her if she'd been used to it, but a dead weight on her neck because she wasn't.

They reached the alley and took a minute to catch their breath.

"We'll have to stay hidden here until dark," the boy told her. "Can't risk you on the street like that. You're built pretty well, and your skin and features are exotic. Even if nobody grabs you for a wife, you are bound to obey any command except sex from any adult."

She now understood his meaning. Any woman still nude at her age would be considered under some kind of divine punishment; her exotic looks—normal Caucasian, but these people were related to American Indians—would confirm that fact to some. No one would feel in the least guilty, and a lot would feel tempted, about making her a domestic slave; and since The Risk, she was bound to do as the natives did— she'd have to obey.

"But where will we go?" she asked him.

"Back to the house, for now," he replied.

She shook her head. "That's not where the job is. I'd just be a prisoner there. No, my answer's in that temple."

"You think there *is* an answer?" the boy asked her skeptically. "If our Holy Elder doesn't like your Holy Elder, then that's that."

She sighed and sat back down. "Maybe, but there *is* an answer. The Holy Spirit as much as told me there was. He said I could solve my problem by studying the Holy Covenant."

The boy and girl both chuckled. "But that's the standard answer to anybody with problems," he told her.

"Maybe it is," she admitted, "but I got the feeling that there really *is* an answer, if I can just figure it out."

They mulled over the possibilities. Stealing was out, of course. She had to be pure as the driven snow— she couldn't violate the Holy Covenant now even if she were willing to accept the consequences. And even if someone else did, the act of stealing itself would mean immediate divine punishment; they might lose their arms after the theft, and their legs if they tried to get away. Of course, *she* wouldn't have to, but she couldn't do the deed herself.

A pretty puzzle.

And time was running out, too—not only an hour every Zolkarian day, but she was now a walking time bomb in this culture who dared not even show herself in public.

The boy went out with some of the coins from the morning's work and returned with some homemade bread, mustard, and sliced meat. The stuff tasted awful, but they were all starving, and there was nothing left at the end of the meal.

Still, the first problem remained. Under the Holy Covenant, how could you gain something that the owner didn't want you to have?

Then, suddenly, she had the answer. "Of course!" she murmured, and snapped her fingers. "I really *do* feel dumb now, Shadow of the City, for not seeing it at the start. It's been right in front of us all along!"

He didn't understand; more, the fact that a *woman* had come up with something *he* didn't understand disturbed him.

"If I can get to the Holy Elder, speak to him even briefly, I can get the jewel," she told them confidently.

The boy seemed to brighten a bit. "But how are you gonna get to him? You had enough problems before— and now . . ." He let the thought trail off, but it was a good point. No matter how she ultimately solved the acquisition problem, she first had to get to the demon.

One at a time, she thought. "The Holy Elder is also bound by the Holy Covenant, is he not?" she pressed eagerly.

They both nodded. "Of course," the boy responded. "He is the only man completely without sin."

"Then my scheme will work," she responded confidently. "If only I can get inside that temple."

"Don't see how," the boy said glumly.

Wait a minute! she thought suddenly. *Maybe I'm going at this too hard, making mountains where they don't exist.* Study the Holy Covenant, the Holy Spirit had told her. The Covenant! That was the key again. She looked at Shadow of the City.

"What is Mogart paying you for this?" she asked.

His eyebrows rose. "Who?"

"My—uh, boss, I guess. The spirit. What's to be your reward?"

The boy sighed. "All the cubes of onyx in the ceremony are to become gold," he told her. "But only when you get back with the jewel." He looked up at her, a strange expression on his face. "Don't you see? With that much gold, I can buy my way into a trade and stay free!"

She nodded, considering that. She understood now what all this meant to him, and that he'd help no matter what. However, one final thing was still troubling her. "Shadow of the City? Why does the Great Spirit allow you to deal with and serve other spirits? I would think doing so would be against the rules."

He chuckled. "It would if we were doing anything crazy like selling our souls or doing acts for the spirits against the Holy Covenant. But we're not. We're just guides."

And that was true. The Holy Covenant was quite literal and specific, but it allowed for nothing outside the experience of its framer, be it the Holy Spirit or some alien, world-building University Department. Spirits just weren't in the script, so what he did was permissible.

She sighed. "It'll be dusk soon. That'll be the best time for me to act, I think. We're going to settle this whole business before the night is out."

"How are you gonna get into the temple?" the boy asked.

She smiled. "I'm going to climb those stairs out there and go up to that big wooden door and knock." She explained the rest to him, and he considered it.

"That just might work," he admitted. "So all we have to do is give you cover and protection until you get up there."

She nodded. "Then just go home. If I'm unsuccessful, you'll never see me again. If I succeed, I guarantee you I'll make certain you get your gold."

The girl, who had said absolutely nothing all day but had through the conversation of the other two figured out most of what was going to go on, sighed. "Nothin' to do but wait for dark." She then lay down on a small patch of grass and seemed to go to sleep. Both the boy and Jill McCulloch stared at her for a moment.

4

It was dusk. Already it was so dark in the alleyway that they could barely see one another, and they almost hurt themselves climbing over dimly seen junk and one another to reach the street.

The boy went first, peered around, then turned to Jill. "All right, let's go. Only a few people around."

She would have preferred none, but she took a deep breath, exhaled, and walked out into the street boldly and determinedly, walked across and into the little park, the children shadowing her at a slight distance.

Suddenly a man came into view, noticed her, and called, "Hello, there!"

That was a cue for the girl, who ran straight at the man and went into her full begging and pleading act.

Jill walked on as the girl's pleadings and the man's protestations rose behind her. She had reached the steps, dark and foreboding in the gathering gloom, and she started up, not even trying to think of how far it was to the torch that flickered near the door so far away. It seemed as if she climbed forever; she had no idea of the number of steps and once or twice had to rest a little and catch her breath, all the time cursing herself slightly under her breath for getting out of condition.

Just when it seemed she'd never make the top, suddenly there she was, on a broad, flat porch in front of the heavy oaken door gilded with gold. She stood there a second, then turned one last time to look at the city and the park below. She couldn't make out much in the gloom, although the city itself shone with lights from thousands of dwellings. Definitely a big place. She hoped that the kids had made it home.

The die was cast now. There was no turning back. Either she had guessed correctly or she had had it. *Either way, here goes,* she thought determinedly, walked up to the door, and pounded on it with all her might. She pounded for quite some time, until she was afraid that there was no one in the temple itself to hear her, but she kept at it. Finally she heard the sound of something rattling on the other side. Quite suddenly and unexpectedly, a small block of wood was pulled out of the door to the side, just above her, revealing an eyehole.

"Daughter, by what right do you demand entrance to the most holy temple at this hour?" a gruff and angry voice asked.

"In the name of charity, mercy, and the Holy Spirit," she responded confidently. "I was directed here by the Holy Spirit himself, in a matter of great urgency for the Holy Elder involving the lives of countless people. I must gain entrance and an audience with him."

The man on the other side considered that. "His Holiness has audiences on Magdays. Come back then."

She wasn't to be easily put off. "This matter is of the greatest urgency, and the Holy Spirit himself directed me here. You know that what I say must be true by Holy Covenant. A matter of life and death for many people will not wait until Magday. I demand entrance!"

That's telling him! she thought smugly. She felt better now, convinced that she was on the right track.

But still the door remained shut.

She could hear others now, grumbling and calling in the interior as to what was the matter, and muffled replies from the man behind the door, but she couldn't make out the words. So glad to be on the offensive after feeling so long a helpless victim, she wasn't about to wait for the resolution of their argument.

"Have you, a keeper of the holy temple, so little regard for the Holy Covenant?" she shouted at the peephole. "Is it possible that even within the most holy temple there are those who lack charity, mercy, or compassion for others? If it be so, then may the Great Spirit strike you down now, for to live in a world without such things would be worse than death!"

That idea seemed to unnerve the man. "All right, all right, just hold on," he grumbled, and she could hear fumbling with latches. Suddenly the door swung open on well-oiled hinges with barely a sound, and a blast of cool air struck her and made her shiver.

A man stood there, dressed not in the robes of the common city dwellers but in a robe of the deepest red, gilt-edged with silver and gold, and wearing not sandals but heavy professional boots. His head was covered in a hood of the same material as the robe, making his face a dark mystery.

"Enter, daughter, and we'll see what we can do," said the man. His mysterious visage and the darkness and coolness beyond made her heart skip a beat, but she didn't let it show. She strode confidently into the chamber, head high, right up to the man.

He wasn't just big, he was huge. She had to crane her neck just to look into the hood, and that didn't help much. It was as if he wore a black mask.

"Now, then," he said in that gruff voice of his, "just what is all this about? What is your name, daughter, and the reason for such unwomanly behavior and dishonorable nakedness?"

"My name is Jill McCulloch. I am from another world than that of Zolkar, and I come on a mission of mercy for my people that only the Holy Elder himself can help resolve. Every minute that I delay is a minute less for my people. I must see His Holiness as soon as possible!"

There was no reaction or expression from the hooded man for a moment, then he sighed. "All right. What you say is manifestly impossible and against all logic and reason, but the fact that you say it and in the name of the Holy Spirit tells me that it must be true. His Holiness is in meditations now; following this, I will convey to him what you have told me. Then it will be up to him to make the final decision. I can do no more." He turned. "Follow me," he said, and she had no choice but to follow.

Behind her the great door shut apparently of its own volition, silent until it hit the latches but then booming and echoing around the interior. She regretted later that she was able to see nothing of the temple itself.

They went down dark, damp corridors dimly lit by small torches for quite a way. The temperature grew slightly colder as they descended some stairs and entered a small room. Inside was a straw cot, a tiny fireplace that put out little heat, and just about nothing else.

"Your word that you will wait here," the man insisted.

She nodded. "I will sit here until I see the Holy Elder," she replied defiantly and lay back on the cot. When the other had gone, she tried to make some sort of makeshift blanket out of her ample hair and exhaled loudly.

Well, I'm in, she thought to herself. *Now to go the rest of the way.*

Despite the chill and the atmosphere of the place, the release of tension and the long day overcame her, and she drifted in spite of herself into a light sleep.

She was conscious, suddenly, of someone in the room and awoke with a start. A man stood there, dressed much as the other had been and also masked, but he was slightly smaller and had a higher voice. She noted that the fire was out and the small candle burned quite a bit lower than she had remembered. But she had no idea how long she had slept.

Some of her initial confidence had worn off, but she was still game. She wanted out of this crazy place, and soon—no matter what.

"His Holiness will see you," the man told her, then turned and walked out. The cold stone felt like ice but she quickly followed.

They descended further into the labyrinth of stone, and the lower they went the colder it became. She had no idea where they were going or what was at the other end, but she knew for a certainty that she would develop pneumonia if this kept up any longer.

Finally they reached a small door, and her guide stopped and knocked softly three times. For the first time Jill reflected on the absence of other people—they had passed none—and, just as interesting, the lack of even the remote sounds of other people.

The guide knocked again, whereupon they heard a muffled response which the red-garbed man took to be assent. He pulled open the door and entered, Jill following, through a back antechamber and into a large room that was surprisingly different than anything she had seen in Zolkar. It was a large room, with a big roaring fireplace, woven rugs on the floor and also on the walls, and a great deal of comfortable-looking furniture, padded chairs and raised tables included. It looked like a staid board room from her world; it was out of place here.

The guide mistook her amazement for ignorance. "You sit on those," he told her, pointing to red-upholstered chairs. "Choose one, sit in it, and wait."

She shrugged. It was warmer in here by far, although certainly cooler than she'd like, and she chose a large stuffed chair near the fire. She relaxed, feeling more normal and comfortable than she had in a long time, then turned to ask the guide how long the wait would be—and discovered that he had vanished. She was alone in the room.

She looked around. Or was she alone? It was a large place, and there was a lot of furniture and stuff here. She had the odd feeling that she was being examined.

Then from across the room, a door opened and a little man stepped through. He wore the same gilded robe and boots as the others, but his robe was the purest white, like white silk. He walked funny. Although his face, too, was hard to see, she knew, just from the size of the man and his gait, that this was, in fact, the man she wanted to see.

Study the Holy Covenant, the voice of the Holy Spirit had told her, and she had, and now here she was. Now if her plan would only continue to hold up!

The white-robed man approached and took a chair facing hers.

"Mogart sent you, of course," said the demon.

His statement caught her a little off guard, but she recovered quickly. His voice was the same as Mogart's, only different—a little softer, a little kinder, which was very good indeed.

She nodded to the demon. "Yes, he did."

"To steal my little gem," the Holy Elder said rather than asked.

"For the gem, yes," she admitted, "but not to steal it. For you to give it to me, freely and of your own will."

The demon chuckled. "Now, why on all the earths should I do that? He's been trying to get enough of the things to get himself off that miserable little existence plane of yours for thousands of years. Got a few, too, in his time, but never got enough and never managed to keep them. He's a rogue and a scoundrel, my dear. Just to assuage his boredom, he has been the source of uncounted misery on your world—demonism, possession, devil worship—you name it and he's behind it. He has an incredibly powerful mind, more powerful than perhaps any other I have known—but it's crossed the border, crossed it millennia ago, that border between greatness and madness. No, my dear, I cannot think of any circumstances under which I would give you the gem—it is, after all, also *my* only way home to the University."

"I don't think our world is so miserable," she retorted. "Zolkar isn't a place I would want to spend my life."

The demon chuckled. "Why not? Why do people live, anyway? A little bit of happiness, a little bit of love, of satisfaction in accomplishment, then they are gone. We have been trying to perfect the perfect society for over a billion years, and I freely admit Zolkar is not it, but it is far better than most. Everyone here knows exactly where he stands, his role in society and his place in it. He is brought up to accept it and make the most of it. Missing here are two things which are horrors of your world—uncertainty and fear. I know of no other place on any plane where it is perfectly safe for one such as you to walk a city street at midnight. Is your world with its little petty wars and miseries and overt, violent tyranny so much better? Do not your people desperately seek a God, and go amok because a technological society has no fixed rules? What is so wrong with Zolkar?"

She didn't have to think about that one. "It's totally stagnant," she told him.

The demon nodded. "It is that, which is, of course, one of the flaws we are trying to correct. But your own political philosophies of utopianism aim toward a technological version of this goal that is far worse—man into insect, or, worse and more probable, man into machine. Please do not go sanctimonious on me about your civilization. A heaven there I leave a question mark, but even without Mogart you would have a Hell."

She let the remark pass. Arguing fine points of philosophy wasn't getting the job done.

"Getting back to the jewel—the amplifier," she said. "You are bound by the Holy Covenant here even as I am and as all the rest are?"

The white hood nodded. "Of course. The jewels and our knowledge might give us an edge or additional capabilities in any world, but we are bound by its rules." His voice started becoming a little uneasy, as if he scented a trap but was too fascinated to flee.

She smiled inwardly. Her scheme was going to work!

"My world is dying," she told the Holy Elder in as somber a tone as she could manage. "In a matter of hours by its time frame, days here, a giant asteroid will crash into the Earth in that plane. There is precious little left of civilization and humanity even now —then it will be too late. Everything has been tried, and everything has failed." She went on to tell, straightforwardly, the story of meeting Mogart in the Reno bar and the last-ditch attempt to gain enough jewels to stop the asteroid.

When she finished, the Holy Elder sat there in silence for some time. Finally he said, "You realize, of course, that the same number of amplifiers required to do what you need can also do almost anything to your plane? Mogart might well be able to stop the destruction with six of them, but in doing so you would be handing the devil the keys to Heaven. The price might be dear indeed."

"Dear!" she exploded. "Dearer than what? My friends and relatives are gone—my world is already gone! Still perhaps a few thousand around the globe, maybe a million, are facing terrible death. Can you think of anything more terrible to me than the extinction of my planet and my people?"

The demon sighed. "No, I cannot," he admitted. "But I'm certain Mogart could."

"If he's so dreadful, why don't *you* come and help save us?" she pleaded. "Surely you could do what was necessary."

"Anybody could with six amplifiers," the demon agreed. "Even you, if you knew how to use them. But

I cannot. I am limited to this world and the University, as Mogart is to yours. Nor is the destruction important in the scheme of things. It is a large universe that you have, you know, and you are such an infinitesimal part of it."

That started her again. "You say you're bound by Holy Covenant, yet you talk so glibly of condemning millions to death. It doesn't matter, you say. Let them die. Is *that* the morality of the Holy Spirit and the Holy Covenant?" She was on her feet now, and her spirit was on fire. "I think not! You will give me the jewel because you must! With it we may still lose, but without it we will most certainly die! You *will* give it to me, or you will be answerable for all the deaths of my people! You will give it to me because you have no other choice!"

She stood there in front of the white-robed figure, waiting. It was done. She had shot her wad.

Finally he sighed, got up, and faced her through his white mask. "You know," he said, "you would make an excellent philosophy player yourself. Mogart chose well. You are correct, of course. The devil has found the one way to my power, and I must turn the jewel over. Wait here and I will get it."

He walked out, and she held her breath, not even daring to sit back down. She'd believe he would give her the jewel when she saw it, had it in her hands.

The Holy Elder returned with a cedar box, plain and small, and walked up to her. A taloned hand flipped a latch on the box and popped the lid open. Inside, lying in velvet, was the living jewel that pulsed with unearthly fire.

She reached out for it, and as she did he said, "Remember—there *are* worse fates than death, and you may experience them."

"I'll take that chance," she replied, and took the jewel in her hands. It burned but she clutched it tightly.

"If possible, I will get this back to you," she told him.

He laughed. "I shall not lose sleep in expectation

of that. It's not so bad, though. I haven't left this temple in over a century as it is."

"You should," she replied. "Go out into the streets and see how the common people live or don't live—particularly the feudal serfs and the beggar children of the city. You have been here so long that you have stagnated yourself. Even within the rules of the Holy Covenant there is room for great improvement, modernization, and change for the better. Perhaps you should tend to some of it."

He shrugged. "Maybe you're right. I'll sleep on it, anyway."

She clutched the burning jewel in her hands and shut all else from her mind.

"Take me to Asmodeus Mogart!" she commanded, and vanished from the room.

Main Line +2076

ASMODEUS MOGART WAS DRUNK, NOT DRUNK ENOUGH for him, but far too much for anyone else to stand him. This didn't matter, though; although the small Reno bar still stood, he'd remained a little out of phase with it—enough so that he was, in fact, in his appointed plane, but with a far accelerated time rate. This gave him complete access to the booze stocks while the few people and the holocaust building outside seemed to stand still. It was illusion, of course, and he knew it; but it was a pleasant illusion.

A slight note of sobriety intruded into his general feeling of well-being when he suddenly caught the irony of himself, an immortal being who had been here since the beginnings of time for this phase, trying to grab a few more precious minutes, hours, even days of life of this now-dying planet's existence for himself.

There was nothing else for him. Either those two young people came across with the goods or it was the end for him. He wouldn't go back, ever—not to the kind of high-technology lobotomies they'd use—never! Walk around smiling at everyone and tending the little animals and happy and unthinking and unfeeling . . .

"Never!" he roared, and poured himself another drink.

Suddenly there was a sharp pop as air was displaced, and he turned, startled, to see the woman—he couldn't even remember her name—standing inside the chalk pentagram on the floor, looking as if she'd never been away. For a moment she was frozen, as if she were a three-dimensional color still photograph, but, quite suddenly, she was filled with animation and turned to face him.

"I have it!" she shouted proudly, and tossed him the jewel.

Mogart was stunned. *So many random factors,* he thought, *yet here it is!* His good fortune was almost beyond belief.

"Anybody chasing you for this?" he asked worriedly.

She shook her head. "Nope. Nobody. I got it fair, square, and clean, which is about the only thing you can do in Zolkar."

Hope suddenly flickered again inside him. "But it's only the second," he pointed out, as much to himself as to the woman. "Four more must be acquired before there is enough power. Even three will not do."

Almost as one, Mogart and Jill McCulloch looked at the clock behind the bar.

It was seven forty-five on the evening of the last day.

He sighed and pocketed the gem. "Let's be off—we have no time to lose," he said, and walked unsteadily toward the pentagram she had never left. He staggered a bit as he entered it, and she had to catch him.

"You sure you're all right?" she asked worriedly.

He brushed it off. "Never better!" he announced a bit too loudly. "Let's away!" Both vanished from the bar.

Their world had nine hours and fifteen minutes to live.

Main Line +1502

"Here"

1

MAC WALTERS FELT THE SHOVE AND WAS SUDDENLY thrust forward from the void in which he had been seemingly suspended into bright sunlight. He felt slightly dizzy and fell to the hard, claylike ground. It took him several seconds to get hold of himself and stand up.

Wherever this place was, it wasn't the world's most appetizing. It was hilly, hard, dry, and the only vegetation of note was a lot of scraggly desert grass and sagebrush. It was terribly hot, and there were no clouds in the sky to block the rays of the sun. He was also nude, which was unexpected. He felt totally alone, exposed, unarmed, and uninformed in a hostile and alien environment.

Now what the hell do I do? he wondered silently.

He looked up and around. Some birds or something, over just beyond the next rocky hill, were circling around and occasionally dipping below his line of sight. He cocked an ear and listened carefully.

Nothing. Nothing but the sound of birds occasionally screeching far off and a very slight sound, almost a hissing noise, that he couldn't make out. *Not snakes,* he decided. Something natural—more like the wind, although there was certainly none on this dry, parched landscape.

Mogart should have told me more about what to expect, he growled to himself. How was he supposed to find the jewel, let alone get it from the little man's counterpart here? There didn't even seem to be any people.

63

He decided to see where the birds were coming from, got up, and started off. The ground felt oddly springy, not at all like the hard clay it appeared to be. Salamanders raced to and fro from sparse grassy plot to grassy plot, paying him no notice at all.

There's something wrong here, he told himself as he tried to think, to figure out what it was.

He was halfway to the rocky hill beyond which the birds still occasionally flittered when he realized the discontinuity: *I have no shadow!* he thought, startled.

Idly he kicked a small pebble with his bare feet. The pebble didn't move—or if it did, it didn't move much. His foot seemed to pass right through it.

What the hell is going on here? he wondered, confused and a little anxious.

He made his way up the hill toward the birds. He felt gravity, and he felt the hill in that slightly soft, unreal way, but he disturbed nothing in his climb. It was an easy grade, anyway; he was at the top in a few minutes.

The hissing noise was the sound of a small river twisting and bending through the parched land. It was an old river, meandering all over the place, yet slow and shallow. It emerged from a great red-rock cleft in a hill to his left, ambled past in a canyon perhaps ten meters below the surrounding land, and vanished into the land in the distance, its twists and turns making it nearly impossible to follow.

Still, hidden in the canyon was a thick line of trees and almost swamplike vegetation. In a dry land where there was water, life clung to the moisture and thrived in abnormally crowded conditions.

He made his way down the hillside to the bank just above the river. The water itself looked about a hundred meters across and was muddy, but judging from the occasional rocks in the middle, it appeared to be no more than thigh-deep at its worst. He decided not to chance it unless he had to—no telling what was under that muddy coating.

There appeared to be a trail of sorts partially overgrown with weeds from the riverbank, and he followed it, noting that he neither disturbed the vegetation nor found it substantial to his touch. The trail led past pools of stagnant water buzzing with dragonflies and other insects; the birds that swept to and fro from sky to river seemed to nest in the small but thick trees that lined the banks.

Neither the insects nor the birds seemed able to see him.

The trail, if in fact it was such, seemed to lead back up toward the red-rock canyon. He stopped a moment, trying to decide what to do. He felt lost, helpless.

This is no way to go into something you don't know or understand, he decided. But what, then, to do?

He was still standing there, uncertain and disgusted, when he heard a voice call his name.

"Walters! Mac Walters! Where are you?"

There was no mistaking the reedy tenor—it was Mogart.

"Here! Down here!" he shouted back, a corner of his mind noting that even his shout did not disturb the surrounding wildlife.

"Just stay there! I'm coming to you!" Mogart responded. Walters shrugged and waited. At least this was *something.*

It took the ungainly Mogart quite a bit longer to negotiate the hill than it had Walters, and when the demon was within sight it was clear that Mogart was definitely not human. "Demon" was, in fact, the most accurate descriptive term for the strange little man. But he was a demon in very poor condition, Walters decided as Mogart approached huffing and puffing from the little bit of exertion.

"Sorry I couldn't be here immediately," the demon apologized. "It took a bit of time to get your counterpart settled. Fortunately, the time differential was wide enough so that your wait wasn't *too* long."

"It seemed damned long to me," Walters grumped. "So now what do we do? I don't even seem to be real in this world."

"You aren't—yet," Mogart told him, explaining the temporal out-of-phase relationship as he had to Jill

McCulloch. "Come, let's follow the path and discover where you have to go."

They walked on for some time, into the canyon whose walls rose ever more imposingly on both sides as the river's width narrowed and its depth increased.

"What is this place?" Walters asked the one who had brought him there.

Mogart sighed. "Earth. Same pattern. Only in this frame our dear little planet was an afterthought—not part of the project at all, which had to do with some very different sort of creatures developing on Venus. Because the Probabilities Department needed Venus, they had to have the whole planetary system, so life evolved here in spite of rather than because of the plan. This was a problem to the project people, of course, since human beings would evolve and reach a high-technology point where they might be able to interfere with the Venus project. To make certain this didn't happen, when humanity had reached a certain stage of development, some biological work was done essentially to freeze them, stabilize them culturally, at that level. Ah! There they are—I think you can see what I mean better than I could explain it."

They stopped and looked up the canyon. In a wide cleft, near a small trickling waterfall just across the river, was a small community of people. Although tanned extremely brown by the hot sun, they looked basically Mediterranean or Semitic. All seemed squarish of build, hard and muscular. Although the largest of them was a head shorter than Walters' own one hundred and ninety-plus centimeters, they looked tough. The bodies, both male and female, were extremely hairy, and the men's beards, which didn't seem long, were nonetheless thick, giving the appearance of a jet-black lion's mane. Their hair was long and scraggly, their gait slightly stooped, and they wore no clothes.

"They look like a bunch of apes," Walters remarked.

Mogart nodded. "More or less. They're smart apes—they have a language that's rather simple yet can convey fairly complex ideas; they have a clearly defined cultural pattern, which is essentially instinctual; they use simple tools and have rather marked if very primitive religious beliefs. It was the instinct that froze the society—human beings like yourself have essentially none. When the social and cultural traits were made hereditary, the society froze at this level."

Walters nodded numbly, feeling a bit sick. The thought of a civilization like Mogart's that had the power to do this to an entire race—and did so without feeling any remorse at all—was uncomfortable indeed. But, most importantly, here was a pretty convincing demonstration that Mogart's people would cheerfully let his own world get smashed to bits if doing so didn't interfere with their plans.

"If this isn't part of a project, as you call it, then what's one of your people doing here?" Walters asked.

Mogart smiled weakly. "Balthazar is . . . er, well, a bit ill, I'm afraid," he began uncertainly. He caught Walters' look and continued. "Oh, he won't hurt you. No, not that. But he's quite mad. He loves to suffer, and there's a lot of that in this society."

Mac's eyebrows rose. "A masochist?"

"A masochist, yes, in every sense of the word."

"But how does he get along in this society?" the big man pressed. "I mean, they don't wear any clothes, and you would certainly stand out even more than I in that group. I wouldn't think they'd accept him, except as a devil or a god."

"Ordinarily you'd be right," Mogart agreed, "but he had himself surgically altered to look more human. Without anesthetic, I might add. But I don't dare go any closer than this—he'd sense me. You'll still recognize him, though, if you see him. Don't worry about that." He paused, looking around. "Now we have to see if we can find you a likely subject for integration without exposing myself." He explained that it would be necessary to place the human into the body of another native to this world.

They continued along the bank, going away from the group.

"Ordinarily I try and have someone from the race on tap to help explain things," Mogart told him, "but this culture's too primitive to allow that. I think integration will give you all the information you need. Ah!

That's what I was looking for!" A clawed hand extended itself and Walters' gaze followed it. Just around the bend from the tribe of humans he saw a dark shape.

"Don't worry, they can't see us or hear us," Mogart soothed, and together they approached.

A young man was crouching by the river, drinking some of the muddy water and washing himself off with it. He was extremely muscular and ruggedly handsome, although he had numerous ugly scars and welts all over his body.

"An unattended young male," Mogart explained. "In order to get any tribal standing, he has to beat one of the male tribal leaders, thereby displacing him. Pecking order is determined by how good a fighter you are, and rank is shown by the number of wives and children you have. He's had a number of inconclusive fights, obviously—but he's lost, which makes him the slave of the loser. He's obviously escaped from the tribe and now haunts it, working out, until he can go back and mount a new challenge. He'll have to do."

Walters looked him over. "You mean I'm going to become him?"

The demon nodded. "You'll have all your knowledge, memories, skills, and personality, but you'll be in his body with *his* instinctual knowledge and past experience to draw on. Time is short—roughly two days here equals an hour back home, and we have four more stones to collect. Remember, all you need do is have the gem in your possession and say my name. It will bring you back to the bar."

Walters nodded. "Okay, I'm as ready as I'll ever be."

"Just walk up to him," Mogart said, "and touch him."

Walters approached the man, who had finished washing and was turning as if to walk back up to some hidden nest or nook. The unseen human reached out, then hesitated a moment.

"Remember, if you fail you are here for the rest of your life—there will be no bar to return to," Mogart warned. "Now, touch him!"

It was an order and a compulsion. Walters touched the primitive man. He felt a sensation like an electric shock, and suddenly the young primitive looked up, confused, then fell dizzily to the ground.

Mogart looked satisfied. "By all the gods, I need a drink!" he swore, and vanished.

2

Mac Walters awoke and sat up groggily. The ground was wet and clammy, and he was in some underbrush. For a moment he was confused; images seemed to blur and thoughts were duplicated. Suddenly he became fully aware and looked around, startled. He hadn't really believed Mogart when the demon had said he'd be inside another's body, but there was no mistaking it.

The body was powerful and in excellent condition, that was a fact. But it was different—filled with small aches and pains that he understood probably had been in his own body as well but, being in different places, were more noticeable in this one. Vision, hearing, smelling—all seemed slightly better and slightly different, although subtly so.

He was still checking out such things when something, some sixth sense, shouted a warning to him. Instantly the newly acquired instinctive protective reactions came into play; he was up and quickly off to seek cover behind some nearby large rocks. It was done so fast and so totally without thinking that he was through all the motions before he even realized it. Curious, he cautiously peered out from his hiding place, ears and nose particularly searching for what had made him run and hide. Then he heard them coming up the canyon. Not a lot of people, no more than a match-pack. But, of course, that was what it had to be.

Someone was challenging a leader to combat for position.

The group of men came around the bend—no, check that, four men and one elderly woman. The woman was obviously the senior wife of the leader, representing his wives and children. If the man lost, she would return with the new winner and there would be a formal family exchange.

Looking at her, Walters wondered why they bothered. She was old, scarred, saggy, with a bad limp and gray hair. She looked more like a wicked witch than somebody anyone would want to marry. He wondered how many husbands the woman had had.

It was easy to pick which was the dominant male—he had an aura of arrogance and displayed a look of confident contempt. Two of the men were obviously slaves, one for each of the combatants. They had a stake in this fight as well—the loser lost all he had, but the slaves of the loser were freed of further service.

The challenger was no newcomer: although younger than the man he was to fight, he'd been through a lot. Massive scars covered his body, and his nose looked as if it had been broken half a dozen times. Unlike the leader male, the challenger was serious, almost grave.

This was no ordinary challenge, Mac realized suddenly. The leader was the chief of the tribe—and the challenger was going for the whole thing. This would be more than interesting. The easiest way to gain unhampered access to the demon and his gem would be to become chief. Mac didn't have to hold on to the position, only have it for a matter of hours at most.

The slaves carried a supply of weapons—large poles that looked like two meter-long clubs, stone axes bound to wooden handles with strips of skin or bark, and nasty-looking sharp stone spears similarly bound to thin but long bamboolike poles. All the weapons were dumped in a single heap between the two fighters. The two slaves and the elderly wife then walked back, far from the fighting, and took seats. Now only the two fighters stood facing each other, the challenger's back to the river, about three meters apart. The pile of weapons was about equidistant between the two men.

Then, for the first time, the chief spoke. "Bakh fight Malk?" he asked ritually.

The other bowed. "Bakh be chief. Malk old. No good now."

Malk seemed to smile. He never lost his aura of

superiority, and that *had* to be unsettling to the challenger. *This may be primitive, but it is subtle,* Walters decided. The old chief knew psychology.

"Bakh show white hair," the chief noted, trading age insult for age insult. "Bakh lose, cost be high. No man no more."

Mac puzzled over this for a minute. Obviously you were allowed only so many challenges no matter what, and Bakh was down to his last one. Did the remark mean that he would be killed if he lost?

Whatever it meant, the comment seemed to infuriate the challenger. "Oh?" he sneered. "Then Bakh say same to Malk."

Walters understood now that they were setting the terms of the fight beyond that prescribed by the law of the tribe. This was not standard, then—they were upping the stakes. *These men must hate each other a great deal,* he decided.

"Bakh say Malk be slave of woman, do woman work to death-sleep," the challenger added.

A little of the confident veneer wavered just a moment in the chief's demeanor, but he quickly recovered. Mac realized with growing fascination that this was a war of nerves, that they were adding promise of a horrible existence on top of horrible existence to the loser. You could back out, probably, up to the moment of the fight—although you probably lost your honor and therefore all you owned. He wondered how many fights for top spots ended without a blow being struck.

The chief nodded to his challenger. "Bakh same," he replied in a tone that added the "of course" not in their language.

They went on a bit longer, until finally there seemed nothing else to threaten. It was over. Both men nodded acceptance of the terms and turned to the slaves and the old woman, who nodded back indicating that they had heard the exchange, understood it, and would see the challenge carried out. Then the men turned back to face each other.

"Fight," the chief said, totally without expression—and it was on.

The two men warily circled each other and the weapons for a while, each trying to feel the other out. Suddenly Bakh, the challenger, darted in and grabbed a club. Malk laughed and circled the challenger, standing amid the weapons pile. As long as Bakh held that position, the old chief could not get a club or axe or spear himself, but he really didn't have to. It was the challenger's job to beat him, and he was content to wait for the attack. There was no time limit, judges, or referees here. The chief could afford to wait.

"Malk coward!" sneered Bakh, lowering the club a little. "Malk no want fight Bakh. Malk old, be old woman!"

The taunts were obviously designed to provoke an angry and unthinking reaction, but the old chief hadn't gotten to where he was by being stupid. His self-control, in fact, appeared almost complete.

Bakh suddenly realized this and switched tactics. He shifted the club to his left hand and picked up a spear carefully. The object was clear to all: a spear could be thrown.

But while he shifted and leaned down to get the spear, there was a momentary pause when his eyes moved, ever so briefly, off the old chief.

Malk saw it and leaped, his body ramming into the other man with much force and causing both to go sprawling. *They are quick, that's for sure,* Mac thought. Somehow, as he crashed into the challenger and rolled, the chief had managed to pick up an axe.

Like expert gymnasts, they were on their feet in moments. Bakh had lost his bid for the spear, but the club had dropped near him and he picked it up quickly.

Malk stepped back, letting Bakh press in on him, taking the challenger away from the now-scattered weapons. He felt the axe in his hand, tested it for balance, right hand still at his side.

Bakh's strategy was obvious—he was pressing the old chief against the canyon wall. Malk realized it, too, and decided to move. With a deft action the axe flipped underhand from his hand directly at the head of the challenger. But Bakh saw it and deflected the axe with his club, which he held like a quarterstaff. The deflection threw him off balance, though, and Malk seized the opening to leap again at the challenger. The club went up in a defensive motion, but only the chief's left hand grabbed it; his right went hard into Bakh's suddenly undefended crotch.

The challenger yowled with pain, a scream that echoed down the canyon, and dropped the club as he doubled over. Malk was ready; as the club dropped he caught it, shifted it to his right hand, and brought it down on Bakh's head—hard.

It was no contest. The challenger collapsed in a heap. His scalp was bleeding, but as the others rushed up to check they saw that he was still alive.

Malk caught his breath; he was breathing hard, and the adrenalin was already starting to fade from his system. He turned to one of the slaves. "Priest!" he ordered. The slave took off at a run down the canyon, back toward the tribe.

Everybody must have been waiting just out of sight for the results, for the slave returned with the priest in a matter of moments. The priest differed from the others. He was about their size, but much thinner and bonier; he walked oddly and was tremendously scarred from head to foot. He wore a piece of bone through his nose, bone through his ears, and a necklace made up of nobody knew what. He carried a container made from skin of some kind under his arm, and he approached the scene of the fight hurriedly.

He stopped, examined the unconscious loser, and sighed. "Priest wait for Bakh wake?" he asked, his voice tinged with anticipation.

The chief looked at him in disgust. "No, Bakh brave. Do now!"

The priest's expression changed to disappointment. He sighed and pulled from the pouch a series of extremely sharp stones and what looked like herbs of one kind or another, then proceeded with a gruesome mutilation of the fallen foe which included the removal of the man's thumbs and tongue, and castration. At least now Mac Walters understood the terrible terms invoked and the price paid for losing. He turned away, much too sickened to continue watching.

He knew a few things now, though. The young man whose body he wore had lost fights without mutilation, so it was far less costly to fight someone low in rank. He thought he could take the chief, but he wasn't sure; and the chief was a lot more experienced and blood-thirsty than he. Too much of a risk.

He also knew now that the demon was in fact with the tribe, that he was the high priest and witch doctor, and that he was, among other things, a sadist as well as a masochist.

Mac Walters decided he needed time to think this thing through.

3

Although time was of the essence, as Mogart had said, Mac Walters decided early on that if the world was going to be saved, he was going to be one of the saved if at all possible. That meant not rushing into things where death could be just a minor little occur-rence if that damned demon had him on the wrong end of those nasty sharp stones and needles.

He waited until everyone had gone, then walked back, away from the direction of the tribe, trying to spot the man's hideout. This body occupation was less than perfect; he felt as if he were in familiar surround-ings, and new scenes looked very normal to him. But he couldn't remember specific facts the man wouldn't even have had to think about.

Finally, though, he saw what he was looking for near the other end of the canyon, about halfway up the wall of red rock. It was not an easy climb, but he seemed to know the steps and holds automatically, and finally reached a small cave hidden from view by a jagged outcrop. It was dry and hard and not very homey, but it would do. Inside he found evidence that the man had lived there for some time—remains of excrement, which didn't thrill him, some dried-out grasses that made at least a makeshift cushion to sleep on—not *much* better than the bare rock, but a little. And some strangled birds.

The man would have to be pretty damned quick to catch birds, he thought. There seemed no way to cook them, though; a fire would betray his position even if he had had a fire source, he realized. He was still too much Mac Walters for his own good, he realized sourly, and settled down to get some sleep while wondering how hungry he would have to be before he'd eat raw dead birds.

Hungry was what he was when he awoke shortly before dawn, but not *that* hungry. He knew he would have to reconnoiter the tribe a bit more before making his move and hoped that, perhaps, they'd leave something edible within snatching range.

Spying on them was easy. He just climbed farther up to the top of the canyon, then, crouching low, walked carefully down until he was across from and above the main tribal area.

They were nomadic, no doubt about that. Their pits were crude and shallow, their weapons and implements also crude and carried tied on a yoke of thin logs designed for humans, not animals. They *had* domesticated the dog, which was bad. That meant there would be no getting close to them without a lot of barking and maybe worse. Horses, cows, or any sign of agriculture were absent, though. They were hunters and gatherers.

He felt genuinely sorry for them. They were people, just like himself, really—but cruelly and permanently trapped in the early part of the Old Stone Age, locked in an artificial heredity-mandated social system that absolutely prohibited the new and revolutionary idea.

They *did* seem to have fire in those pits, though; thin wisps of smoke curled from the dozens scattered around the cleft floor. He wondered how they made or carried their fires—*flint, probably,* he decided. This area was dry enough so that you could start a fire without much patience if you had flint.

The tribal organization was also easily observed. A large number of women and children, most still asleep, flanked both sides of the waterfall, and there was a clear space around them for several meters. Their own territory was marked by an old spear stuck in the ground with what looked like a human skull impaled on it. A couple of early-rising women in the chief's group seemed to be pounding or grinding something on nearby rocks and watching the large fire pits. *Breakfast, of course,* he concluded hungrily.

Flanking the chief's area were several younger men —*slaves, probably,* he guessed. The other areas were organized in much the same way, in a descending order of magnitude. Far from the cleft and the water source, separated from the rest, were a number of young men in a group by themselves. *The unattached male surplus,* he thought.

As the sun rose higher and its light started to filter down into the canyon itself, the community began to wake up.

The day progressed, with Mac just watching, getting hungrier and hungrier, but learning.

The women prepared the foods, dug the pits, tended the fires, even maintained a very primitive, public pit toilet. The family men hunted, fished with crude nets made of bark and skin, and generally worked together to find a food supply, be it deer or lizard, fish or certain kinds of marsh grasses. The food was brought back, then the men were allowed to pick their needs based on their tribal rank. The surplus males, who also were required to hunt, got what was left over.

The men spent the rest of their time—if, as on this day, they were lucky enough to gather enough food early—making and tending their weapons, shaping stones as tools for the women, and a few even indulged in elaborate sand paintings or more simplified drawings on the canyon walls. Chief Malk himself seemed to be the one who taught the young men the art of fighting—an act of extreme bravery, considering he was training the people who would, certainly, one day challenge, beat, and replace him. *But then,* Mac reflected, *you never play poker with the man who taught you.* There was not only the matter of experience but the one or two tricks he kept to himself that would do you in.

Malk's primary enemy, he realized, was age or crippling injury. There were no old men or obvious cripples among any there except for a few slaves of the chief who were, like the unfortunate Bakh, kept around as object lessons.

One day Malk *would* be too old or too slow, or would have an accident and break a limb and wind up on the losing end of a challenge. So would the lesser-ranking males. The older females seemed to keep their position, but not the men. They had a very limited time of power, then fell into disgrace, disfigurement, and probably quick suicide. It was a terribly uncertain life; even a bad cold could do Malk in.

Mac wondered idly what the average life span of a chief really was.

By midafternoon, he no longer wondered how hungry he'd have to be to eat raw birds—or raw anything else for that matter. He forced himself to do it and to trap and strip a couple of lizards as well. He felt better, although he still preferred his food cooked and would have preferred something more substantial.

He knew one thing—he couldn't keep up this routine very long. Better to go down and get it over with, trusting to his football training and his college wrestling experience to see him through. He left the cave and walked, boldly this time, toward the tribe. He was still a way off when he saw a young woman slip into the river to wash off. She turned, saw him, and her mouth dropped open in surprise. He approached her curiously.

"Dend be crazy! Bad spirit in Dend!" she uttered in complete wonder. He was obviously expected to know her.

"Dend win fight that comes," he responded, hoping he sounded confident. The exchange was a little unsettling. He could internally verbalize anything he wanted, but apparently he could vocalize only what this language allowed—and that really wasn't much.

He walked on. This late in the day most people were back in their areas. He hit the young men's area first, and they looked up at him with surprise and shock on their faces. He guessed that Dend must have gotten beaten pretty badly the last time and been run out of town on a rail or some equivalent.

He wasn't going much farther. The first, outer area was composed of groups of no more than four wives and one or two slaves. He had seen the pro leagues; he would be satisfied with a spot on the lowest of the amateur clubs.

They gave him wide berth, knowing what he must be there to do. The males in particular seemed frozen, waiting to see who he would pick. He, in turn, looked them over, trying to select his victim. Two he dismissed immediately. They hardly had a mark or scar on them and so were obviously damned good fighters on their way up. He wanted one of younger years who was fairly well marked up and had the look of complacency rather than ambition.

He found no such man, and he understood why almost immediately. In the lowest rank you always had all those young, unattached men looking for a way into society. Only in the middle ranks would such a complacent one be found, and he'd probably be pretty damned good.

Mac noticed that one of the men stood a little uncomfortably, as if he had some sort of physical problem. He was young but well scarred—a better bet than most, Mac decided. Since it was his move and he was already committed, he walked over to the gimpy-legged man. Standing up straight, trying the best look of arrogance he could muster, he pointed at the man and said, "Dend challenge!"

It was a good thing the girl had called him by name; the language had no personal pronouns.

The other males visibly relaxed, and one or two went back to eating or being preened or whatever it was they had been doing when he arrived.

The gimpy-legged man grinned evilly, exposing broken and crooked teeth. "Fight now?" he came back, looking not the least bit worried. Then he added, "Run now—like fight-that-was?"

Walters understood suddenly why there was so much amazement and contempt at his return. This Dend had turned coward and run the last time.

"Fight now," he emphasized. The other man nodded and turned to walk down to the river. Mac was confused. "Weapons?" he asked.

The little man grinned that evil grin again, stopped, and held up his powerful-looking arms. "Guml no need weapons for *Dend*," he responded, pronouncing the last word as if it were a dead skunk that needed quick burial before it stank up the place.

The rules were slightly different in the lower ranks, Mac discovered. First, the unattached young men were permitted to watch—an open invitation to challenge the winner after spotting his weak points, Mac noted.

Guml's slight limp didn't seem to bother or limit him in the least, much to Mac's disappointment.

The young men formed a wide circle around the two fighters; he and Guml stood facing each other, sizing each other up. The other man had good balance despite his injury, and there was no mistaking the power in his bulging arm and leg muscles. Mac felt as if he were back on the line, in a sort of nudist pro football game, one-on-one.

"Fight!" Guml snarled, and without any of the ceremony or ritual Mac had earlier witnessed, the fight was on. He was thankful they hadn't traded challenges, anyway. Nonetheless, he had the same problem Bakh had had, in one respect—Guml didn't have to expose himself to attack, but could afford to wait for the challenger.

Mac put his arms in the blocker's position and charged with a bloodcurdling scream. The combination of sudden charge and scream caught the other man off guard. Mac was on him before he could twist away, and in another second they were on the ground, grappling for position, rolling over and over. The circle of young men, curiously quiet for spectators, made room for them.

Mac felt incredibly strong viselike fingers on his throat and pushed out hard against the other's strong neck, trying to break the grip. Almost reflexively, he brought his knee up toward the other man's groin. Guml was too good for that, though; he released his grip and twisted, catching Mac's knee, and using his whole body as a lever, threw the challenger to the ground hard.

What followed was almost classical wrestling, Guml on top, hands and knees keeping Walters' body pressed against the ground. Mac couldn't break the grip in this position; but, unlike wrestling where pinning would do it, Guml would have to move off one of the pressure points for the *coup de grâce*. Mac waited, knowing he would have only a split second before it would be all over. He guessed the shot would be the man's right arm—his legs weren't his strongest suit, and he was right-handed.

Mac was right. He felt the pressure suddenly let up and twisted and rolled, spilling the other man to the ground. Mac wasn't about to let the man get up. He pounced on him, grabbing him arm under throat, and squeezed hard. He could hear Guml groan and try to breathe as all his air was cut off; he had the tribesman at the Adam's apple from a position atop his back— almost perfect.

But Guml wasn't through. Somehow, by sheer force of will, he got an arm up and got hold of some of Mac's long black hair and pulled with all his ebbing strength.

The move was unexpected, and Walters dropped his grip as he moved to free himself from the sudden pain. Guml wasn't in good condition, though, and could barely twist out from under while still gasping for breath. Yet, for a moment the tribesman was free, and he rolled as Mac came back to pounce on him once more.

The man from another world was confident now and jumped on the still-gasping tribesman with enthusiasm, grabbing him again by the throat. But this time he had his two powerful hands around the vulnerable area and kept the victim face up.

The victim was ready, though; a huge hand came up with a large rock in it and struck Mac on the side of the head with a powerful blow that drew blood. He let go and rolled over, stunned from the force of the unexpected attack. All he could think of was, *That's cheating!* Then a second blow hit him, then a third, and he was plunged into a terrible darkness.

4

It was well past dark when Mac Walters awoke. His head hurt like hell, and there was dried and caked blood in his hair. He groaned.

Guml heard him and sauntered over, looking down. Even by moonlight the man had an evil grin. "Dend fight good," the man with the limp acknowledged. "Lose good fight. Slave now—next year try Guml."

Mac couldn't think clearly. Too many workmen were using hammers to knock holes in his head. He could not remember ever having such pain. Still, he managed, "Guml break law to win." In this limited language "law" and "rule" were the same.

Guml chuckled. "No break law. No law for Guml break." He walked away, still chuckling.

Mac tried to get up, found it too much of an effort, and sank back down, breathing deeply to try to alleviate the pain. Sleep would be the only healer, he knew. He didn't want to try that sadistic witch doctor from a position of weakness, and so he was helpless for the moment. He could only consider the fact that he'd been the victim of a cultural loophole he hadn't foreseen. Clearly, in this society, you could get away with anything if there was no rule expressly forbidding it.

The next day was a learning experience. He discovered, first of all, that his fight had earned him a portion of respect from the other low-rank slaves and unattached young men, but that did him little good. The rules governing a loss were quite specific in this closed society and enforced by *all* the males regardless of rank. He was obligated to be a slave, to take Guml's orders and carry them out, and not to challenge anybody else to a fight for at least a year—the period of time when this nomadic tribe would again return to this canyon cleft.

The duties weren't too difficult—to help the women with the heavy stuff, which was considered demeaning by the other men but was nothing much to him, and to help keep the place marked out as Guml's as clean and neat as possible. He was also to help in the daily hunting and gathering with the other men, but since slaves did most of the labor and there was no dearth of slaves, the work even there was light. The toughest thing was that he had to try as hard as possible to ignore the women, and they had to ignore him. The penalty for any sort of sexual fraternization between a slave and a woman was the loss of the ability to make use of those urges.

His situation wouldn't have been tough even then, but time was pressing. He was stuck in a dead-end job and three days had already passed. An hour and a half of the eight his world had left to live. Time was running out on him rather quickly, and he was still far from his goal.

The witch doctor was glimpsed only occasionally, despite the smallness of the tribe. He kept mostly to himself, didn't take part in the hunt, and was left pretty much alone. The tribe was convinced he had great magical powers—which he probably did, using the jewel—and was in personal daily contact with the Sun God. He was also greatly feared for his sadism and sadomasochism, the last of which nonetheless brought a measure of respect from even the top males of the tribe. Anyone who could take such self-inflicted punishment and seem to like it was obviously incredibly brave, even if more than a little bit nuts.

By the evening of the third day on this world, Mac Walters knew he had to get out. This Dend hadn't escaped before, he'd run and dishonored himself. Now he would have to accomplish a true escape, although if caught the penalties would be anything but pleasant. Guml would be able to do anything to him he wanted, and the tribesman would be a dangerous man to be completely at the mercy of, with all the rules off.

Throughout the first day a woman who looked middle-aged and ugly as sin had showed him great kindness; while cleaning and stoking her fire pit she'd given him some good-tasting cooked berries—something a slave would never get to touch, ordinarily—and showed other kindnesses. She told him he reminded her of her dead son, and that was fine with him. It made life easier, and not even Guml would think there was any sexual hanky-panky with a woman this old and ugly. Her name was Oona, and by the middle of the third day she was so deep into her fussings that she often referred to Mac as "Oona-son" and was consistently more motherly.

As Mac expected, Guml found the relationship more humorous than anything else and allowed it. He seemed grateful to get Oona off his own back; he was far too busy with some younger and more attractive women.

The hunt on the third day in this strange, primitive world did not go well, though. They became a little ambitious and decided to tackle a herd of antelope watering downstream. Mac stayed well back, since he was new to all this, but that proved no safe refuge as he saw the graceful, long-horned, deerlike creatures leap ten meters or more in their panic. One leaped in his direction and cleared most of the men.

Mac was tough, all right, and he knew how to take a fall from his football days. Otherwise, two hundred kilos of deer would have pounded him into the ground and broken most of his bones. As it was, the weight was mostly on the left shoulder, briefly. It hurt like hell, but he suffered only a bad bruise and sprain and not a break. They had to carry him back to camp, but he refused medical help. He could just imagine what that witch doctor would do with him. Two other men weren't so lucky. One would be cremated that evening; the other, one of the unattached young men, would soon join him.

Oona fussed and fumed over him; even Guml was concerned, since he had a measure of respect for this brave man. Mac's "master" sent the woman for some broad, dry leaves that were kept in the chief's pouch, and, with Malk's permission, he was permitted to grind a portion of the leaves into a clay-fashioned crude pipe.

It was not marijuana, with which Mac was familiar,

but something infinitely stronger. It was potentially addictive, since it was closely rationed and used primarily for easing pain. The sinking young man was given all he wanted.

For Mac, the effect was like an explosion in his head, followed by the rapid falling off of pain to an ecstatically pleasant numbness; all seemed right and wonderful, the surroundings and colors seemed beautiful. He felt an incredible sense of well-being such as he had never known.

The next morning the shoulder still hurt like hell and there was only a slight rosy afterglow from the drug, but the sleep allowed by the drug had done wonders for him. Not for the more seriously injured man, though. There would be another cremation at the new dusk.

Hurt though he was, Mac was determined that he would not be around to witness the act if he could help it. *The fourth day,* he kept thinking. *Two hours gone. A quarter of the time.*

As a man injured in the line of duty, so to speak, he was not now expected to work. Instead he spent most of the time trying to keep Oona from fussing over him and looking for a way out. By late afternoon he had the germ of a plan. It wasn't complete, but it would accomplish what he needed. In a way, the injury, although still aggravating, was the best thing that could have happened to him.

He would have to make his move tonight, he decided. Time was running out all too quickly. Time! Already four days—two precious hours shot. If this plan didn't work, or if it did but he couldn't get the jewel, he was as good as dead. And so was his world.

He believed he'd been inconspicuous, but as he waited for darkness to overtake the campsite Oona slid up to him and offered to massage his shoulder. It ached and he needed it, so he let her begin.

After a little of the soothing rubdown, the woman said in a low whisper, "Dend be going leave clan." It wasn't a question but a statement.

He sighed and his mind raced. She must have trailed

him today and watched his movements, what he was studying, all of it, and put two and two together. Although she'd been useful, she was getting to be a real pain—and a danger. He considered his answer, knowing that if he lied she'd just spy on him all night.

"Dend leave when dark," he admitted. "Oona no stop leave?"

"Oona leave, go where Dend go," she replied unhesitatingly.

He was surprised. Not only had he not counted on this, but she would most certainly get in the way. She had been nice to him; she wouldn't understand what he was doing with the witch doctor, and she would certainly be out on a limb if he managed to get the jewel and then left. *The trouble with this language is that it allows you to communicate action but not to hold subtle arguments.*

"Oona no leave. Not good. Dend come back to fight in year," he attempted.

"Oona leave, go where Dend go," she persisted.

He gave up. A big argument would draw attention to him; if he left her behind, she might raise an alarm just to have him returned. *Okay, Oona, old mother hen, you dug your own hole,* he thought.

Through dusk and into darkness he feigned increasing pain but refused to smoke the magic leaves. There was enough sympathy and respect for him that nobody was suspicious; nobody questioned him.

Oona meanwhile gathered up a few things in a skin pouch and waited. It was well into the night; even the moon was below the canyon walls by the time he was ready. Just about everybody was asleep, and furious snores echoed off the canyon walls. Even Oona was dropping off. Mac rose as quietly as possible and started away. Suddenly she looked up, saw him going, and began to follow. He cursed a little under his breath but could do nothing to stop her.

It was remarkably easy to escape. The only reason more slaves hadn't done it was, first, this was an instinctually tribal people who were not suited to going it alone, and second, the life of a slave was neither that terribly bad nor a permanent condition. One had more to lose from escaping, particularly because there was just about nothing to escape *to*.

Oona remained quiet. She didn't even utter a sound when she saw him make his way back toward the far left base of the canyon instead of away downriver, although her face showed extreme confusion.

He had no weapons, but passing near a fire pit that had gone out, he grabbed a thick piece of wood that would serve as a club. He also steered clear of the dogs, which would challenge him if he came too close to their owners' territories. They were his worst fear, since if just one got set off they all would, and everybody would be awake. They were the tribal guard.

The witch doctor's area was apart from the others, and he kept no dog. Dogs didn't like the witch doctor any more than the people did—less, it seemed. That was the other worry.

And there he was—sleeping there on a collection of netting, dead to the world. Mac was happy to see it. This was the first indication he had that demons slept. The surgery this one had undergone to make him more human was very good indeed, but he still walked and even slept with his legs at the odd angle more appropriate to his own cloven-hoofed race.

Now to the task. A jewel like Mogart's would glow in the eerie darkness even if a tiny portion of it was exposed to air, Mac felt sure of that. The one he had seen had appeared to have a life of its own. Mac looked around, concerned now. His plan had seemed very simple, but somehow he'd known it wouldn't be. Seeing no other artifacts, he felt certain the jewel had to be in the skin bag with the herbs and sharp stones that was the demon's medical kit. Surely so essential a thing as the jewel would not be left behind in some buried spot. It was his badge of authority with these savages and, most important, his only way out of unforeseen tight situations. It just *had* to be here.

The demon slept soundly. Mac crept close to him, club at the ready, reaching the skin bag that was a mere hand's span from the witch doctor's face. He picked it up, stepped back a bit, and opened the bag in anticipation.

There was no glowing gem.

He dumped the contents of the bag onto the ground and felt inside again for hidden compartments. There were none. The jewel wasn't in the bag; it wasn't around anyplace he could see, and since the demon was nude, as they all were, it wasn't in his clothing, either. The witch doctor still wore his bone jewelry, but that was hardly a likely hiding place. None of the bones was large enough to contain or conceal the gem.

There was nothing else Mac could do. If he couldn't find the gem, then the demon would have to tell him where it was. He judged the distance, angle, and velocity required, and hoped he wasn't making a big mistake. Raising the club, he brought it down hard on the demon's skull.

The witch doctor started as if shocked; his eyes and mouth flew open. For a fleeting moment Mac feared that he would cry out an alarm, but then the eyes rolled upward, closed again, and he sagged visibly.

So demons can also be knocked cold. That's handy to know, too, Mac Walters thought.

Being as careful as he could, he hoisted the body, which was surprisingly light, over his back and good shoulder and turned. Oona just stood there, mouth open, knowing what she was seeing but totally unable to comprehend any of it.

Mac didn't care. His burden still made his bad shoulder hurt like hell, and he wanted out of there as quickly as possible.

The demon groaned and opened his eyes. Things were terribly blurry, and his head pounded. Finally he made out two dim shapes and tried to focus on them. He was in a cave, he knew that. He tried to move his arms and legs and found them bound with strong vines.

Balthazar smiled suddenly. Bound and spirited away! What fun! A man's face came close to his and he could make out the features. *This is Guml's slave, Dend,* he thought, wondering just what was going on here.

"Where stone that burns?" Dend demanded.

It took Balthazar a second to comprehend. This fellow meant the amplifier! He chuckled. "Why Dend want stone that burns?" he asked, both curious and amused. "No good but to spirit priests. *Kill* Dend."

Now it was the other man's turn to laugh. "No kill Dend. Dend no want." Mac Walters hesitated now, trying to decide whether to blow the whole bit: *Oh, hell,* he thought sourly, *what harm could it do? At least this creature will know he isn't dealing with an ignorant savage. That will save time.*

"Mogart want stone that burns," he told the demon.

Balthazar gasped. "Mogart!" His mind was clearing quickly now. "Then Dend not Dend."

Walters shook his head. "Dend *not* Dend," he confirmed.

The demon was still digesting that fact when he saw there was a third person in the cave—an old woman, it looked like. She walked forward now, and he saw that in her hand she held a burning ember, its flame extinguished but still glowing red in the almost total darkness of the cave.

"Baal give stone that burns Dend!" she ordered in a tone that surprised both of them. Mac hadn't even known that she was going to get involved, and he looked wonderingly at her wrinkled and scarred face by the light of the ember. There was sheer hatred in her eyes and expression, that was for sure.

Oona might not know what the hell was going on, but she definitely had reasons to hate this demonic witch doctor.

Balthazar was equally surprised. "Oona!" he exclaimed.

Now it was Mac Walters' turn to be confused. These two obviously knew each other, and pretty well.

Without hesitation, she touched the ember to Balthazar's skin just below the hip. It sizzled and made a sickening stench; even Walters was stunned by her unhesitating brutality.

The demon's reaction, however, was not at all expected. Instead of yelling and screaming in pain, he almost seemed to lean into the glowing wooden wand, and his face took on a look of rapturous delight.

"No, Oona!" Mac shouted, and grabbed the burning

ember from her hand. "Baal *like* hurt!" It was true.
Here was one very sick mind.

She hesitated a moment, looked at her victim, and
saw that this was so. She threw up her hands in disgust. Plainly she was feeling the same helplessness Mac
himself felt.

*How the hell do you torture a secret out of a mas-
ochist like this?*

The situation was worse than that, really. Holding
the ember and shaking it a bit to keep it glowing, he
held it near where Oona had thrust it into the demon's
side.

The charred flesh was already starting to heal.

*How long had Mogart said he'd been on Earth?
Since the beginnings,* Mac thought glumly. They
couldn't be killed, and their injuries healed quickly.
The scars on Balthazar were obviously a touch of au-
thenticity added by the surgeons, rather than true ones.

Not only could the son of a bitch be tortured in-
definitely, but he'd love every minute of it.

Mac understood Oona's frustration. Whatever this
creature had done to make her hate him so, there was
obviously no way to get even. No way at all. That jewel
seemed to be as unattainable as ever.

Even the demon sensed the frustration, and started
to chuckle in the dark.

Oona was so mad she stalked out of the cave, leaving the two alone. Balthazar sensed this, looked up,
and said, "Dend put hand on Bual, talk more good."

Walters considered it. A trick, perhaps? Some way
for the demon to get at him? He sighed. *Might as well,*
he decided, and put his hand on Balthazar's shoulder.

There was no feeling, no sensation out of the ordinary, and after a few seconds Mac took his hand
away, confused.

"That's much better," said Balthazar in flawless,
middle-American English. "The language of these people can be *so* cumbersome sometimes."

Walters' jaw dropped. He was speechless for a
moment.

Balthazar sensed his wonderment. "Oh, come, come.
You can talk to me as well. I merely had to match your

soul to the known patterns of Mogart's world. I spent some time there a few thousand years ago, but it got too cultured and structured for me. I still take a look at it from time to time, though. There's some interesting devil worship going on there, and a bunch of talented amateurs manage to break through occasionally and summon me."

"Then you really *are* demons," Walters breathed.

Balthazar shrugged. "Magic is any phenomenon that is misunderstood. When sufficient mental force and desire are properly focused into, say, a pentagram, even by using ridiculous mumbo jumbo which helps concentration, these factors can call one or another of us who are, shall we say, *simpático* with the basic spirits of the callers. There are several of them in your world, although the number has fallen off in recent years."

"I need your jewel," Walters told the creature flatly. "My world is about to be destroyed by a collision with an asteroid, and only Mogart with enough power in his hands can stop it."

The demon shrugged again. "Too bad. I sympathize. But I'm not much on doing something for nothing, and there's nothing you can offer me to make me part with the only means I have of contacting, or being reached by, other continuums. This life is all well and good, but it gets to be a bore sometimes. No, I'm afraid you'll do without my jewel, and I am prepared to wait here in this cave until you die of old age if need be. Why not just forget this silliness and throw in with me? I've had some success establishing devil worship here— with me as the devil, of course. You could be a high priest for this tribe. Put your soul under my command and you won't have a bad life here."

Mac Walters snorted. "I don't think I'd want to preside over any religion *you* were at the heart of, even if I weren't already under Mogart."

Balthazar smiled. "But as you said yourself, Mogart is on a world that is swiftly coming to an end. He'll never go back; he'll kill himself first, the only way we can die. I need only outwait him—and you."

"Why, you——!" Walters snarled in fury, and put his hands around the other's throat and squeezed.

"Tighter! Tighter! Oh, please!" the demon choked, but he wasn't kidding. He really *did* enjoy this sort of thing.

Walters let go. "The woman—Oona. Tell me, why does *she* hate you?" he asked.

Balthazar coughed a little and caught his breath. "I have certain needs that others must fulfill," the demon told him. "With the jewel I have a certain power over others. Oona was one of the first I chose when I arrived here. She was pretty then, very desirable. She did as I commanded—she had no choice. The rites are, ah, rather strenuous. Within a year she was used up, the crone you see now."

Mac Walters heard the demon, and the hairs on his scalp tingled slightly. He felt sick. What sort of hideous, hellish rites did this demon command?

"How long ago?" he asked Balthazar. "How old is she?"

The demon shrugged. "I told you I haven't been with this tribe very long. A year, I suppose. She must be around twenty, I'd guess."

Mac Walters hit the demon hard on the jaw, not once but several times. The demon loved it, of course; but doing it made Mac feel a little better. Finally his shoulder, which had been agonizing for hours, just couldn't take it any more. In terrible pain, he whirled in disgust and walked out to the mouth of the cave, to where Oona was.

She looked up at him, seeing his obvious discomfort. "Down on belly!" she commanded. "Oona rub."

He shook his head from side to side, barely noting that, away from the demon, he was still in the other language frame. "No. Hurt be going." Still, he sank down with a sigh and leaned against the rock outcrop that protected them from view by any canyon-level searchers. He looked up at the sky. Soon it would be dawn of the fifth day.

He looked over at the woman. She looked old, terribly old and scarred and haunted, yet Balthazar had said she'd been a young beauty only a year before. No wonder she hated him!

"No can hurt Baal," she concluded, saying the obvious. "Leave Baal in cave. Dend-Oona go far, make Dend-Oona clan." She turned and looked hauntingly at the cave. "Baal hurt Oona, take young, pretty time, but Oona still make lots babies."

He sighed. So that was it. Wasted, ruined by the demon, she had returned ugly and ancient-looking, no longer desired by any of the men. Guml had had to take her back in since she was one of his wives, but nobody would give her a second look with so many unspoiled women about.

This explained a lot. She must have sensed in Mac something new, different from the other men. She knew he'd try to escape, and if he did, then it provided her with the only escape she had as well.

He felt enormous pity for her, but there was literally nothing he could do. The only thing even remotely possible was to get that jewel from Balthazar. Doing so would not help Oona, but it would help prevent future Oonas. The demon would still be both sick and immortal, but that would not translate into power if the jewel were removed. And it would keep him out of other planes where sadomasochistic devil worshippers might summon him to spread his sickness.

But how the hell did you torture a secret out of a sadomasochist? That would be the only way—to threaten him with something he just couldn't stand.

Mac's mind raced. *Let's see. If somebody is a sadomasochist, then you are incredibly kind to them, right? They can't stand that.* He sighed. How could you do that here? Balthazar was a prisoner, which suited him. Left to his own devices, he could inflict pain on himself, and if you were kind enough to remove his restraints it'd be even worse. He might even have some residual power, jewel or no.

And any scheme of that type would take time, lots of time. Time Mac didn't have; time that was running out.

He heard Oona fooling with something and looked over at her. She had that pouch she'd filled, and it was stuffed from the looks of it. From it she took some crushed narcotic weed and a clay pipe—the pipe he'd used the night before. She was preparing it to ease his pain.

Suddenly an idea came to him. "Oona!" he whispered excitedly, reaching over and taking the pouch. It was full of the stuff. Lots of it. For the first time in a long while, Mac Walters smiled. Here was his weapon—this and the demon's ignorance of his true circumstance.

"No hurt when smoke," Oona said soothingly.

His smile became a grin which she had mistaken for pain. The shoulder was bad, but it was forgotten now. He nodded to her. "No hurt when smoke!" he agreed, and pointed to the cave.

She understood almost immediately, and a faint grin appeared on her ravished face as well. "Ooooh . . ." she breathed.

Mac stood up with her help and went back into the cave. False dawn was upon them, and there was some light now. The demon had fallen asleep and had to be shaken to wake up. Mac Walters also checked the vine bindings to make sure they were secure.

The demon awoke and looked around, then yawned. "More fun and games?" he asked in English. Oona, preparing the leaves, seemed a little confused by the strange sounds, but ignored them.

"My turn," Walters replied. "Ever smoke the drug they use for pain around here?"

The demon sniffed. "Noxious stuff. Wouldn't touch it."

"I thought as much," Walters said, partly to himself. "Well, you see Oona over there? She's got a lot of it, and we're going to make a little fire in here and use some brush to block the cave entrance. You'll breathe it and feel no pain at all."

The demon laughed menacingly. "Very clever, but I am of strong mind. I can stand it."

Mac tried to match the menacingly confident tones of Balthazar. "Oh, not just now. We have lots of it—a whole grove of it that I spotted on my way in here. It's an awfully common weed, it seems." An extra tone that sounded somewhat sadistic itself crept into his voice. "How long do you think Oona can live?"

The demon looked worried. "If nothing happened, twenty, thirty, maybe more years. Why?" Realization was creeping into his voice, but he dared not think it.

"Not much time for an immortal," Walters shot back. "Twenty, thirty, forty years of being mildly drugged, feeling wonderfully high, unable to feel any pain. But that won't be all. I think the stuff's addictive. She'll only have to drug you for a few weeks at most, I think, and you'll be hooked. You'll *have* to have it. No pain, nothing but pleasant sensations, always."

The demon began sweating. He seemed nervous and scared, but he tried to think himself out of his predicament. "It's horrible! But you're right, Walters. Forty years—by the Gods of Teikelal! Horrible! But I can stand it! My people can't become addicted to your stuff!"

And then Mac Walters laughed. "Good try, Balthazar, but your people are the prototypes for all the worlds you created—in your own image, more or less. *You forget that Mogart is an alcoholic!*"

Oona couldn't understand what was being said, but she couldn't mistake the witch doctor's expression, his mixture of hatred and pure fear, the kind of expression heretofore found only on his victims. She held up a bowl of crushed leaves and took a lighted bit of tinder she'd just obtained by patient striking of flint. She touched it to the leaves and blew on it until they caught, slowly, a little reddish glowing patch in the middle of the bowl giving off a thin wispy smoke. With sheer enjoyment she thrust it under the demon's nose. He twisted and turned, but Mac's powerful grip held him now.

At the first whiff he recoiled; his voice became a strangled whisper, a whimper almost. "Take it away!" he pleaded. "Take it away! I'll do it! The jewel is yours!"

Walters smiled and gestured to Oona to remove the bowl.

"Five seconds," the man from another world told

him. "You have five seconds to tell me where the jewel is. Otherwise I walk out of here and leave the two of you alone for the day!"

Balthazar was only too anxious. "There's a pouch—a skin flap, a cavity between my genitals and my ass! It's in there!"

So that was it! Walters spread the demon on the floor and got a good wrestling position on him despite his bonds. He reached down, felt around, and found the pouch. It took a little doing to haul the jewel out, but he managed it.

The jewel looked just like Mogart's.

Mac released the demon. "One thing I don't understand," he said to him. "If you had it all the time, why didn't you use it?"

"I—I would have," the demon admitted, "but that would have taken some twisting with these bonds, and I didn't see the need. There would be time, later, when I would be alone and would not have to betray the location to you."

Oona looked pleased but confused. Mac turned to face her. "Oona, I wish I could help you, at least tell you what I have to do now—but there's no way."

She couldn't understand a word of what he was saying, but something in his tone and expression got through.

"Dend not Dend," he told her. "Dend come back, no remember Oona."

She seemed to understand, although there was a tear or two in her eyes. In her own terms, he was a spirit in Dend's body, an enemy spirit to that of the witch doctor; and now he had won, now he had to go.

He smiled compassionately and kissed her lightly on the forehead, then turned to go.

"Hey! Mogart man! Untie me! I have kept my end of the bargain!" the demon shouted anxiously. "You can't leave me here with *her*!"

Mac Walters turned, and a strange look appeared on his primitive face.

"No break law," he responded in the language of these people. "No law for Dend break."

Oona started laughing, laughing deep and hard, as she reached over to the bowl and glowing ember.

The screams of the demon and the almost unholy laughter would scare the hell out of any searchers below rather than attract them. And even if they were brave enough to investigate, hell, they'd probably love to watch the bastard squirm.

The sun was just coming up over the canyon wall, and Mac felt its warmth start to bathe the cold canyon walls and glisten off the slow, lazy river below.

He sighed and gripped the jewel tightly in his right hand.

"Take me to Asmodeus Mogart!" he commanded.

The bright sun, the warmth, and the canyon vanished.

Main Line +2076

THE BAR APPEARED MUCH AS HE'D LEFT IT. THE PEOple had changed position slightly; the bartender was starting to pour a beer that would take a long, long time to reach the glass, but that was about it.

Mac Walters turned but didn't leave the chalk pentagram on the floor. He spotted Mogart at a bar stool, nursing a large and barely diluted Scotch.

"Hey! Mogart! I got your damned jewel!" he called.

Mogart jumped, slightly startled, then turned slowly, lifting his head to see the source of the commotion.

"Wa—Waltersh!" he called, suddenly remembering who the man was.

Mac Walters held up the jewel and tossed it to Mogart. Drunk as the demon obviously was, he nonetheless caught it and looked at it wonderingly. "Be damned," Mogart muttered. "That makes three!"

Walters' eyebrows went up. "Three? Then the girl

got one?" He should have been elated, but it kind of hurt his male ego to have been beaten to the punch. *Maybe she had a faster time line,* he consoled himself.

Mogart stood up and struggled uncertainly over to the pentagram.

"You shertainly took yer time," he accused.

Walters felt his sense of victory deflate and looked at the clock. They'd left at—what? Six-fifteen or so. It was now almost nine o'clock.

The big man sighed. "Well, let's get me to the next one as fast as we can, huh?"

Mogart stepped into the pentagram. "Up, up, and away!" he shouted.

Both vanished from the bar that had not seen them in the first place. To those inside, less than a tenth of a second had passed from Walters' appearance to his disappearance. Time moved very, very slowly in the bar at Mogart's time rate, the fastest he could exist at and still be able to get the booze and translate it to his time speed.

But time still moved.

Main Line +1302

Makiva

1

"AN EASY ONE THIS TIME, ALTHOUGH DEADLY DANgerous," Asmodeus Mogart told Jill McCulloch as they materialized around a city street scene—or, to be more correct, the scene materialized around them. It was chilly and damp, not at all what she'd been used to. She shivered.

"Let's get on with this," she urged him. "I'm freezing to death!"

He grinned and motioned her to follow him.

It was another primitive world—nonindustrial, anyway—but obviously a lot more culturally advanced and cosmopolitan than the world of the Holy Spirit. Still, the men in robes and cloaks and hoods and the women in similar garb reminded her of her previous experiences. "No gods from the sky punishing sinners around here, are there?" she asked hopefully.

Mogart chuckled. "Oh, no. None of that. Gods and devils and spirits and spells galore, but no all-knowing, all-seeing being or system that I know of. You can lie and cheat and steal—even kill—to your heart's content here, subject only to the same thing *we* are used to: don't get caught."

She passed on responding to his cynical view of crime and instead pressed him for more concrete information. "Why was this world set up, and what're the details?"

Mogart stopped in the middle of a busy street, allowing pedestrians and occasional horses and oxen-pulled carts to go through him. She was almost as blasé as he by this point and didn't let it bother her.

"Makiva is one of about a hundred or so planes set up with differing rules of magic," he told her. "Most of the worlds below the two-thousand mark are basically nontechnological, those above it increasingly more so. Most, like this one, were established to prove this or that social or economic theory or point. To be perfectly honest, I can't remember what the point was here, but here it is all the same. Expect a lot of real elemental spirits—air spirits, earth spirits, fire spirits, and the like. Spells, curses, witches, warlocks, wizards, and sorcerers, too. If you're told somebody has the evil eye, they probably *do*. And if you disturb a hex sign you'll get hexed." He paused and looked around, surveying the busy scene, then continued.

"Since ignorance of magic by the common people is magic's greatest strength—along with belief in magic, of course—most people don't know any more about it than you do. Just take every little piece of superstitious behavior and belief you see and hear literally, and you have it. Big-time practitioners of magic train for years to do it right. They better, or they're dead!"

Mogart seemed to get some amusement from that. "It's all very mathematical, very logical, and very precise—but don't worry about it. Come."

They walked up the street, continuing to ignore and be ignored by the crowds of the city's streets and marketplaces. Finally they reached the harbor—small but deep and picturesque, filled with exotic-looking sailing ships of all shapes and sizes. Low mountains ringed the harbor, and the city's houses and streets went right up the sides. Mogart stopped by the stone sea wall on the road down to the harbor and pointed up to the highest peak on the other side.

"Look up there," he instructed. She followed his gaze and saw a massive castle of black rock sitting almost on top of the peak; for perhaps fifty meters below it there was a sheer cliff before the land started to taper, and even then it was some distance before there were roads and houses. "That is Castle Zondar," he told her. "It is the seat of government for the city and surrounding lands, and also the treasury building. Few people live there, though, since it's not very comfortable and is guarded by all sorts of spells. The doors and gates, for example, are so well protected that no one not there on proper business may enter. They just can't get through, even if the door is opened for them."

She gulped. "You mean my man is in there?"

He nodded. "Yes, indeed. Asothoth is his name, but that hardly matters. He is there, kept there, because of his unique anatomy. The locals consider him a demon. He's no threat, though. Long ago, to ease his boring exile, he took to powerful drugs as I seized upon alcohol. They supply him with enough to keep him in a permanent stupor. After a couple of hundred years of this they've come to believe that terrible things will happen if they should *not* keep him drugged, and he is a hopeless addict, anyway."

She nodded. "Then what makes you think he still has the jewel?"

Mogart shrugged. "I don't know if he has it or not. But we are drawn to the things like bees to nectar. I feel its magnetism even from here, far away and out of time sync. Indeed, it is only this force that keeps me from just walking in and grabbing it myself. It is keyed to Asothoth, therefore I could not touch it without his permission, unless it were given to me far from him by a third party. A safeguard, you understand."

Jill McCulloch understood. "I'm the third party, then."

The demon nodded. "It is easier to scout this place because of his disability, however. I'm considered sort of a god of drinking here, and so I know the place well. Follow me."

They walked a short way from the harbor and entered an inn whose bar and cafe seemed to be doing a fair business. It wasn't to the eating and drinking part of the establishment that they went, though, but up the stairs and down a long, dark hall past numbered rooms. It was a fairly large inn, probably serving seamen and tourists—if there were such things here— equally. Finally they reached a door near the rear, Number 16, and Mogart did the usual act of walking right through the door. Jill was prepared this time and followed.

It was a small room, a single. There was a small nightstand with an oil lamp and a pan half filled with water, a small flowered rug, a shuttered window, and a low, narrow bed that rested on a hardwood frame. The mattress, at least, seemed to be thick and filled with feathers—no straw this trip.

On the bed a woman lay asleep. She was young, lithe, with a fine athletic figure. Her legs were long and well developed; she might have been a dancer or a gymnast. Her hair was cut short, making her face look like that of a young teen-age boy, although she was clearly in her early twenties. The fact that her skin had a slightly weathered look and that her hands and feet bore tough calluses indicated that she was not just a demure young woman in town on a holiday— that and the fact that she was in this inn, in a room such as this, alone, and sound asleep at midday.

"This is Yoni," Mogart told Jill. "She's been useful to me once or twice, although the time rate here is such that people come and go too quickly to form lasting attachments. You get a little over four days here to the hour back home, so you have some leeway."

Jill nodded. "She is an athlete?"

"You might say that," Mogart replied. "She is a thief. A damned good one. If *she* could bring me the jewel I'd hire her, but it's not possible. Only someone from another plane may hold a jewel for long without it shorting and killing them. It has to be that way—otherwise somebody clever could lift one, and then where would the University be? And, of course, with *you* I know you'll bring the jewel to me, not try it yourself. So into Yoni you go, all your old skills coming into play to go steal the jewel."

She hesitated. "Wait a minute, Mogart. First of all, if the gates are hexed closed, how do I get in? Second, where in that Gothic monstrosity is the jewel? And, finally, why did you say this one was easy but dangerous?"

Asmodeus Mogart laughed dryly. "All right, all right. First, the jewel just has to be somewhere in the black tower that faces the sea and doubles as a lighthouse. More specific I cannot be. It's easy because you won't have to worry about Asothoth, and dangerous because the tower and castle are guarded by both human and demonic forces. This inn's a thieves' hangout after dark. You're an outsider—a newcomer—so they won't expect you to know much of anything. But you have the Thieves' Guild mark there—see on her left thumb? It's a magical sign, so nobody but other Guild members can see it. Look at it and remember it—so you'll know who's who yourself."

She leaned over and looked. On the woman's thumb was an unmistakable but intricate star pattern, geometric and elaborate. She wouldn't have to remember it, though, since it would be there for her to see—she and no one else but a fellow thief. Good enough.

"I'd suggest pumping for information about the castle," Mogart advised. "It's a tempting target because of its great treasury, its gold and precious gems."

Jill turned and looked him squarely in the eye. "If that's so, why aren't they all burgling it?"

Mogart shrugged. "A few have succeeded—those capable of scaling the walls and cliff. Then you have to get past the human and supernatural guardians and traps. I fear you will have to kill on this trip. It's just too dangerous. Most thieves dream of doing it but don't have the guts."

"No guide?" she asked him.

He shook his head. "Recruit your own. Get your information, then act. Get help if you think you need it, or go it alone. But be prepared to show your bravery and agility, even to your fellow thieves. They respect only strength, skill, and a good blade. Now, touch her and let me get a drink."

Jill turned back to the sleeping woman, reached out and touched her shoulder.

There was blackness.

2

She awoke, feeling pretty good, a little after sunset. Although the shutters had kept out most of the light, enough had come in to illuminate the room slightly. But now it was almost pitch-black, and she sat up on the side of the bed and tried to remember where everything was in the little room.

Feeling her way cautiously, she located the nightstand and the lamp and water basin. Feeling around— and almost knocking the basin over—she felt what seemed to be several long, thin wooden matches. She struck one against the wooden wall and it flared immediately to life. She touched it to the wick, and soon the room glowed and took form. The amount of light the lamp threw off was surprisingly good.

After washing her face with the stale water to wake up completely, she looked around for clothes, which she found over a chair. Clearly these people didn't take baths often, and Yoni traveled light. The outfit smelled. A small leather purse hanging from a black belt showed that it was bulging with gold coins, though. Simple system. When you needed a new outfit, you just stole enough to buy it and tossed the other one away.

The clothes were tight-fitting and reminded her of ballet or gymnastics uniforms—a black cloth pullover shirt with long sleeves, black pants of the same material, and high slip-on black boots. In addition to the coins, the purse, which was designed to hang from the belt, contained a rolled-up pair of black gloves, a mirror and comb, and some boot-black. She guessed that that last item was used as much for darkening faces as for polishing boots.

Also on the belt, hanging down from the buckle itself, was a sheath containing a small and nasty-looking sharp-pointed dagger.

After donning the outfit she removed the dagger and evaluated its balance, heft—all the things she thought she might have to do with it. It felt very good and natural in her hand, almost as if it had a will of its own. She practiced drawing it a few times and surprised herself with the speed at which she had it out and ready.

She'd inherited the beggar girl's gift for getting money in that first body; now, hopefully, she'd inherited Yoni's skill with dagger and perhaps sword. She reminded herself that the owners of these bodies were still there, somewhere, in the back of her mind. Yoni's reflexes and sense of self-preservation would be essential in a pinch.

She checked herself out and liked what she saw. Now, *this* woman was close to her in size, condition, and athletic ability—and was younger. She felt almost normal. She walked to the door, opened it, blew out the light, and moved down the hall and descended the stairs. The bar and cafe were becoming crowded. A peak period was obviously coming up. She could tell even from this distance that Mogart had underrated this place as a thieves' hangout—it seemed as if everyone, even the bartender and serving maids, had a black mark on his thumb.

If anything, this was the Thieves' Guild Union Hall.

They came in all shapes and sizes. Men outnumbered women about three to one, but there still seemed a fair share of female customers with black marks, daggers or swords, and business on their faces. They were also from different lands. Some odd tongues floated in the atmosphere thick with smoke and the odors of heavy eating and drinking, and even odder accents were discernible in the conversations she could understand.

Most of the people of the city had been short to medium and dark. In here she saw individuals who could have been Scandinavian, or Irish and Italian, English and Slav.

She spied a small table that had just been vacated, headed across the room toward it quickly, then sat down and surveyed the scene as a serving woman cleared away the remains and wiped the table. Knives were there in abundance, and some spoons of an odd depth and squarish shape; but forks were not a part of the culture, that was clear.

The sandwich, though, seemed to have been invented here in a way. Several people were munching on meat thickly sliced between halves of large hard rolls.

"A roast beef sandwich and an ale," she told the waitress, and that was that except to wait, look, listen, and reflect that this was one *hell* of an improvement over the enforced piety of Zolkar. Basic, even somewhat primitive, this world might be—but it was a living, breathing primitivism, such as might have existed in ancient Greece or Rome.

She let the threads of conversations float to her. Most were sheer nonsense, but they conveyed the life and vitality of this place, and that, for now, was enough.

". . . Ningauble and Sheela! Ningauble and Sheela!" a huge Nordic-looking man was complaining to his partner, a small, dark man dressed in gray cloak and hood. "By all the black gods, aren't we *ever* going to be left alone . . . ?"

". . . well, we got on the mathematics of magic, and, suddenly, there I was, in the middle of Spenser's *Faerie Queene*. So I—what? Who's Spenser? Well, I—never mind, just drop it . . ."

A huge Germanic type was singing a little ditty for some friends.

> ". . . three brave hearts
> and three brave lions . . ."

"Oh, knock it off," a tall, blond-haired man snapped to the singer.

The big man laughed. "By Crom, Holger, you got no sense of humor when it comes to you!" General laughter.

". . . I like not the look of this place," a tall, strikingly beautiful woman told her male companion. "It is a thieves' den, I think."

"Judge not, my lady," her handsome and bearded companion reproved. "Remember that Christos Himself was nailed between two of them."

There was more, none of it clear and all of it, somehow, vital and alive. These people had seen a lot and experienced enough excitement for a dozen lifetimes. Their energy swirled and congealed in the smoke and odor of the room; there was a spark, a sizzling presence here because of them.

The ale and roast beef came, and the latter proved excellent despite an unordered addition of fried green peppers and onions and some sort of hot sauce. The mixture tasted wonderful and fresh, so much a contrast to the plastic food of her own world. She felt as if she belonged, could live here happily the rest of her life.

And that was a trap as sinister as any demon, she realized, for she dared not live here. She must get the jewel from that dark tower out there and return to Mogart as quickly as possible, or she would abandon her world.

A man entered, dressed in dark green from head to foot and with soft boots of the same color. He wore a short-sword on a belt and had on a small green hat with a feather in it. He reminded her of a short Robin Hood.

He surveyed the scene, apparently looking for someone he knew or at least an empty seat near someone he'd feel comfortable with. His eyes fell on her and on the conspicuously empty chair across from her, and then he started across the crowded cafe in her direction. She watched him, more curious than alarmed. Still, she shifted her sandwich to her left hand and let the right drop to her lap, near the dagger.

He had the thumb of the Guild, but that meant little—only that you had better not leave your purse in plain sight. Coming up to her, he stopped, removed his cap, and bowed slightly.

"Pardon—there are no empty places this night. Might I join you?" he asked in a polite and cultured voice.

It would have been easy to brush him off, but she needed information, and information came from people. She kept her right hand on her lap, though.

"By all means, sir, take the seat," she invited. "I am called Yoni."

He bowed again and sat comfortably. "Sugrin Paibrush," he replied. "I can tell by your speech that you are not of the city. I should have remembered one of such loveliness here before in any event. Norbig?"

The flattery had little effect, but he was pleasant enough company. "Tussain," she replied. Now where the hell had that expression come from, she wondered. Clearly this Yoni was a much stronger personality than the beggar girl had been. She looked at his green garb. "Poacher?"

He laughed. "Oh, my, no! Requires you be an expert bowman and fleet of foot as well. I work mostly in the country, though, where green is the best disguise."

He didn't have to say any more, even if he were so inclined. A highwayman, without a doubt.

After a moment's silence he continued to press the conversation. "And what brings you to our fair city? Not much pickin's around here. Too many *criminals* running about, you know." His eyes showed merriment, and the sarcastic tone in his voice was quite funny. She laughed and relaxed, starting to like him.

They talked a bit more. She finished her sandwich and he ordered a full beef dinner, and she began to feel comfortable with him. The magical thieves' mark made life a lot easier here. He was full of witty and fantastic stories, and if most of them or most all of them weren't true, they were nonetheless entertaining.

"And what of you?" he asked her.

She shrugged. "Nothing much to tell—no fantastic tales." She thought a moment. "Well, perhaps one rather difficult one." In general terms she told of stealing a precious gem from a land where sin was impossible.

He loved it. "Wonderful!" he gushed, then became a little more serious. "But now, truly. You are young, you are attractive, and you are very well off and very independent of tone and manner. Such a one as you would be dead if she were not exceptional at her trade. What brings you to this place? Vacation? Stopover?"

She thought a moment. "I told you about stealing the gem. I have, ah, an incredible contract with an eager buyer for more of them. One is here, and I mean to have it."

That piqued his interest a bit. "Oh? Where?"

"Castle Zondar," she replied almost in a whisper.

The humor and merriment drained out of him, and for a moment he just stared at her. Finally he asked, "Are you serious?" He turned and waved a hand around at the assembly of thieves and adventurers. "Look at them. Some of the best are in this room, you know. Some of the best there are. They've battled demons and demigods, faced down terrible sorceries and helped conquer whole kingdoms. I'm pretty good at the trade and live quite well, and I've never been caught —yet I am a flea, a gnat as compared to possibly a third of these. And none of these men and women will try that tower." He shook his head slowly from side to side. "No, I'd say no matter how good you are, you have an impossible contract. Break it. Forget it. Try something simpler, like fighting rogue elephants with wet noodles. It's safer and surer."

She didn't like the sound of that, but she had no choice. "What's so hard? I can climb a wall. I've done as much or worse, even climbing some *real* mountains. As you surmised, Sir Sugrin, I *am* good."

He smiled wanly. "It's not the getting *in* that's the problem—the guards and such will let you do that, at least if you're good. Not that they will open the treasury and say, 'Here it is,' but it's not impossible. It's the getting *out* that's impossible. Alarms, demonic guardians triggered by theft—impossible. They will have you, and death will be something desired but denied after that."

She considered his information. "Then maybe it's not so impossible," she responded. "You see, I'm there only to steal one thing, and if I get it in my hands I do not have to get out. The gem will transport me in an instant to my buyer."

He thought about it. "A magic stone, then. Hmmm . . . Maybe. But the risks are still too great, and there is a lot of countermagic up there. Safer to go to one of the southern kingdoms and score big and live a life of luxury if you're that good, in any event."

"I'll think about your advice," she told him. "But in the meantime, I'm a stranger here in need of equipment. Just in case I decide to try, anyway. Where would I get it?"

"The Guild Hall, of course," he replied. "Let me finish my meal, and then I'll take you over there. It's not far, and they should be open about now."

He ate with relish and insisted on paying the tab. Since she pretty well guessed that any advice and equipment from a Thieves' Guild would hardly be free, she did not object.

They walked out into the darkness. Quite a large number of people stood about, but he took her away from the bustling bars and dives toward the small warehouse district of the harbor. All the time he kept up a running commentary on his philosophy of life, love, fun, and danger. When they turned another corner into a narrow alley between two large, two-story grain warehouses, she began to grow a little nervous and suspicious. "I thought you said it wasn't far."

"It's not," he replied, his voice coming from slightly to one side and behind her. She cursed herself for letting him drop behind. "In fact, it's the warehouse at the end, just across the brightly lit street up ahead.

You can see the two gargoyles on either side holding torches in their mouths."

She saw the building, but also noticed something else. "That looks like only a block or two down from the inn—on the same street!" She turned to face him and found herself pinned to the wall with a short-sword at her throat. Sugrin Paibrush was grinning in the darkness.

"Right you are, my girl!" he agreed. "But such is not for you. Cutpursing, perhaps, decoying, perhaps a nice little bank—but not the castle, no, not that. If you'll just remove and toss me your purse, we can be done with this. I will have saved you from a fate worse than death and, at the same time, reaped reward for my goodness. Easy, now, though! I shouldn't like to have to slit such a pretty throat!"

She sighed and inwardly cursed herself for being so sloppily trusting. She had no doubt that this man was, in his own way, quite honorable. He would let her go if he got the money, would kill her if she did not yield, and if he got the money, would feel wonderful about doing such a good deed.

Her hands moved to unfasten the purse from her belt. Suddenly she stepped to one side, battled down the sword on its flat, and spun the highwayman half-way around. Quickly, in a blur, she took advantage of the split second he was off balance, and using the wall as a brace, pushed off into him, feet shooting out in midair and landing right in his belly. He went down and the sword dropped free of his hand and clattered harmlessly to the ground. Quickly she somersaulted over him, landing on her feet, somehow drawing her deadly dagger at the same time, and was kneeling down with it at his throat before he could recover.

Paibrush was stunned, not so much by the fight as by how easily the tables had turned. No less stunned was Jill McCulloch, who hadn't remembered doing any of it until she'd completed the maneuvers and still couldn't believe that she'd actually performed them. Clearly this Yoni had an incredible instinct for self-preservation that fully matched her skills and agility.

"And now, Sir Sugrin, we shall proceed with the

theft," she announced triumphantly, dagger still at his jugular. "Just rip your own purse loose and toss it to your right, near your sword."

He smiled, seemed to shrug, and did as instructed.

"I warn you that I toss this dagger as well as I wield it," she said, then released him and in a flash dashed over to the sword and purse.

Paibrush rose unsteadily to his feet, his face still reflecting his surprise and embarrassment. "Hustled!" He swore to himself in disgust. "Twenty-two years in the business and I let myself get hustled!"

She laughed. He still wasn't much of a threat, but he could be. She felt his sword—a fine, well-balanced weapon that was surprisingly light, almost as if made from aluminum yet with a blade as hard as steel.

"And now, sir, if you will remove your jerkin and breeches," she ordered.

He looked shocked. "My what?"

"Your clothes. Oh, you may keep the hat and boots —I shouldn't want you to catch cold. The rest you will remove and toss to me—do it! *Now!* Or I shall have no need of removing them!"

He removed the shirt easily, baring a hairy chest, but took some additional prodding to take off his pants. As she'd guessed, underwear wasn't in style on this world. She stood back and looked at him as he stood embarrassed in his nakedness. "Cute," she decided.

"B-but—look here! You can't leave me like this!" he protested. "What is the point of this?"

She laughed. "I want no one coming up in back of me when I carry out my errands this night, particularly no one who bears me a grudge. This will keep you busy until you can discover a sheet or potato-sack. I'll leave the clothes at the Guild Hall."

That plan seemed to upset him more than anything. "No! Please! Toss them in the gutter, sink them in the harbor—but not at the Guild Hall! I couldn't *stand* the humiliation," he pleaded.

She laughed again and started to back off with her booty. "Very well, then—under the light on the street up there. Good luck and thank you, Sir Sugrin, for all the help you have been this night to me."

He stood and watched her go, and as she made the street, gave a little wave, and turned, dropping the clothes just *across* from the intersection, some reflections overcame his mortification. She really *was* good, he thought. She really *might* make it . . .

In the meantime, he hoped no one stole his clothes before the early morning hours, when the streets would be deserted enough for him to retrieve them.

3

The Thieves' Guild headquarters was pretty conspicuous despite its lack of signs. Paibrush had explained its visibility as something tolerated by most local authorities, since that way they knew who the thieves were, and often had need of their services themselves. There was, of course, the additional problem that spells protected the building just as other spells protected the castle. No one without the mark on his thumb could enter it; and, being a gathering place for thieves, it was probably the safest, most protected, most burglarproof building in the city.

She entered without resistance, noting the two men on the other side of the street, one leaning against a lamppost and the other pretending to look in a shop window. They were obviously cops. It didn't matter— she'd been known as a thief the moment she hit town, of course. And from what Paibrush had said, nobody who entered the Guild Hall left with anything but what they had entered with—except money, of course. It was always a good trick to enter the hall in full view of the officials, slip out by one of the dozens of secret ways designed into the place, do the job, slip back in the same way, then emerge. The perfect alibi.

The building itself was quite something, too. Its entranceway looked like that of dozens of small office buildings; there was a receptionist to direct you, complete with hand-pumped compressed air tubes to fire messages to the various offices and departments. There was also a Directory well posted on a central support pillar, and a large message board.

Jill scanned the message board. It contained all sorts of "I'm here, where are you" type notices, notes about arrests and convictions, and even ads for jobs. "Ocean-based pirate crew forming. Barbarians preferred, sailing experience essential," one read. There were lots of others.

The Directory showed the scope of the Guild. There were specific departments for Cutpursing and Pick-pockets, Blackmailers, Highwaymen and Robbers, and so on down a list of larcenies. She found Burglary and Grand Theft, then scanned the internal departments. One group would help case the place, another would outfit you, consider and work out your plan and make suggestions—or even come up with a plan if you didn't have one—and even fence the goods afterward. You could even check your balance in a foreign numbered account and make deposits and withdrawals on it. The network was incredible.

There was also, she noted, a board of honor and ethics, a disciplinary and enforcement squad, as well as social auxiliaries for sporting events, banquets, and the like.

Talk about organized crime, she thought as she read the list.

About the only thing that protected the public was the fact that you could very easily get caught—and torture and death were the rule, as the long list of In Memoriam opposite the Directory attested. No one-to-five with time off for good behavior at a minimum-security prison farm here. It was a sobering thought.

The receptionist was efficient and directed her to the proper department with a minimum of trouble. The first step was a junior clerk who looked more like a beginning bank teller than an official in the Thieves' Guild.

"And where are you talking about?" he asked pleasantly.

"Castle Zondar," she told him.

He hesitated a moment. "You realize that the castle is considered a three-star risk?" He scribbled notes down on a house form that was beautifully printed in a kind of Old English or Germanic script.

She nodded. "I am aware of the dangers," she assured him.

He shrugged. "The danger isn't much of a problem. It's the low potential for success. You'll have to have at least the basic fees up front, you know, to cover our expenses, and you are specifically excluded from our group hospitalization and life insurance policies."

"I expected as much," she answered truthfully. "What sort of fees are we talking about?"

He took out another pad, mostly blank, and an abacus and started figuring. A lot of stuff was listed. He paused several times to ask additional information.

"General sortie or specific objective?"

"Specific objective," she responded.

He nodded to himself. "That's a *little* better. Single object, then? Piece of art for a private collector? You'll get a good discount if so, since you won't have to bother with our fencing, and you wouldn't need to pay for smuggling and transport unless—until—you come back with the goods."

"Something like that—as good as that, anyway. A talisman of no value to anyone except my employer that just happens to be there."

"Small?"

"Very," she agreed.

That seemed to please him even more, and the list soon contained a lot of cross-outs and corrections. Finally he was finished and turned to her.

"All right. Basic layout of the place, twenty. Briefing on guard schedules, basic spells, and known supernatural guardians, thirty-five. Ropes, pitons, miscellaneous climbing equipment, along with the proper spells to render them most effective and least visible, twenty-five. Associated magic repellers, ten. Standard set—but I hope you understand that, considering the failure rate, there's obviously a bunch we don't know about, so don't put too much stock in them. Surcharge for three stars, one hundred. That comes to one hundred ninety exactly, plus five percent tax, one ninety-nine fifty, payable to the cashier in Room Twelve."

"Tax?" she responded incredulously.

He shrugged. "Since the local authorities can't come

in, they have no way of estimating the property tax on the building. We got around that by accepting their bid for a sales tax. Don't worry—the payment can't be specifically traced to you."

She shrugged and sighed. This was not her idea of crime at all.

Yoni's purse held only twenty-nine of the gold pieces, far short, but Paibrush's contained seventy-five. Enough for the fee and a good dinner if she wanted it, and that was about it. *Oh, well,* she thought to herself, *if I get the jewel I won't need the gold, anyway—and if I don't I almost certainly won't need money.*

She stood up and went down the hall to Room 12, taking the intricately coded itemized price sheet with her. The cashier looked at it, took and counted her money, then wrote out a series of receipts for each service, placing his signature and a wax seal on each.

"Go to the rooms indicated, in order," he instructed.

Jill sighed and turned to go. She felt as if she were getting a driver's license rather than being briefed for a crime.

The first place was Layout. They actually had the blueprints of the castle there, which surprised her. The woman in charge noted her reaction. "Why not? After all, it takes *years* to build a castle—forty-six to build Zondar—and in all that time you *know* somebody can steal the best-guarded blueprints."

That was a point.

The woman offered hypnotism to allow Jill to memorize the plans, but she turned it down. She didn't really want to be hypnotized—no telling what would come out—and besides, it cost ten gold pieces and she didn't have them, anyway.

The blueprints were good enough. They showed the correct passageways in the maze of the castle, and also indicated where most of the traps were. It was very easy to get around in there if you knew the layout—it had to be. Although the castle had a very small permanent population, during the day almost two hundred civil servants worked in one part or another. She wondered why one or more of those workers hadn't turned thief, but the woman in Layout scoffed. "They undergo hypnotic spells when they leave, to scramble all their knowledge up. Besides, if you work for the government you can steal so much more than we could, anyway—why bother?"

Again, that was a point well taken.

Satisfied after a while that she had the basic design features down pat—and there were some pretty nasty ones if you chose the wrong door or corridor at a number of junctions—she thanked the woman and moved on.

Next was a thin, elderly man who somehow reminded her more of a Shakespearean actor than a functionary in a place like this. It took all kinds, of course, but Jill wondered whether the place was staffed with former thieves or if, in fact, this was just another office job to these people who never themselves had to take a risk.

The elderly man headed Briefing. After greeting her, he went back to an enormous file cabinet, rummaged through a drawer, and came up with a thick folder. "Castle Zondar's one of the ones we keep up front, since everybody wants to hear about it," he explained in a melodious baritone. "Not too many go through with it, though." He paused a moment. "Going up the cliff face?"

"Yes," she told him. "And I'm interested only in the tower—the Hall of the Sleeper, to be exact."

A bushy white eyebrow shot up. "That's interesting," he replied. "Well, we suggest going to the tower directly, then, bypassing all the other crap. It means an extra fifty-meter climb, which is rough; but doing it that way bypasses a lot of foolishness as well. There is a guard position on top of the tower, and patrolling guards at the tower base on the roof of the castle. Get as far over to the right as possible and angle yourself so that once you're onto the tower proper, you'll be out of sight of the lower guards. There are no shortcuts, though. You can enter only at the top or along the guard wall."

Jill looked at his diagrams and recalled the blueprints. That would mean a sheer climb of almost a hundred and ten meters straight up, the last fifty on a curved surface! She protested as much to the briefer.

"That's true," he admitted, "but then you only have to go down two levels rather than up fourteen with all the attendant risks not only of discovery but of tripping alarms, running into people—or things worse than people. The top guard basically tends the lighthouse at the top, and he's the only human you'd have to bother with under normal circumstances. He guards against an attack by air—sorcerers can do some interesting things, sometimes with as simple a thing as a carpet—by a simple trick. The fuel to the lighthouse is carefully measured and metered to last only ten minutes, after which a complex mechanism must be operated in the proper sequence. Otherwise the light goes out and, quite literally, all hell will break loose. There are two rather enormous gaunts, for example, bound to the top, circling around the tower. They won't bother you as long as the light burns, and they won't pick you off the side, either. They are, in effect, incorporeal as long as the light shines. Let the light go out and they will land, devouring everything on top."

She gulped a little. "What *is* a gaunt, anyway?"

He shrugged. "Who knows? Amorphous black creatures of sorcery that eat flesh. Need any more details? I've never known anyone to meet up with one and live, so that's the best I can tell you."

"That's enough," she assured him. "So the light has to burn until I'm down in the tower."

"All the time, if you intend to get out," he responded. "The guard is almost certainly just a bored and perfectly ordinary watchman. Just wait on the side of the wall until he goes and rekindles the lamp. Climb up onto the tower, get around, and when he comes out just pace him around the tower and go in and down. No reason he should have to know you're there until you're on the way out, if he doesn't have to."

There was more, and it was all practical advice given in a simple, matter-of-fact way. Finally, the briefing was over.

"Tell me," she said hesitantly. "I've explained generally what I'm after, where—the whole thing. In all honesty, what do you think my chances are, assuming I'm good and in the proper condition for this?"

The man shrugged. "Getting in, I'd say excellent. Getting down to the Hall of the Sleeper, fair to good. Getting into the Hall, fair. Finding what you're after there—well, who knows? If it's there, probably fair to good. Getting out again, poor. Getting back down the side and to town here—hell, I wouldn't bet a button on that."

That was exactly what she wanted to hear, for all her information showed that the major problems were in escaping; the primary security both human and supernatural was also geared to catching whoever had managed to get in.

But she didn't have to get out.

She hoped.

Spells and Charms turned out to be a short class on basic stuff anybody could do—some for luck, some for silence, a number for misdirection, and the like. She was delighted when she tried a couple and they worked —although she was warned that, first, the spells were no panacea, and second, they required concentrated willpower which might not be possible if, say, you were surrounded by a host of armed guards trying to kill you.

In general, a cross repelled vampires only if you first had a chance to pull it out and, second, if the vampire was a Christian. There were no vampires likely in the tower, but the principle was the same.

The climbing equipment was perfect and well made for the type of stone involved. The pitons, for example, were fastened with a type of glue that supposedly would hold a hundred kilograms and therefore prevented the need to bang holes noisily in solid granite.

The magic repellers turned out to be a series of small blessings and numerous charms that would protect her, it was claimed, from some of the more basic, routine stuff.

Jill felt set—but by the time she was through the crash course, it was after five in the morning and dawn was fast approaching. She would not be able to go after the gem until the next night, and she had almost no money.

The larcenous part of her brain that contained the unusually strong Yoni came up with a simple remedy. Returning to her room at the inn, she decided that she could practice and also get some needed cash in a simple way. She took a couple of the pitons and the glue, crawled out her window, and hand-walked two stories up on the pitons to the next room. She opened the shutters slightly, crept in—thankful that this society also hadn't invented the glass window or screens —and snatched the purse of an obese middle-aged couple still snoring soundly. They had really bolted their door and barricaded it with a chair besides, but that didn't matter.

Going back, one of the pitons loosened and came off in her hand. It wasn't critical—she made the leap to the next one easily—but it was a nerve-racking experience. The damned things had to be in just right, obviously, or the glue wouldn't hold. It didn't occur to her until she was back in the room that if the piton she'd jumped to had also loosened, she'd have fallen a good nine or ten meters to the stone alleyway below.

And when she *did* think of it, it did nothing to help her sleep at all. *A hundred-and-ten-meter climb on those pitons,* she kept thinking.

Finally, though, she *did* get to sleep.

4

The next evening they were still buzzing about the robbery in the inn. But since the couple weren't certain where they'd been burgled—Jill had left a couple of coins in the purse and put everything exactly right and taken in all the pitons—the glue came loose somehow when she mumbled a few little words—no suspicion was pointed at anyone. The police were essentially going through the motions, anyway, in the belief that any idiot tourists who wanted to stay in a known thieves' hangout for the thrills and experience got what they deserved.

She looked around for Paibrush, but he didn't reappear. She started to worry about him a bit. If he really were the vengeful kind, he could easily tip the castle that she was coming and give her description. That would be a violation of the thieves' honor code and could cause him horrible trouble, but that would happen only if she survived to file a complaint. He didn't seem the type, but one never knew. One more worry.

She went to the Guild Hall early, shortly after sundown, for a final refresher and also to complain to the Equipment Department about the piton. All she got for that was a lecture on clean, smooth surfaces—the inn was masonry, not granite—and a snide comment to the effect that anybody who'd use granite piton glue on porous rock deserved what she got. She dropped the subject.

The Guild Hall had more exits than an ant farm, all underground. She walked for what seemed like kilometers, including some very long stair climbs, with an elderly guide and finally wound up coming out of the cliff almost directly below the castle.

The pitons were in a sack—enough, they'd claimed, for the distance and made of the same light yet super-hard alloy as the swords. She was certain that such a metal did not exist back home. The glue was puttylike and had been preapplied to the pitons; it would not come off, and it would not stick to anything except rock, which simplified matters. There were some advantages to this institutionalized criminality after all.

The guide wished her luck and was quickly gone. She was alone at the cliff base, her only light a crescent moon and the lighthouse beacon which shone more out than up. She blackened her face and pulled on the black skin-tight gloves and felt ready. The gloves were made of a rubberlike material; they wouldn't slip.

The climb proved relatively easy, and, true to Equipment's promise, no piton glue failed, although she gingerly tested each one before pulling herself up to it. Each was almost a meter long, a dull tube really, and easy to work with. Several times they clattered in the large sack, but although she was certain on many occasions that someone must have heard her, there were no alarms. At no time was she particularly worried about falling. The climb was easier than a lot of the gymnastics stuff she'd done, and a lot easier than some mountains she'd climbed in Alaska just for fun. No snow, almost no wind, and no oxygen problems.

Taking it slow and easy, she made the guard wall at the tower's base in a little over an hour. Several times she saw the heads and shoulders of guardsmen who were armed with what looked like crossbows. One even looked out, but none seemed aware of her presence.

Following the suggestions, Jill angled herself around to the right side of the tower, which was located at the seaward corner. She could proceed straight up now and barely be seen by the men on the walls. But it was bright as day up here thanks to the light in the tower, and that made her feel totally exposed. *There's a measure of luck in anything dangerous, though,* she told herself.

Her luck held. She made the top of the tower in another twenty minutes or so. Once, only once, she dropped a piton, but thankfully it fell away from the tower and castle, and the noise of its fall by the time it struck something solid was muffled by the sounds of the ocean.

The light itself was a giant polished mirror before which was the hot oil flame, its heat and smoke suffocating at times. It rotated by having an ox tied to a lever that turned the whole light on a turntable of some sort. How they got the ox up there and down again was a mystery. There was the expected residue of working oxen, but not thick and not old, and no real sign of a big feeding and watering area.

The guard, who definitely *did* look bored, yawned as he followed the ox around. He wore a sword, but no other weapons were apparent—mostly just uniform, she guessed.

She waited there on her uncertain perch just below the top of the wall, letting her ears tell her when it might be safe to look by the sound of the ox. The man stuck with the animal. There was very little else he could do, since there was barely enough room for the animal to walk around, and if he stood still the beast would only run him over in a couple of minutes. Besides, the smoke was terrible and the flame damned hot —but if he stayed behind the ox, he had the mirror between him and the flame, which helped a little.

Finally, the man walked inside to pump his pumps and move his levers to let more fuel into the lamp reservoir. It was hot and uncomfortable, and he did it quickly. Jill didn't move the first time, since she wanted to see just what his routine was. What he did was come out and take the shortest path to the rear of the ox. That was handy.

Just as a watched pot never seems to boil, a watched lamp reservoir never seems to go down. Soon Jill's feet and leg muscles started to ache like mad, and imagination—at least she hoped it was just her imagination—started making the piton feel loose and uneven, as if it were about to drop off. She maintained her self-control, though, and when the man finally went back in to prime the lamp reservoir again, she moved up and out in front of the ox, which gave her a slight glimpse but didn't stop its monotonous walk. She crept silently ahead until she was sure she was far enough around so that the man wouldn't be able to see her ahead or, she hoped, just across. The lamp was terribly hot; she began perspiring immediately.

As soon as the man walked out to make his way back to his shield behind the ox, she rolled into the light structure and belly-crawled quickly to the small stone stairway opening. *This is going to be tight and rough,* she thought, but there was nothing else she could do. Momentarily she would be within two meters of the flame.

Using the mirror as a shield, she got up quickly and made for the stairs at just the right point. The heat was intense, unbearable; she was certain that she couldn't withstand it for more than a few seconds. But she made it down into the hole perfectly, then paused to catch her breath and let her body temperature cool down. She was drenched with perspiration and felt as if she had a high fever. She hoped she wasn't on fire.

It was dark below except for a shaft of light coming from the opening above. She could see the base of the turntable near her and hear its creaky turning, even hear the sounds of man and animal on their long walk to nowhere just above—but there were no alarms.

No human being could stand duty like the lighthouse keeper for very long. Jill felt confident that the guard was changed frequently, perhaps as frequently as every one to two hours. It didn't matter. She intended to wait for the guard change here, on the steps. It was a free ticket down.

It was not, mercifully, a very long wait. She heard him first—a noise, someone moving far below—then heard the clanging of some chains and the lifting of some gates. She was exhausted, but this was only the beginning, and she forced herself into action.

Finally there was a torch visible below, and when it was clearly in someone's hand she moved swiftly and silently over, judged the distance to the bottom part of the turntable, then leaped for it and held on with both hands. It was hot, but bearably hot. She had conceived this notion when she'd seen that this bottom part was made of thick hardwood. Had it been metal, it would certainly have been too hot to hold on to and would have forced a new plan.

She turned slowly with the light and waited nervously for the man with the torch to pass. For the briefest of moments the top of the tower would be lighted by that torch and she would be exposed. She hoped that the man was neither expecting the extraordinary nor looking for it.

He wasn't. He was tall and thin, a gaunt man dressed as the other had been. His expression told her how much he hated going to work now. She had a bad moment when he stopped just below the opening to the top to wait for the shielded side to come around, but he was looking up there, to the light, and not at her.

Finally he passed, and she was behind him, hanging in the darkness. Her arms ached and the heat transferred from the top started to get to her, but she held on.

A man with lighthouse duty doesn't stick around and talk much to his replacement when he's relieved, so it was only a minute or two before the original guard came down the steps, torch in hand. He was far too smoked up and heated up to be looking for visitors, and passed right by her. She let him get just ahead and below and swung herself back to the stairs, thankful for the slight glow from his torch and the light above. As she had hoped, the noise of the light itself masked her. The torch never wavered—and now she followed it, getting as close to the relieved guard as she dared.

At the first level there was a gate and then a flat floor. Doors to several small chambers were revealed in the torchlight. She didn't like the iron gate at all, nor the fact that the guard took a big key off his belt and moved to unlock it. The noise seemed to disturb whoever or whatever was in the rooms. She could hear a gibbering and hissing and a lot of banging sounds, like an inhuman army of ghouls and other creatures clamoring for release. It scared the hell out of her but didn't seem to ruffle the guard at all.

The key and gate were a different matter. There seemed only one key on his belt, so it was safe to assume that, even if there were more locks and gates, this key would fit. But she would need it—and that meant getting the guard.

She didn't really have the size or strength to knock the man cold with a piton, blackjack style. That meant the dagger. She drew it, then hesitated as Mogart's voice seemed to echo in the back of her mind from some distant space and time.

"Ever kill anyone, either of you? . . . Do you think you could do so? Could you kill if, by doing so, you could stop that thing up there from hitting the Earth, maybe even reverse a lot of what has happened here?"

Well, here it was. The man had the key in the lock, was turning it. Now or never. An innocent man, just doing his job, maybe with a wife and kids somewhere.

As in the alley with Paibrush, a force seemed to

surge through her; the dagger went up, cocked, and sped unerringly to its target. The man stiffened and cried out in surprise and pain, then collapsed in a heap on the floor. He was still moving, though, still breathing. The commotion hadn't been heard by others above or below, but it certainly was heard by whatever lurked behind the doors. They seemed driven into a frenzy.

Jill was quickly beside him, and he groaned as she reached down and took the key off his belt, then turned him slightly so she could pull out the dagger and wipe it on his clothing. There was a lot of blood, and for a moment she thought she was going to be sick.

Then, suddenly, the body started undergoing a terrible transformation as she watched. It seemed to shrink and twist a bit and turn black; the man's eyes suddenly glowed a deep red and his face became something horrible, inhuman, more like a gargoyle than a human being.

She was horrified and stepped back. He seemed to be growing stronger as he changed, becoming more and more a gargoyle that radiated pure hate and evil but without a trace of humanity.

It's going to get up and come after me! Jill thought suddenly, then took out a piton and pounded the creature's loathsome head with all her remaining strength, again and again and yet again! Blood and a terrible, clear ichor seemed to ooze as the thing screamed and was joined by the screams of others just beyond the doors on this level, yet it would not die.

Suddenly a corner of her mind whispered, "The vampire syndrome." Her mind raced as she tried to remember what you did to kill a gargoyle. The briefing —like a vampire, sure!

When she stopped hitting the thing, a black, clawed arm reached out and grabbed her leg. Its head had split open and an eyeball dangled from its socket, yet the creature was still very much alive. She could not break the grip that was trying to unbalance her with certain success, perhaps hold her for help or throw her against the stone, but she managed to reach the thing's sword and pulled it.

The gargoyle saw what she was doing with its one good eye and snarled, pulling and twisting. She brought the sword down first on the arm and neatly severed it —but, if anything, that had strengthened its grip on her! She was down now, next to the thing, and the other arm shot out to get hold of her throat. She still had her sword arm free and brought it down again on the neck. Blood and ichor spurted everywhere and the head rolled, but still the other arm shot out.

She forced herself to ignore its blind thrust and drove the sword deep into the thing's belly. The severed head screamed with agony; the body shuddered and was suddenly still. The severed arm that had cut off circulation in her leg stiffened, loosened, and dropped lifelessly.

Sever its head and then drive wood or metal through its chest, they'd said. Well, it had worked.

She was hurt now, and the horrible pounding on the doors around her didn't help any. She imagined a gargoyle horde, mad with blood-lust, trying to beat their way through to her.

Cloth, part of one boot, and some flesh had been torn away by the arm. It hurt like hell, but she couldn't stop. Not now. Rising painfully to her feet, limping badly, Jill put the key in the lock, turned it, and opened the gate wide. She somehow hauled herself through the mess to the other side, then shut the gate and locked it behind her. For a moment she had considered removing the sword from the creature. It would be a handy thing to have, particularly considering how tremendously light and balanced the swords here were and her fencing background, but she decided to leave it. The thing had not changed until she'd removed the dagger from its back. Removing the sword probably wouldn't reanimate the parts, but she couldn't take the chance.

Suddenly she realized that she'd left the torch in the holder on the other side of the gate where the gargoyle had put it. She had to go through the gate again, reach over and retrieve the torch, then lock the gate again. The whole thing was extremely unpleasant.

The doors had little eyeholes in them, she saw, but

decided not to pull any latches back on this side. She'd had enough of the denizens of the upper tower already, and she wanted no more.

There was another gate on the floor of this level, blocking her way down. For a moment she was afraid that it would be impassable, that the watch-devils were confined to this floor. But the large key fit and she swung the gate up quietly, moved farther down the stone stairs, then pulled the grate shut and relocked it. If they took these kind of precautions, she wasn't going to question them.

There was yet a third gate at the bottom, but this, too, yielded to the key, for which she was thankful. The Equipment people had included some metal-cutting wire, but it would have been broad daylight before she could have sawed through just one of those bars of grillwork.

The next level looked a lot more normal, but she was taking little for granted in a place where even ordinary-looking men were not what they seemed. There were no funny noises here; this had more the smell and feel of a place closed for the night. The Hall of the Sleeper was behind the large set of double doors to her right, if the information from the Guild was correct. The doors were locked, but with a different key than the one she had swiped. Again Equipment had come through with a skeleton key that was supposed to work on all standard locks. She hoped it did. She had no experience as a locksmith or as a regular burglar, so if the key failed, the only alternative was to chop the doors down. Rustlings, mewings, and murmurings of possible human or inhuman origin echoed all around from the shaft leading down. Some of the noises sounded extremely close—which figured, since the plans had shown that the city's main treasury started only two floors below and continued for three floors after that. She might have some time before those below wondered where the ghoulish guard who'd been relieved was, but any loud noises now would bring enemies at the run. Nervously she put the skeleton key into the lock and turned it to the right. Nothing. For a moment panic rose within her, then she twisted it to the left.

Something clicked.

She opened the door cautiously, not knowing what to expect.

She saw quickly that she did not need a torch; the Hall was small but well lit by oil lamps with long wicks and reservoirs hidden behind colored glass. They gave the room an eerie if beautiful illumination, reminding her of nothing so much as a church interior.

There were no furnishings; the whole atmosphere was reverential, in fact. Against the far wall were massive and thick golden drapes drawn across a room cavity. Cautiously she walked over to them, noting the pull ropes. She was about to draw the curtains when she noticed that the ropes only seemed to merge with the drapes; in actuality, they went just a hair farther, into a disguised cavity in the ceiling.

Booby-trapped, she thought.

She stood back and tried to figure out what to do. There could be anything on the other side of those drapes, but whatever was there was considered important enough to have this room devoted to it and to have alarms to protect it. Now she looked around, checking for signs of other traps throughout the room.

There were several. The floor was sort of a checkerboard tile, each square about a meter square. Some of them seemed to ride a little above the rest, as if on springs or a plunger. She marveled that she hadn't stepped on any of them before noticing them.

Suddenly she feared that the whole room was some sort of trap, that any touch of the drapes would cause some sort of alarm to go off, some kind of trap to be sprung. That was entirely possible, but she prayed that this was not so.

Still, there were no alarms on the door or immediately in the hall, which indicated that only the area behind the drapes was considered worth guarding at all. That made sense if the sleeping demon were there —but whether the traps were mechanical or supernatural in their effect, they were totally mechanical in operation. Somewhere there had to be an off switch—

just had to be. It couldn't be too elaborate, either, since the demon would have to be fed the drug at regular intervals. She searched for it.

Suddenly a strange, eerie chuckling issued from behind the drapes, growing slowly in intensity until its menace bounced off the walls.

Jill turned frantically, dagger drawn; but there was no sign of anyone. Slowly, cautiously, making sure she didn't touch any of the booby-trapped tiles, she approached the curtained-off alcove.

"All right! Show yourself, be you man or demon!" she challenged.

Suddenly the curtains opened with great force, revealing the contents of the alcove beyond. As she'd suspected, the demon lay there in a great, sumptuous bed beneath satin sheets. The bed itself appeared to be of solid gold; at its foot was a cedar chest on top of which was a smaller box. Two crossed fencing swords hung on the wall beyond, perfectly framed by drapes.

And something else. Something that stood there between her and the sleeper, glowering menacingly as the lights shrank, coming more into view as the room lapsed into near darkness.

It was the ghostly outline of a man dressed in an ancient and outlandish costume—only the barest of outlines, though, sort of bluish white in the dim light. The face, only a dim mask that was like the photographic negative of an outline of a face, still retained some of the rough-hewn character it must have worn in life. The eyes seemed to have tiny gleaming dots of light for pupils.

"Boo," said the ghost playfully.

She tossed the dagger at its strange face, and it sailed right through and stuck in the far wall just below the crossed sabers.

The ghost's head turned and noted the accuracy and the aim, and its head seemed to nod approvingly. "Faith and be damned!" it swore in a thick Irish brogue. "That's mighty fine aim for a slip of a lass like ye!" It turned back and faced her. "Now, what brings ye here in the middle of the night? Old happy dust, here, he don't have much worth stealin', as I can attest."

"Who and what are you?" she asked sharply. "And what is your intent?"

The ghost chuckled. "Intent, is it? Why, as to who I am, I'm the remains of Patrick O'Toole, my dear. The important part, of course. Like ye, I came a'questin' old droopy's little treasures, and here I have remained these fifty-seven years more or less, awaitin' ye."

Her face hardened. "You've guessed, then, what I seek, or know its true value?"

Again the robust laugh. "Aye, my darlin', for who better than a spirit to see that ye carry not one but two within yer pretty and bountiful self?" O'Toole turned and pointed a ghostly finger at the small box. "There it be, all for the takin', though the takin' ain't so easy, y'see."

"You're not—weren't—from this world, either, were you?" she surmised more than asked. "The Irish are more kin to my own world."

He shrugged. "And to many others, I'd wager," he replied. "Nay, I'm not from this world. I was plucked from the gallows by this fellow's cousin and plopped here as ye were, and into this very room did I creep, and here did I meet another as ye have met me. Poor divil—he'd been here more'n a century and was quite mad, for, y'see, 'tis a most borin' haunt. They dope him in the daytime, when I'm not about, so all ye see on this job are burglars, and, faith, yer the first!"

"But you didn't get the jewel," she pointed out. "What happened?"

There was a trace of a smile on his ghostly visage. "Well, this fellow was mad indeed, but he was good—so very, very good. Ye hav'ta be good to get here at all, and he was better. They have a spell on the place, ye see, that traps yer spirit and keeps it from final rest until someone takes yer place. It's a bit hard to kill a ghost, ye see, so this fellow runs me through and here I've sat."

She considered his story, but there was a hole in it. "But you had to be like me, in another body," she pointed out. "There should be *two* of you if you didn't reach the jewel—and the other fellow should be here, not you, if you did."

Again that ghostly yet charming smile. "True enough," he admitted, "except ye forget that the one inside ye is not really a party to the theft. I never reached the jewel—got run clean through, I did. The host went to his reward, and here I sit, a'waitin' for ye." He paused for a moment. "It'll be easier on ye, though, since I know the one inside ye is a party to the theft by consent, unlike my poor dullard, who never knew what was what until he died."

The ghost turned, walked in back of the sleeping, drugged demon, and took the sabers down from their mount. "So I'll be freed, and ye'll have company 'til the next try," he added.

She smiled wryly, realizing that the ghost was going to offer her a sword. Clearly the rules required a fight; the ghost could not commit outright murder, although since it couldn't be killed what it planned amounted to the same thing. "Why not just run me through and be done with it?" she asked sharply. "Must we go through this farce?"

He seemed almost apologetic. "But, darlin', don't y'see, yer invitin' suicide, and that's a worse fate than bein' cooped up here. Where do ye think those hideous beasties with the shells of men they use around here come from? Besides, anybody who can get this far deserves a fight, and I'd love to do it one last time." He hefted each of the blades, picked one, then tossed the other to her. She caught it, tested it out, and decided it was as fine a saber as she'd ever had in her hand, although the first with no foil. This was *her* element, at least. Fencing she knew well, and she didn't need to win, only to maneuver to the box and grab the jewel.

He seemed to follow her thoughts and her gaze to the box. "I know what yer thinkin'," he said, "and it's true enough if yer not a fair-minded lass. 'Tis true ye might, if yer good enough, get to the gem and flee, but that will still leave one for me and that's quite enough."

A portion of her mind seemed to wiggle and squirm as the thought hit home. O'Toole was right—she had based all her calculations on getting in and letting the jewel get her out—but what of Yoni? Even had O'Toole not intervened, she had condemned the woman to getting out on her own, a task even the Guild thought nearly impossible.

Here was something that obviously hadn't been explained to Yoni properly, either. She felt the other woman's anger and fear as faint echoes in her mind.

"I have to do it," she told not only the ghost but, in an apologetic way, Yoni as well. "My world is threatened with great doom if I do not get the jewel, and its survival is more important than anyone's life, including my own."

O'Toole was still standing there, but now had assumed a fencer's position. She stepped up on the platform beyond the curtain and faced him, also at the ready.

They began. A few feints, testing each other out, then becoming a bit more serious. Feint-thrust-parry! Feint! Thrust! Parry! Back and forth they dueled, gathering increasing admiration for each other's skills.

"One thing!" she yelled at him even as they continued to fence and dance, she trying to get near the box, he trying to prevent her, and both trying to avoid the bed with the demon upon it. "Tell me the name of the master who sent you here! Was it Mogart?"

He never let down his guard and, in fact, started pressing his attack, yet he answered, "Nay, lass, I know not a Mogart. 'Twas old Theritus the tempter who sent me, ten thousand curses on his immortal hellish soul!"

Somehow that made her feel better. She surged with added vigor and started pressing him back. While it was true that he had no physical substance, the sword did, and required force to wield it and mass to support it, which meant that she might as well be fighting a live man. The only problem was, even if she stabbed him through the heart she would do no damage to him, only open herself to a deadly counterthrust.

"The hell with this!" she snapped, and jumped upon the bed. The demon in it stirred and mumbled a few meaningless noises but did not awaken.

The maneuver had taken O'Toole by surprise and

he'd lunged forward, then had to turn to face her. As soon as he did, she jumped back onto the floor—only then was she where she needed to be, allowing him to press as she retreated, parrying his attempts, backing up slowly, carefully, toward the foot of the bed and the little chest.

The old ghost was impressed. "Bless me! Why didn't I think of that?" he seemed to scold himself. "Up on old druggie's bed and about! What a fool ye are, O'Toole!"

She was back to where she had to be, and, if anything, the Irish ghost had eased off, laid back to allow her to use her free hand to flip open the box. The jewel was in there, lying on a bed of yellow satin. She'd almost expected it not to be.

All at once she realized that the ghost was not pressing at all. He was *letting* her take the jewel! She turned, sword still *en garde,* and looked in wonder at the specter. "Why?" she asked him.

Again the Irish chuckle. "Faith, lass, ye duel as well as any I've ever fought, and better than any man I can think of! I'm not heartless, either. Ye *earned* yer way past me with the blade, and ye need the bauble for good purpose. When ye leave, I'll still have my exchange, and we'll see how good the other lass is as well!"

She thought about it. Here she was, the jewel in her hand, and a gallant and likable ghost was allowing her a getaway at the price of another's innocent life. No, more than that, for she would condemn Yoni to perhaps centuries here, alone with the drugged demon. There *had* to be an answer! There *had* to be!

O'Toole seemed puzzled. "What's the matter, lass? Conscience? 'Tis a bad thing to have. It always gets in the way. Do it, lass! I grow increasingly impatient to break these bonds, and I'll not wait until close to daylight and be robbed of my freedom when she's good as dead, anyway. Do it—or stay and join her! Choose now!"

She felt like a trapped rat whose only means of escape was to feed its mate to the cat, yet O'Toole was right. She could not delay.

"I'm sorry," she began, speaking to Yoni trapped inside, when all of a sudden an idea came to her—one gamble, one risk, one possibility. "I'm sorry— O'Toole," she said softly, then shouted quickly, "Jewel! Take me to my room at the inn!"

The world blinked, and then, quite suddenly, she was immersed in darkness. She still held the sword and used it to feel her way around wherever she was.

She'd taken the one gamble—that, being an alien on this world, the jewel that obeyed her order to take her to Mogart would obey other orders as well. It had been a dangerous thesis; if she had been wrong, it could have killed her or trapped her somewhere in between the worlds.

The fact that she still held the sword told her that she was still Yoni, still in Yoni's body. There were solid things in the blackness, and a path between. She felt her way with the sword, then found a wall and walked to it, feeling along it with her hands. She pushed when something seemed loose, and a shutter opened.

She looked out on the street below the room at the inn, dimly lit by oil lamps. "Oh, thank God!" she breathed, and sank down, crying softly for a while.

Her other hand held the jewel. She looked at it glowing in the dark.

It started to burn her.

"Goodbye and thank you, Yoni the Thief," she said aloud. "May good fortune follow you."

Inside her head, there seemed to be a feeling of thanks and relief.

The jewel was terribly hot now; she had to go before it killed the woman it had been used to save.

"Take me to Asmodeus Mogart!" Jill McCulloch demanded.

The nothingness took on a new texture as she sped back to her world. She'd learned some valuable things, though, this time out, although some seemed of doubtful use. She'd learned that human beings, too, could command the jewels.

She'd learned something about herself, too. She

hoped it would not be tested again, for next time there might be no demon in man's skin or magical way out.

She prayed that she be spared that most terrible of choices.

Main Line +2076

MOGART WAS EASY TO LOCATE IN THE BAR.

"I went down to the Saint James Infirmary," he was bawling, horribly out of tune, *"to see my poor bay-be there!"*

"Mogart!" Jill McCulloch yelled to him. "Sober up!"

Mogart clutched a drink uncertainly, spilling a little. He didn't seem to hear her. "Damn, can never 'member the rest of it." He swigged on the glass, then looked up, seemed to brighten. "Oh, yeah." He mumbled to himself, then started, *"Come to me my melancholy baby!"*

"Asmodeus Mogart!" she practically screamed at him. "It's me! Jill McCulloch! I have the jewel!"

He halted in midword, seemed to realize that he was not alone in this time frame, and looked around to see her standing there. He grinned stupidly.

"Hi, there, girlie! Have a drink and siddown!"

She had not left the chalk pentagram on the floor the last time, and decided not to leave it this time, either. She suspected that to do so would require setting up another, and Mogart was in no condition for that.

She held up the jewel, which burned no longer, for she was now in her own body and holding an alien jewel. "Look, Mogart! See what I've got!" she invited.

He looked, couldn't seem to focus, then looked again and seemed to see it. He grinned drunkenly, got up from the stool, and started making his way to her with extreme difficulty.

"A jewel!" he exclaimed, amazed, then stopped and stood unsteadily a few feet from her. "It—it *is* one, isn't it?"

"It is," she affirmed, then glanced at the clock. It was almost midnight. Mogart had been wrong about the time differential.

The drunken demon reached for the jewel, missed it, finally grabbed it on the second try, and looked at it in bleary amazement. "Bedamned," he mumbled. "Lemme shee, now." He reached into his pocket, missed it three times, finally found it and got into it by using his other hand to steady the coat, and brought out the other jewels.

Jill McCulloch's heart leaped. Four! He had *four!* That meant that the man, Mac whatever his name was, had gotten one! Two to go, and almost five hours on the clock. They could make it!

Mogart seemed to be just staring at the jewels, and she suddenly realized that he'd gone to sleep like that, standing up and holding the glowing orbs.

"Mogart!" she yelled at the top of her lungs.

He started. "Umh? Huh?" he managed, and shook his head for a moment, then looked up at her. "Yesh?"

"Send me after the next jewel! We have a chance to get all six!"

He seemed to struggle with himself, to bring himself together. It was a losing proposition, but he did manage to pocket the jewels on the first try.

"Shorry," he mumbled apologetically. "I—I drink, y'know. I—I don' think I can go with you thish time, you'll have to go yourself," he added. "I'd just screw things up."

"But you've *got* to!" she pleaded. "How will I know whose body to use or what the rules are?"

He shrugged. "Itsh a counterpart world," he told her. "Same short of shtuff as this one. Alternate ideas —controls and all that sort of rot. Magic works, machines don't, otherwisch the same. You don' need no body 'cause you're already there!" he explained mysteriously.

She wasn't sure she liked this, but she had no choice. "Walters!" she shouted at him, suddenly remembering the man's last name. "If Walters gets back, send him to me!"

Mogart nodded. "Why not?" he said. "Sho go—got lotsa time there. One hour, one week. Lotsa time. But Theritus, he loves the good life but he's dangerous, like me." He drew himself up straight, but the figure was more ludicrous than terrifying.

"Asmodeus, King of the Demons!" he proclaimed, and fell flat on his face. The drink and glass shattered and splattered everywhere.

He looked up at her drunkenly. "Before you go, can you please help me?"

"I don't think I should get out of the pentagram," she responded dubiously.

"Oh, no, no, don't get out," he murmured. "Just tell me one thing—do you know the next four lines to *Saint James Infirmary?*"

She sighed, exasperated. "Yes, sure I do," she told him.

"Excellent!" he cried triumphantly. "Now go!"

There was blackness.

Main Line +2000
Training Ground #4

1

"I DARE NOT EVEN ENTER THIS PLANE," MOGART HAD told him as they'd traveled. "Of all the problems, this is the one that I fear the most. It is a training area for adepts in the Probabilities Department—not very large as universes go, and tremendously malleable. Unlike most of the planes, this one has no fixed rules. It is designed to respond to the willpower of the utilizer. Thus, you're going to encounter not an old sot or a nut case but someone fully in good with the powers that be."

Mac was nervous about that. "Then with the jewel and no weaknesses, I'll be a sitting duck for him," he'd objected.

"Not at all," the demon had responded. "The jewel is of no consequence here except to get you in or out. Nor did I say that brother Abaddon had no weaknesses. He has a great many that might well be his undoing in the future, but the one most prominent and the one you can make the most use of is that he is a compulsive gambler. It's only because he is that we are risking this one. And he is honorable, as things go. If you wager with him he will play by the rules and will honor the terms of the wager. Beware, though —he loves loopholes, and he will take advantage of any you leave him."

Mac Walters had smiled bitterly, thinking of the rules of the fight back in that other, primitive world. "I'll take care on that score. But what am I to expect? What sort of rules apply here?"

"No rules at all, except what is made by willpower. All that you will see and hear is created in another's mind. You will find that you, too, will be able to do the same thing if you can concentrate and place your requirements in clear terms in your own mind. Don't try a contest of wills, though. Abaddon has the advantage in mental training and experience. First look over the place and test yourself out. There are a lot of leftovers from other training exercises, and more than likely he'll just consider you one of those. Then, when you think you are ready, seek him out—challenge him, appeal to his sporting interests. A contest under clearly defined rules for the jewel. He'll leap at it. The rest, though —winning it, I mean—that's up to you."

There had been more, of course. These training levels were used between testing out new jobs and concepts as refresher courses for active experimenters. That was what Abaddon was doing now. It was, in many ways, a sophisticated equivalent of target practice for a marksman. Now Mac entered the plane, not in anyone else's body but as himself, for the training ground was open.

If there was a hell, he decided, this might be it— the real thing. A gray nothingness spread from horizon to horizon; the ground was featureless as well, with the appearance of dull gray tile but with the feel and consistency of hard-packed dirt. There was no moon, no stars, no sun, although an eerie bright twilight permeated everything. There was no problem seeing where you were going, but there didn't seem anyplace to go.

Yet, somehow, even the stagnant and heavy air around him seemed to be charged with some sort of energy, some kind of electricity he sensed but could not otherwise identify. There was nothing to see, hear, smell, taste, or touch—yet it was there, all the same, and could be felt by some inner part of his brain.

The line "and the Earth was without form or void" came unbidden into his mind, and Mac realized that this must be what it had been like. He resisted the temptation to proclaim "Let there be light!" For all the evidence to the contrary, Mogart had told him he was not alone here, and he was almost afraid that if he said something like that, the living energy all around him would obey and give him away.

He stopped and considered what Mogart had said. The energy *would* be obedient to him if he learned how to use it. You only had to be specific in your mind as to what you wanted; great computers of some sort, filled with every bit of knowledge necessary to creation, were here, or could be tapped from here. If you wanted a tree you need only have a clear idea of the tree you wanted—the physiology, chemistry, all the other material necessary to that tree would be provided. You could change that formula, of course, but only if you so directed.

He considered that. It might do to experiment on some scale before going any further. He held out his hand, looked at it, and said commandingly, "Let there be an apple in my hand!"

Nothing happened.

For a moment he was thrown for a loss. Mogart had made the process sound so simple and basic. He thought furiously, trying to see the flaw. He held out his hand again, concentrated all his attention on it, and ordered, "Let there be a large, juicy red McIntosh apple in my hand!"

Still nothing. He began to worry. Maybe Mogart had been wrong, it wouldn't work for himself or anybody but demons. Maybe there was some magic formula or something.

He relaxed, began some deep-breathing exercises, tried to clear his mind of everything. He closed his eyes and tried to think only of a big, juicy red apple, nothing else. An apple. An apple in his hand.

He started to feel some kind of disturbance in the energy flow, touching him, flowing through him and concentrating in his right hand. It trickled down his arm like warm water; the sensation was not unpleasant, and he did not resist it.

And then he felt something in his hand. He opened his eyes and looked down. He held an apple exactly like the one he'd visualized. Even though he had not only tried for it but hoped for it, he still was amazed. It *felt* like an apple, it *looked* like an apple—and all he'd done was dream it up. He put it to his mouth and bit into it.

Well, if there was one thing for certain, he wouldn't starve in this plane. The trouble, he decided, was concentration. You had to be able to visualize the thing you wanted, which certainly limited you to your own experiences and sensations—and also took a little time. Under some sort of pressure doing so might not be possible.

This concept explained a lot of so-called "magic" and sorcery through the ages, though. Anyone could do it if he were attuned to it. All the magical spells and formulae and paraphernalia associated with magic might be thought of as aids to concentration. It would not be easy to reach beyond the artificially set natural laws of a universe to circumvent them. One might even disrupt things enough to call attention to oneself and notify a repairman, so to speak, to stop you.

Such a repairman might well be one of Mogart's own race—a demon. Somehow, he felt, he'd stumbled on the basic explanation for the supernatural in his own world and perhaps many others. A subconscious attunement, for example, might bring about poltergeist phenomena, anything you wanted. It was a fascinating and potentially useful concept.

Here, on the testing ground, where no natural laws were imposed, the way was open.

He spent some time practicing. Getting the knack was neither easy nor automatic. It might become so if he had a lot of time—but, after a while, he got enough of the hang of it to create the things he thought of. Small things, to be sure, but elaborate nonetheless, in that a fir tree, for example, was something complex, living, and yet there because he willed it. He was not satisfied, but his small successes would have to do. Mogart hadn't indicated the time rate for this place, and he couldn't wait forever in any event. Somewhere in this vast expanse of nothingness was a demon with a jewel he had to have.

He decided to start walking, but stopped short as he scanned the place from horizon to horizon and saw nothing to aim for. Last time Mogart had led him almost to the exact spot. And then he saw it.

It wasn't much, just a dull glow on the horizon to his left. For a moment he wasn't positive that his imagination wasn't playing tricks on him. But he had nothing else to aim at, anyway, so he started walking toward the glow. It took him over an hour to close in on it. But the closer he came, the more certain he was that this had to be the place, and he became wary.

It was a town, that was for sure. It looked a little like something out of an old western movie—a couple or three blocks square with a main street of rutted dirt lined with storefronts and watering troughs and hitching posts. From a large building that had to be the saloon came the sound of a piano and with it the sound of human activity, of people being merry.

He wished now that he had a gun, some sort of protection. No telling who or what was in the town —perhaps a "leftover" of somebody else's practice session, perhaps even Abaddon himself. He stood still, visualizing a pistol and holster with gunbelt, and felt the energy flow and the proper form take place around his waist. The gun was wrong, though, he decided, too much in the western period suggested by the town. But what kind of pistol did he want? One that was accurate, wouldn't easily run out of ammunition, and would be light and easy to use without kicking like the .45 caliber thing he held. He tried again, retaining the shape if possible but otherwise wishing for the properties of a laser-based pistol he'd seen once in a science-fiction movie. He had no idea if such a thing actually existed, but that made no difference if he could get his idea across.

The pistol changed. Outwardly it still looked like a .45 circa 1880, but its barrel was solidly plugged with a screenlike seal, and inside he could see some sort of rod. It also felt a lot lighter, almost like a plastic toy.

He was still a way from the town. He looked over to his right, materialized a wooden stake, then took aim and fired. There was a whine and a beam of ruby-colored light reached out. He missed the stake but managed to use the beam to bring it quickly to bear. The stake shimmered and vanished.

He released the trigger and looked again at the pistol. Pretty good. He added a small lever on it that allowed him to stun if it were up and disintegrate if it were down, and then holstered the weapon. He was beginning to enjoy this magic stuff. Satisfied, he walked into the town.

There were torchlights and kerosene lanterns all about; the place was pretty well lit up in the permanent twilight. It sounded busy, too—the sounds of an active and living town were all around him. And yet there were no people on the street, no animals—although he heard the occasional sound of a horse or dog—nothing. Feeling like a character in an old movie, he headed for the brightly lit saloon from which the sounds of laughter and lots of people milling about emanated. As he approached the swinging double doors, though, he could see nothing but light inside. When he stepped through, all sound stopped, and not because everyone had turned to see a stranger.

There was no one in the hall. No one at all. Card tables had hands dealt and money lay on the tables; cigarettes and cigars smoldered in ashtrays as if put down just a moment before, and half-touched drinks were lining the bar. A roulette wheel was still turning to his left, and he heard it slow and the ball drop into its slot.

Now what the hell? he thought anxiously, looking around.

He walked around the large room looking for someone, anyone. He walked upstairs and checked the rooms—more still-lit smokes and the appearance that people had been there only moments earlier, but not a living thing to be seen.

He walked back down to the deserted bar, confused. Either a deserted or an active town he could have taken, but one in which there was the semblance of life without the living was unnerving indeed.

He returned to the street, and ten steps from the saloon door he heard the sounds of furious yet normal activity resume there. He was tempted to go back but decided not to.

There was a sign saying CAFE across the street, and he went over to it and opened the door. Again there were no people. Yet on the counter were mugs of coffee and other beverages that were still hot, and glasses of cooler stuff still felt cold. Two steaks were sizzling on the open-pit grill; they were not burned to a crisp but cooking rather nicely, as if someone had just flipped them over. Blood and juice still oozed from the fork holes.

A sudden whistle startled him. He whirled and drew his gun, but saw that the noise came from a teapot that had just reached the boiling point.

Wait a minute, he told himself nervously. *Just reached the boiling point?*

He heard some noise coming from a back room, like water being pumped, and rushed to it. It stopped just as he pushed through the door. There *was* a well pump there, and it was still dripping with the runoff into a bucket hung on the spout that was now half full. There were no exits from the back room except a small window that obviously hadn't been opened in a long time.

He walked back into the cafe, shaking his head and trying to get a grip on himself when he stopped short.

The steaks were on a plate next to the pit now, still sizzling but done. The water was off the flame and no longer boiling.

Behind him he heard the pump start again.

He walked quickly out into the street once more. He felt more comfortable there, at least—he could see a greater distance on all sides. He didn't have the feeling that anyone was watching him, just a sense of isolation from human contact. It was as if this town lived all around him but not where he was.

He saw a little church at the end of the street, away from the other buildings a bit, and he walked toward it. It sounded as if some sort of service were going on, except that instead of hymns, the sound of the choir reminded him of a Gregorian chant.

Or witchcraft ritual, perhaps?

He reached the church, which, he noticed, had no cross on it. As he expected, when he opened the massive doors there was no chanting, no people inside at all.

He turned, pistol still in hand, and walked around to the side of the building. The service, naturally, started up again and sounded very, very real, if a bit eerie.

To one side was a small graveyard. He approached it and tried to make out the inscriptions on the crude wooden slabs. Again no sign of crosses or of Stars of David or of any other known religion adorned them.

He cursed under his breath. Naturally the inscriptions were in a language he couldn't read, even an alphabet that looked very odd indeed.

He sighed and was about to return to town when he thought he heard movement off to his left, further inside the cemetery. That perked his interest and put him more on guard. For the first time he had the sensation of something living, something physically present, lurking there somewhere between the tombstones, watching him.

He flicked the small lever on his pistol to stun and walked slowly to the side of the cemetery nearest the church, then carefully started moving past rows of wooden tombstones. He could see nothing, but it wasn't well lit here, anyway. Nobody burns lights in a graveyard, and the uniform twilight with its lack of a light source prevented shadows from any natural source. He considered that, reached out his left hand, and materialized a small burning torch. Its light was not the best, but it was an improvement. The flickering flame's shadow-making ability, particularly among the slabs and against the church wall, gave the scene an even more eerie cast.

Suddenly a small, dark figure bolted from behind a slab just as Mac was approaching it.

"Hold it!" Mac shouted and aimed the pistol. The figure did not heed his warning, so he pressed the trigger, using the pencil-thin beam to find its mark. It struck the figure just on the other side of the graveyard and bathed it in an eerie reddish glow. The stun worked; the figure collapsed in a heap and remained still. Mac almost broke a record getting to the figure, then gasped when he reached it and turned it over.

It was a girl. Not a woman-type girl, a small one of perhaps nine or ten, barefoot and dressed in an obviously handmade shirt and pants. Her hair was cut short, her complexion was dark, and her features were vaguely Chinese or something similar.

He sat and waited for her to recover, planting the torch in a recess in the ground that he had ordered and holding the pistol lightly. The church service continued. He wondered if they ever stopped chanting.

He'd waited perhaps five minutes when he suddenly cursed himself again. He had no idea how long "stun" worked—he hadn't specified it. On the other hand, she had been knocked down by a weapon of his own will, so that meant she could also be brought around in the same way. He stared at her and his mind ordered her to wake up.

She stirred, groaned, sat up, and shook her head, looking confused. Then, suddenly, she became aware of him and her head turned slowly to look at him for the first time under these conditions. She gasped; her expression showed abject terror.

"Don't be afraid," he soothed, glad to find another living being. "I won't hurt you."

Confusion reigned again on her face, although the look of terror was not at all diminished. *"Bu kasha liu briesto,"* she rasped through a fear-constricted throat. It seemed to be a plea.

"Oh, boy!" Mac Walters said aloud disgustedly. There had never been any reason to expect that someone here would speak English. He fervently wished he could understand her and she him.

"Bu kasha liu harm," she said in that same pleading voice.

Suddenly his head came up. *Harm? Then maybe . . .*

"I'm not going to hurt you," he told her again.

She plainly didn't believe him, but at least now she understood him. "Please, master, I did not mean to come to your holy place," she explained desperately. "Duru, my chicken, he got away today and I was just looking for him, just trying to find him, and accidentally came here. This was a forest yesterday, not a town." She started to cry.

Mac realized suddenly that he was able to understand her. This *was* a strange world. He relaxed the pistol a little. "I don't have anything to do with this town," he told her as gently as possible. "I don't know as much about this place as you do. And I'm nobody's master but my own."

Still, he thought, *if this was a forest yesterday and is a town today, it is somebody's doing. Abaddon? Almost certainly—but where?*

At any rate, she still didn't believe him. She waited to see what he was going to say or do next.

"Where are you from?" he asked her. "I didn't see anything but this town anywhere."

She looked, if anything, even more fearful and

certainly hesitant. "I'm from Brobis," she explained, as if that told him anything.

"Never heard of it," he admitted. "No matter. What do you know of this place here? I mean, where are the people?"

A little of the fear lessened in her and she looked at him curiously. "You really don't know? You aren't just playing with me?"

"I'm perfectly serious," he assured her. "I never saw this town until a few minutes ago, and I certainly have no idea what or where a Brobis is. You're the first living thing I've run into since I got here."

"I still think you might be a *simulacrum* or a demon in disguise," she warned, "but if you're not, you'd better put out that torch and get outta here quick as you can. There's a demon here, and he'll hex you and steal your soul and use you for his toy unless you do."

He decided to take a part of that advice and nullified the torch in his mind. It ceased to exist.

Her terror was back. "You *are* one of Them!" she whispered fearfully. "Oh, I wish I had listened to Daddy!"

Again he felt the need to calm her down. "No, I'm not one of Them, whoever they are. Not a demon, anyway, and I was born of real people just like you. You might call me a . . . magician, let's say."

"Magicians get their power from demons," she retorted. "Same thing."

In a way she had him there. Without Mogart he wouldn't be here, and he bore Mogart's brand on his palm.

"Some demons aren't as bad as others," he told her. "The demon I work for wouldn't scare anybody. He's a falling-down drunk. The other demons made him live with my people as one of my people, and now my home is about to be destroyed. The other demons won't help us, so we're trying to help ourselves."

She looked a little dubious. "You can't trust *any* demons," she stated flatly. "They don't care about people at all, or if they do, they treat them like toys.

You oughta know that. Go ahead, do with me what you want. I'm in your power."

He gave up. Clearly the girl's universe didn't allow for such as he. He gestured back at the church and the town. "Are there real people there? Can you see them?"

She shrugged. "Bunch o' ghosts, I think. They're there—you just can't tell it. Living beings break the spell around 'em."

He nodded. *That* he could understand. Ghosts— or perhaps real people, it made no difference in this case—inhabited the town, but when another mind not part of its creation came into their proximity, they did not exist for that immediate area. That explained a lot. He just hoped he was as invisible to them as they were to him.

Clearly the girl could be no more help to him, though, and would be better out of the way. If this was Abaddon's town, and Mac had every reason to believe it was, then his next step was the most dangerous of all.

"Go home," he told her. "Don't come back around here as long as there's any action. It'll be safer for you." He holstered his pistol.

She sat there a minute, apparently not realizing she'd just been freed. Finally she gaped at him. "You mean you're letting me go? Just like that?" She was still suspicious but had visibly relaxed a little. "Why?"

"My business isn't with you or your people," he told her. "It's with the demon in this town. You can only get hurt here."

She couldn't seem to believe it. "What're you gonna do?"

"Seek him out. Find him. I understand he likes wagers. I have one for him he might find appealing. Now—go!"

She was on her feet, still staring at him in wonder. "You really *aren't* from here, are you? A living man with blood and unpledged soul? And you walked in here on your own? Not knowing anything? You're *crazy!*"

"Not crazy," he replied. "Desperate. Now—get out of here!" He stood up.

"Blood . . . life . . . soul," the girl repeated with wonder. As she did so she suddenly grinned, exposing not nice teeth but nasty, sharp fangs such as a carnivore might have. Her eyes shone inhumanly, and her form seemed to alter slightly into something neither human nor little-girl-like at all. That it had once been the girl there was no question. Her general size and features remained, but this thing was darker —its ears were pointed, animal-like, and it seemed to have long, nasty claws and— Were those bat wings, tiny bat wings, growing from its back?

He was startled, even a little scared, at this demonic transformation. And yet within him stirred something even stronger, an anger born of feeling like a foolish sucker. He'd been had! Softened up by the town and soothed by the little girl. He was mad as hell, and the pistol flew into his hand.

The creature looked at the pistol and laughed. "You got me the first time because I wasn't prepared for it," she rasped. It was still the girl's voice but now somehow changed slightly, more throaty and full. It sounded more like that of an old woman than a small girl. "That thing can't hurt me now."

"What are you?" he challenged, deciding that a brave front was best. Besides, he was mad and becoming madder. "Are you a part of *this?*" He gestured toward the town with his pistol, flicking the lever from stun to disintegrate.

"This is Hell, you idiot," snarled the creature. "All that dwell here are the souls of those who pledged or were pledged to the Demon Lords in world after world. In life I was sacrificed to My Lord Mammon, and I belong to Him. Now I will claim you despite your silly gun. You cannot kill the dead, and particularly not in Hell itself!"

Her tone and look were menacing, but it didn't escape him that she was still talking and not charging him. The pistol *had* stunned her; she hadn't expected that and wasn't really sure just what it could or could not do to her. The logic behind her words came to him quickly in the adrenal flush of the standoff. Somewhere, in some world, this poor girl had been sacrificed to a particularly nasty demon in some sort of black-magic ritual, and she'd since been the creature of that demon here at the training site. No matter that he had an understanding of how these universes were set up and knew the rationale behind the magic, this girl didn't know that. Hers was the world of the purely supernatural, and frankly, it didn't matter what kind of term you put on it. Her concepts were as valid for her as his were for him. What had tripped her up was that his pistol was created out of the rules of this world, by him, for use against the creatures of this world. In a dark graveyard on his world, or probably on hers, she'd be right—but not here. Here there was a different set of rules, and the dead could die if he so willed it. He certainly hoped so.

"What do you intend to do with me?" he asked softly. In a way he felt pity for the girl and anger for the demon who had done this to her.

"You have blood . . . fresh blood," she responded hungrily, beginning to sound like a heroin addict in sight of a quick fix. "I shall drink it and gain your power, and you shall be to me in my service as I am in the service of the Lord Mammon." She shifted a little but still did not attack, and her eyes remained on the pistol.

"I serve Asmodeus," he told her, and showed the brand on his hand. "You cannot claim me for Mammon."

She considered the argument but rejected it. "You live and that is enough. I will take you now. You will become my husband and show me those things of love and sex that I was not allowed to grow to discover for myself!"

He felt real pity for her now. She'd been cheated of everything.

"I cannot," he said softly. "I'm sorry." He pulled the trigger on the pistol.

She *was* prepared, he had to give her that. She was enveloped in the glow but fought it fiercely. Still, his own willpower supported the blast, his own command that it work—and she had felt only the stun, not the full force of the beam. She struggled against it, but it was winning; the glow began closing in, eating at her. She writhed and screamed and spit, then ran for the graveyard. He kept the blast on her, a blast that should have eliminated her in the first millisecond. She made the second grave in the fourth row, seemed to reach out for the tombstone, wistfully, hopefully, and faded into the earth of the graveyard in front of it.

The beam closed in on her, became smaller, ever smaller, and he heard her cries abruptly cut off as the field closed to a single bright dot at the end of the pencil. He released the trigger and stood there a moment, shaking slightly. Finally he went over to the grave she'd tried so desperately to get into and willed himself able to read the inscription.

"Meka Chau," it read. "Born 17 Sept. 1874, Rangoon. Died 4 April 1883, Kubai, her soul pledged."

Suddenly he became aware of other noises in the graveyard, noises that had been partially masked by the chanting. This was a cemetery of the living dead, he realized. Mac turned and walked quickly back to town, consoling himself that at least she would suffer no more.

He barged into the church or whatever it was, stopping the service in the chilly silence he was now expecting. He was still mad and doubly determined to get this over with.

He walked about two-thirds of the way up the aisle and stopped, facing the altar. It was, he noted, exactly that, though it looked more like a place to sacrifice people than anything else. Behind it was a black-painted stage framed by black curtains which bordered the stone sacrificial altar and gave everything just the right theatrical touch. Clearly Abaddon was trying out different decors for whatever project he had in mind.

"Abaddon!" he called, his voice echoing through the hollow, empty church. "Abaddon, I call upon you to appear to me! I have a wager for you!"

He waited as the echoes died down. For a moment he wasn't sure he'd been heard—or was perhaps being ignored. Then with a sudden force the rear doors of the church, which he'd closed behind him, burst open with a bang, and a great wind swept in and down the aisle, almost knocking him to the floor.

The torches that illuminated the church flared as if they had suddenly been fed by jets of pure oxygen. The effect was a roaring-fire noise that dominated the interior of the building.

As he stood there expectantly, the chanting returned—coming from countless voices both male and female in the choir loft. They were so realistic-sounding that he could almost swear he saw the chanters there.

The noises and sensations of a lot of people were inside now, in the pews, sitting there all around him. The choir chanted one word over and over, one name in a reverent summons: "A-bad-don! A-bad-don!" it called.

Over the altar stone, a writhing, twisting shape that was neither matter nor energy but a little of both began to emerge against the black backdrop. A face was forming there—huge, gigantic, monstrously animalistic and leeringly evil—a satanic, goatlike head that seemed to radiate both pure power and absolute evil.

Mac was impressed, he had to admit that.

The choir continued its chanting of the name, but now in joyful greeting rather than as a summons, and the unseen congregation joined in in hushed whispers of respect.

The chanting grew faster, ever faster, until finally it was a frenzied, near-insane plea. The choir was at a fever pitch, overcome with emotion, intoning faster, ever faster . . .

"A-bad-don! A-bad-don! Abaddon! Abaddon! A-baddonabaddonabaddon!"

Then, suddenly, the fury was over, all was still. Yet within the silence was an overpowering sense of expectation, of waiting for something to happen.

The image behind the altar spoke. "Who summons Abaddon?" it demanded, its tone powerful, tremendously deep, and overwhelmingly ancient in its feel.

Mac Walters tried to imagine the effect of this act on a real congregation. Hell, he might have converted himself!

"I did!" he shouted at the head.

"From whom do you come, and whence?" the great, evil head demanded to know. "And by what boldness do you face Abaddon?"

"I come from Asmodeus, also called Mogart," he shouted back. "I come as his agent with a proposition, a wager, a contest. Now cut out this great showmanship and let's talk it over! Your display is all very impressive, but leave that for the dumb masses."

The fury of the great head was terrible to behold. "You *dare* mock Abaddon, Prince of Darkness? Why should the great and all-powerful Abaddon not just strike you into oblivion from where you stand and get on with his business?"

That worried Mac a little. This show of bravado was all well and good, but the demon could in fact just get rid of him with a mental flick of his finger— and he might believe in all this. After having seen two others of his kind, Mac wouldn't be at all surprised.

"As I remember it, Asmodeus is King of the Demons, second only to Lucifer Makrieg himself in the demonic pantheon," he responded boldly. "In short, he outranks you if you want to keep this up. But I was told that the great Abaddon was fond of the wager and the challenge of gaming. I come with a proposition for such a game from Asmodeus himself, as you can see from his mark on my palm. If I was wrong, if the great Abaddon has no stomach for a fair wager and desires only sure things, then I will leave and report so."

Mac hesitated a second, almost afraid that he'd overplayed his hand with the taunt, made the creature mad.

The evil, leering goat's head seemed to be thinking over the proposition. Finally it asked, in that awe-inspiring voice it had, "If this is so, then why did Asmodeus send a representative and not come himself? Why must I deal through a vassal?"

Mac started to feel better. The demon wouldn't be

asking questions if he weren't at least interested. Mac controlled his enthusiasm slightly, though, reminding himself that Abaddon was only considering the offer. He hadn't accepted it, still hadn't even considered dropping the Black-Sabbath act. Mac wondered where the demon really was and experienced a sudden feeling of uncertainty. What if this were all part of the setup? What if the demon really wasn't anywhere around, and this thing was just another creature of the demon's imagination?

"You know very well where Mogart is," he told the head flatly, letting a little disgust and resignation creep into his voice. "He's back in a bar on his plane, drunk as a skunk."

The head seemed frozen for a moment. Then, slowly at first, then building, it started to laugh uncontrollably, until peals of deep, rich laughter almost shook the foundations of the building. Then in an instant the creature was gone, leaving only the echoes of its mirth, but there was another sound, the sound of a thin, reedy voice still chuckling—near him.

Mac whirled. Sitting not two pews in back of him, on the aisle, was the demon prince Abaddon himself. He was still laughing, and he looked and sounded exactly like Asmodeus Mogart.

The demon, who was wearing a flowered aloha shirt and baggy jeans with boots, grinned at him and applauded slightly. "Very, very good!" he chuckled, then looked around thoughtfully at the church. "Obviously the act still needs a little polishing, though."

It was Mac's turn to smile. "Oh, I wouldn't say so. If somebody didn't know about the University and the Department of Probabilities and some of the real laws of existence, then they'd be scared shitless by all this. I am deeply impressed, anyway."

The demon smiled, accepting the flattery and obviously enjoying it. "I've let things slip the last few centuries," he explained. "Office work. I let my people —my contacts—on the various planes go their own way a little too long. No miracles or manifestations for a while, and the cult tends to die out if there are others to take its place. Now I have nobody left to do my legwork for me, let me keep track of what's going on up and down the Main Line, get the stuff I need—things like that. It's like starting from scratch. I can't tell you what a blow to the ego it is to find out that most planes don't even remember my name unless it's in some arcane book of demonology."

Walters nodded, suddenly understanding what all this was about. The jewels were repellers of a sort; each insured that the physical presence of a demon couldn't coexist in proximity to another demon on the same plane. "Proximity" probably meant the whole planet. But they could get close—he remembered Mogart in that primitive world. "Out of phase," he'd called it. Ghostlike, unseen—but with the jewels, the amplifiers, they could make their influence felt. They could establish a cult, then use it as their eyes and ears in each plane they were interested in, keeping an eye on other projects as well as on their fellow demons —particularly the renegades—and having the cult obtain ideas developed on one plane that could be useful on another, perhaps even products.

Demonology, Mac reflected, was sadly unromantic from the other side of the pentagram.

"So what's the old sot got in mind?" Abaddon prodded. His mood was still light, and Mac hoped it would remain so. "He was never much of a sportsman himself. Couldn't stay sober."

Quickly Walters explained the situation—the collision, the short time, the need for six jewels.

Abaddon nodded. "I can see his point. He'd rather die than go home, he's got no means of space travel to get him out of the target area, and the only alternative would be to spend eternity forever out of phase—you can't drink there, either. So he's trying to create an Eye of Baal, huh? That'd do it. But I've never seen one formed outside of University sanction. Hell, with an Eye of Baal even *you* could become Zeus atop Olympus—that's right, isn't it? I haven't got the wrong world?"

"Right world," Mac assured him. "But it's our only hope."

Abaddon became thoughtful. "How many's he got?"

"I've seen three," Mac told the demon. "Probably by now my counterpart has another. I hope so, anyway. Probably four."

Abaddon was impressed. "That many? In so short a time? My, my! Whatever happened to security? Oh, I guess we just underestimated Mogart. He seems to have done his homework on all counts. So now you're here to bet me for my jewel, huh? Number five of six?"

"Or perhaps number six," the human responded. "After all, I have no idea what my counterpart is doing, how well or whatever, since we're running at such different time rates."

Abaddon reached into his pants pocket and brought out the jewel. Mac's heart leaped at seeing it. So close! So very, very close!

Abaddon read his thoughts and laughed. "I know, I know! But you can't take it from me—not here. Not anywhere, really. I have to *give* it to you. You know that. Either that or else not be in any position to stop you—and this is my element, not yours."

"I know that," Mac grumbled. He did—but he didn't have to like it. "That's why I suggested the wager. A contest, with your jewel the prize."

Abaddon put the jewel away. "So I'm to take the risk and also put up the only prize? Come on, now! What's in it for me if *I* win?"

Mac had considered this possibility on his way into the town and was ready to respond. "Look, I know you're still in good graces and all that," he began, "but tell me, doesn't an Eye of Baal tempt you— even a little bit?"

The demon stared at him for a minute, then suddenly a twinkling started in his eyes and spread through his whole face. He laughed evilly, a human-proportioned, high-pitched echo of his great phony laughter.

"If I lose, my world's dead and, as you said, so is Mogart," Mac pressed. "That means four, maybe five jewels at the very least. It also means that both my counterpart and I won't have a home to come back to but will have a proven track record of getting the goods. Even if we're one short, we could wait until you found the right time and place and go after it."

"You'd work for me?" the demon asked, his tone definitely interested. "And you can speak for this counterpart individual?"

He shrugged. "What choice would she have? No Mogart, no home world. A job's a job and a demon's a demon."

Abaddon nodded thoughtfully. "You're right, of course. Amazingly, you're right. An Eye of Baal." He looked up at Mac Walters. "So what's the wager?"

Halfway there! The human exulted. "Simple, really. You will place the jewel somewhere near here—in a known place, that is. I'd then have to get it without getting killed and within, say, a given local time limit. I'd just as soon *not* get killed even if I lose."

"You against me?" The demon was incredulous. "Hell, man, I can wilt you where you stand. You know that. I've been doing this sort of thing for about four billion of your years!"

Mac shook his head. "No, that'd be unfair and you admit it. Choose a champion—another human. Show him the ropes here if he needs it." He was improvising now. "Let's make it a race, your champion against me for the jewel. Make him anybody you want, but somebody from my world or at least close to my world so we start out without any physical or mental handicaps. A fair race to a predetermined point. If I get there, I get your jewel. If he gets there first, then you have Mogart's number and, if I'm still alive, my services and probably those of the woman working with me. Fair enough?"

The demon thought the proposal over. "Yes, indeed, it does sort of appeal to me," he murmured, more to himself than to Mac. He looked up at the human. "Shall we agree to that and start this? No time limits, though. You against my champion. I guarantee he'll be from your world. I can reach back a bit into the past if necessary to get one—time is a bit more fluid for those of us not tied to the plane involved. We'll start from here and make the objective a monument, a statue of me, let's say, that I'll put a bit away from here. Let's see—you use kilometers, don't you? We'll make it at the end of a road seven kilometers from this church."

"Your champion gets no more information on its location than I do—all even?" Mac prompted.

"Of course! A wager's no fun if the race is fixed. Profitable, maybe, but no fun. I won't cheat you, and if you win I'll pay off. One thing, though—if you get killed, it won't end you. If you die here you'll simply become one of the local living dead under my orders, so even if you lose that way, you'll be in my service."

Mac shivered slightly, remembering the poor girl. An eternity like that—he wasn't going to die if he could help it. He took a deep breath and swallowed hard. "You're on. Let's do it."

Abaddon rose and put out his hand. "Shake on it?"

Walters looked bemused. "What? No blood pacts?"

"On an agreement, a wager, between honorable gentlemen? Don't be ridiculous," Abaddon scoffed. They shook hands.

"Let's go down to the cafe and get a bite to eat while I summon my champion," the demon suggested. "Then we'll be ready to start this." He paused and his voice became tinged with excitement. "This is really going to be *something!*"

Mac followed him, feeling a bit hungry and remembering those steaks. "You sound confident," he noted. "What if I win? You'll be trapped here."

"I never take a wager I don't intend to win," the demon responded lightly. "But still, this isn't a bad place to be stuck—anything you want is yours. And sooner or later, in a few thousand years or so, somebody else will be through to sharpen up his skills, so it's not forever." He patted Mac on the rump. "But I don't intend to lose. I intend to have a great deal of fun!"

Halfway there, yes, Mac Walters told himself. But something in the demon's manner suggested that the second half would be much tougher than it looked.

2

"Are there really people here, or is this just more of the act?" Mac Walters asked the demon prince Abaddon over steak, baked potato, and coffee in the cafe.

Abaddon smiled. "Well, yes and yes. Yes, there are real people here and yes, it's all part of the act." He became serious and common-sensical in tone and expression, as if lecturing a novice or new student. "You see, creating inanimate objects and special effects is easy. Here in the training area anybody can do it, and on the stable planes those of us with amplifiers can do it, although only to a minor degree. To give you an idea as to the power of the jewels, six will certainly deflect a rogue planet and sixty are used to create a stable plane. But living things—that's a bit different. In the creation process we can, of course, establish the building blocks for the evolution of life by any rules we choose and let it take its course. We can also, with the jewels, affect things which are already alive. There is, however, a binder force, if you will—it's difficult to put it in layman's terms—in all living things, and there is an enormous but finite amount of it. It's this force, stabilized by the *persona* of Mac Walters, that travels the planes and enters other bodies, not the physical you. Only we Main Liners, who are the only naturally created plane's inhabitants—at least I think and hope so—can and must travel and take our physical selves along. In most cases this force is dispersed upon death, but not always. If the personality is particularly strong it might survive intact—a ghost, if you will—or partially, as an elemental insane force, a poltergeist or some such phenomenon, at least for a time."

He paused to polish off the rest of his food and swig some coffee. He looked neither anxious nor worried, which bothered Mac considerably, since he was staking his jewel on the coming contest.

"But here, you see," the demon continued, "there was no creation as such. Anyone who dies here is stuck here and is usable by the living who enter. Most are sacrifices, people and animals who pledged themselves or were pledged to us in rites, plucked a fraction of a second before true death by one of us and brought here, and in some cases just people picked at random as needed. People disappear all the time in every world—no real problem."

He pulled two cigars from his coat pocket, offered Mac one—which was declined—then lit his in the interesting manner of having his index finger burst into flame. Mac tried not to be unnerved, and it suddenly occurred to him that the demon might be trying to psych him out.

Abaddon inhaled and blew out a big cloud of purple-gray smoke. "Of course," he added, "there are some planes where nobody really dies—ones which have reincarnation and the like, and one where the best of the faithful become demigods and get to do their own minicreations. Then there are a plethora of planes where magic works, and so we have vampires and other creatures of the night. Quite a number on the minus line that aren't anything close to human, too, and where death has different meanings. It keeps things from getting boring, anyway.

"So, to return to your question, there are lots of 'people' here, in that form. For the town I don't need their physical forms, only what is necessary to assure that the normal functions of the town run as if it were real, and that I have. That answer your question?"

Mac suppressed a chuckle. "I'd almost forgotten that I'd asked a question, but thanks. What about that girl in the graveyard?"

The demon looked startled. "Girl? In *my* graveyard?"

Quickly Mac told Abaddon of his encounter with the living dead.

"Hmmm . . ." the demon said thoughtfully. "Lots of that sort of thing around, of course, but I didn't know it was here. Mammon and some of the others take their demonic roles too seriously, to the point of believing in them themselves. We're all a little crazy, Walters, in our own way—all the responsibility and living an impossibly long time do it, I suppose."

"You seem pretty sane and levelheaded to me," the human noted.

The compliment pleased Abaddon. "Thanks. Sometimes I feel like I'm the only really sane one left. Still," he added, pausing for effect, a twinkle now in his eye, "I made this dumb wager with you, didn't I?"

Mac decided he didn't really want to comment on that. He was about to change the subject when a man materialized just inside the entrance to the cafe. There was a little bang when he appeared, and a slight smell of ozone. He looked at the two sitting there with some curiosity and a bit of suspicion, but not with any great fear or alarm.

"Was ist das?" he asked in a nasty-sounding tenor. *"Gott in Himmel! Ich bin—"* He sounded slightly angry.

"English, please, my friend," Abaddon told the newcomer in a conversational tone.

The newcomer looked mildly surprised. "English? Well, all right, then, whatever," he said in a gentle upper-class British accent. He was still mad. "What the bloody hell took you so long, Abaddon? I thought I'd had it with that bloody planet about to go bump!"

Mac surveyed the man with more than idle interest now. Obviously this man was from his own world in real time and was, therefore, probably his competitor.

He was a tall, thin, muscular man who appeared to be in his mid-forties. His hair and bushy mustache were a premature gray, as were his equally bushy eyebrows, which seemed to connect at the apex of the bridge on his nose. He looked more classically Slavic than German, though.

"Calm yourself, my friend," Abaddon soothed. "I would not forget *you,* at least."

"You cut it pretty damn close, almost too close," the newcomer grouched, but he had softened a bit from his previous anger as the realization came that, close or not, he *had* been spared.

"Come! Sit! Eat if you wish. We have just finished, but you should not go hungry," the demon invited.

"Thanks, but no, thank you," the man responded.

"I had my last meal an hour or so ago—everything I ever wanted to eat, even a bottle of Rothschild 'forty-seven. If I get hungry again I can always whip up something else to eat *here*."

That was bad. It meant that this stranger knew the demons for what they were and implied that he also well understood how to use this training ground. Abaddon had called in an old-timer, his best. Mac turned to the demon and whispered, "Aren't you even going to introduce us?"

The demon laughed. "Well, bless me! Of course! Mac Walters, this is—let me get it right—Dr. Hans Martin Kroeger, head of the secret police of the GDR."

"GDR?" Mac responded, a bit puzzled.

"East Germany," snapped Kroeger impatiently. "Besides, that was only my current identity, and it's gone now with the planet. I prefer my classical name, which I have not been able to use in a very long time. I am Boreas." He said the last as if the name should have meant something to Mac. When it didn't he looked doubly annoyed.

"Look, see? That's the trouble with that world today, anyway. Just as well it was blown away. He's never even heard of me," the man complained. "Americans," he mumbled under his breath.

Abaddon leaned over and half whispered to Mac. "He was one of your plane's leading sorcerers and alchemists. One of the best minds of what you would call the early Middle Ages."

That gave Mac a start. "And he's still *alive?*"

Boreas shrugged and gave a curious half-smile in Abaddon's direction. "One of my own developed processes," he told him, "although I dare say it pays to have friends."

The demon dismissed the topic with a gesture. "Well, come over and sit, anyway. I have a job for you for high stakes. If you want to enjoy *this* life, you'll have to win."

Boreas was suddenly tense. He came over and sat, fixing steel-gray eyes on the demon; his finely etched Slavic face, rough-hewn and almost triangular beneath the bushy mustache, was all business. "So you *were* going to leave me to die there," he said in a low but steady tone that conveyed acid. "You only pulled me because I was needed."

Abaddon sighed. "Look, I could argue with you, I know, but why bother? The result's the same no matter what."

"He didn't even know the Earth was in trouble until I told him," Mac put in, hoping to drive a further wedge. Instead his comment seemed to ease the sorcerer's mind considerably.

"All right, then. I know you've been out of touch. Hell—when was it last? Sometime in the seventeen hundreds, I think."

"Earlier," the demon responded. "Besides, with all my people you've talked to over the centuries, I'm the one who saved you."

"Fair enough," Boreas admitted. "So what's this little game all about?"

"That's exactly what it is," Abaddon told him. "A game." Quickly he explained what was going on, what Mac was doing there, the stakes and the general rules they'd agreed upon.

"Sounds fair enough," the sorcerer agreed. "I'm ready any time."

Mac was somewhat appalled by the man. There was something inherently evil in him, something that radiated a sense of the sinister. Yet here he was readily agreeing to a contest which, if he won, would doom his native world, and Mac said as much.

"Harumph!" The sorcerer snorted. "So what's worth saving about it? With the technocrats in full charge it was rapidly moving either toward nuclear self-destruction or to being a sterile world of robotic people. No character, no stomach. I don't know why you're so keen on it. Maybe a few dozen of all the billions would do the same for you—and they're all dead now, anyway. All the greats are gone, too— Hitler, Stalin, Mao, the best of a bad lot. Look who's replaced them! Colorless little men turned out in a bureaucracy factory, so lacking in anything that even the people they rule can hardly remember their names and faces! So here, with this deal, I team up with a powerful man who's also my gateway to thousands of other worlds and with a crack at a piece of the action on an Eye of Baal. Don't give me any of that duty crap. Your own popular democracy would gleefully murder you if you were the slightest bit of inconvenience to it. Don't bother to refute that—just think about a half million dead in Vietnam and let's get back to the business at hand!"

Mac Walters had no intention of responding to the tirade, yet it disturbed him. Why *was* he doing this, anyway? All that he'd learned on this mission so far was just how insignificant the human race really was, created playthings and perhaps byproducts of some inhuman scientific team's project. Rats in a specially constructed maze, no more. Even the religions were shams, all of them. If you received life after death, it would still be as the plaything of some godlike demonic professor like Abaddon, perhaps as a subhuman monster like the girl in the graveyard. He could understand Boreas now, a little—the man was ready to make the best of a humiliating position. And yet, and yet—that understanding worried him. There *had* to be something more to being a human being than Boreas and the demons had made it out to be. Something more. The fact that the rats had been created and placed in the maze did not automatically make them inferior, just less powerful. But only at the moment—not absolutely less powerful. These demons had the edge because of superior technology and eons of experience—yet they did not seem any smarter than the average person he knew.

Perhaps the rats could triumph over the maze and turn the tables on the experimenters. *He* had plundered one of their precious amplifiers; the girl, Jill, had also done so at least once. If the lab is burning down and the rats save themselves, what, then, did *that* say about their relative positions? He wasn't sure, but it must mean something. It just *had* to mean something!

"Shall we establish the specifics?" Abaddon suggested. When the other two men nodded he continued.

"All right. We'll start right outside the cafe here, in the street. Both of you will begin naked and un-armed, although what you do once the contest is be-gun is up to you. Seven kilometers down the road will be a life-sized granite statue of me. To make the game more interesting, I'll put the jewel in my outstretched stone palm. There is no time limit. The first man to the jewel will touch it and say the name he must— you, Mr. Walters, will say Asmodeus and so take it to him; you, Boreas, will utter my name. You know the thing will destroy you if you don't, so I have no fear there. I will establish conditions whereby no one but you two or myself can touch the jewel, so no matter what stray souls are around, they can't queer the deal. In addition, there will be no teleporting and no growing wings or levitation flying. You must make it the hard way. If either of you kills the other, the survivor wins, of course; if both of you are killed, then I still win."

That last got to Mac. "And you will not in any way set up anything to kill either of us," he added. "You will not interfere in any way to help or hurt either of us, even to give your man, here, information."

"Fair enough," the demon agreed. "I will be a spectator, nothing more, once the race is under way. But you could still kill each other, you know, or be done in by leftovers on this plane pledged to others, like your little girl ghoul. I can't do much about them."

That sounded fair enough. "Let's do it," Mac said flatly.

The three of them got up and went outside. The ghostly choir was still chanting in the church down the street, and other ghosts seemed to be living it up in the saloon across the way.

Abaddon smiled, snapped his fingers, and they were both naked. Mac's useful side arm was gone as well. *It doesn't matter,* he told himself. *I can wish it back in a second.*

"I said I would not interfere in any way once the race began, and I will not," the demon told them. Mac was barely listening. Boreas had the body of a youthful man, reminding him of a linebacker for the Green Bay Packers.

"Seven kilometers down the road you are facing," the demon reminded them. "Ready?" Both men tensed visibly.

Abaddon smiled wickedly and snapped his fingers once again.

Suddenly they were no longer in the tiny western town facing a bleak and featureless dirt road. There was traffic and crowds and noise and sky and tall buildings all around.

"That's cheating!" Mac screamed, but it was too late.

"Go!" yelled the demon gleefully.

He was honorable, yes. He would not interfere after they had begun. Before, though— Mac felt he'd been had, and could only console himself that Boreas must be equally confused.

Both men, naked as the day they were born, were standing on a grassy knoll in the warm sunshine under a blue sky. They were in an exact copy of the Battery in New York City, facing uptown—people, traffic, and all—and the little old ladies were already appropriately shocked.

The street they were facing was the foot of Broadway.

3

It *was* a fair complication. Boreas looked as shocked as he did. The difference was that the sorcerer recovered a split second before Mac, dropped to the grass, and suddenly there was a gun in his hand. He fired.

Mac dropped and rolled as people screamed and scattered in all directions. He poised for a second, sure now that he'd lost at the start and that a second shot would finish him.

It didn't come. He looked up to see a veritable horde of cops, guns drawn, running toward them, then risked a quick glance at where Boreas should be, very near him.

The sorcerer wasn't there. There were people running all around, but no one who looked remotely like the demon's agent. Mac didn't waste any time now; the cops were closing in on him as well and he was still naked and exposed. Clearly Boreas didn't want to risk being shot by the cops and had changed into someone who could blend into the crowd. Mac decided he'd better do the same. No teleporting was one of the rules, and no flying; but, Manhattan or not, this was really still the training ground and he could still influence things.

Suddenly he was up, a pistol in his hand, and running toward an empty spot on the grass near him. The transformation had been instantaneous and was accompanied by a wish that the cops would not notice it.

They didn't. They caught up to him and surrounded the same empty space he'd reached, and they all looked puzzled.

Mac Walters, now just one of the uniformed cops, looked puzzled, too. He glanced around for any sign of his foe but saw none. That was bad. He wondered how familiar the European was with New York— probably very much so, which was why Abaddon had picked it.

As for him, he'd only been in New York for games, and they hadn't been in Manhattan. His business was a western one; he'd just never had occasion to really be in the city any more.

It also took him some time to extricate himself from the masses of cops. He noticed that some were wearing walkie-talkies, added one to his own belt, then wished a call for him to report back to his squad car. It helped.

As he walked across the park he considered the possibilities. Why not a squad car? The street was Broadway and there Broadway was. Just get into the car, turn on the light and siren, and off he'd go.

He saw one by the curb, lights still flashing, and headed toward it. Just a few meters before he reached the car, though, it blew up in a tremendous ball of smoke and flame. The force of the explosion knocked him down, and he got back to his feet unsteadily but growing angry now. Boreas! That son of a bitch was somewhere around and actually *toying* with him! Apparently the bastard thought the game so easily won, the opponent so poor, that he would play a while before the kill.

And maybe he was right, unless . . . Mac looked around, spotted a steel grate that had a rumbling noise issuing from it, a noise that was almost completely covered by the conflagration—which was also again attracting cops and passersby.

I wish I were made of smoke and sucked right down that grate! he thought angrily.

In a split second, almost before he realized that his wish had come true, he was pulled to and down through the grating.

A young stockbroker type with tweed suit and horn-rimmed glasses standing nearby yelled something angrily, turned to smoke, and followed him.

Mac Walters drifted lazily over the crowds waiting for the subway and congratulated himself. By all rights he should have been dead now; sheer luck and Boreas's overconfidence had allowed him to escape. Now he could simply turn into anyone he wanted to, blend with the crowd down there, and make it fairly quickly to Times Square. A map behind some plastic on a post in back of the platform gave him a color-coded guide to the New York subway system. He looked it over, found he had to be on the other side of the platform, and lazily drifted that way.

He knew he should be elated; even if the sorcerer were around here himself, drifting invisibly as Mac was, it would be impossible now for Boreas to get a clear fix on him. And yet something in the back of his mind nagged at him, a certain feeling he couldn't shake that he'd made a mistake somewhere. Not an error in this—he knew that he was free of Boreas unless he did something stupid. Something else. He tried to think, pressured suddenly by the rumbling far off in the tube that told him that a train was coming. It would be easy now; just step on the train, ride to Times Square—perhaps with Boreas himself aboard—and make the final race to the jewel. Simple. Direct.

Or was it? He brought himself up short. He was still alive because Boreas was better at the wizard game than he was. At any time the sorcerer could simply have left him and sped the seven easy kilometers up Broadway, leaving him in his dust, particularly after the strange man had vanished as the cops closed in. Boreas hadn't—that was too easy for him. He'd stayed, playing with exploding police cars and the like, enjoying himself and rejoicing in his total superiority over Mac Walters, bumbling amateur.

Boreas would be on that subway only if he *knew* his opponent was, too—and perhaps not even then. If he lost Mac he'd head straight for the jewel to protect himself. Maybe he was already heading there now!

Mac felt momentary panic. The only way to make sure that Boreas didn't get there before he did was to expose himself, keep the other man intent on playing with him rather than attaining the objective. Boreas's arrogant overconfidence was the only thing Mac had going for himself. With a discorporate sigh, he materialized as himself in the crowd waiting for the subway.

Mac glanced nervously around, aware of his extreme vulnerability as a target and of his opponent's almost total anonymity. He felt more naked and helpless than he had in the primitive world. What was even worse was that he had to pray for an attempt on him to occur; if he peacefully boarded the train and had an uneventful ride, then the odds were he had already lost.

The train stopped and he got on with a group of men and women and grabbed a metal strap. All the seats were taken, and a fair crowd of standees pressed against him. It was uncomfortable, particularly since in every face he seemed to see the sardonic eyes of Boreas.

The experience was unnerving, the feeling that all around you were ready to pounce, to kill you in any one of a thousand different ways, coupled with the fervent prayer that they truly *were* evil and malevolent and would try to do that very thing.

The train was rolling barely a minute when he got his wish. A little old lady who must have been eighty if she was a day lurched into him, looked up with pure meanness in her eyes, and spat into his face. The action was so unexpected that he didn't recover for a couple of seconds.

"Pooh and fie on you!" she cackled. "You're a bad, bad man!"

Several other standees nodded in agreement, and in a matter of a few seconds more they were all looking at him with pure hatred in their faces and chanting, "Bad man! Bad man!"

Then the little old lady stomped on his foot. Somebody else poked him in the stomach—he was being attacked from all sides. It gave him little chance to think or concentrate, but it added a quick sense of desperation to his moves. He went back to mist again, and the crowd fell into itself, still chanting, kicking, poking, and shoving.

Boreas wouldn't be taken aback for very long, he knew. Suddenly he heard a sound as if someone had switched on a giant vacuum cleaner, and he felt himself being pulled back, out of the train, back toward the Battery. He became solid once again, standing in the darkened tunnel as the lights of the subway train receded rapidly.

The giant suction continued for a minute or so, then abruptly stopped, leaving instead an eerie silence. He looked around, considering what to do next. There seemed to be no openings to the street from wherever he was, making the mist routine suddenly less useful. No teleporting had been the rule; he couldn't just wish himself to the surface. He shrugged and started walking after the now-vanished train, searching for an outlet to the surface.

There was a humming noise and he realized after a moment that it was the third rail that supplied the electrical power for the trains. He shied away from it. *Wouldn't do to escape Boreas and do yourself in,* he thought nervously.

Suddenly the tunnel ahead of him constricted; the tube was now closed, but centered in the pinched area was a pair of human-looking but gigantic lips. They smiled at him.

He stopped and stared at them, trying to think. *Boreas—he must be here, somewhere, in the tunnel with me!*

"This has been most entertaining," the giant lips told him in a ghostly parody of the sorcerer's voice that echoed down the subway tunnel. When the mouth opened he could see the rest of the tunnel through its "throat." *That should mean something,* he told himself, but he couldn't grab onto it.

"Yes, most entertaining indeed," the lips continued. "However, it is time to end this now—you are so incompetent, my dear fellow, that you take the challenge out of it!"

He glanced around for the real Boreas but saw nothing. A rat, probably, skulking in the darkness, smiling at him. *Well—why not?*

So Mac became a rat. Everything, the giant lips included, loomed huge around him, and he started running at high speed for the dark corner. As he almost reached the deepest part of the shadows a pair of large, luminous yellow eyes leered back at him. He barely had time to cut and run before a huge cat was upon him. He felt a sting in his tail and desperation set in as he was yanked up into the air, held by the cat's sharp, toothy grip on his rat's tail.

He made himself into a Saint Bernard dog. The cat, taken unawares, almost choked on the monstrous, furry tail it grasped, and its smaller jaw was almost wrenched from its socket by the huge thing it now no longer could grip.

Mac's victory was short-lived, however. He barely had time to turn to face his assailant when the cat was replaced by a giant, monstrous spider, a hairy tarantula nearly filling the tunnel, facing him down, holding him between the wall of lips and any kind of escape.

There was silence for a moment as Boreas savored his victory. The giant spider's sting dripped with deadly, paralyzing venom. Mac realized that he could never best the man in a contest like this; experience and confidence in his powers and abilities automatically made the sorcerer his superior. He thought desperately for a solution, a way out, as the lips opened to reveal nasty-looking teeth. The spider began a slow advance. He could still see the intact tunnel through the open mouth of the wall of lips, emergency lights trailing off into the distance. So near and yet so far.

Or was it? He remembered the subway map once again. The line branched off quickly from the other lines that also started at the Battery. But although other lines might join this one and run parallel to it, that tunnel on the other side of the gaping, mocking mouth was a direct line to where he needed to go.

As the first of the spider's huge legs almost touched him and the mandibles of the creature snapped in obvious relish, Mac knew what he had to do. He ran sideways toward the third rail, and as he reached it there was a brilliant white light and he vanished.

The lips vanished as well, as did the spider, leaving an enraged Boreas suddenly puzzled. Where could Walters have gone? Not to mist—he had guarded against that. Not to invisibility—he would hear and sense the breathing. That brilliant flash . . . What could it have meant?

Instantly the answer was clear to him and he cursed himself for a fool. Walters had become a creature of pure energy and was riding the third rail in electrical form!

Damn!

Stalled by his lack of knowledge of just where the tunnel led and unwilling to take a chance on following the man without knowing the byways of the electrical system, Boreas summoned a special subway car and started riding at top speed toward Times Square Station.

Mac Walters cursed as he became himself once again. At the speed electricity traveled, he had traversed the entire line from beginning to end and back again over thirty thousand times in the few seconds he had ridden the rail. He picked a station, materialized, emerged, and found himself across from Central Park.

A quick check told him that he was some sixteen or seventeen blocks north of his goal. He ran from the park into Columbus Circle, willed a police car at the curb and jumped in, following his original plan.

He quickly discovered that a police car with lights and siren going full blast meant absolutely nothing to New York traffic. It took him a precious two minutes to calm down enough to see and be able to use the solution.

He willed the streets clear of all traffic and ordered the lights to obey him. It took less than two more minutes to roar into Times Square.

Emerging on 43rd Street, Boreas realized immediately by the absence of automobile traffic that Walters had already gotten there. As for Mac, he stopped short at 46th Street, staring into the square. There should have been a statue of Abaddon there, the jewel ready for plucking. There wasn't. Times Square, although bereft of auto traffic, was as it always had been, and there was no sign of a statue of Abaddon anywhere.

Wisely deciding to abandon the police car short of his goal, Mac Walters made his way quickly down Seventh Avenue toward its junction with Broadway that formed Times Square. He was glad he hadn't also banned pedestrians; the crowds gave him some protection without slowing him up very much, since they had the streets as well as the broad sidewalks to use.

If Mac was confused, the confusion was mirrored on the face of Boreas, who looked around at the square from the opposite side, searching for the statue. It *had* to be there, it just *had* to be—and Walters hadn't reached it yet, that was clear, since the demon's metropolitan construction was still there.

There were ads all over the place, huge billboards for everything from Broadway shows to coffee, cigarettes, airlines, and the like. He scanned them, hoping that, perhaps, the statue might be concealed within one of the giant displays, or as an ornament on the side of one of the buildings.

Mac had the same thought and stopped just short of the square to figure out where the clever demon might have hidden it. For a second he feared that he had been double-crossed, that Abaddon had gone back on his word, but he quickly dismissed that thought from his mind, if for no other reason than that the alternatives were unthinkable.

It was Boreas who saw the key first by virtue of his slightly southern orientation. As it had always had, back when it had been the Allied Chemical Building and even earlier, as a newspaper headquarters, the triangular building jutting into the square from the north had an electronic sign around it which supposedly displayed the headline news. The sign was there all right—and it was, in a way, performing its usual function.

In flashing lights across one side, around the triangular edge and down the other side of the building, the words flashed:

"MAC WALTERS AND BOREAS BOTH REACHED TIMES SQUARE JUST MOMENTS AGO," the sign read. "SKYTOP BATTLE EXPECTED ATOP THIS BUILDING ANY MOMENT NOW."

Boreas grinned and looked up. High atop the building was a polelike structure that was used, although he didn't know it, to signal the coming in of the New Year. Atop that pole was, recognizably, a large manlike shape in jet-black.

Boreas looked around nervously. He couldn't spot Walters, and if he negated the people in the square he would expose himself as well. *The other man,* he thought, *could be speeding to the top of the building in its elevator right now! If not, he is here in the street somewhere. Better to take the shortcut that would accomplish an insurance rear-guard action and forestall the possibility of an elevator rush now.*

He chose the giant spider again, first because it could climb the outer walls of the building in a flash, and also because its horrible visage would induce panic in the crowds, panic that might engulf a Mac Walters should he still be in the street. It was a good plan, but it had a major flaw: it would work totally to his advantage only if Walters was, even now, trying to race for the statue.

The truth was that Asmodeus's man was still half a block back from the square itself and hadn't noticed the electronic writing. Suddenly the horror that was the giant tarantula rose in front of him about two blocks down and started moving his way.

There were terrible screams and shouts of sheer panic, and the crowds started trampling themselves in their flight from the terrifying creature. They ran in all directions, and there were a lot of exits from Times Square, but a solid wall of people nonetheless threatened to engulf Mac in another few seconds.

Boreas was taking no chances, though. As soon as he became the creature he headed straight for the proper building and started to climb. This activity told Mac exactly where the statue had to be.

If Boreas wanted to play horror movies, then horror movies it would be. In a flash Mac Walters became King Kong, a larger-than-the-movies King Kong, towering over the buildings, almost half as tall as the structures of Rockefeller Center only a few blocks away. He could see all the way to the Hudson to the west, though, and noted, in the back of his mind, that the world seemed to end there, leaving only a blank grayness beyond the river. He wondered for the briefest of seconds whether or not New Jersey was actually there or whether the construct merely ended at the river. With New Jersey it was impossible to say.

He actually looked down slightly to see the statue perched atop the building and adjusted his height accordingly. At that second the giant spider came up over the other side and onto the roof.

Boreas hadn't seen the giant ape materialize; he'd been much too busy climbing. Now he watched as a huge ape's hand started to close on the entire statue, jewel and all. There was little time to lose. With the hand almost on the object of the search, jet fighters roared out of the sky and shot rockets at the giant ape.

The explosions and sounds startled Mac Walters; one rocket almost hit his rear end and he roared in pain. The hand that was about to grasp the statue jerked reflexively and knocked the whole thing over. It toppled into Times Square itself, deserted now of people, and landed with a crash. The statue itself separated from the mast and flew through the front window of a restaurant.

The spider was back over the side in a flash, but that was only to give it some operating room. With his size, Mac was only a few steps from the goal even now.

Boreas accepted that fact and changed himself into a King Kong as well. Now there were *two* giant ape-like figures, one on either side of the old landmark.

Mac dropped quickly to all fours and made himself small once again. Merely the act of assuming that position before he shrank brought him to within ten meters of the statue, now resting partway in the restaurant window.

Boreas, still the giant ape, roared his defiance and glee and in two steps started to bend down for the statue. There was another roaring sound, and four well-placed rockets from jet fighters all found their mark on his rear end.

Even as the sorcerer howled in giant pain and straightened up in reflex action to the hits, Mac approached the statue. He climbed over it unmindful of the broken window glass and reached out for the burning jewel that the demonic figure grasped in its right hand. Mac turned his head for just a second and saw Boreas, human once again, only ten steps from the window and running hard. He wanted no part of a last-minute fight with the sorcerer and gambled precious seconds in a last-stop effort.

The sky was abruptly blackened by millions of flapping shapes, and the empty square echoed with the thunderous sound of millions of beating wings reverberating again and again from the buildings and signs. And then every pigeon in the city of New York relieved itself at one and the same time with unerring accuracy, fairly drowning Boreas in pigeon dung.

Mac Walters reached out, grasped the jewel, and started to yell Mogart's name in triumph.

In a flash New York was gone, the sky was gone, all was gone. They were once again on a gray plain in the never-never land of the training ground. Boreas was seated on the hard ground, still spitting out and cleaning off pigeon dung. Mac held the jewel and saw the figure of Abaddon between him and his defeated opponent.

"Fairly done and fairly won, Mr. Walters," the demon approved. "I congratulate you." His expression turned deeply threatening, grim and furious, as demonic as legends had made him, when he turned to glare at the unfortunate Boreas. "And as for *you*," he sneered. "You had it easily won and you threw it away in your misplaced egotism! You shall pay for this dearly, Boreas!"

The sorcerer just glowered at the demon and said nothing.

"Now, wait a minute, Abaddon!" Mac protested. "That's not fair! Sure he lost, sure he made the mistakes, but you really can't blame him in the end."

The demon whirled. "And why not?" he growled.

"Out of all the possible human beings you could have used, *you* picked *him*," Mac pointed out. "You knew him well enough to pick him, so you knew his weaknesses as well. You've got no one to blame but yourself, and I thank you for the sporting chance that gave me the opportunity to win. He has no faults, though, that aren't reflections of your own."

The demon stopped short, considering the argument, then shrugged. "Perhaps you're right. I'll think on it until the next training mission comes by. Perhaps I can learn something by seeing my own faults reflected in my followers."

"You're a fair and honest man and a good sport for all the curves you threw me," Mac told him. "I wish you good fortune in the future."

The demon smiled at the flattery. "I thank you most sincerely," he told the man. "Now, go with your prize

—and watch out for old Asmodeus! Take care that when you complete your Eye of Baal, you don't get something different than you bargained for. Unlike me, he is neither a good sport nor a man of his word."

"I'll remember," Mac assured him, then turned his mind to the jewel in his hand. "Take me to Asmodeus Mogart!" he ordered—and vanished.

Abaddon sighed and turned to Boreas, who was still covered in pigeon droppings. A wet cloth materialized in the demon's hand and he threw it to the man.

"Clean yourself up," he snapped. "It might be ten thousand years before we get rescued, and I have other plans for you."

Boreas did not look either grateful or amused.

Main Line +2076

MAC WALTERS MATERIALIZED AGAIN IN THE PENTA-gram chalked on the floor of the Reno bar.

Mogart, he saw, was on the floor in front of the bar. He had a martini glass and seemed to be lapping up the liquid like a dog.

"Hey! Mogart! I got another one!" the man shouted.

Mogart stirred and looked blearily in the direction of the noise. His eyes wouldn't focus and the whole room seemed to be spinning.

"Mogart! Snap out of it! Come take the jewel so I can get going for the next one!" Mac Walters yelled insistently.

"Keep yer—*hic!*—shirt on, awright, awright," Mogart mumbled. He tried to get up, couldn't, then looked again at the man. There seemed to be seven or eight of him, and they were all spinning around slightly.

Finally he said, "Jus'—*hic!*—roll the thing t'me," and sank back down once again.

Mac sighed and tossed the jewel at the demon. It rested only a hand's spread away from Mogart, yet it took the demon four tries before he grabbed it and looked at it curiously.

Even now he wasn't so drunk that he couldn't think, albeit slowly.

"Thash five!" he said wonderingly.

Mac Walters' heart skipped a beat. Five! Only one to go! The fact that the woman had beaten him again didn't bother him this time.

"Mogart! Where's the girl—what's her name?"

The demon heard him through a fog. "Shill McCug —Shill McCogh—McCullow—what the hell!" he mumbled. "Off to the wars, a'coursh. One, two, three, four, five, only one to go!" he almost sang, and a stupid smile appeared on his face.

"Send me to help her, then!" Walters urged. "Time's wasting!"

Mogart managed to grab a leg of a bar stool and slowly and painfully pulled himself up to the level of the bar. On his second try he stood upright with the help of the bar's support and looked again at the man in the pentagram. Standing only made him feel worse—there were eight of Mac now, and they were all hanging from the ceiling.

"I am, obvioushly, in no condishon to take you," the demon pointed out. "Ish a counterpart world, though. You should get along. I'll shend you wherever she ish and you can take it from there." He reached over, grabbed a gin bottle on the third try, then poured the liquid all over while trying to hit a glass from a distance of almost four centimeters.

"Oh, yeah, gotta warn ya," he managed. "Ya both gotta be t'gether to get back on the jewel. 'Member that!"

"I'll remember," Mac assured the demon. "Nothing else you want to tell me?"

"I'll shend you to her," Mogart mumbled. "She'll tell you. Go!"

Mac Walters vanished.

Asmodeus Mogart detected movement to one side and turned, suddenly alarmed. He took a moment to calm down, realizing now that he was seeing his own reflection in the mirror behind the bar.

There were a lot of him, too, and they were all spinning around.

He picked up the glass partly filled with gin, tried for his mouth, succeeded by taking it slowly, and drained the glass. He looked back at the reflection in the mirror.

"Asmodeus, King of the Demons!" he snapped bitterly and threw the glass at the mirror. It struck and made a crack that would still take three subjective hours to widen into something you could see.

The clock read almost one A.M. on the last day of Earth.

Main Line +1076
Chicago

1

IT WAS DARK, BUT THAT DIDN'T SEEM TO MATTER. He was only vaguely aware of the darkness; his vision, catlike, penetrated every nook and cranny of the small apartment in which he found himself.

He felt good, really good—without aches or pains of any sort, even the most minor ones that everybody always had with them but ignored for that very reason.

He was in the living room of somebody's one-bedroom apartment. It was odd, too: the carpeting was wall-to-wall and quite professional, the furniture of fine quality woods, very homey and very luxurious —yet the kitchen alcove held a wood stove and icebox rather than refrigerator. Furthermore, he could tell by the remnants of soot and odor that some large fire elsewhere in the building was used to keep the place warm in winter, rather than any modern heating system. The lamps, too, were quite stylish and modern, but a look inside showed that they had glass tubes instead of bulbs, tubes filled with water and with oil on top in which a wick floated.

In short, it looked like a perfectly normal Earth-modern apartment for his own time and native area— but one in which electricity had never been discovered. It was the most ultramodern, nontechnologically based example he could think of. And yet, and yet— The curtains were finely woven, as were the rugs and many other artifacts. Far too finely done and evenly seamed to be the work of anything but machines. It was a puzzle, one which he, at the moment, had no way of solving.

A photograph on a table caught his cat's eyes. It was the old-fashioned type, like those taken back in the early or mid-1800s, but it clearly showed the face of a woman who was somehow very familiar.

The woman—Jill—it was *her* face!

His spirits lifted. He moved to the bedroom, trying to be careful and quiet. No sense in getting shot as a burglar.

The room had an unpleasant odor that seemed to thicken the air, suffocating him. He stifled the impulse to cough and rubbed his watering eyes.

She lay on the bed, asleep under a sheet. There was no mistaking her. Until seeing the photograph, he had almost forgotten her features, but now they came fully back into his mind. It was Jill McCulloch all right, no question about it. He moved toward the bed, intent on gently shaking her awake.

She turned a little, seeming to hear him coming. Unseen by him, an eyelid rose just slightly, and as she turned she grasped an object hidden by the sheet. He was almost to the bed now, reaching out, ready to shake her, when she suddenly whirled off the opposite side and jumped up, standing, facing him, something in her hand.

"Hey! Wait! I—" he called out, but she was having

none of it. She brought the object in her hand up into view and thrust it forward. It was in the shape of a cross and glowed with a tremendously powerful radiation, shooting out, blinding him with its radiance and, at the same time, giving off a terrible radioactive heat that burned like fire. He raised his hands to cover his eyes, but that helped only a little.

"Get thee away from my door and my house, vampire," commanded the woman. "By this cross I command you flee!"

He was thrown for a complete loop. "Holy shit, Jill! It's me—Mac! Mac Walters! From Mogart!" he cried out. The pain was becoming intense.

She hesitated and the cross wavered slightly. Although to her the cross had neither radiation nor luminescence, she herself was mostly blinded by the darkness. She could see him, but not distinctly.

"Wait there a moment," she ordered, "while I light a lamp, and don't make any funny moves!"

"I'll stay right here," he promised her, "but my Lord! Put that thing away!"

She didn't lower the cross very much, but with her free hand she felt for a wooden match on the nightstand, struck it, and touched it to the oil candle sitting there. Only then did she closely examine her visitor.

"It *is* you!" she breathed, still a little uncertainly. She'd seen the man for so short a time and, by her reckoning, many days before. Still, he did in fact look familiar. "How the hell did you become a vampire?" The cross dropped to her side, taking most of the heat off, but she kept it tightly in her grip, ready for instant use.

He shook his head wonderingly. "I—I didn't know I *was* a vampire until you told me. I still can't believe it. I—I don't know what to say."

Jill McCulloch considered that. "How long have you been here?"

"Just arrived," he told her. "I materialized in your living room."

"You got the jewel?"

He nodded. "This is the last one." A horrible thought suddenly occurred to him. "Hey! Mogart never told me the time frame here! We might not have enough to make it!"

That thought unnerved her as well. "What time was it in Reno when you left?"

He thought a moment. "Around one in the morning. Why?"

"Well, I've been here almost two weeks and that represents only a couple of hours on the clock. I think we've got time. It makes no difference, anyway —we have to get this one, and either we're in time when we get it or we aren't."

He cleared his throat nervously. "Ah—Mogart was drunk—dead drunk, incredibly looped, when I got there. He said you would brief me."

She nodded, relaxing a little. "He was in pretty bad shape when I was there. But—a vampire! This complicates things!"

He had to agree with her on that but said nothing.

"Okay, here it is. You're in Chicago, Illinois, U.S.A. Things here are pretty much a parallel of what we know, except that this is what Mogart called a counterpart world—that is, a world set up to run as close to ours as possible yet with certain basic underlying changes, I suppose to see how much events and people would change under different circumstances."

"I noticed there was no electricity," he responded.

She nodded. "No electricity, no major machines at all. But there's magic here and lots of it. Also elves, pixies, gnomes—you name it. They produce an awful lot of the manufactured goods and certain power and services. There are also plenty of magicians with various powers and skills, both white and black magic variety. Much of the human magic is based on training and willpower. If you know how to wish for something and have the mind to produce it, it's done. The stronger the mind the more powerful the spell."

He shook his head slowly in disbelief. "And vampires, too."

"And vampires, too," she agreed. "Not very many of them. The cops have a squad out just to catch them, but you have about the same percentage of being a vampire victim as, say, getting robbed or raped. It's something you fear, but the fear doesn't dominate your life."

His mind was already racing. The vampire should have the legendary powers as well as weaknesses. Such power could be useful.

"What about the demon and the jewel?" he asked her.

She sighed. "I know who he's with—the demon's name is Theritus, by the way—but not exactly where. That's what's caused me a problem. I was hoping you'd show up. As a vampire, though . . ."

"Fill me in," he told her, getting to serious business.

"There's a Mafia boss, name of Constanza, who lives in Cicero. He's a big rackets boss, known not only for a massive smuggling-and-drug empire but also for providing certain illegal magical supplies and services. He's hated even by the other bosses, but somehow a few years ago he ran into Theritus and imprisoned him. Demons can be bound by a strong magician, kept against their wills and forced to do things for the binder, just like in the old legends. Looks like he actually knew how to do it—or had somebody who did. Theritus is bound and living somewhere in the city here. Constanza owns half of it or more, including the police department."

"And you haven't been able to find him?"

She shook her head. "He's well buried. I materialized near the Loop, so that might be a clue. I've worked and worked on it. About a week ago I managed to get a lead on where his magical files were kept—they'd reveal the particulars."

"But you haven't gotten to them yet?" he guessed.

She sighed in frustration. "Oh, yes, I got in, with the help of a half-baked disbarred magician; but he wasn't nearly up to what Constanza can buy, and my sources weren't too discriminating, either. While I was in the building and my inept magician friend was still working on the spells for a lock, who should come busting in but a Chief Necromancer for the F.B.I.! There was a terrible facedown between the feds and some demonic guardians, but the feds won out. I was a floor away and I heard it all. Of course, out went the files. While I was trying to make my own getaway, some of the mob's men got me."

They had been none too gentle with her. For a while they thought she was a fed herself; she'd acquitted herself as an expert swordswoman by intercepting two guards on the lower floors and had done a very nice job neutralizing a minor demon. They took her out a tunnel the feds didn't cover and then off to Cicero; she never saw her magician friend again.

An empathic mesmerist had been brought in and she was questioned extensively. It was impossible not to answer, and the mesmerist guaranteed that she could not lie even if she were fighting him—he smelled lies. She'd spilled the whole story.

The hoods hadn't believed her, anyway—it was just too fantastic a story—so they kept her there, a prisoner, awaiting the return of Constanza from Miami. Word of the raid brought him back in less than three days.

He turned out to be quite different from what she had expected. She didn't really know what he should look like—old and ugly, certainly, with evil eyes and a scarred face. He was none of that. He seemed to be no more than forty, and a young, healthy, tanned forty at that. He was extremely handsome and gentlemanly suave.

They had sat at dinner, sipping fine wine and eating exquisitely cooked pheasant. "Some more wine, my dear?" he had suggested. "It is an excellent vintage—few today can savor its excellence."

"Thank you, no," she responded politely. "I appreciate the offer, but I'm quite full. I must say, though, that you are a gracious and charming host, not at all what I would expect from a . . . a—" She stalled there.

He smiled. "A gangster? But, my dear, the roots of this organization go back to the union of Italy in eighteen seventy-one, when the nobles of the old Kingdom of the Two Sicilies were ousted for the Corsican conquerers. They fled here, a land that was still open and growing, and established a shadow kingdom that

was a reflection of their former lives. Here nobility
was money, not birth—so my ancestors went into
business, providing goods and services which people
really wanted, even if they openly professed they
wished them banned. No one has ever been forced
to make an illegal bet at gunpoint, nor do squads go
out into the street shanghaiing poor, innocent young
men to patronize brothels, and no man borrows from
a loan shark if he has good credit and pays his bills
on time, to name but three examples. By providing
these services, huge sums were raised; armies of 'soldiers' were put together; the nobility truly reestablished
itself and looked after its own. We have our family
feuds and internal rivalries, even wars, but these are
all kept pretty much within the family and away from
the innocents. The demand for our services has grown
so great, our family now includes Jews and Blacks
and Poles and Chinese as well. I see no reason why
we should not be expected to be civilized human beings
—we are, after all, aristocracy!"

There was a flaw somewhere in his justification,
but she decided to wait a while to find it. There were
more pressing matters now. "What will you do with
me?" she asked softly.

He grinned again and sipped his wine. "As you
know, I was raided recently. A result of our family
squabbles. One of my brother businessmen who wants
a lot more managed to bribe or torture a key person
or two in my service to reveal the existence of some
vital records. Because of my pet demon he has been
unable to assault me directly—so he assaults me thus.
I plan to fool and foil him. I can run my share of
the kingdom from afar, but not *too* afar, and certainly
not from prison."

His eyes narrowed to slits and his face became
grim. "I had such a perfect place all established. My
own private little city-state in the Southwest, in the
Chihuahuan District of Mexico. I moved most of my
operations there, in fact, and enjoyed it for many
years."

She tried to reconstruct things a bit. On *this* Earth,
Mexico had never lost its northern possessions; Chi-

huahua ran north from Monterrey through most of west Texas, southern New Mexico, and all of Arizona.

Constanza's face clouded. "But I was outdone only a few months ago by what, it is now clear, was the opening of a full campaign against me. The local people, farmers mostly, never liked me or my rule. I maintained a magnificent castle overlooking a river that was the only one for hundreds of miles around. I purchased the dam controlling the river and thus controlled its flow. They were dependent on me, but I was, I think, a just ruler." His face beamed at the memory. "Ah, it was like the old days in Naples must have been before the Corsicans! I ruled several thousand subjects, fairly but sternly." His face clouded again, became almost angry-looking. "And yet they acted against me!"

Jill suppressed a grim smile. It wasn't difficult to see that such a man as this would enjoy reestablishing feudalism, and even less difficult to guess that frontier farmers wouldn't want to surrender their lands, reclaimed with sweat from the desert, and move on.

"The C.I.A., that's part of what did me in," Constanza continued. "I can see it now. My enemy, an unprincipled common wretch named Julius Goldfarb, obviously had the information he needed well in advance and sought to cut off my retreat. First they cut off my retreat, then raided my files. I am as one with his back to the door, and without time to establish yet another safe enclave. I must either flee the continent—putting me away from control—or go to prison. There is only one other way—break that wretched spell on my southwestern headquarters."

She was fascinated by the story but puzzled. "So what does this have to do with me?"

He smiled again and lit a big cigar. "Well, you see, the spell was a basic one, intended mostly to keep me *out*. It was, in other words, a quickie, and those have flaws in them. The spell was simple enough: 'No man shall cross the boundary of this domain,' followed by the domain itself—including the dam. This kept me and my soldiers out, and, armed, the men inside, cut off from any hope of reinforcements, were easily beaten. The spell is sound—a necromancer of the highest classes was used, along with some new procedures, which is why I know the C.I.A. was involved. None of my sorcerers or even the nonhumans and halflings in my power can prevail against it."

"Why not a nonhuman army, then?" she wondered aloud. "After all, the spell wouldn't keep *them* out. And don't tell me your captive demon couldn't punch holes in it."

He chuckled. "The nonhumans and halflings come under different rules, surely you must know that. They would not put together an army for any save their own kind. And as for the demon—well, he is confined by a powerful spell, but he is confined to one spot. If I move him I free him—and he'll hardly work for me after that. Far from the scene, he can do nothing to neutralize a spell—he must be there to find the mathematics of the spell itself before he can undo it. Thus, he, too, is out. But there is still a way to recapture the place, and if it is done in my name, my experts feel certain that the spell will fall. One group who could be collected into an army and would not be hampered by the spell."

She was confused and said so.

"The spell said, 'No *man* shall cross,'" he reminded her.

She saw what he was driving at. "Oh," she responded. "And you want me to join your army of Amazons?"

He laughed now. "No, no. You miss half the point! I want you to *lead* it."

She was taken aback. "In the first place, I'm no general—I've never even killed anyone human. In the second place, what makes you think I would do it for you even if I could?"

His dark eyes twinkled merrily. "Well, you see, I can recruit such a force by coercion—a massive collection of women bound to obey by powerful spells. But there is no one I can trust to lead them and carry out my orders. Most of the women best qualified to do so are also too dangerous—give them command of an army like that and they might well just take over and start their *own* kingdom, not hand it over to me. The problem has been unsolvable until you dropped in so unexpectedly." He snapped his fingers.

In the background, ghostlike, she heard her own voice, sounding drugged or numbed, answering questions, telling of her problem and her adventures in other worlds.

"Dr. Lambeth's crystal ball showed me your entire interrogation," Constanza told her. "You have been through a lot. You are brave, clever, resourceful. And, more important, you absolutely *must* have something only I can produce for you—the demon's powerful amulet."

"You would trade the jewel for this?" she responded unbelievingly. "And surrender your demon's power?"

Constanza shrugged. "He is useless to me now. So far, my lawyers have kept the feds out of my magical holdings, but it is only a matter of weeks. They will break in sometime, under powerful counterspells, and with experts who know how to banish demons. I am losing him anyway, Miss McCulloch. I am strong enough to rule without him now." He leaned forward and stared hard into her eyes. "You will lead my female army, McCulloch, and you will force the surrender of the will of the people inside the boundary or kill everyone. And then, thus breaking the spell, you will surrender the castle and its domains freely to me in exchange for the jewel. If you do not, then you will not get the jewel; Theritus will be banished from this plane, and you will be stuck and your own world destroyed. You *will* do it, Miss McCulloch. You have no choice in the matter. You needn't know military strategy, there will be those with you who do. Nor do you need to soil your hands with blood. You need only order the killing. And *you will do so!*"

"He gave me this apartment," Jill continued, facing Mac Walters across the bed, "and tomorrow I'm off. I have no choice, as he said, Mac. I'm going to have to kill a valley of peaceful farmers and turn what's left over to Constanza. And I'll have to do it five days from today, unless *you* can locate the demon and get the jewel before that." Tears stood in her eyes. "I don't see any way out. It's a question of the lives on our world or the innocent lives here. I'd hoped you could still work on the demon angle here and save me —but as a vampire, well, I don't know."

He considered the situation. "Look, this has its advantages and disadvantages," he told her. "The two biggest disadvantages are this Vampire Squad you mentioned, which I'm going to dismiss since it's probably not any better than any other cop squad, and the fact that I can operate only in darkness. Look, what's the month and day?"

She looked puzzled. "September fourteenth. Why?"

His head bobbed up and down in satisfaction. "That means almost equal daylight and darkness, so I have some operating room. And if the rules hold all the way here, I have tremendous powers of movement, of invulnerability, and probably a lot more once I learn the rules. I can get in places you can't and obtain information you couldn't. I think I can give it a good try."

She seemed slightly heartened. "I hope so, Mac. I don't want to have to make the choice."

"When do you leave?"

"In the morning. Why?"

Mac suddenly remembered Mogart's warning. "We both have to be at the same place to get us both back to Reno," he told her. "If I get the jewel, how will I find you?"

"That's an easy one," she assured him. "If either of us gets the jewel, we just order it to take us to the other and only *then* to Mogart."

"That makes sense," Mac responded. "Abaddon told me that anybody, even one of us, could use this Eye of Baal—six jewels. Okay, then. So where do I start?"

She gestured toward the living room. "Go in there. I'll follow."

He chuckled. "Still afraid of the big bad vampire?"

"Can't be too careful," she replied. "After all, you're very powerful, but you're also like a dope addict, subject to compulsions beyond your ability to countermand. The nicest people become vampires, Mac. I can't take chances."

He agreed and they moved into the living room. To prove his trustworthiness, he even struck and lit the candles in the other room. She rummaged through a desk and brought out a folder from a briefcase.

"They brought all my stuff here without even going through it," she told him. "These are the police reports, gossip, names of the people he obviously owns, a list of his properties in the city here." She put the folder on the coffee table and backed away slowly. He reached over and picked it up.

"This'll be a big help," he told her seriously. "Look, I know I'm making you uncomfortable, so I'll go now. But—if it's possible to get this jewel, I'll get it. Keep your hopes up. We're too close to the end to fail now!"

"Yes, we'll get the jewel, Mac," she replied softly, "but with how much blood on it? *That* is the problem."

2

Finding his coffin proved to be easy. As sunup neared, he felt the pull of the burial place as if some great magnet were turned on and he were clad in an iron suit. It was in an alcove of a drainage pipe, up out of the way of the muck. He was satisfied with the location; it was unlikely his coffin would be discovered during the few days left.

He slept deeply and, as far as he could tell, dreamlessly.

He awoke feeling hungry as hell. He crawled out of the drain alcove, not certain what he was going to do next but knowing that he needed food badly—and remembering just what that food was.

To his surprise he was not alone in the canal. There was a pretty young woman in a fashionable dress and a small man attired, as he was, in a conventional suit and tie. They looked ordinary, as did he; no fancy opera clothes and cape. He could see why the Vampire Squad might have its work cut out for it in figuring out who was who.

He watched, fascinated despite his hunger, as the woman turned herself into a wolf and loped off. The man, however, spotted him and gave a look of surprise. He walked over to Mac, who was still wondering what the hell to do.

"Hey! Aren't you Mac Walters?" the other vampire asked him.

Mac wasn't just surprised, he was stunned. "Uh—yeah," he managed.

"I'll be damned," the man said, then added, "No, I already *am* that. Wow! I figured you'd have to get out of Denver—too many people know your face—but I never expected to find you in Chicago!" He put out his hand and Mac shook it.

"Uh—excuse me, but—should I know you?" he asked sheepishly.

The other vampire chuckled. "Oh, my! No! Of course not! But, you see, back at Super Bowl time I was much better situated with a nice house and all. Morey Kurtz was a real estate salesman in life, and, as luck would have it, he managed to salt away a lot in Swiss bank accounts before he passed away. Had a nice block of houses mostly for folks in our condition over on the South Side. He hired a crystal-ball man to rerun the game for us. We all knew you'd become one of us. Poor Morey—the Vamp Squad finally got him, tipped by the property-tax assessor."

The man was rambling and more than a little odd, but then again, anybody in this situation might be expected to be worse than that, Mac decided. He remembered his Dracula films. And the man might be useful.

"I—I've had some real memory problems since—since I died," Mac told him lamely. "Can you tell me what you're talking about? Why I became a vampire?"

The man moved his head in an understanding manner. "That's too bad, but don't be upset by the memory thing. Happens to the best of us. Well, you remember you ran for one hundred and twenty-two yards against Dallas and caught for fifty more. There you were in L.A.—equal crowd for and against you. When you didn't get up early in the fourth quarter after Billy Thompson gave you that hit, everybody seemed to feel you were a goner—only the Denver fans prayed that you'd live and the Dallas fans hoped you'd croak, seeing as how you were responsible for them goin' down the tubes. The mixture of the two wills got you when you croaked on the field. They were, freakishly, about exactly even, as I figure it— so both sides got their wish."

The current situation was a little unsettling, but Mac remembered what Jill had told him—magic was mostly willpower, the relative strength of the mind— a modified version of Abaddon's training ground, on a smaller level of individual accomplishment, of course. Here conflicting mass wills for him to live or die had caused him to become one of the living dead.

He sighed, surprised he seemed to breathe at all, and eyed the little man again. "Well, I'm new to this vampire business and, like I said, a little fuzzy on it. What do we do and how do we do it?"

The vampire shrugged. "The usual. Oh, some get into this big power trip and turn people into vampire slaves and like that, but the cops are pretty good at gettin' those nuts. Me, I figure I make the best of a bad situation. I'm lucky—like you, I wasn't made by any other vampire, so I have nobody to boss me around. I get enough blood to keep me goin'—you got to do it, it's like opium—so I find several victims and take maybe a pint from each. Doesn't hurt them and helps me, it only takes a little longer. Then I relax, maybe go to an all-night games arcade, play a little solitaire, or find a good crap game someplace. Mostly I just take it easy and enjoy what little I can of life. If it gets hot I'll move, maybe someday go to a resort area or somethin'."

"These victims of yours—they let you take their blood?" Mac asked incredulously.

The man laughed. "Oh, hell, no! All you need is eye contact and you got 'em hypnotized—women and kids are the easiest for men. Easy as fallin' off a log.

Only don't get no pattern or use the same area night after night, or the Vamp Squad will get you."

"That woman—she turned into a wolf. Can we?" Mac prodded.

"Oh, sure," the man told him. "Just will it. Also a cloud of white smoke or a bat. Handy sometimes. Just watch out that nobody tracks you back here, stay away from crosses if you were a Christian, or a Star of David or Seal of Solomon if you were Jewish, and remember that running water will drown you. Also, you'll find it hard to enter private dwellings if you aren't invited—there are ways around it, like hypnotizing somebody near a window to invite you in, but it's tough and usually a bother." He turned and looked out at the tall buildings going off in all directions. "Hell, in a city this size there are always a lot of folks out late, not just the fools but the ones who work nights, too. Take it easy, don't draw attention, cover your ass, and you'll be fine."

Mac nodded, still bewildered and numbed by all this, and thanked the little man. As they parted he called back, "Hey! Tell me something! If you weren't made by another vampire, you must've had an experience similar to mine—an equal number of people loving you and hating you. What sort of work did you do?"

The man laughed bitterly. "How fickle is fame far from home," he mumbled. "Why, man, I was once the Mayor of Philadelphia!"

Vampirism was definitely not common, and people often ignored its perils as they did other perils of the city at night. Just as in Mac's own world people insisted on waiting alone on dark street corners, hitchhiking on lonely roads, and walking through mugger-infested parks, so, too, did the citizens of Chicago—a small percentage of them, anyway—brave the added risk of the vampire.

He had to allow himself the luxury of this one night, even if time were pressing terribly. He found, in fact, that his craving for blood became overpowering, and he finally encountered a victim without even thinking about it, held her in a hypnotic grip that came to him almost completely without effort, and drank some of her blood without being in the least repelled by it. He was conscientious, though, as the little man had instructed him. He took only enough, never too much, and though his victims fainted afterward, he always left them in as comfortable and unexposed positions as possible and always with a strong pulse.

The blood had an odd effect on him, too. The more he drank, the stronger he seemed to be, the headier and braver he became. It was more than food, it was a mild stimulant and very mild intoxicant, and he resolved to watch his consumption in the future. Overconfidence could lead to carelessness, and carelessness killed. He would be dealing with people who would know the protections and would guard themselves, particularly those in the upper echelons who would know where a Mafia don would keep a demon.

He also practiced the hypnosis and transformation tricks until he could perform them automatically and risked taking on a couple of men. One he could not control and had to depend on his incredible superhuman strength and transformation to get away; a second man was taken almost as easily as the women victims. Again it was a matter of emotion and willpower.

By sunup he was certain he had it all down pat, at least as much as he could master in the limited time allowed him. He also considered the parallels in his own life between this world and his own. In his own world he had quit rather than play that last season, even though he had felt that his team would go to the Super Bowl and be winners—an experience denied him. He had been smart and quit. His counterpart had given in to the temptation and died in that game. He wondered about that. His own world's Dallas had its own Billy Thompson. If he had played . . .

The thought was still in his mind when sunrise brought sleep.

3

Jill McCulloch was impressed. They rode to the station in a huge and ornate coach seemingly fit for the King of England and pulled by a team of eight Clydesdale-like horses. With her was Constanza, his ever-present bodyguards, and O'Malley, who looked like a typical Irish politician and was anything but.

Even master sorcerers in this world wore three-button suits and carefully knotted ties.

About the only thing that betrayed O'Malley's dumb-boxer impression was his eyes—steely blue-gray, hard, and alive with a tremendous intellect that seemed to see inside you. They were cold eyes, too, the eyes of a man who knows he is superior to the bulk of the human race and cares about them about as much as the exterminator cares about house flies. She'd asked him why he bothered to be in the employ of Constanza or of anyone, for that matter, and he'd just smiled and replied, "You see, miss, I have everything I need in the material world—I just love my craft, and as I lack ambition in worldly matters, it is people like Mr. Constanza who give me the challenges to practice it."

She had been surprised when she'd first discovered that this world had steam engines and steam trains. They looked like something out of the 1880s, and even then their boilers seemed too bloated and their wheels of odd size and even more unusual distribution, but they were close to what the old western movies showed for all that. Now, as the coach pulled into Union Station and moved to a private entrance for first-class passengers, the incongruity of these engines in an otherwise nontechnological society struck her full on.

"I can't understand, if you have these, why you haven't gotten to electricity or at least to gas lighting for the cities," she remarked to Constanza, who knew of her other-worldly origin from the interrogations.

He smiled. "Well, you see, things are different here," he explained. "Electricity is used in small doses, yes, for very minor things. But if this society were dependent on electricity, any good magician could disrupt its flow either specifically or generally. A society dependent on power so easily controlled by elemental spirits would be a captive one. As for the gas—" he sighed "—it's like most petroleum in the ground. The gnomes simply will not permit much drilling, let alone the pipelines necessary to bring it out. Most of it is in the strongholds to the west, too, and southwest, where the Indians have millennia-old alliances with the gnomes. Maybe someday we'll be able to compromise, but not now."

She thought that there was an awful lot she still didn't know about this world and probably never would and dismissed it.

They emerged from the carriage and walked into the station, the bodyguards fanning out and clearing the way, even opening doors for them. Constanza had a private car waiting at the end of the train and they boarded. Beyond, on the platform, large groups of men and women in Victorian modes of dress were boarding the regular cars as well. Some glanced back to the opulence at the rear, while newsboys ran up and down hawking papers and shouting headlines that sounded to Jill as if something like the fairy gold workers were on strike demanding AFL-CIO representation.

A minute or so after they had boarded, the train pulled out. The ride was a little shaky at the start but became much smoother once they left the railyards, much smoother than the trains of Jill's own world. They were heading west.

The private car had everything from a small bedroom to a flush toilet, plush, fur-covered seats, and even a small pool table down at one end that converted into a card table. A bodyguard mixed drinks from a hand-tooled leather-covered bar and brought them to Jill, Constanza, and O'Malley.

"So what happens now?" she asked them. They hadn't been very specific up to now, probably to minimize the risk of leaks. Constanza still hadn't found out where his rival had obtained the information on the files.

"First we head west, then southwest," Constanza told her. "We'll go off the main line at Kansas City and take the branch for Dodge, a dead end, you understand, because it's a railhead for cattle. You'll be quite comfortable on the trip. The two cars forward are also mine—one is a dining car with a superb chef in my employ; the other, a first-class accommodations car with private bedrooms for you and Mr. O'Malley here, and quarters for my staff. From Dodge we will travel by coach and horseback to the Mexican border, and there I will camp until word comes. Then it's O'Malley's turn with you, and I have only a vague notion of what he will do. From that point, though, you will be on your own."

She didn't relish the thought of being alone with O'Malley, but, as Constanza kept reminding her cheerily, she had little choice in the matter.

"This Amazon army—where is it located?" she asked them.

"Not Amazons, just women in my service," the don responded. "They will meet us along the way—or, rather, you. I wouldn't worry about it. Your role in this is quite simple and effortless."

Effortless, she thought sourly. Perhaps. To order a mass slaughter, to make certain that every last man, woman, and child in a town and its surrounding farm land were killed, then to turn over the land to Constanza "freely and of my own will," thus regaining for him his stronghold and for her the jewel.

"You have the jewel with you?" she probed.

Constanza chuckled. "No, of course not. As you yourself must be aware, it would kill any of us."

"Then what assurance do I have that you will give it to me when I have completed this—this massacre?"

"Mine, Miss McCulloch," O'Malley's low, uncharacteristically operatic voice intoned. "Theritus is held by a spell of my own device. He *must* obey me. For my spell we shall work a bargain—you had a similar pledge with Asmodeus, did you not, where he swore you to service?"

She nodded and he continued.

"A bargain's a bargain. You will agree to liberate the land and I shall agree to turn over the stone in payment. It will be handed to you at the gates of the Citadel. I must honor that part or the Dark Ones will claim my soul on the spot, and Don Constanza must allow me to do so because he requires my service to make the Citadel secure once again."

She glanced over at Constanza and saw he was trying to conceal his irritation at that remark. It irked him to be in need of someone he could not buy, threaten, or control.

The train rolled on.

A day and a half later they were in Dodge City, Kansas, a town that looked very much like it must have looked when the West was being tamed and legends like Wyatt Earp and Bat Masterson ran it. They wasted no time there, though, heading west almost immediately in a wagon train and luxury coach.

There was only a sign at the border, which they reached an hour or so after sunset. She was surprised at that. International borders were not normally so lightly guarded, even in her own North America.

"There's no need," O'Malley explained. "The spells are far more effective than any fence and network of guards. Smugglers and illegals will find it difficult if not lethal to cross. We have the proper seals from Mexico; we can pass."

And pass they did. Jill felt a slight tingling as they moved by the border sign, as if she'd just gone through an enormous spider web, but it quickly evaporated. Clearly there *was* some sort of barrier there, and she was thankful that they hadn't had to fight their way across.

Constanza set up camp—a large tent village for himself, his bodyguards, and his cooking staff—and offered a last dinner. But O'Malley refused all food and drink, as he had all day, and forbade Jill to take anything, either.

"Now we will go," he told them. She looked nervously around; the stars were incredibly bright, so bright that their numbers defied any rational attempt to count them, but otherwise it was very, very dark, almost absolute darkness.

Still, Constanza did not protest and snapped his fingers. A bodyguard brought up two good-looking horses and a pack mule loaded with two sacks of something indistinguishable.

"You know how to ride, I hope?" O'Malley asked her.

She nodded. Once having exchanged her Victorian dress for a shirt and jeans, she felt more normal and more human. "May as well get this over with," she mumbled in reply and mounted.

Constanza came up to her. "God be with you," he said sincerely, and offered his hand.

She looked at him strangely. *He can't be serious,* she thought. But he *was* serious—his own private world saw no contradictions.

She spurned his hand. "I'll do your killing for you," she told him, "but not in the name of God, nor in your name, either, but only for the sake of my people." She looked up at O'Malley. "Let's get out of here before I get sick."

Constanza seemed not at all offended. He shrugged and walked off. O'Malley kicked his horse into action and pulled on the rope in his free hand that was attached to the mule's harness. "Stick close and to the road," the sorcerer warned.

In minutes the glow from Constanza's camp was gone, leaving them alone with the brilliant Milky Way and the darkness, yet she could swear that she heard, somewhere behind her, Constanza laughing, laughing hard at some sort of self-satisfying joke.

The joke on her.

They rode for what seemed like hours. Her legs quickly became very sore, and she felt muscles start to ache that she'd forgotten she had. Jill knew how to ride, yes, but it had been two years or more since she'd had to do so and she'd gone soft in all the wrong places. Also, she was becoming increasingly hungry and thirsty.

She had just about reached the point of total surrender when she was going to stop in the middle of the darkness and tell O'Malley that she could travel no farther until food, drink, and rest were provided, when he stopped all by himself.

"This is a good enough spot," he said, more to himself than to her, and dismounted. She followed, weariness mixed with blessed relief from the pain flowing into her. She sat down on the ground, finding the dirt road preferable to the almost impossibly tall grass that seemed to line it, and waited. She heard O'Malley fumbling with the packs on the mule and then heard him doing something in the dark over to one side, just off the road in the grass. She wondered how he could see to do anything at all.

Finally he was ready and walked unerringly up to her, his strange eyes oddly reflective of any stray bits of light, almost like a cat's eyes yet with some kind of internal luminescence as well. He had changed clothes, she saw as he drew to within a meter of her. Gone were the tailored shirt and pants and the fancy, polished riding boots; now he wore a garment that looked more like a dark blue robe and a matching blue skullcap.

"It is time, Miss McCulloch," he said softly. "Please rise and come with me."

Jill looked at him but didn't move immediately. She was bone-tired.

"Please. It must be done now," he urged softly.

"All right, all right," she grumbled, and got up, taking his extended hand for support.

She followed the man in the darkness, wondering what was going to come next.

As they walked to one side of the road she saw that here the grass was gone, the ground barren, hard dirt. As she took her fifth or sixth step on the flat area, braziers suddenly flared into life, illuminating the place in an eerie blend of colors—blue, red, yellow, orange, and green, all bright and sparkling and reaching upward into the night. Five colors, five flaring braziers, arranged in a five-pointed shape. A border had been drawn in the dirt, she saw, and the braziers had come to life as she had stepped over that boundary.

A pentagram.

O'Malley also walked into the pentagram and over to a small table in its center. Motioning Jill to stand in front of the little folding table with a box on it, he stood behind, reached into the box, and pulled out a wand of some sort. It started to glow in his right hand, and he seemed to check it out to see if it was working properly. Then he looked up at her.

"Remove all your clothing, please," he instructed.

She flinched. Even Constanza hadn't taken any sexual advantage of her. "I'll do no such thing," she told him.

He sighed. "Please, Miss McCulloch! We must remove all foreign objects. Remember, please, that I am not casting a spell over you, simply striking a bargain. The spell is for the work that has to be done. I assure you your virtue is safe with me."

She didn't like the way he had said that. Not as if he were merely disinterested in her, but as if the idea —and she—were of no consequence to him.

"Miss McCulloch, if I were so inclined I could turn you in a matter of seconds into a panting love-slave or anything else I chose. That is not the job here, nor my interest, nor the interest of my employer. Now, for the last time, will you please disrobe and throw all your clothing outside the pentagram without leaving it yourself?"

She sighed. The trouble was, she could believe everything he was saying was true. She did as instructed and saw him nod approval, not of her but only of her action. He was preoccupied with other matters.

Although it was mid-September, the air was not chilly; either the climate was warmer in this world or there was a strong snap of Indian summer in the air.

Soon O'Malley was ready. He closed the box lid and faced her, holding the wand in his hand. It resembled a thin version of an aircraft wand, a flashlight with a long plastic tube of yellow. Yet she knew they had no flashlights here, nor batteries to store energy.

"From this point, just stand there facing me," he

instructed. "Say or do nothing until and unless I specifically ask you for a response. Clear?"

She nodded.

O'Malley began. At first it was a prayerful chant, then it rose in pitch, becoming a call, almost a summons. The language was vaguely Latin-sounding, yet the words made no kind of sense to her at all.

"Siruptis vergobum una toma maculum Tobit!" he chanted, and the wand waved all over the place. He chanted the same phrase again, and yet again, and continued making odd motions with the wand.

For a moment there seemed to be no effect at all, just a silly-looking man standing in front of a table in the middle of nowhere chanting mumbo jumbo. But, quite abruptly, things started to happen.

The braziers, for one thing, already flaring to two or three meters, all shot up to tremendous heights—ten, twenty meters high like sparkling fountains. Eerie shadows played against the inside of the pentagram, over both her and the wizard. For the first time she noticed that only the area inside the borders was illuminated. There was nothing but darkness beyond.

The wand began to glow fiercely as well, and O'Malley changed his chant to an even more impossible language and an even eerier sound.

"Iä! Iä! Yog-Sothoth! Upschar pfagn!" he repeated again and again. The air seemed to swirl and thicken within the pentagram, and there came a sensation, a feeling, no more, of unseen powerful forces, forces evil and beyond the understanding of humanity, descending, closing in, surrounding them on all sides. Despite the cooling night air she found herself perspiring nervously.

O'Malley seemed satisfied rather than scared and switched again, this time to English, although what he was saying made as little sense as the gibberish.

"The Old Ones were, the Old Ones are, and the Old Ones shall be," he chanted as if reciting a litany. "Not in the spaces we know, but between them. They walk serene and primal, undimensioned and to us unseen. Yog-Sothoth knows the gate. Yog-Sothoth is the gate. Yog-Sothoth is the key and guardian of the gate.

Yog-Sothoth is the key to the gate where the spheres meet. Man rules where They ruled once; They shall rule where man rules now. After summer is winter and after winter, summer. O great Keeper of the Key, send us thy servant!"

And from the spaces around and outside the pentagram she sensed life, life of a sort terribly alien to her, so much so that her mind could not accept this life as it was and protected her with blurred images. There were many of them, looking like soap bubbles but radiating that feeling of being totally alien and incomprehensible, and hidden from her by her own mind as bubble shapes.

And now O'Malley received an answer from the shapes, a shrill piping as if from thousands of inhuman and nonhuman creatures all shouting, *"Tekeli-li! Tekeli-li!"*

She had seen and experienced the magic of the University engineers, the godlike power of the holy world and the rigidly structured wizardry of the castle, the Thieves' Guild, and the demons and ghosts of the tower. She had seen the magic of this counterpart world in which elves, gnomes, and faerie cohabited with man and spells were tests of will—but this was unlike any of that. This was alien, so alien as to be incomprehensible; so alien that she knew, instinctively, that no Department of Probabilities in some far-off time line had dreamed it up. These were *real*, not constructs. These were at the root of O'Malley's powers, why he was the master magician of them all, how he could hold even a demon from the zero time line completely in thrall, helpless despite his jewel of power. These were the counterparts of the demons, the alien creatures of enormous power that lived between the worlds and inhabited the dimensional spaces between the levels of reality. The former masters of reality, perhaps the creators of the demons themselves, bound and thrown out, if O'Malley's chant could be accepted, by—what? The jewels, the power amplifiers, the means that some demon slave of these foul creatures had developed by which to break free, to revolt, to join together so many that they exiled their former masters to half-planes and insubstantial realities. Pressed back by the joining of—how many? If six could move a planet, what might six thousand jewels do, or six million? Locked away until greed and lust for limitless power by such as O'Malley might pierce the veil and draw them hither.

"Hear me, O servants of the Mighty and Omnipotent Keeper of the Gates!" O'Malley called to them, raising his arms in supplication. "Feed me the power to serve, that I might serve Him Who Is Not to Be Named through your master and through you! I call the power unto myself, for I need His blessing and His power for a mortal task, that my position might be increased and my service tenfold increased in value! Let the power flow to me!"

The call agitated the "bubbles" to a fever pitch; they screamed their strange piping call all the more. And now she could feel it—feel the power flow from all sides of the pentagram, closing in. The barrier of the pentagram kept the creatures out, but not the tremendous surge of force.

The wand came up and again started tracing a symbol in the air, a complex symbol based on the five-pointed star. Only now, as the light traced the symbol, it remained in the air in front of O'Malley like a glowing yellow sign without support. She felt the power surge flow into it, felt the enormous force it absorbed as surely as if she could see it, yet nothing visibly changed.

Then the sorcerer stepped up to the symbol still hanging in the air, stepped up to it and placed his head into it. He did not penetrate; it seemed to her as if his head had vanished and his broad shoulders had acquired the eerie sign for a head.

"Jill McCulloch!" his voice came at her. It was recognizably O'Malley's, yet it seemed huge, deep, and not quite human any more. "Here is the bargain. You shall accept command of the forces that I shall place at your disposal; you shall lead them where I direct, and you shall besiege the Citadel that I designate. Not one human life shall you order spared; you shall order the death of all humans inside the compound, and you shall see that it is carried out. Once it is, you shall summon me by stating my name three times at the gates. If you do this, I will deliver unto you the jewel which you seek to use as you see fit. Do you agree to this bargain, freely and of your own will do you make it with me?"

She had no choice, yet she hesitated. This was no bargain with an Asmodeus Mogart, it was a bargain with the sworn and ancient enemies of all the humans, demons and her own kind equally.

O'Malley, or the thing that O'Malley had become, sensed her hesitation and a vision started to appear in her mind—a vision of the great asteroid filling the skies of Earth, of oceans crashing inland, cities destroyed, millions—no—billions of lives swept away, their faces showing terror at the destruction, their faces, too, a mirror of her friends and relatives, those to whom she had been closest in life. With the vision came a strong thought, an argument.

All this has happened, it seemed to tell her. *All this is the fate of your world. But winter becomes summer after a while; what seems like permanent desolation come December is reborn in April's warmth and May's sweet rains. What is done may be undone if you so wish, Jill McCulloch. Without shedding of blood there is no remission. Blood must flow that blood be saved. It is your choice, Jill McCulloch. Your choice alone. Choose now, Jill McCulloch,* the voice inside her commanded. *Which lives will you choose? Do you accept the terms of my bargain?*

There was no choice. "I accept," she choked, holding back tears.

"Know now the spell that I shall weave," O'Malley's strangely distorted voice proclaimed. "Be you strong and agile, the best of the best of a warrior race. Feel the force and power of command flow into you, and feel the building of superior identity! Command, O Queen of Women, all of your sex who are the dissatisfied, the lost, the ones without direction, the yearning ones and the ones beyond yearning, the ones who dare to hope and the ones beyond hope! The outcasts, the misfits, the empty of soul and spirit! Draw them to yourself as a magnet draws iron, and command them with force of will! Command with invulnerable force! You have the power now!"

And she felt the power flow into her; felt herself grow strong and hard, knew and flexed the enormous forces now placed at her command. She was Jill McCulloch, yes, but she was far more than that now—the Queen of Darkness.

It was done. The alien shapes receded into the blackness until only the faintest echoes of their weird cry seemed to linger in the dead air; the flames of many colors sank and withdrew into their holders, giving off but a pale glow now. The magic symbol traced in the air faded and dissipated like smoke into the faintly flowing colors of the pentagram and then was gone for good.

O'Malley was soaking wet and looked dead tired, as if some vital spark had gone from him, yet his eyes retained their nonhuman glow and that feeling of tremendous power and intellect. He looked at her across the little table and placed the wand almost absently in the box atop that table, closing the lid.

"Now you know I must keep the bargain," he said softly, his voice a faint whisper. "What I have done cannot be undone, and I dare not loose such a force as you upon this world. You must win the jewel and leave."

The figure to whom he spoke bore only a superficial resemblance to the Jill McCulloch who had entered the pentagram. It was a warrior queen who stood there, incomparably beautiful beyond man's fantasies, with long blue-black hair and flashing black eyes. Tall, bronze, she radiated a strength and power beyond any human's.

She felt it, knew that she was now more than human, a goddess of tremendous power, and flashed an evil smile at the sorcerer.

"You need not remind me of our bargain," she responded sharply to him, the royalty of absolute confidence and command in her voice. "But you should know, too, what you have wrought. No man commands me, nor any human. I do what I do because *I* choose to do it, not because you order it. Least of all by your order, for you have sold out and betrayed your own race for power."

He grinned wearily. "I'll not bandy words with you. You now know who my masters are, and *what* they are. You know that nothing human can withstand them and that your power flows from them through me. I cannot turn it off, but I can summon them again."

The threat didn't disturb her in the least, yet she was curious about one other thing that seemed to connect with that threat.

"Tell me, Wizard, this one thing: with such power at your command that you can do such as this and present that power so casually, why cannot your alien friends break the spell? Why must one such as I do it?"

He considered the question and his answer carefully. "Let us just say," he replied slowly, "that just as we humans do not always act in concert, so, too, the other side is not unanimous and shares with us one common ground only—love of power and fear of power in others."

She nodded in understanding. "In other words, they fight with one another over who should be the ruler when they return—and other humans are betting on different favorites, including the one who cast this spell."

He nodded wearily and picked up a small bag under the table. It contained water and he drank deeply but carefully, coughing once or twice nonetheless.

"That's why you're doing this," she pressed as full comprehension struck her. "Constanza means nothing to you. It's to break the spell of a rival!" Her new, bright eyes bored into him. "There is something in the Citadel that interests your master and that has been denied it by this spell. The C.I.A. had nothing to do with it! Your own rivals cast that spell to deny you something there, and it was *you* who betrayed Constanza to force this! You! What's in there that you want?"

He was plainly weary and sank to the ground with a sigh. "What I wish is none of your concern, for you will leave this plane when the job is done. Let us just say it isn't a thing, it's the place itself—a thin spot, as it were, between their world and ours. That is why I influenced Constanza to build there in the first place. As to the betrayal, does one betray a rose when he replants it, or an ant in an ant farm by killing its queen? Only when I sensed your passage through the planes did all this develop; I traced you, I probed you, and I led you here. Does it make a difference? You are here to save your own world, a place alien to me. No matter what happens here, it is of no consequence to you."

She felt fury, a fury mixed with contempt, for this man who knew all and yet chose against his own kind. He and his rival sorcerers who stumbled on the truth had somehow contacted these alien creatures and bargained with them, and were now fighting a war with one another in which all humanity other than themselves was just a pawn in their power games.

She would go now and leave this miserable creature. She would go and spill blood in his cause for the jewel she now knew he could and would give her.

But if there were any way to deny him his spoils, she would take it, for although she was a Queen of Forces, she was still of human issue and the enemy of what he stood for. He could not undo her power; he had admitted as much. Perhaps the man, Mac Walters, might secure the jewel before she had to fulfill the bargain. Perhaps, then, *he* could return to save their world and she would be loosed fully upon this one with the power and knowledge she now possessed.

She was Queen of Women, and it hurt like hell to know that whether or not she could do anything depended on the actions of a man.

4

For two days Mac Walters had studied the information from Jill's own canvassing, and for two nights he had gone forth to look over the area himself in one or more of his many guises. It was a big city; a demon could be anywhere within it and permanently hidden, and there seemed no way to break through the brick and concrete barriers and the hundreds of square kilometers of civilization spreading out in a star-shaped pattern from the edge of Lake Michigan.

There were rumors, yes. He hadn't even needed Jill's information to pick those up—that the Boss of Bosses, Constanza, had a true demon held in thrall somewhere within the city limits of Chicago who did his bidding and devoured the souls of his enemies. But where?

Constanza's enemies wanted to know as well, as did the federal government. The only thing that had come out was that the demon was held by a pentagram but had freedom and creature comforts within his prison. But what sort of pentagram?

"Creature comforts" implied a large area, much larger than a chalk circle on the floor of a bar or even the standard magician's working area. How large could a pentagram be? Or, perhaps the question should be: how large could a pentagram be without its being obvious or giving the demon too much freedom to move?

Mac had spent his nights checking over Constanza's known property, finding nothing. The rival gangs and the feds were checking that angle, too, and he knew that the mob boss wasn't stupid. There were other areas not under his direct control, though; these, under other, lesser figures, would have to be ruled out. He couldn't trust anyone with this kind of secret who might turn out to be a rival or sell him out to a rival, and all the mob bosses paid big money to black magicians to protect themselves from assaults on that score.

Constanza's magician was named O'Malley, Mac

learned, but that didn't help much. O'Malley himself lived in a comfortable house with lots of servants up on the North Shore, but the property was actually Constanza's. As far as Mac could determine, O'Malley owned nothing he didn't carry with him and spurned money and most material possessions. Wealth simply wasn't important to him, and Constanza could give him whatever he wanted or needed.

Still, it had to have been O'Malley's power that had trapped the demon; it had to be O'Malley's power that maintained the prison. Constanza would not be the one to give the demon commands; he would command O'Malley, who would then face the demon.

That implied that the demon would have to be somewhere close to where the magician usually lived.

As a bat, Mac Walters approached O'Malley's lakeshore house again. He'd flown over it many times before, but to no avail. Clearly, the place was large but built on a shallow foundation to avoid any troubles with the creatures of the underworld. In front of the three-story house, which must have had twenty or more rooms, was a long, bright green lawn dotted with some shade trees leading down to the lake itself, where an artificial beach had been constructed and a small pier built.

The feds at least had gone over the house, but he decided to have a look of his own. In his mist form he could penetrate places that might be missed by even the best human investigators. He let the air currents lift him and turn him up and to the left, toward the house. He avoided the lake itself, since it was running water—he could fly over it, but should he ever allow himself to touch it, it would suck him in, engulf and drown him. It glowed dangerously to his vampire's eye, a threatening reddish glow broken only by the black dots of the thirty or more yachts and fishing boats tied up just inside the breakwater, shelter for the craft of the very rich who lived along this area.

The house was not vacant. A staff of thirty or more young men and women ran the place at all times and maintained it in tip-top condition. They were too close to being perfect physical specimens to be merely the hired help. That much was apparent from his peeks inside the windows. The men were extraordinarily handsome and muscular, like some sort of Mr. America contestants' gathering, and the women were all incredibly beautiful. He wondered idly whether they were human at all, if they were not some supernatural forms conjured up by this most powerful of wizards. It took some time for him to observe them through the windows, going about their duties and in most cases making ready for bed, and to conclude that they were, in fact, real people—albeit possibly made more so than they were by magical aids—and not the nonhuman. They behaved too normally, even with one another, and betrayed the usual human emotions of boredom, of cursing when they stumbled, that sort of thing, to be supernatural perfection.

It did not surprise him that there were no religious artifacts like crosses about. O'Malley, it was rumored, was a former Catholic bishop who'd "crossed over" to the black side when passed over for promotion. Such religious artifacts as would disturb him would also disturb O'Malley.

The lack of other safeguards surprised him a little, but this reeked more of O'Malley's overconfidence than of any sinister traps. Mac had discovered the unwillingness of his fellow vampires to come near this place. O'Malley was tremendously powerful and his vengeance could reach throughout the world. Nobody dared cross him.

Nobody but somebody who didn't plan to be on this world very long.

He could not get into the house on his own; someone would have to help him, this he knew. He checked the second- and third-floor balconies and the widow's walk around the attic. The staff roomed upstairs, and many were just preparing for bed or were already asleep. One room, in which four beautiful sex symbols slept in flimsy nightgowns, particularly interested him. Three were asleep in their beds, but the fourth tossed and turned and seemed to be having problems.

Mac alighted on the balcony and turned back into his human form.

He could not enter, could not raise the window, although it was half raised as it was to accommodate a screen. It wouldn't have mattered if the window had instead been wide-open French doors—he had to be invited. There were ways, though, to finagle an invitation.

Not having taken blood from the woman, he had no real control over her, yet he did have great mental powers. He rejected merely tapping on the window—doing so might just raise an alarm or wake the others. He concentrated hard on the restless woman in her bed, projecting one simple thought, one action, that he needed.

It is stifling hot, he projected. *You need some fresh air!*

For a minute or two he was unsure that he was getting through; you just couldn't tell about such things. Then he saw the woman sigh, sit up on the side of her bed, and rub her eyes. He kept projecting.

Finally she stood up, looking sleepy but uncomfortable, and walked over toward the window. Now here she was—looking out, breathing in the fresher air. He stepped in front of her quickly and made instant eye contact. His movement was so sudden that she had no time to react; once eye contact was made, he had her.

Open the window quietly and remove the screen, he ordered, not vocally but directly from his mind to hers.

She carefully, yet unthinkingly, did as instructed, then returned, stepped back from the window, and gazed at him expectantly, arms slightly outstretched, inviting him in.

He entered the house quietly and looked nervously at the other three women, still sleeping soundly. He could control all four, but only by taking blood from all of them. That would take time. It was past midnight now; he had only a few hours to prowl the house. Still, he needed one ally here, one person he could call upon by mental command if necessary. He went up to the woman, embraced her, and puncturing her neck low, drank some of her blood.

She was his slave now; unlike those whom he usually fed upon in the city, he had taken from her not merely blood but a portion of her life force. Her thoughts were what he wished them to be, her mind and its contents his to tap no matter what.

Never had he encountered so vacuous a brain. She was not just an unliberated woman, she probably couldn't spell either "liberated" or "woman." Her world was the house, her thoughts on service, and her mental activity on such a low level that she actually *enjoyed* waxing floors and making beds. Worse, these duties weren't at all dull to her but were almost a challenge.

There was no sign of a spell or supernatural tampering. O'Malley or Constanza had obviously recruited such people as the perfect servants. That there were such people—so desirable on the outside and on the inside so much a cross between a puppy dog and a trained monkey—disturbed Mac slightly.

She knew the house, though; it was her world. After taking the plan and what little else was there, he had her replace the screen, close the window down to it, and return to bed and get to sleep. He left the room quickly; once in, it would be easy to get out.

He searched the place from top to bottom, finding much out of the ordinary but nothing whatsoever to indicate that a demon might be kept there. He found hidden passageways all over, and one cleverly concealed chamber held not only a sacrificial altar with stains, indicating that it was used on occasion, but also eerie potions and paraphernalia that went far beyond those of a common sorcerer. There were pentagrams aplenty as well, some of which he found impossible to cross, but none that couldn't be completely canvassed and none large enough for what would be necessary.

Worse, for all his versatility at snooping, Mac knew deep inside that he was retracing well-worn ground and that none of this could be concealed from the feds' sorcerers, either. Reluctantly he had to conclude that the demon was not in the house nor on the grounds, nor was there any sign of his ever having been there—no records or other clues to point the way.

Records! he thought sourly. The feds had seized the records of all the magical spells used by Constanza, a potentially devastating blow in the long run, but the investigators might need years to unravel them. At least they still hadn't discovered the demon's prison, that was clear—so there was still a chance.

He flowed under the front door as a mist, changed to a bat, and beat the dawn back to his culvert hiding place by only a few minutes. He kept thinking that something was wrong with what he'd seen—that there was a clue there if only he could figure it out. He sat in his coffin trying to think as lethargy overtook him with the dawn. Just before he slept he thought he might have it, but if so, it slipped away into oblivion.

He didn't think of Jill McCulloch at all.

5

At dawn she had started riding to the north and they had begun to come to her. The prior spells of O'Malley had summoned them to this desolate place and armed and motivated them with his force of will, yet she was required to lead them.

Women . . . a trickle at first, coming across the plains on horseback toward her, then more, and still more, until a force of more than five hundred women had joined her, their horses' hooves beating like thunder against the distant mountains.

They were of all shapes and sizes and races; although they acted proud and single-minded as a great force, they seemed to have no true will of their own other than to follow her and to obey her commands as wild creatures of the forest were said to obey the pipes of Pan.

She knew them, even through their different clothes and habits and accents; they were the dispossessed, the spiritual outcasts of this world. They were the cruelly treated, the abused, the lesbians, and the malcontents—the square pegs existing in this ordered society either by birth or by circumstance. They were armed with swords and daggers, yes, but also with nasty-looking repeating rifles. Two drove a sleek wagon that carried more ammunition and supplies. Jill, herself, wore nothing except a great silver sword on a copper link belt; she needed nothing more, even for protection against the elements. Her aura of power and total command precluded any other threats.

They rode through some small towns, mostly American farm settlements, and none spoke with them nor tried to stop them. Their power was awesome, her will unstoppable. They took only water from the towns, drawing sparse rations from tins in a supply wagon. As she passed through each town, slowly, proudly, a few of the women among the townspeople would lay down whatever they were doing, come out, and take a horse and join them. Sometimes the men near them would cry out their names in fear or anguish and occasionally run after them, but the women would pay no further attention to those left behind. A withering glance from Jill would stop them in their tracks. She radiated both awe and fear; mere humans were powerless to stop her or contest her will.

As O'Malley had promised, she was a power, an elemental force loosed disruptively in the world, yet a force that was required to draw and hold and bind these women for the task. It was too much power; little wonder the sorcerer had waited for one who would voluntarily have to leave this place.

Isolated women also joined them on the road; mostly Indian women, and women from various secluded farms and settlements far from them. She was calling to them like a magnet if they qualified, and they kept coming.

For herself, she was torn by her sense of time passing them by, of gaining the jewel too late if she did not make all speed with her force. This was tempered by her unwillingness to shed innocent blood, particularly in O'Malley's cause. These conflicting desires, to take things slowly and put off the hour of decision on the one hand and to get her mission over with on the other, caused her the most disturbance. The power and confidence felt good as well; she would love to remain, to stalk this land with her elemental forces, to seek out and attack those forces which O'Malley served and stamp them out.

The road turned west at dusk and led into the mountains which rose up like a solid wall from the Great Plains. She decided to press on to more level ground, at least a plateau, where her people could be fed and bedded down.

They came over a rise and Jill stopped, looking down at a flat region between two mountains. Her night vision was exceptional; she was the Queen of Darkness, and her magnetism drew and guided the force of women behind her.

Down in the valley she saw a single farmhouse with a small barn next to it, and it was burning.

She stared hard at the scene, at the hundreds upon hundreds of tiny figures lurking in the darkness around the burning farm. Too tiny. She spurred her mount and she and her army descended into the valley. She needed to give no order to draw weapons and be on the ready.

She had been right, she saw as they drew closer. This was not an Indian attack—that sort of thing had gone out with the Wild West here as well, replaced by Indian farmers and game managers in enclavelike countries who, themselves, had rid the plains of the barbarian nomads.

The attackers were gnomes.

Instantly she knew that their guns would have no effect on the squat, meter-high, bearded ancient creatures that circled the farm. They had set it afire by propelling flaming torches with catapults, but had not been able to go in themselves. Why?

And then she saw a fence, a fence of iron built around the structures. It was iron and its alloy, steel, which they were powerless against; they had simply set the place afire and waited for the inhabitants to come out. If the people crossed the fence line, they would be captives or victims of the gnomes; if they didn't, the gnomes, who, like people, were diurnal, could simply starve them to death in a siege or shoot wooden and copper spears and arrows at them from the outside.

But everyone in the women's force she led held iron and steel swords. She slowed and turned back to her force. "Draw swords! Cold iron only," she snapped crisply, and the order was passed back. Normal military tactics were included with the spell that bound them; they spread out, creating a solid wall ten deep, and advanced.

The gnomes saw them and formed a line across the road between them and the burning farm. Their eyes reflected the spreading fires, and their almost comic fairy-tale appearance was offset by grim and determined expressions in those eyes and behind those beards.

They looked less human close up; more stonelike and with an alien construction to their bone structure.

Jill stopped and faced the gnome force. She had no fear of them as such, since she greatly outnumbered them and possessed the weapon they most feared; but gnomes were magical creatures that had powers beyond those of humankind. She was immune to them, she knew that intuitively, although her female force was not. The gnomes could cost her dearly in injuries and lives before she reached her goal.

"What is the meaning of this?" she shouted imperiously to the lead gnome.

"It is none of your affair, Spirit Queen," snarled the gnome in a gruff, low voice that was unexpected from the small creature. "Go about your business and proceed unharmed, but do not interfere in our work!" The threatening tone was unmistakable.

She looked at the house. It was a conflagration now, yet she sensed someone in there still lived, somehow, and could be gotten out before the walls collapsed; someone who was now one of her own.

"I claim the life that remains for my own," she told the gnome. "Stand aside. I will take what is mine and proceed."

"It is not your right," snapped the gnome leader.

"All lives in yon structure are forfeit to the Collective!"

She was conscious that time was running out. Her first major decision on life was at hand, yet she responded. "Collective? Why do you attack the humans now, gnome? Was it not agreed long ago by treaty that your domain is not ours nor ours yours? How dare you break it!"

The gnome leader laughed. "Treaties! Bah! Treaties between the bourgeoisie humans who enjoy the fruits of proletarian labor while returning no labor to those Underearth. The time for revolution is at hand! We have nothing to lose but our chains!" A roar of approval went up from his gnome force.

Holy smokes! she thought. *Radical communist gnomes?*

"Is this the start of your revolution, small one?" she retorted aloud. "If so, we shall see just how well prepared you are." She drew her sword from its hilt, holding it high in the air. As one, the rest of her force followed her lead.

The action scared the hell out of the gnomes. Even the leader, who was good at bluff, gulped. Cold steel. Gnomes reproduced only once in a century, and cold steel, with its iron base, was the only substance that could kill them. They could not afford a war—or revolution—of attrition, particularly not these few against so many.

There was hatred in the gnome's eyes, but it was mixed with a certain knowledge of defeat as well. He made one last attempt.

"This is not the revolution—that is still coming, creeping over all the Underearth," he told her. "These people received our goods and repaid us by drilling a well deep into our domain, without our permission, and with a drill of *steel!* They killed one of us!"

She understood now what had brought this confrontation about. These farmers were young and dumb; a sign on the gate read TALL TREES COMMUNE. City kids playing at independence, forgetting, in their utopian dreams, that in a modern society interdependence was the rule. They had forgotten the interdependence between human and gnome, and they had paid for it.

"There is but one left," she told the gnome. "She will join us. You have been avenged many times over. Go, now!" She started forward.

The gnomes stood their ground for a moment, then, after a signal from their leader, gave way to her. Jill jumped the fence and bounded quickly off her horse, who was kept from panicking only by being under her mental control.

She stalked into the house and the flames receded from her. Much of the place was burning; it was incredible that some of the structure should still be relatively, although very temporarily, untouched. Back in the kitchen, in a trough of water, was the lone survivor, a water-soaked blanket over her head. It was already becoming unbearably hot, even for Jill; the smoke, too, was thick and acrid. There were only moments left.

She pulled the blanket off the trough and saw the woman, already unconscious from smoke inhalation. Jill was afraid she was too late, but she had to try. She lifted the woman out of the water and kicked open the back door.

Seconds later the flaming roof caved in. Jill looked back briefly and let out some breath.

She put the woman down on the cool grass and started mouth-to-mouth resuscitation. Pressing on the woman, she realized for the first time that the fire victim was not only pregnant but in a very advanced stage. She pumped air in carefully, steadily, then bent low over the woman's face and breathed in, out, in, out, tasting the smoke. She willed the woman to live, gave her tiny spark of life a supercharge by transferring energy from herself inside as she breathed.

The woman coughed, groaned, then started gasping and wheezing.

Several of the women in Jill's force approached, and she turned to them. "Get her to a wagon!" she ordered. "Those among us with any kind of medical skills should attend to her. We will camp on the farm land just beyond the fence tonight."

They hastened to do her bidding, bowing slightly in

deference. She got up and walked back to the gnomes.

"How many lived there?" she demanded to know.

"Ten—five males and five females," the gnome replied. He looked around, still trying to sound haughty, defiant. "We have decided that nine for one is atonement. We will consider this matter closed. The well, however, shall not be used. We shall seal and destroy it."

She had to admire his nerve. He was still talking as if he had a choice in this.

"We agree," she responded, allowing him his pride. "Now you will return to your domain and we shall keep to ours."

The little creature nodded and started to turn to go, then turned back to her. "Answer me one question, if you will," he said in a curious and respectful tone. He gestured to the women now setting up camp in the fields. "Whither is such a strange force as this bound, and to what purpose?"

She smiled at his obvious prodding for information. "I should answer you that you should keep going, that it is none of your affair," she taunted, "but I will ask you this question in turn. How far from this spot are the lands and castle known as the Citadel?"

He looked at her strangely. "You are a free spirit, not bound," he noted. "The others are under spells, yes, but not you, nor is your soul with lein. Why would you go against such peaceful folk as those when your victory is one for such evil?"

It was odd to hear him take so moral a tone after he'd just murdered nine human beings by burning them to death.

"But was the spell not cast by one equally as evil?" she retorted, throwing the ball back to him.

He looked genuinely surprised. "Do you not know, then? Not all the elemental forces between the worlds are evil. You speak as if man vanquished them, but it was not so. We—human, gnome, faerie, all the denizens who now live upon this earth—were the byproducts of that struggle, not the victors but the inheritors. They were vanquished in civil war, not by the efforts of others. This world is where the battle was won, not anything more. The others still rule the spaces between the worlds of our own universe—they have no need of Earth. They who still rule the light and the darkness aided the spell you would break. I beg you, do not do so, for beneath the Citadel lies the gate to evil most foul!"

"I will take your words to heart," she told him, "but I beg you to remember that even free souls are not fully free, nor are all chains visible. I bid you goodbye." She turned and started walking toward her women now camping in the fields. After a few seconds she turned and looked back.

There was no one there. The gnomes had completely vanished.

She made her way to the food wagon where the pregnant woman—no more than a girl, really, she saw —lay. They had removed and burned her scorched dress and covered her with a blanket. She was still in shock. An older woman was tending her, wiping her brow and occasionally trying to force some water into her mouth.

The women of the force spoke little except in their duties, yet they responded to the girl as ordered. The older woman looked up and nodded slightly in deference to her Queen.

"How is she?" Jill wanted to know.

The older woman shook her head. "I don't know. Still in some shock, of course. She occasionally calls out a man's name—Michael, I believe—and gets upset, then relapses as you see her."

"The child?"

"Still lives, I believe," the woman, obviously a former nurse, told her. "She is far advanced, and with this shock to her system the child could come at any time."

Jill stood there thinking for a minute. "Can she travel, at least in the food wagon?"

The woman shrugged. "I know not, Mistress. I should not like to move her, and such movement over any great distance might kill her or the child or both."

"She will *not* die," Jill said confidently. "You will stay with her and attend to her. I will have need of her

—alive." She turned and walked off, wishing she were as confident as she sounded.

The gnome had not answered her question as to how far the Citadel was, but it had to be fairly close by, as he'd known too much about it.

If so, and if the fates held, that pregnant, delirious girl in the wagon just might be the key to salvaging at least a partial victory for her, although it would not wash the blood off her hands.

They reached the Citadel area before noon on the next day. There was no mistaking it—a broad, deep, rich valley scattered with prosperous-looking farms and with one small town built on a low rise in its center. An ancient, Moorish-looking castle dominated the area from above.

The road continued down into the valley, past huge stone gates that were only remains of a former guard wall. These people no longer needed gates.

A new road branched off along the side of the mountain and continued all the way down the length of the valley, then seemed to cross over the dam that backed up blue river water and to follow the other side back to the original road. Clearly the poor highway department had been thrown for a loss when it discovered that no men could cross or even enter the valley, and had done the best it could. A huge sign at the branch proclaimed, in Spanish and English, that one's highway taxes were at work.

"Remain here," Jill commanded her force. "I will go down and give them one opportunity to avoid carnage."

She approached the gates slowly, apprehensively. Here it would be no ordinary spell like the one at the border, and she had only Constanza's word that it would not affect her.

His word proved correct, and although her horse had some problems, it was successful in the end. A gelding, she noticed for the first time. She made a mental note to see if there were any stallions among the women's horses before any attack. Some of them were sure to be, but then, infantry would be needed, anyway.

Spirits and nonhumans of any kind were obviously barred from the place as well. It seemed to have quite an underground plumbing system, and one building looked like a small gas plant.

Word had gone ahead, though, probably via the gnomes in some way or another. The inhabitants waited for her in a great crowd in the small town square, and they viewed her visage with awe when she moved slowly up to them. For the first time some of them were really afraid.

She surveyed them pityingly. Shopkeepers and farmers, men, women, and children. Not a fighter among them. Here and there she saw people with rifles and swords and even some old fencing rapiers, but nothing that could withstand an onslaught such as she could mount.

They knew it, too; she could see it in their eyes. Her force was visible along the mountain road above them.

She was surprised to see the men, considering the spell, but guessed that it would apply to them only if they left.

An old man, standing tall and straight despite his years, dressed in his best Sunday suit and peering at her through thick bifocals perched atop a bushy white mustache, came forward and faced her, looking grave and scared.

"Why?" he asked, his voice quivering.

It was a question she didn't want to hear, but it demanded an answer. These people *deserved* an answer.

"I come not from your world but from another far away," she told them. "My world is dying. It will be dead soon and gone to dust, kicked into the sun by a wandering moon. My people have only one hope of salvation, and that hope is to obtain a magic stone that is in the hands of the Wizard O'Malley. His price to save five billion lives is the several hundred of yours."

There was dead silence for a moment in the square; not even the children stirred or made a sound. Finally the old man sighed sadly and said, "Well, that's it, then. You must do what you must do—and so must we."

"You cannot win," Jill pointed out. "You know that. No piece of land is worth such blood. The road goes off in the other direction. If all of you leave, then the spell will be broken the same way as if we had fought."

The old man turned and looked at the silent crowd, then back at her. "Do you know who we are?" he asked her, emotion rising in his voice. "We are the poor and the children of the poor. Of the tens of thousands of us who began, we are the few survivors. Chased, shot, burned, raped, and pillaged in place after place, we finally came here, to a valley that even the Indians and the Little People shunned. It was acid, barren, a badlands hell. We had little food, we had no more money; our few pitiful cows were dying, our horses broken and done in. We had no means of going farther, and no hope of survival. We had only our own souls."

He paused and removed his glasses, wiping them with a big red handkerchief as an excuse to wipe his misty eyes unobtrusively, then replaced them and continued.

"We built that dam out of the earth and rock without magical aids," he told her. "We went over the mountains and carried out wagons of sod, pulling the wagons in human teams since we hadn't the animals to use. In two generations, without outside aid and with the blood of two-thirds of our number, we built this place. We held it and we loved it and we fed it as it fed us. My family is buried in this soil, and the fathers and mothers and sisters and brothers of all these people as well.

"When Constanza came he tried to get us to move and could not. He built that mighty castle there—we could not stop him, but we hated him. He had no right to this land, and no blood of his was in it that gave him rights over it or us. We sought our liberation, we prayed for it as a body, and our prayers were answered. A creature came from Heaven, shining with a light that paled the stars, while Constanza and his chiefs were away. The spell was laid, and the rest of the staff of that castle he called the Citadel then added their blood to this valley. It is a place of evil and the evil lingers, but it is contained, trapped beneath that hill. We do not enter it, we leave it undisturbed." He paused again, looked back at the people in the square, then back up at her.

"You ask us to leave this place," he concluded, "yet we cannot. We are this place and it is us. We have no place else to go, nor any desire nor purpose elsewhere. We built this place and made it, and it is our only world. You might as well ask us to leave this planet. We will die, if necessary, but all men must. But *we will die here!*"

She felt like crying but didn't dare. Instead she said, "That is true for you. I understand and accept it. But not the younger parents, surely, and their children. They have a chance at life—they *deserve* a chance at life."

The old man looked again into her eyes, and she saw within them a strength beyond the fear and nervousness, a strength that was inside him, inside all of them, that somehow made them greater than they seemed.

"They are the fruits of this valley; they will not transplant easily," the old man told her.

"Still, consider it," she urged. "All of you. You cannot win. There will be no miracles from Heaven this time. I will stay my advance until dawn tomorrow. That is the most time I can allow. I beg you, at least the parents of the children too young to decide, to leave. We will not stop you, and I promise we will do our utmost to take care of those who go. Consider it until dawn. After that, I can make no more decisions; it will be out of my hands."

The old man smiled warmly and reached out, actually taking her hand. He spoke for them all, she sensed that.

"I'm so sorry you must do this," he said softly, kindly, gently, with pity. "So very sorry for you."

She looked at him in complete surprise. *He* was pitying *her!*

"What do you mean?" she managed.

He smiled kindly and patted her hand. "For us it will be a brief moment. For you it will be a lifetime."

She turned and spurred her horse to increase its speed away from the town, through the gates, up the road, past the sign. She slowed only to regain control of herself. It would not do for the others to see their goddess crying.

She turned and looked back down at the peaceful green valley and the distant town, then rode into the rapidly established hillside camp, up to the food wagon where the pregnant girl lay, still semicomatose. The nurse poked her head out the back.

"Has the child come yet?" Jill asked her.

The woman shook her head. "False labor twice, but no birth yet. It cannot be long."

Jill stared at the nurse. "Now, listen carefully to my commands and obey them to the letter. A great deal depends on this." And in the back of her mind something shouted: *Oh, Mac Walters, find the gem tonight and spare me!*

6

It was night again, and again he circled near O'Malley's estate, trying to think. Theritus simply *had* to be close to the house, he just *had* to be. But where? Not under the ground—Mac had checked that angle. Nor in the house or the beach houses, either. Nowhere. He'd even checked out many of the other estates up and down the north beach area, but they were even less likely havens. They were mostly millionaires' places and far, far too public to hide Theritus.

Using his hypnotic powers to question random people only confirmed this; no one had seen anyone who looked like the demon anywhere around, at any time.

Still, I'm missing something, Mac told himself as he flew aimlessly up and down the beach. There was a clue here, something he'd seen that was important, if he could only figure it out.

He almost stopped dead in the air and started falling. Not something he'd seen, but something he had *not* seen!

There had been an altar, a full magical room that was used for sacrifices and for casting many of O'Malley's best spells. It had that used look, that feel of magic and dark forces.

But there had been no paraphernalia of the magician there, not even spares, assuming he took some with him. No magic books, either—no potions or signs or formulae of any sort. Mac didn't care how powerful the sorcerer was, he couldn't possibly carry everything in his head—and you didn't dare make even a tiny mistake in his business. And yet that room was where he did his evil work. That meant that the things he required had to be close by, so close as to be on instant call as needed.

Mac was sure he had the answer within his grasp, if only he could take the last little step the evidence demanded. Where was Sherlock Holmes when you really needed him?

Burial? No, that was out. It would take a metal container to safeguard all of it, and the denizens of the Underearth were very jealous of that and clearly had authorized no such burial—nor could O'Malley have trusted them in any case. Not there. Not in the house. Not on the grounds. Not in the immediate neighborhood, either. Yet the stuff had to be very close by . . .

Under water? He considered that, turning his gaze to the lethal-looking lake. No, not under water, either, since again O'Malley would have to trust the sea-sprites and freshwater mermaids, not to mention the major water elementals. He didn't dare sink the stuff —it would no longer be his, but the property of the water worlders by law and treaty.

The boats!

Mac cursed himself for a fool. A yacht basin. Three hundred-plus yachts out there, all neatly anchored, with a speedboat tied to O'Malley's pier. The perfect hiding place for the records and books and all the magical stuff O'Malley would use—close by, easily accessible, but should the cover ever be blown, explosive charges would destroy the stuff as well as send it to the bottom.

He studied the boats well, wishing just this once he could get to the Hall of Records when it was open to see which boats in the batch were registered to Constanza, O'Malley, or one of their fronts. But that wasn't any good, anyway—it would take days just to unearth the faces behind those fronts.

The lake glowed its lethal color against which the ships were silhouetted perfectly. He edged over as close as he dared, at one point actually skimming the water about five meters up. He felt the effect even from where he was—a sapping of strength, a general malaise. He could not cross the water on his own, he knew that.

And cross it to where? he wondered. On one of those three hundred ships out there was Theritus and the jewel, of that he was now certain. The problem was that he didn't know which one—and it was sure to be guarded.

He studied the boats again carefully. For the first time he realized that circumstances had placed him at a disadvantage in being a vampire. He considered the woman in the house but rejected that idea. She would do his bidding, of course, but he could not *bēcome* her; even after finding the demon he would have to figure out how to get the jewel from him.

He racked his memory. It had been a long time since he'd seen *Dracula* on television. Had that master vampire been stopped by running water? If Mac remembered it right, the Count was from Rumania but the movie was set in England. How had he reached England? How had he returned?

Of course! He'd shipped himself as freight on a ship! He'd even killed the crew and beached the ship! He *could* travel over running water!

Mac alighted near the speedboat. The keys weren't in it, of course. He stopped short. What was he thinking of? It might *look* like a speedboat, but it couldn't be, not in *this* world. They didn't have internal-combustion engines.

Not a rowboat, though. There was a steering wheel, a pilot's seat, and—

"Well I'll be doubly damned!" he swore aloud. "Pedals!"

It was like riding a bicycle—easy once he got the hang of it with his superior strength. He was down a bit from the sapping feeling the water around him gave him, but still stronger than an ordinary man, and in life he'd been an athlete. He was nervous, though: first that some guard might notice the boat was missing, or that somebody might spot him; and also because if he fell or was pushed overboard, that would be the end of him.

He had to put both possibilities out of his mind; he still had to find out which boat was which.

It turned out to be fairly easy. First there were the guards with submachine guns occasionally walking up and down the decks of nearby ships—but the real tip-off was the line in the water. He was almost on it before he realized it—a rope or something kept afloat with marker buoys. All the guards were on boats outside the line, which went from that boat to that boat to that boat to that boat to that boat and back again.

A pentagram. A pentagram in the water, with another ship in the center, a big luxury ship with two masts and a smokestack as well—a two-way side-wheeler-and-sail combo.

But first he had to get past those guards.

They hadn't spotted him, despite the torches around, because he'd been cautious as well as lucky. Guarding is one of the most boring businesses there is. You can't be as dumb as those house servants, since you might be called upon to foil some very clever thief or cop or interloper, yet you had about the same thrills as that girl who waxed floors. Less even.

Those men were there, but they weren't looking for anything.

He pulled up close to one of the boats and hoped he had judged the distance correctly. He made a mighty leap and clung like a spider to the hull of the yacht. The small boat was pushed away by the force of the leap and he made some noise when he grabbed onto the hull, but that couldn't be helped.

He hoped the noise would be put down by the guards as just the sounds of boats at anchor, but no such luck. A man was coming along the deck directly above him at a dead run, a directional lantern in one hand and a submachine gun in the other. He peered anxiously over the side, then spied the small boat drifting away and became suspicious.

A strong arm suddenly grabbed the man's neck and held it in a viselike grip; he was pushed backward before the power of the vampire's grip on his windpipe. He could not cry out. His eyes bulged and his tongue swelled, and suddenly his eyes rolled and he sank limply onto the deck. Mac didn't know whether he'd killed the man or not, but he no longer cared. He crept along the deck, all too conscious of the glaring torchlights that turned the area of the basin almost into daylight.

He wondered idly if he could fly and then decided not to risk it. There were still a lot of problems, he saw. They'd left the place less heavily guarded than they could have—no more guarded than such a collection of fancy shipping should be—to avoid attracting attention to their hideaway. And yet— There were still three guards around, possibly more if there were any on the central ship, and that central ship was about ten meters from any other craft. Ten meters! He couldn't fly over there, close as it was—he dared not risk doing so over water. He had lost his small boat, too. He couldn't even risk raising anchor on this one, since it was part of the pentagram. He hardly wanted to free the demon, loose him before he got what he'd come for.

The ships were unnaturally steady, anyway, probably held to the shallow lake floor by concrete posts. It wouldn't do for storm or ice to disrupt the protection, either.

The pentagram was even more cleverly designed than he'd thought. It was designed not to keep people out but to keep people *in*. You had to have some special counter, like the guards, to walk out, although the guards could probably take you out. That, too, was bad. He had perhaps four hours to complete all this or he'd be trapped here at sunup, unable to return to the culvert.

He'd have to abandon subtlety and depend on the fact that the pentagram was supposed to work to keep the nonhumans out and that the guards were there to keep people out. Nobody had considered vampires.

He looked around nervously. None of the other guards had apparently seen or heard anything out of the ordinary, but he would have to cross the distance to the central key boat in full torchlight and with nothing to hide behind. The machine guns the men had couldn't hurt him, but they would have impact, perhaps enough impact to knock him into the water. He examined the yacht itself—deserted, of course, probably used only for the guard's quarters. He checked below and found signs that at least two others lived there—probably not the other guards but the rest of the shift now off in town. Down in the hold, below the water line, he saw that he'd guessed correctly. Two huge steel and concrete pilings, fixed in concrete, came up through the bottom of the hull. There was a trickling of water which convinced him to get out of there. He wanted no part of water regardless of how shallow and still it was.

Mac also found the massive dynamite charges as well, which confirmed his overall hypothesis about this boat. There was no doubt—the wire was the pentagram and the ship in the center was where the demon was being held.

This yacht would be a beauty if it weren't so firmly fixed to its spot—a three-masted schooner with every conceivable luxury. He considered the masts. Accepting the fact that he could not cross the ten meters to his target ship undetected, he had to grant that all hell would break loose. That meant eliminating the other guards if at all possible. Well, he had the dead guard's submachine gun. If he could just make enough of a disturbance to bring them all out into the open, then cut loose on them . . . It might work. But still, how would he cross the ten meters?

He spent a quiet hour trying to figure out the means, and even more time, after he had come up with a solution, wishing he knew more about physics or at least something about lumberjacking.

It took still more time to set it all up. The dynamite in the hold was bound together with straps in groups of six sticks, all connected from their blasting caps to a common copper wire. The wire branched at several points, each leading to a plunger-type detonator that used static electricity generated by the plunger, causing interaction with fine metal brushes to provide the motive spark. A simple system, and with this many detonators a cornered guard could trigger them from almost anyplace on the ship and, with a nice little delay circuit in the emitter of the plunger box, have at least a few seconds to get away.

The system did not seem to be booby-trapped. Mac gingerly removed one stick and its blasting cap from the assembly after cutting the binding straps, then cut the copper wire after the junction. It took a lot of time and effort to follow the wire to its plunger box and then to get the wire, which was wire-stapled, to come free. Finally he had it and reached the second big problem in his plan.

Placing the single charge would be easy, although he had no idea just how much of an explosion one stick would make. A hell of a bang, he guessed, if the old movies were right. He intended to blow up the mast nearest the target ship—he hoped without breaking the pentagram or sinking the yacht—and take advantage of the disturbance to use the guards and the mast itself to cross to the target ship. The only problem was, where did you plant the charge in order to take out the mast and have it fall in the direction you wanted? How, in fact, could you contain the dynamite blast so that it wouldn't spend its force equally in all directions and splinter the 16+-meter mast?

At least he didn't have to worry yet about the guard being missed. Once or twice others had called for him, but, upon receiving no answer, had assumed he was goofing off below decks, perhaps grabbing a catnap. It seemed to be a common enough practice among

them that they thought nothing of it. They were secure
here; any attack would come from massed federal
boats moving in hard or rival gangsters with guns blazing.

They hadn't counted on a lone outsider.

There was enough room around the mast support
hole in the upper superstructure to plant the stick of
dynamite if he could decide where to put it. He remembered seeing some logging once where the tree
had fallen toward the largest cut. That meant, if all
things held, placing the dynamite between the mast
and the target boat. This he did, dampening it from
underneath as best he could with pillows, bedding,
whatever he could get his hands on.

Satisfied, finally, that he'd done all he could, he ran
the copper wire outside and got down near the stern
of the boat. He had no desire to be blown overboard
by the force of the explosion. He held the guard's submachine gun, he was as ready as he'd ever be.

He pumped the plunger up and down from a prone
position. It started to whine, and he saw a small meter
on the top climb rapidly into the red zone. When it
reached that point, he let go and braced himself.

The brushes inside continued to interact for a few
seconds, then the whine started to decline and the
meter started to drop. He worried now that he hadn't
adequately understood the mechanism, that the wire
had come loose, that the dynamite had fallen from its
position—anything that would prevent an explosion.

The whine continued to diminish and the seconds
dragged on. He grew panicky but wasn't about to
move as long as any sound issued from the box. He
remembered tales of people having been blown apart
when they'd gotten up to check about why some explosive hadn't gone off. Not that he could be blown
apart, but he could be thrown into the water. Even a
stake through the heart seemed preferable to drowning.

And then it went off. The explosion was louder and
of a magnitude stronger than his wildest imaginings;
the whole ship shook despite its foundation, and a
large part of the bridge superstructure flew in all di-

rections. The mast itself was snapped like a twig and blown backward from the bottom. It fell forward, as he'd hoped, but crashed over into the water, missing the target boat by the smallest of margins, perhaps a meter from the stern. It simply wasn't long enough— the added six meters didn't quite compensate for its distance behind the bridge nor for the distance it would be blown back at the base.

It would have to do, he decided. The explosion's roar was still echoing from the shore, and lights began coming on all over the place. The guards on the picket boats rushed on deck, as he'd hoped. He stood up and opened up on the nearest one, cutting him down, then leaped to the roof of the ship's superstructure and continued firing at every moving creature he could see on the ships. The right and wrong of killing the men had never entered his mind. These were mobsters, anyway.

One guard had a chance to get back to cover and opened up on him. The bullets struck him and whirled him around; they didn't hurt, but they knocked him off his feet and made him drop his own gun. He lay there a moment, then crawled carefully forward to the weapon and grabbed onto it.

There were shouts from shore now, and from the target boat came a call: "What's happening out there? What's going on?" It was a woman's voice.

The guard who'd cut him down naturally assumed he was dead, and after checking to see if anyone else was lurking about, he stood up and peered at the other ship, trying to get a make on his attacker.

He was the only one left. Mac jumped up, shooting, and cut him down. The guard carried a look of absolute disbelief to his death.

Realizing that help would be on the way at any moment, Mac Walters knew he had little time to spare. He looked at the mast, cockeyed from his position to about a meter from the target boat, and changed into a bat. He hadn't the strength to fly the distance, and there were better shapes for this that he couldn't master; but being a bat made him an almost invisible target, and its legs provided perfect if slow traction. Furthermore, the bat also had a perfect sense of balance and position.

He made it faster than he'd thought possible. Confused reinforcements were still getting into boats on the shore by the time he reached the closest point of mast to target. He knew what he needed now and changed into a great gray wolf. Taking only seconds to figure angle and get a footing, he leaped for the low rail of the target ship's lower deck and barely cleared the rails.

A woman screamed. He immediately changed back to himself and ran inside the nearest door. Two stunningly beautiful but fully capable women stood there, both holding submachine guns on him.

"All right, bud, hold it right there," one, a redhead, snapped at him.

"Yeah, or we'll cut you down and don't think we won't," chimed in the blond.

He had no doubt that they would, but time was running out. He made eye contact with the redhead, got it, and forced through his mental orders without the other woman even realizing it.

He turned to the blond. "Put down your gun," he ordered quietly, trying to control his excitement and nervousness. She looked puzzled, then, following his gesture, saw that the redhead was now pointing her weapon at her.

To her credit she didn't drop her gun but turned back to him. "What kind of magic . . . ?" She started, looking him determinedly in the eye.

That was a mistake. Wishing he had time to take one of their minds and learn more about the ship, he walked past them. They would continue to stand guard; he wouldn't like to be the next person who tried to get through there.

There were a lot of people on this ship. A white-clad black man who might have been the chef or steward poked his head out of a cabin door as Mac stalked imperiously down a corridor, and then reached out to grab him. It did little good; the strength of a vampire is beyond mortal men, and the man was rudely tossed back into his cabin and slammed against the bulkhead.

Mac found a stairway, tossed two ordinary and frightened-looking men down it with a grab and a pull by each arm, and went up a deck. If this one followed the pattern, the main room should be amidships on this deck.

It was. It was also decked out like a sultan's palace —incredibly ornate, almost overdone in its luxury. If this was Theritus's prison, O'Malley had made it a very comfortable one.

"Theritus! Demon! Are you here?" he shouted loudly.

A woman with a pistol appeared at the far end, braced herself, and fired a full volley of shots at him. He flinched when they hit him but stood his ground and stormed toward her. She tried to turn and run, but he was too fast. He caught her, turned her around, and looked fiercely into her frightened eyes.

"Where is the demon?" he thundered. "You will tell me!"

"Ca—captain's cabin," she managed.

"You will take me!" He held her so that she presented something of a shield, hoping they wouldn't fire for fear of hitting her. These constant attacks on him were slowing him up.

There wasn't a great distance to go, though, and they encountered no more trouble. She pointed toward an oaken door forward, just underneath the bridge. "He is in there," she told him.

He had no doubt that she was telling the truth; he held her at least tenuously in his hypnotic grip. He turned her again and looked deeply into her eyes.

"You will find a weapon and you will allow no one to disturb us," he commanded.

There was no questioning. "Yes, Master," she responded and walked off.

He approached the door and decided not to stand on ceremony. He grabbed the handle and pulled it open with such force that it came right off its hinges, the lock flying.

It was a truly luxurious cabin, too, and on its heart-shaped bed sat the demon, wearing a nightshirt, holding an unclad woman in each arm. The women looked terrified; the demon looked puzzled.

"What is the meaning of this?" Theritus hissed, not in the least intimidated.

"I'm from Asmodeus Mogart," Mac told him. "His life and my world are threatened. We need your jewel to save it. I'm here to get it!"

Theritus laughed. It sounded more like the barking of a small dog. "And what makes you think, bold sir, that I will hand it over?" he responded haughtily.

"It's all over and you know it," Mac pointed out. "It's been a good life up to now, but O'Malley's pledged your jewel to my partner for some dirty work he wants done. The feds will find this place now no matter what—the explosion and gunfire will guarantee it. Your good life's over."

"Then the cops will break the pentagram, freeing me," retorted the demon, who still hadn't let go of his bed companions. "They cannot hold me."

"That's why O'Malley will get your jewel to my partner," the vampire argued. "He's got nothing to lose. Give it to me now and save even more lives!" *Including mine,* Mac thought glumly.

The demon considered his words, sensing their truth. "There's no way O'Malley, even O'Malley, could get the jewel without my permission, unless . . ." His voice trailed off as he thought it over, talking more to himself than to Mac. "Unless he sends the shoggoths to kill me!" he shouted excitedly. He released his grip on the women and leaped over one to the floor. He looked genuinely frightened.

"You don't understand. O'Malley's master is the enemy of my people, of all people everywhere," he babbled, sounding and looking like a man becoming unhinged by nerves. "That's how he trapped me! If he sends the shoggoths—they'll be sent directly to this pentagram! I have to get out of here!"

Mac didn't understand him but knew he somehow had an advantage. "Okay, then—give me the jewel. You can't get out of here with it, but maybe if *I* wished us *both* out of here, it would work!"

The demon looked thunderstruck. "Of course! Of course! You aren't under his spell!" He turned, fumbled in a drawer, and took out a small jewel box. He walked toward the stranger, then hesitated.

"Once I give you this—you won't leave me?" he asked nervously.

"I give you my word," promised Mac.

The demon handed him the box. Mac tripped the catch and opened it, then unwrapped an object bound in layers of satin. Outside there were the yells and screams of many people, the sounds of a lot of running in his direction on the ship and around it, and the sounds of a lot of shots.

"Quickly! Touch my arm!" Mac ordered the demon, who did as instructed. Even so, he looked around at the women and the cabin. "Too bad," he murmured. "It was the best racket I've ever been in."

"Jewel! Take us to the gully near my hideout!" Mac ordered.

A gunman reached the door, saw the two of them, and turned his machine gun in their direction. The women on the bed screamed in terror and shouted, "No! No!"

Mac and Theritus vanished.

Theritus's goatlike feet were sinking in the mud. It was raining slightly near the culvert. He was still in shock of some kind, but he was thinking through it. He turned to the vampire.

"All right—hand me the jewel back now!" he ordered.

Mac Walters looked at him strangely. "Are you kidding? I told you *I* needed this."

"Give it back!" the demon screeched angrily and leaped at him. Mac easily sidestepped the lunge, and the creature went face down into the mud and lay there, unmoving.

For a moment Mac thought he'd killed him, or at least knocked him cold. He carefully pocketed the jewel and approached the mud-caked body. The rain had soaked the nightshirt clean through, leaving no doubt that Theritus had a tail.

The demon wasn't dead or out. He was crying, in fact. As Mac put a hand on him he looked up into the vampire's face. There was madness in the demon's own features, madness mixed with fear.

"Please!" he pleaded. "I beg you! Without that stone I am trapped here, unprotected, too close to the Ancient Ones. This is a thin area! Can't you understand that?"

Mac didn't, but he realized that there was pure terror in the demon now, something he'd never seen in the creatures before.

"You mean there's something here that can kill even you, no matter what," he said rather than asked.

The demon nodded. "Yes, yes—that's it exactly."

Mac Walters thought it over. Time! This was wasting so much time! An idea came to him.

"Theritus, could I drop you somewhere else, say a training level, and get back here?"

The frantic expression faded entirely and the demon looked thoughtful. "Why, yes, surely—if you know the right number to the levels."

Mac nodded. "Look, I left Abaddon in a training area. I think I can reach it and drop you. Now—how the hell do I get back to this one to pick up my partner?"

The demon brightened. Mac didn't know what the creature was scared of, but he was certain he didn't want to meet it.

"All right, all right—take me there! Anywhere! When you want to come back here, just tell the jewel to come to Main Line plus one thousand and seventy-six. That's here."

"One thousand and seventy-six," Mac repeated. "Okay—let's get out of this rain." He reached out and grabbed the demon's hand. "Take us to the training level now occupied by Abaddon but at least one kilometer from him!" he commanded. They both vanished again.

The training ground was the same gray nothingness he remembered it as being—and over there was the western town, still going.

Only now this barren land was populated. Heavily populated by all sorts of people, nonpeople, creatures, and demonic figures. A whole host of them.

The training ground did not change you. Mac was still a vampire, still dead—and as such, he could see the dead. He wanted out and fast.

And yet—how much time had this detour taken? He couldn't take a chance on its having been too long; dawn had been close by when he left.

"Jewel!" he commanded. "Take me to my coffin inside the culvert on level one thousand and seventy-six!"

He vanished.

As he traveled the gray spaces he began to wonder what could possibly frighten a demon, and nervously realized that he'd taken the creature's word for it that level one thousand and seventy-six was the right one. What if he'd been double-crossed? He worried—then appeared literally lying in his culvert hideaway. He'd bet right now all down the line. It *was* daylight out there—he could feel the lethargy overtaking him already.

Were it not for Jill, he'd return to Mogart immediately, but he couldn't leave her here, couldn't abandon her after what she'd done. Mogart had said that all the time lines on the levels they'd use were vastly speeded up and that the fastest ones were saved for last. He was confident he was in time.

He awoke at dusk but immediately realized that he couldn't put through his plan right away. He didn't know where Jill McCulloch was. Somewhere still in North America, that was certain—and surely not Alaska. Too far for the time. But he couldn't risk going to her yet. It was dusk in Chicago, but not out West, not yet. He'd have to give it two hours to be sure.

He also couldn't be certain what he'd run into there. He needed to renew his strength with blood first, and that would use up the time.

Finally it was seven-thirty in the evening, and he

decided to chance it. He removed the jewel and looked at it.

"Jewel—take me to Jill McCulloch!" he commanded, tensely waiting for the shift, ready to try to shout a countering command if he felt the sun's rays. He didn't. There was an afterglow beyond the mountains, but the sun itself had set.

She sat there on a large stone just outside a huge and ancient gate. She looked blank, as if everything within her was worn out, spent. Still, she radiated power—she looked different, greater, stronger, truly beautiful. Clearly somebody had worked a hell of a spell on her.

"Jill!" he shouted excitedly. "It's me—Mac! I got the jewel!" He held it up; it glowed like a living thing, pulsing in the twilight.

She looked up slowly, as if only seeming to hear him. Finally her eyes came to rest on the jewel.

"So you got it after all," she said lifelessly.

He was puzzled. "What's the matter?"

She gestured behind her with her head, and he walked up to the gate and looked out on the valley, the town, and the castle.

"Oh, my Lord!" was all he could say.

The carnage was absolute. They'd put up only token resistance, that was clear. There were a number of women's bodies around that obviously did not belong with the rest, but the kinship of the majority was evident.

Young men, old men, boys, girls, women young and old as well, even babies clutched in their arms. Spread out across the field, all dead, all of them.

Fires burned across the valley. A large force composed entirely of women was camped there, seeing to and checking out everything.

Jill was on her feet and at his side. "I gave them until dawn to clear out," she said woodenly. "When they didn't go, I gave them until noon. They still wouldn't go. They couldn't fight—they had only twenty rifles among them and a few old swords—and put up little resistance. That old man over there—he was the governor." She pointed to a body lying sprawled like a rag doll near the gate. "He met us at the gate. He looked up into my eyes as we rode in. And you know what he said to me? He said, 'We forgive you!' *We forgive you!*"

She was sobbing now, and sank back down for a moment. He let her be by herself as he tried to imagine what it had been like.

Suddenly she flared up at him. "Why couldn't you have gotten here sooner?" she almost screamed at him. "Why did you take so long?"

He hadn't known that a vampire could become sick to his stomach.

"Because I was afraid," he half whispered in reply. "Because I had thought so much of getting this jewel, had gone through so many close shaves, that I didn't think when I should have. Call me tired, call me stupid, anything you want—but blame me, Jill, not yourself."

She snorted in self-derision. "No, Mac. Thanks for trying, but I have to face it myself. I—I just couldn't trust you to get the jewel where I'd failed. I didn't think you could do it, and so I didn't wait for you. I should have remembered you could work only at night. I should have remembered that you got two of them yourself, as I did. I should have waited." She looked up at him again. "You got the jewel too late, didn't you? You had to get back to your grave or whatever. I understand."

He put his arm around her and pulled her to her feet. "We'll share the blame on this one," he said kindly. "I just didn't comprehend fully what they were making you do. You see, when I got back it was daylight. I didn't know how far into the day it was—but it might have been only a little bit. We're in the West, aren't we?"

"Somewhere near where Denver should be."

He nodded glumly. "So take your guilt and live with it, as I must. I should have gambled. I should have returned not to Chicago but to you, here, in the West, where it might not have been sunup yet."

She sighed. "We'll never know, will we? We'll just have to live with it."

He nodded again. "Want to go now? I think we'd better put a move on. If the deaths of these people are to make any sense at all, have any purpose at all, we must save our own world."

She hesitated a moment. "No, there's one more thing that has to be taken care of now. *Two* things." She turned and yelled toward the gate, "Sound assembly just inside the gate! I want everyone there except the medical people!"

Horns blew and were answered by other horns and by their echoes. The women of O'Malley's magically created force started to move toward them from all over the valley.

Mac was puzzled. "What . . . ?" was all he could manage.

She smiled bitterly. "We had completed our conquest by two this afternoon, canvassed and checked the last of the valley people by four. But I didn't immediately summon O'Malley to transfer the place and demand payment. Know why?"

He shook his head, completely confused.

"The spell on this place was firm: no man could pass that gate or its border so long as one born in the valley lived." She pointed back at the castle, almost invisible to her in the gathering darkness. "Up there was Constanza's headquarters, and the gateway for a monstrous evil, an alien intelligence that is the enemy of humanity on all levels," she told him. "O'Malley is a traitor to all of us. He serves the enemy. He was trying to open that gate, to let those alien horrors in, when he was fouled up. He was called away and, while away, was kept out by the spell. He expected to use me to get back to that gate, to open it, to unleash that alien power back into human levels where it could get all of us. He mustn't be allowed back. None of his kind must be allowed back."

Mac was still confused, although what she told him explained a little of Theritus's pure terror. "But I still don't see . . ." he began, but she cut him off.

"I called O'Malley just before you arrived," she told him. "I think he's coming now—see the torches and coaches? That's the whole Constanza party. Just lie back in the shadows and let me do what I have to do."

He was more confused than ever and felt more helpless. His sense of accomplishment, of victory, had been dashed by this massacre and the guilt it engendered. Now here he was, the object in his pocket, ready to go back and proclaim total victory—and he was a helpless bystander to events happening around him.

We've saved the world—our world! he told himself. *Then why do I suddenly feel like I've lost the game?*

O'Malley led the procession, a look of total satisfaction on his face. Constanza followed on a magnificent palomino, also looking well satisfied. Jill stood in the middle of the road, just meters from the ancient gate, and they halted in front of her.

"By right of conquest, I give this land to you," she told them. "All who inhabited it have been slain."

O'Malley nodded. "I'm aware of that. I have a peculiar—er—sensitivity to these people. There is no more life force of the Elder Gods present, only ordinary people, the ones you brought in with you. You have fulfilled your end of the bargain."

She smiled evilly at him, and something in her eyes shouted the hate and contempt she felt for him. "And now I will take my reward!" she responded.

O'Malley looked slightly puzzled and bemused. "Why, you've already got it!" he answered. "Your man, or whatever he is, got it last night! He's here, outside the gate—I sense his alien presence, and the presence of the jewel."

"But you didn't pay me with it—he took it!" Jill pointed out. "That was not our bargain!"

O'Malley suddenly seemed disturbed; Constanza's look of utter confusion matched Mac's in the shadows. Neither man knew what the hell was going on here, yet both had the feeling something very important was.

"The terms," she taunted the sorcerer. "Remember the terms? I'll quote them to you from memory. They were: 'You shall accept command of the forces that I shall place at your disposal; you shall lead them where I direct, and you shall besiege the Citadel that I designate. Not one human life shall you order spared; you shall order the death of all humans inside the compound, and you shall see that it is carried out. Once it is, you shall summon me by stating my name three times at the gates.' " She paused and stared up at him. "This I have done to the letter," she pointed out. "But that was only one side. You then said, 'If you do this, I will deliver unto you the jewel which you seek to use as you see fit.' That was the bargain. I have done my half. You must now do yours! I demand it!"

O'Malley now looked nervous, even frightened. He fumbled at his collar as if to loosen his tie, and sweat started beading up all along his forehead.

"Just wait a minute!" he protested. "You tricked me! You know what I meant!"

A grin was on her face now, but it held no humor, only satisfaction.

"A bargain is a bargain," she taunted. "How many bargains have you made and then welched on because of trickery or semantics, O'Malley? Hundreds, I'll bet. Maybe thousands! When you make a compact with the devil, you had better beware the fine print!"

Mac looked at the sorcerer, his first real look at him in person. There was real fear there, the same kind of abject terror he'd seen on the face of Theritus.

"Fulfill your bargain or forfeit!" Jill McCulloch demanded.

"I can't! You know that, you bitch!" shrieked the sorcerer. "Let me go! Anything! I'll give you anything! Anything you want! Name it! You are already a goddess—I'll make you Queen of the world! Name it! Limitless power! Yours!" He was babbling incoherently now, frantic, and suddenly he looked up into the darkness, up and around, as if seeing hundreds of dark and shapeless horrors all around him.

And there *was* something there. The horses stirred nervously, and the air seemed to thicken into something solid, something indefinable and yet a *presence,* an alien presence they could all feel rather than see.

Mac strained in the darkness, trying to see with his perfect night vision what the wizard saw, but there was nothing—just true living blackness, impenetrable even to his vampire's sight.

"I want you to present me with the jewel!" Jill screamed at O'Malley. "Fulfill or forfeit! I demand my payment *now!*"

There *were* shapes there, Mac was sure of it. Shapes of—what? He strained, but all he could make out was vagueness, hundreds of bubblelike shapes that wouldn't stay in focus long enough for him to determine what they really represented.

Constanza had moved back, far away from the sorcerer, as had the whole party.

And now came the voices from the blackness, a weird, alien piping sound that could not be made by anything in their experience. Hundreds—no, thousands—of piping alien things all crying out, *"Tekeli-li! Tekeli-li!"*

They closed in on O'Malley, who still sat atop his saddle, paralyzed by a fear greater than any that the watchers had ever seen or known.

The dark shapes closed in on him as he stared in horror, shouting, "No! No! Master! *Iä! Iä! Yog-Sothoth!* Protect thy servant! Oh, no! *Please! No!* Must thy honor cost your faithful servant? *No! Please!*"

The shapes touched him; even his horse seemed frozen, a statue. A blue light suddenly surrounded both man and horse; they seemed to turn into a negative image, like that of a photograph, then wink out.

It was over. The blackness receded; the weird, mocking, alien calls withdrew into whatever place between the worlds they dwelt, and all was suddenly quiet. Of horse and rider there remained only a foul putrescence in the center of the road, nothing more.

Everyone was speechless for a moment, all frozen by the drama. All but Jill. She relaxed, and there was a look of almost total satisfaction on her face, a look that seemed to say, *Well, all right, many good people have died this day, yet their deaths have rid the world of a foul and terrible threat. They counted. Their deaths mean something now.*

Mac understood at last, yet his confusion remained.

She could not have known he had the jewel until he'd arrived—yet she had already called O'Malley. This was the frosting on the cake. Jill still had to serve the cake.

Constanza, to his own credit, was the first to recover. He let out a low breath and whistled. "I never trusted that bastard, anyway," he said calmly. He looked down from his horse at Jill, still standing defiantly in the road. "Looks like we both win," he said pleasantly, almost cheerfully. "I get my lands back and safety and am rid of a most dangerous man—and you have your precious jewel."

"We have both lost," she responded with equal calmness but no cheer. "I have done something to a good and gentle people that will haunt me. And you shall not regain your lands."

His pleasant, self-satisfied expression faded into stony anger. "Do you think you can stop me?" he asked haughtily. "My people are already here, having arrived in the last couple of days. I have an *army* here, a trained army, with all that that implies. Your women were good enough for these farmers"—he almost spit the last word—"but against five hundred good, experienced men with machine guns? Don't make me laugh. Stand aside."

Jill's smile of contentment did not disappear. "I will stand aside, man, and none of my force shall molest you or yours in any way." She walked back down the road, passing Mac against the gate, still hidden from general view in the shadows. "Stay here and keep out of sight!" she hissed. "I'll join you in a minute!"

He shrugged and sighed. He *still* didn't understand what was going on.

Constanza moved forward, his horse skirting the foulness that still remained in the road. Behind him his forces began their descent. He reined up at the outer gate, only meters from the hidden Mac Walters, and dismounted. He was going to do this right—he was going to enter the gates as a conqueror and lord.

He walked up to the opening in the gate and took a step forward.

There was nothing there, yet it was as if he'd struck

a barrier of plate glass. He frowned and tried to force his way in. That didn't work. He took out his pistol and beat upon the opening. It gave off no sound, yet it was solid as a rock.

He was furious. "What have you done, you bitch!" he snarled. "I don't know what the hell you're trying to pull, but it won't work! I heard you turn over the lands, and I know they're all dead or O'Malley wouldn't have had'ta die. *What did you do?*"

She smiled, facing him just a few meters inside the gate. "Listen well," she told him. "You would have heard it before had we not all been making so much noise. Listen now in the silence of the dead and hear!"

Confused, angry, frustrated, Constanza listened, as did all the others. At first he heard nothing, nothing but the residual noise of the gentle wind through the mountains and the fires of the camp and the torches of his own party. But dimly, through the residual level, he heard it. Heard it and understood.

It was a baby's cry.

"Hear it, Constanza?" she asked him, that satisfied tone still in her voice. "You needed an army of women. One thing about them—they sometimes get together with men and have babies, Constanza. We found her along the march—about to give birth and alone. We waited and prayed that she would *not* give birth early, and then we waited some more after the battle until the child was born. A man-child, Constanza. I filled my end of the bargain to the letter. I killed all within the Citadel. But afterward, yes, afterward, I brought in my own. The spell is renewed. He lives and cries out his life. Begone, Constanza. There is no opening for you here, no place to hide. Your armies cannot pass, and you have no O'Malley to raise another. Begone! To exile, which you do not deserve, or to prison, which you most surely do. Exile is far too lenient for you."

Constanza accepted defeat and stepped back from the barrier no one could see. He fingered his pistol, then aimed it through the gate, at her, and fired before Mac could even act.

Nothing happened to her. She stood there and laughed at him.

He fired again and again and again, frantically, until he was out of bullets. Then he just stood there, dumbfounded.

"It's not that easy, Constanza," she called to him. "If it were, you could have reconquered this land with sharpshooters. The spell is renewed. No man may enter or cause harm to this place. Not even you."

The mobster stood there a moment, just staring through the gate at her in concentrated fury. Then, suddenly, his fury was spent. He holstered his pistol, turned, and walked back to his horse, mounting quickly.

He rode up to his forces, past the wagons, past the men, back over the mountain and into the night. His forces hesitated a moment, then turned and followed him.

Jill walked back to her own troops assembled inside as she had ordered. "Listen well to me," she commanded. "I must leave you now, for a time. I must go to save my world. This is *your* land now, and no man can take it from you. You are here because you did not fit into the societies that men had made for you. Now you may make your own. Create your own land here. Nurture it, protect it, love it as the people we have killed loved it. Make something new and wonderful here— if you can, if you dare! Go from this place for a time if you will, *but have your children here!* It is yours now! I free you from any spells placed upon you, but I challenge you!" She hesitated a moment, sensing something.

These women, bound by spell, had been silent, almost automatons to her wishes, and they had killed this day as such, without emotion, with no objective other than to carry out the orders of their Queen.

Many were weeping now.

"Farewell," she concluded, feeling a lump in her throat. "Others need me." She turned and walked down the road, out past the ancient gate, to Mac and the jewel. She didn't look back once, but *he* did—they were all still standing there, still at attention, but more of them were weeping.

Jill was weeping, too, and he tried to comfort her. He took her hand. "Let's go home," he said gently, and pulled the jewel out of his pocket with his other hand.

"Take us both to Asmodeus Mogart!" he commanded.

The world vanished.

Main Line +2076

MAC WALTERS COULDN'T HELP BUT GLANCE OUT THE front door of the bar. He opened it a crack, and a whirlwind of tremendous force almost tore it from his hands. He pulled it shut with great effort. The glance had been a quick one, but it was all he needed to see.

"Jesus!" was all he could manage. "I think we're too late! The world's already ended out there!"

Jill McCulloch looked around anxiously for Asmodeus Mogart. The strange little man was nowhere to be seen, nor were any of the other patrons of the bar or the barman, either.

The two of them looked exactly as they had when they'd entered the bar only a few hours before, objective time.

"I wonder if you're right," she replied grimly. "I don't see Mogart or anybody else anywhere."

Mac shook his head. "He's here someplace. Only the five jewels have kept this place standing at all. If *they're* here, then so is he."

They started searching the nooks and crannies. Jill finally walked around the bar and stopped short.

"Mac! Here he is! Oh, my God!"

Walters bounded over the top of the bar in an instant. Mogart lay face down on the floor, stark naked, his goatlike tail sticking almost straight up in the air.

"Is he dead?" Jill asked worriedly, afraid to confirm her worst fears herself.

Walters knelt down by the demon and gently tried to turn him over. Mogart groaned and issued a loud snore.

Mac Walters grunted. "Damn! Out cold! Stinko! Look—he's still clutching a fifth of Scotch!"

Jill spied the ice-water tap and hastily filled a pitcher usually used for mixing drinks. "We've got to wake him up!" she exclaimed almost hysterically. Seeing the water start to overflow the pitcher, she shut off the tap, aimed the container at Mogart, and turned it upside down over the little man's head.

Mogart reacted. He shivered uncomfortably and gave a shrill, high-pitched snort of annoyance, but he didn't wake up.

Walters grabbed him.

"Mogart! Come on, you bastard! Wake up!" Mac screamed into the little man's face, then shook the frail-looking body violently.

The demon seemed to come out of it, slowly, groggily, and just barely. His eyes opened halfway, revealing pupils wandering off in different directions, and he murmured something unintelligible—and sank back again to the floor.

"More water!" Mac called frantically to Jill, and she hastily filled another pitcher. He took it from her hands and poured it slowly over the little man's head while continuing the shaking motions. Both of the humans were screaming now for Asmodeus Mogart to wake up.

Oh, dear God! No! Jill kept thinking even as she yelled. *He's got to wake up! After all we've just been through!*

Walters slapped the demon a few times in the face, trying to jar him awake. Mogart stirred again, the tail drooped, and he opened his dazed eyes and looked around. He seemed to be having a great deal of trouble focusing on anything.

For the first time, Jill noticed the number of empty

whiskey bottles behind the bar. She could count a dozen at least without even trying. Enough to kill any normal human being. The term "alcoholic" was far too mild to describe Asmodeus Mogart.

"More water!" Mac commanded, and she again filled the pitcher. "I think his eyes are staying open!"

She almost dropped the pitcher in her anxiety. An impossibly violent gust of wind shook the whole building—or was it the wind? It sounded and felt as if the very Earth were crumbling around them.

Again Mac poured the water, and this time Mogart knew what was happening. He screamed and tried to knock away the pitcher.

"Enough! Enough!" he screamed at them in that high-pitched whine. "Begone, foul fiends! Water shall not touch these lips unless well diluted with Scotch!"

"Mogart!" Walters yelled at him, almost nose to nose. "It's us! We have the fifth jewel, Mogart! We have the fifth jewel! You have to save the world!"

A tiny light dawned in his brain. "Oh, yesh, yesh. Da crash. Gotta shtop the crash. Crishy, crashy, crunchy," he sang. "But firsht I gotta shleep," he announced. His eyelids closed, and he tried to turn over.

Jill was ahead of him, pouring more water on his head. Their actions seemed to infuriate him, and his manner changed. His eyes opened wide and glared at her menacingly. "Oh, foul bearer of that putrid liquid," he screamed hoarsely, "I shall turn you into a toad for that!"

He reached over to a shelf behind the bar, knocking a few of the glasses onto the floor, where they shattered with a crash that seemed to please him. He liked the sound so much, in fact, that he started knocking over all the other glasses as well. Then, reaching back, he pulled out one of the jewels—then a second, third, fourth, and a fifth.

He stared at them in fascination, then looked up angrily, facing his tormentors. He tried to stand, but it was too much for him.

Mac turned to Jill anxiously. "Where's the damned jewel? We have to show it to him!"

She started for a minute, then responded, *"You've got it! I never even saw it!"*

He looked momentarily sheepish, then reached into a pocket where he had slipped the thing after rematerializing in the bar.

Mogart saw it, and his jaw dropped. He stared down at the others in his hands and counted, "One . . . two . . . three . . . four . . . five! Five and one makesh shix!" He looked up at Mac, a look of childish anticipation on his face. "Gimme!"

Nervously, Mac Walters handed the demon the sixth jewel. He was not too thrilled by the prospect, though, since he'd been told what six could do—and Mogart was in no condition to do anything right.

The demon stared at his palm full of glowing, throbbing gems for a moment, as if deep in thought. Then he cupped both his hands and let the jewels tumble between them. Abruptly this stopped, and he cupped his hands together and pressed hard, so hard that the effort was obvious in his face. Smoke issued from his closed, joined hands, and Jill and Mac heard a slight hissing sound. Whatever he was doing was obviously painful, as his facial expression and jerky movements indicated, but Mogart didn't seem to mind. A change was coming over him, and the man and woman stepped back, watching the demon in growing wonder.

There was a smile on his face, one of almost inconceivable rapture. He seemed to be growing in stature, to be filling out, becoming the potential of his body in full. The transformation was astonishing. He was no longer a thin and broken drunk but a creature of tremendous power, the image of the devil at his most fearsome.

Suddenly Mogart relaxed and walked out from behind the bar, now in full command of his body and mind. The smile was no longer one of rapture but the look of total satisfaction, of one who has power and the ability to use it. He glanced around, ignoring the two humans, then slowly and deliberately walked around the far end of the bar and over to the door. Each second his metamorphosis became more pronounced; a tiny man before, he was now more than two meters high. A weak, frail man before, his chest was now massive, his arms bulging with muscles. Veins and sinews rippled with each slow movement. His skin had taken on a light bluish cast, and below his waist thick, curly black hair was now covering him like a coarse pair of fur pants. His legs were even more animalistic than they had been, somewhat goatlike yet thick and sturdy, terminating in great cloven hooves. His tail, extended now, whiplike, terminated in a triangular membrane that looked something like a cobra's hood.

"Mogart!" Jill called to him. "The planetoid! You must stop the collision!"

The strange being who only moments before had been a helpless, pitiful drunk turned slowly to face them. Great eyes seemed to blaze with a strange red-black fire; his nose was flatter, his teeth animal-like and those of a carnivore when he smiled at them. He looked at them as if they were some kind of trained animals, not real people at all.

Neither Mac nor Jill could help remembering the warnings they had received from the other demons, that Mogart was not at all what he seemed and would be dangerous beyond their wildest dreams given all the jewels. Mac gripped Jill's hand tightly, and both had the same thought, the same questions: *What have we done? Have we done right?*

"I am not unmindful of the problem of the satellite," he told them in a voice at least two octaves lower than the old Mogart's. "I have been considering how to deal with it." He held up the object in his hands formed by the fusion of the six gems—a perfect larger gem, blazing with that living fire around the edges and shimmering blue-black along its facets.

"Behold the Eye of Baal," he intoned, looking down at it with a mixture of wonder and excitement. "It has been long, far too long, since I have seen one, let alone possessed one."

"You lied to us!" Jill accused him. "You never cared about this world! You just needed somebody to do your dirty work for you!"

He grinned evilly. "Clever one, aren't you? Yes, this is what it is all about, but I think you have yet to perceive the fullness of my genius. Many times through the millennia I have tried to secure an Eye of Baal to replace the one taken from me so long ago. They said I was misusing the power, establishing myself as a self-indulgent god. As if—as if constructs, mere creations of a fertile imagination, artificial creatures formed by superior intelligence and science, had some sort of rights! In the past I failed. Security was too good. It was too easy for them to spot me, and when I sent others they were incompetent. What my envoys lacked, I decided, was motivation. When they had to face the problems, worlds, and creatures you faced, they were working for me, not for themselves, and the difficulties sapped their will to carry out the job." His grin widened.

"Do you think," he continued, "that it was just a coincidence that the two of you were here, in this spot, when you were needed? Did you think you accomplished what you did without help, without training? I planned for years for this! Years! Ever since I detected the gravitational imbalances almost twenty years ago. I picked people, many people, to be my agents. They didn't know it, of course. Using what powers I had, I endowed them with superb bodies and even better minds. Thoughts and motivations planted in their parents', teachers', and all other close-contact people's brains shaped and molded their interests, their personalities, so they would be the people *best* equipped to succeed in the Alternatives. There were thousands of such people, *not just the two of you!*"

Mogart paused, enjoying the delicious shock on their faces, then continued. He was thoroughly delighting in this.

"Such activities took a lot out of me. The jewel and its powers have very definite limits; as hard as it is for you to comprehend, there *are* immutable natural laws applicable to all the universes. What it took out of me left me that pitiful, drunken weakling you saw. Almost too much. The story I told you about being on a drunk for key weeks when I should have been gathering and sending out my agents was true. *All* of it was true, except why I was exiled here. It wasn't for alcoholism, but for what they termed incurable megalomania." He shrugged. "They were probably right. It didn't matter to them. I resisted treatment because megalomania is such a wonderful thing to have. This *is* a working universe—projects go on here. But Earth was just a byproduct of the forces set in motion. As I think I told you, there are no real ongoing projects closer than the Andromeda galaxy. I was safely out of the way. And I accepted exile, since the alternative was a brainwipe, the destruction of my entire personality and memory. I would still be here, a prisoner, had not a number of fortuitous events coincided."

"The asteroid," Jill breathed.

He nodded. "Getting the idea into the right people's heads to try and hold it captive was a problem—the project was so costly! Then it was discovered that the asteroid really *did* contain riches, and the way was cleared. Just as important a factor was that this event should not come about until there was adequate technology to implement the plan. After that the pride and greed that are reflections of me in your race took over."

"You're God?" Mac Walters gasped.

"Of course not, you idiot!" Jill almost hissed at him. "God's a University Department back on the Main Line. He's the *other* one!"

Mogart almost blushed and bowed politely. "At your service," he said mockingly. "Satan, Beelzebub, Old Scratch, Asmodeus—whatever's your pleasure." He grinned. "Megalomania is such a *wonderful* illness!"

"So the jewels, even individually, have a lot more power than you let on," Mac pressed. "I remember now Abaddon's demonic show and his comment that he ran cults on hundreds of worlds with just his jewel. I should have figured it out then."

"Don't feel too bad," Mogart replied. "After all, you had time running out and more pressing puzzles to solve. And don't feel bad about giving me the Eye. After all, there *was* a danger, and only one solution. You had no choice."

"So now what?" Mac asked him. It was a legitimate question.

Mogart gestured with his now-imposing satanic head at the strange product of fusion he held in his right hand. "See that? An Eye of Baal, it's called. The single jewel, as you've now seen, is very powerful. Six of them in close proximity give a minimum of ten to the sixth power output of one. But the fusion is more economical, thus giving me ten to the tenth amplification—roughly ten billion times as much power as one. An Eye can deal with almost anything. It's the power of pure applied thought. Matter to energy, energy to matter, on any scale you want, and by tapping the central Main Line computers, you don't even have to know the composition or formulae. Just think of what you want and you've got it. Only ten of these are needed to create a new Alternative level. Come outside with me! I'll show you!"

The bar still felt as if it were going to be ripped apart, and Mac and Jill watched nervously as the demon reached over and pulled the door right off its hinges, flinging it to one side like a matchstick.

The scene outside was one of utter desolation. The whole city looked as if it had been the victim of some ancient war; buildings that remained standing at all were mere shells; I-80 was down and twisted, the casino and motel signs were long smashed to dust. An evil-smelling wind blew dust and dirt around in swirling maelstroms; there were cracks in the Earth, faults large enough to swallow whole buildings, and it was cold as hell.

It was daylight, but the stars were out, at least the nearest ones. The sky was a deep, dark blue, as it would be during a total eclipse. Mogart stepped into the street confidently and they followed hesitantly, realizing that safety lay only with Mogart. With the jewel gone, the bar, too, would fall victim to the holocaust.

They were almost blown over by the howling winds, and bitter cold ate into them. The very mountains all around them seemed to be trembling.

Jill grabbed Mac's arm for support, coughing, and

managed to look up. The sky—almost a third of it— was filled with a monstrous object hurtling down upon them, cold and black as the deepest night.

Mogart stopped and turned toward the looming specter in the sky, his dark form itself almost as eerie against the bleak ruins of the city of Reno.

But the Eye of Baal shone brightly in his hand. He put both arms out in front of him, tightly clenching his hands together over the Eye, which nonetheless radiated from every visible break in his grip.

Then, raising his arms high as if in supplication to the dark god overhead, staring directly at the great object, he intoned in a voice like thunder, cutting through the pounding wind, commanding the object: *"BEGONE!"*

And it was.

Suddenly the sky was bright; the sun was up there in its normal position for midday, there were no stars visible, and the wind and most of the tremors in the Earth had ceased. It was still bitterly cold, but already they could feel warmth starting once again to bathe the Earth from its mother the sun.

Mogart lowered his arms and turned to them with satisfaction. "See? Minor problems can be dealt with quickly."

"Yeah, but now what?" Mac asked glumly. "Some world you've just saved. Probably only a handful of people left alive—maybe just us. Everything in ruins. You say you prepped hundreds, maybe thousands, of people for the job. Yet when you called, only the two of us showed up. Maybe only the two of us were *able* to show up. That doesn't say much for the rest of humanity."

Mogart nodded agreement. "Yes, I believe there are only a few left, and probably most of these are still on the night side. But that's all right, you see. It is good that the old civilizations are swept away. Now something new can be built, to *my* specifications, in *my* image." That last was said in a tone of smug menace that sent chills through both of them.

The demon turned again, facing the desolation, the hulking shapes of former buildings and the wreckage

of smashed signs. As he looked again at the Eye of
Baal in his right palm, there came a sudden rumble
like a small earthquake. They watched as the ruins in
front of them shimmered, then faded to nothingness,
leaving only a barren plain against the still, unmoving
mountains.

Then there came another sound, like that of a far-
off Chinese gong, and out of the plain a single huge
building arose—a massive fortress gleaming golden in
the restored sunlight, ten stories high at the very minimum. Through the open golden doors to the main hall
they could see a great throne encrusted in precious
gems, adorned with red satin and ermine trim.

Jill McCulloch looked sharply at Mac Walters. "How
much longer do you think you can stand all this bull-
shit?" she asked disgustedly.

"About another second and a half," he replied in the
same tone, feeling the same frustration she was feeling,
thinking of the experiences they had undergone to
bring this petty lunatic to power. The awe was gone,
and fear simply didn't fit the unreality of the situation.

They were angry, and perhaps more than a little
mad themselves.

Mogart walked close to the great palace, studying it
with admiration, chuckling to himself in confident
satisfaction.

Jill moved to Mogart's left. Mac found he had been
standing on a large, partially broken two-by-four that
had been unaffected by the land transformation because it was part of the landscape *behind* Mogart, to
which the demon had not yet paid attention. Mac
reached down and picked up the board, then walked
to Mogart's right.

The demon was oblivious to them. He had totally
forgotten anyone else was there in his ecstasy over
achieving absolute power.

Jill waited until Mac seemed to be in position and
gave her a slight nod. Then, glancing around, she found
a large gray rock and tested its heft; there was a look
of determination on her face.

"Okay, Mogart, this has gone far enough!" Jill yelled
at the demon, and tossed the rock as hard as she could

at his head. It struck him a glancing blow on the left arm, but his expression showed fury and his eyes blazed with contempt as he whirled to face her.

"So!" he snarled. "What is a little earthworm to *me?*" He lifted up the Eye of Baal, and she felt real panic.

Mac made his move, running up on Mogart and swatting the creature's outstretched right hand. The board struck with every ounce of power Mac could muster. Mogart was taken completely off guard; he cried out in fury and surprise, and as he jerked from the blow, the Eye of Baal slipped from his hand and hit the ground, bouncing several times and then rolling to a stop.

Mogart was so furious that he hardly noticed, whirling instead to face his new attacker. He grabbed Mac by his left arm and pulled the human to him violently. Mac was simply outclassed in the muscle department no matter how hard he struggled.

Jill didn't wait to see the great, gnarled blue hands close on the man's throat; she dived for the Eye of Baal and scooped it up into her hands. Something like a great electric shock coursed through her as she gripped the thing. She felt the same enormous, almost limitless power potential that Mogart had experienced flow to every cell of her being. In a way it felt something like that experience in the pentagram with O'Malley, but this was of an incalculable magnitude stronger, power beyond belief and beyond full comprehension. The world seemed to slow. She turned to the two who were fighting—the huge creature and the man, locked in a slow-motion death grip.

She wondered how the hell to work the damned thing.

Mogart had just seemed to wish something and it had been so, the rational corner of her brain whispered to her. She looked at the two men and projected the thought with all her mental might that the two would be repelled from each other.

Nothing happened.

For a moment she couldn't understand why. The power *was* there, and it *could* be tapped; she knew it, felt it pulsing within her from the great fused jewel.

Mogart abruptly realized that he no longer held the Eye. He flung Walters away from him and turned, snarling, advancing on Jill.

Mac groaned and coughed, then looked up to see what was going on. Instantly he sensed she was trying to work the thing and couldn't—and he also guessed why.

"Jill! Look at the jewel, not Mogart!" he managed to cry out in a voice still hoarse from the creature's death grip on his throat.

Her momentary panic subsided as she realized what he meant. It took all her willpower, particularly with the demon only a few paces in front of her and coming on strong, to look away from the charging apparition and at the Eye. She managed, picturing in her mind a simple concept. She felt no sensation, no release, nothing, and braced herself for what could only be the inevitable strong grasp.

"Jill?" She jumped, almost screaming in panic. She stepped back involuntarily and looked away from the jewel.

It was Mac.

It took a few seconds longer for that to sink in. Then, still in some shock, she looked around in all directions.

The great palace was still there, but not Asmodeus Mogart.

Everything drained out of her, and she sat down in the dirt. Mac sighed, understanding, and sat down beside her.

"I—I just wished he'd go away," she told him, "and I guess he did."

Mac nodded. "I don't know where he went, but I'll tell you he just winked out—one moment he's running for you and the next, gone. *Pffft!*"

She suddenly looked up, eyes still dull. "No, I—I think I *do* know where he went. I think I told him to go to Hell."

He considered this. "Hmmm . . . I doubt if you can make an Alternative, even with *that,*" he thought aloud. "So—well, I would say you'd better proclaim a Heaven, too. There's a Hell now even if there wasn't one before. And since he's the devil himself, I don't think we've seen the last of him."

She thought about that and laughed, slowly at first, then in roaring peals. She couldn't stop for several minutes, and tears rolled down her cheeks. Finally, she sighed and lay back on the dirt.

Mac looked at the Eye of Baal, still clutched in her right hand. He pointed to it. "May I see it?" he asked curiously.

Suddenly emotion shot back through her, irrational and strange. "No!" she snapped and quickly stood up, clutching the Eye to her and backing away from him.

He stared at her in amazement. "Oh, come on," was all he could manage.

She was looking at him strangely, as if seeing him for the first time. There was a glint of something not quite right in her expression. Her mouth was slightly open as if she, too, were sensing the changes inside her in wonder. Behind her eyes a mental battle seemed to be going on. Finally she appeared to come to a decision and looked again at the jewel.

He watched, a sickening sensation in his stomach, as she began to undergo a transformation, changing, growing, glowing.

She became, once again, the Queen of Darkness—and more besides. She was Venus, and Aphrodite, and the Queen of the Amazons all rolled up into one. She was a true goddess, radiating and reflecting all the power, awe, and mystery that those imagined deities supposedly possessed.

Mac Walters felt all the primal feelings of the ancients rise within him, all those emotions associated with the presence of a goddess: awe, wonder, fear, worship, and yes, love, too. He felt himself kneeling, then prostrating himself before Her, the supreme, the sublime being who was, in fact, the center of his creation.

And yet something of his modern rational self remained, and deep within a fading corner of rationality there came the thought, unbidden but deeply felt, that said, *Oh, no! Not again!*

The Goddess, sole ruler and Supreme Being of the

ravaged Earth, looked down in satisfaction at Her supplicant. The feeling was tremendous, exhilarating in ways She had never known before. The sight of worship, even by one lone worshipper, fed and nurtured Her heady feelings of omnipotence. She understood now what Mogart had been feeling, what he had striven for and so briefly attained, why he had felt as he'd felt and done what he'd done.

Megalomania was, in fact, a wonderful disease, at least it was when the sufferer really attained the power to match the mentality. Or was it the other way around? *Did* absolute power corrupt absolutely? Was that why so many of the demons were forever imprisoned, kept away from the Main Line and prevented by special safeguards from stealing other jewels? Were those whom she had seen imprisoned in their worlds because they had been so tainted with the disease they couldn't be allowed home?

She put such thoughts from Her mind. *This* was Her home, and *here* was where She had the power.

She turned and looked at Mogart's castle. *So crude,* She thought. *So common. Gods should have no need of fortresses; they lived in beauty.*

Working the Eye of Baal, She altered the structure. Great Grecian columns, sparkling fountains, marbled walkways, and inviting pools dripping with flowers appeared everywhere. Again She felt the headiness of the Eye; to think it was to have it.

She turned back to Walters for a moment. *No use making Mogart's mistake,* She told herself. She walked slowly, majestically, forward, trying to decide what to do with him. *Replace his memories,* She decided, *so that he would never even know, guess, or doubt the power of the Goddess.* She was already making plans. A perfect world, an extension of that valley all over the Earth, happiness, kindness, no want or fear, all presided over by Her, of course. A perfect world, where the mistakes of the past would not be made.

So deeply was She thinking of this new world She was going to create, She failed to see the board with which Mac had struck Mogart. She stepped on it, and it flew out from under Her, as did Her feet.

Her Supreme Holiness, Goddess of the Earth Jill McCulloch, fell flat on Her magnificent fanny.

Mac heard her cry out as she slipped and chanced a look up. She fell hard on her left side, with no chance to break her fall or time to get herself out of it by way of the Eye. The great jewel came loose from her right hand when she opened the hand to try to cushion the fall. As she hit the ground, the jewel rolled almost in front of him.

Incredulous, he picked it up. She realized what had happened almost immediately and jumped quickly to her feet. Mac, fighting back those still-present primal emotions, looked at the glowing orb and thought: *You have no desire for the Eye of Baal. You want me to have it.*

She stopped, looking momentarily confused. In that same moment Mac Walters started feeling what first Mogart and then Jill McCulloch had felt when gripping the Eye of Baal—the sense of stored-up energy, of near limitless power and potential now within him.

He stared hard at her. She was still as incredibly beautiful as she had made herself, and he still felt strong emotions for her.

A queen! he thought triumphantly. *A queen fit for such as I!*

Slowly his shape also changed. He was still himself, but all had been made perfection—the Grecian ideal of manhood. She was awed in spite of herself.

He smiled, seeing in her face that the transformation was perfect. He turned to the Grecian palace she had built. It would do, he decided. Grand and glorious, a seat of ultimate power.

"What will you do now?" she asked in a voice as beautiful and wondrous as her appearance.

He thought a moment. "We shall remake the world, you and I!" he almost shouted in anticipation. "We shall remake it into something better than it was! And while we reign, the people of Earth shall know no want or fear, for we have learned so much and undergone so much that it is only just that we should determine the new way of the world!"

She joined Him, stood beside Him, and together they looked at the glorious palace.

"Where do we begin?" she asked him, sharing his vision.

"At the beginning, probably, which is the first step amateurs face in their attempts to muck things up," came a strange voice behind them.

They whirled and saw that they were no longer alone. Nine creatures stood upon the plain, huge and imposing. All looked much like Mogart had looked when he'd possessed the Eye of Baal—imposing, powerful, like something out of a primal mythos. But there was something else there, too, that had been absent in Mogart: a sense of tremendous dignity and quiet wisdom.

Each wore a great golden chain around his neck, and hanging from each chain was an Eye of Baal.

Five were male, four female, although there was no appreciable difference between them unless you looked in the region of the genitalia.

Mac could only think of Mogart's boast that only ten Eyes were needed to create an entire Alternative level—a whole universe!

And, counting his, there were ten now in this small space.

"Who are you?" he asked, guessing the answer.

"We are the Security Council of the Main Line," responded the one in the middle who had first spoken. "We are the heads of the nine colleges which make up the University. We are the ones who authorize the power jewels to be crafted, and the ones who authorize the creation and destruction of Alternatives." The demon looked him squarely in the eye. "We did not authorize you to have an Eye of Baal."

Mac Walters felt nervous panic rising inside him and fought to control it. "It's mine now! Ours! We went and got it! We worked for it! We *earned* it!"

The creature sighed. "Don't you think this godly horse-trading foolishness has gone far enough? Surely the lessons taught you in your experiences have demonstrated to the rational part of your mind that *no* single human being is capable of handling such power."

"*You* do," Mac responded defensively.

"We do not," the demon told him. "While we hold our positions we live together, eat together, sleep together, do all things together. We do this for a set period of time and then we surrender our power and position. And during this period of time when we *do* have the power, none of us can abuse it without being detected and corrected by the other eight." The creature looked down at the Eye dangling from the thick gold chain. "This is not power. This is *responsibility*. It is what we have and accept, and what you do not. It is why you must surrender the Eye to us, so that it might once more be split and returned to its owners —after those owners undergo a great deal of work and meditation to prove that they deserve it." A clawed hand reached out. "Give the Eye to me."

Walters stepped back a bit. "No! It's mine!"

The creature shook his head. "Why is it yours? More than hers? More than Mogart's? More than the owners of the original gems from which it was crafted?"

"It's mine because I have it," Mac responded defiantly. "Nobody has any right to take it from me!"

The leader sighed. "We can. You must know that, logically. As powerful and godlike as the Eye is, it is not limitless power. Two Eyes can undo one. You face nine. And your own actions prove your unworthiness to use it. Surely there is still a rational part of you that realizes that such power must corrupt the emotions of the wielder even as it did our brother Asmodeus and the woman beside you. Consider what you defy. Nine Eyes are fifty-four jewels in parallel series. Each jewel amplifies by a power of ten, and the efficiency is raised so that there is an additional factor of thirty-six. Ten to the ninetieth power. With one Eye you might rule a galaxy. With nine you might well create one."

There was dead silence, save for the now-gentle wind coming through the mountain passes. Jill McCulloch moved, turning to Mac Walters, who stood as if frozen, and gently removed the Eye from his hand. He offered no protest, although she sensed that he was not under any sort of spell of command. There was simply no purpose in making these creatures use that power. Turning once more, she walked to the creatures standing there in a line, just in front of the bar which had been so much the center of their existence recently, and handed the Eye of Baal to the leader. Then she looked into those incredibly wise and so very tired-looking eyes and asked the question that had to be asked.

"What is to become of our world—and of us?"

The leader's gaze showed deep compassion, compassion mixed with understanding for what they had been through, and why, and what they faced now. It was very different from the feelings generated by any of the other demons they had known. *We know,* it seemed to say. *We're only human, too.*

"When you wished Asmodeus to go to Hell, he naturally appeared immediately in the Board of Ethics hearing room at the University," the old one explained. "You see, Hell is a subjective place—and that was the place he feared the most. It was no trouble at all to get the story out of him—a bit one-sided, I will admit, but our devices were able to sort and balance. He's not really a bad man, you know. Despite his excesses, the similarity between what he would do with the Eye and what either of you would do is rather striking. He is, quite simply, human. That, of course, is the tragedy we all must bear."

They understood, she knew. Understood what it must be like to be just an ordinary individual in a multiplicity of universes where such power existed.

The leader read her thoughts. "He was a philosophy instructor. He was close to us, could see the sort of power being wielded and the type of people who decided it. Just people. Ordinary people, like himself. And he found others—five others—who felt the same, who craved the power and *knew* that they would be better gods than those who acted the part. Like prideful men for all time, they were well-meaning, utopian idealists, really. They really did think, in their conceit, that they would be better at it than we. Like you, they saw the power but did not comprehend the responsibility that goes with it, that must always be present so that the power can be used properly and with respect. They procured power jewels, supposedly to pursue minor projects on some of the neglected or abandoned areas. They were to meet later and fashion an Eye, thence to create their own visions."

All nine seemed to sigh in unison.

"But there were six such, of course, and their visions differed, even as two people look at the same flower and perceive different aspects of it. Each was trapped. They dared not join together because they were jealous and mistrustful of one another; they could not return to the University without their plot being unmasked—as now it has been. They became prisoners of their own scheme, trapped in their own petty greeds and ambitions in the backwaters of reality. Be not deceived by the manner of some of them. They were the five from whom you procured the jewels, and Asmodeus, of course. They have been trying to steal one another's amplifiers for tens of thousands of years now."

Mac Walters seemed to snap out of it. "But *this* is *our* reality," he pointed out, moving his arm in a sweeping gesture. "Desolation. Ruin. Death."

"What is done may be undone," the demon leader replied. "Not exactly, of course, but a close approximation. You wish this area—by which I mean this planet—restored. It is possible. But that is not the full answer to your question, nor can I give it. You must give it. Tell us—how would you wield the power of nine Eyes in regard to your own planet and also to yourselves?"

Jill looked at Mac and saw the same message on his face that she had on hers. "We fought—and killed— to save our world. For all that to mean anything at all, our world must be saved, restored. We realize that now."

"But your society had its evils; it was a race that lived in pain and faced new threats daily. Is this the society you would re-create?"

Mac stepped in. "I think we were fools," he admitted. "We were thinking of godhead and a land of pastoral peace. But such a land has no value if it is imposed from above and maintained by dictatorial power, no matter how benignly applied."

"The more I think of myself a few minutes ago, the more ashamed of myself I am," Jill added. "The first world I went to had this godlike morality, and it was a stagnant, dreary world. I should have remembered. The most perfect society that I saw was the valley I was forced to destroy, and it was not imposed, merely protected. Human beings created it. Not all that world, or all humanity, but it showed that such things are possible if people truly want them and work for them. That is the only enduring type of human utopia."

Mac Walters nodded in agreement. "I, too, saw an imposed, hierarchical society—and hated it, and hated you for imposing the limitations on those people. Now I see that I, too, was ready to do the same sort of thing here, to my own world. Like Jill, I feel a little ashamed of myself."

The demon leader smiled kindly. "Don't be ashamed, either of you, for you have learned some great lessons. You have gained a great wisdom that few would have received from your experiences, and that makes you greater than most human beings. Be proud, for in this moment you have shown yourselves greater than Asmodeus, who is unrepentant. In a few brief days and nights you have learned that millennia could not teach him. Your words gladden us and make our decisions much easier. Your world has been ignored, a backwater—but it did produce such as you. It will no longer be ignored."

"But Mogart said he shaped and trained us," Jill pointed out.

"False," exclaimed the demon leader. "One cannot teach an idiot to read, or a blind man color, or a deaf man a symphony. Mogart is all three. You are not. You are pupils who transcended your teacher."

Jill had a sudden thought. "The others—the ones between the planes, the alien enemy. They were active, very active in the world we left last. Something must be done to stop them."

"We have already considered the information, having drawn it from your minds and from a check of the five planes you visited. They are active *everywhere,* even here. You can never be rid of them or their threat. We are on guard, rest assured. But we learned other things from reading your accounts. A special quality you possess that is the prerequisite for true wisdom. You, McCulloch, upset over the stagnancy of one society and remorseful in the extreme over the deaths of innocents you were forced to carry out. And you, Walters, upset at us for retarding a world that means nothing to you—and taking precious time to get one of our own, whom you had no cause to like or to help, to safety on another plane. That quality is compassion."

The demon looked around once, as if surveying the scene. "It grows late. This is business that takes up far too much of our time. There are over six thousand Alternatives and over seventy trillion projects. We can dwell here no longer. It is time. A consensus is easily reached."

Mac and Jill looked at the nine expectantly, a little hesitantly.

"Hear our words. What if the trajectory of the object had been altered, not for collision, but in the same manner opposite to collision? It would have been captured by the sun at a slower speed and drawn inward to burn. We reach back to that point and make the adjustment *so!*"

Nothing seemed to happen, except that the nine froze for a moment, as if suddenly turned to stone. That state lasted only a few seconds, and then they were once again filled with life.

"It will take weeks for the temporal ripple to reach us here in the present and make the correction," the demon leader explained. "Time is variable but moves in each Alternative in a prescribed manner. I fear you will have a few weeks to yourselves here, unclothed and alone. The castle, I fear, must go." As the creature uttered the words, the castle with its columns, fountains, and flowers vanished.

The creature looked around. "In the ruins here you will find enough food and shelter to keep you until the temporal adjustment is made."

"Then we are to go back," Jill sighed.

The leader nodded. "Back, yes, but not as you were. Never as you were. If these bodies please you more than the ones you had, you may keep them. The only valuable things in a human being are his mind and soul."

Mac laughed. "They won't even recognize us like this," he thought aloud. "But I guess, looking like this, we won't have any trouble finding some kind of place."

"You have a place," the demon replied. "And a job, too. As I told you, Asmodeus is unrepentant. He forfeits his right to a jewel. The others—well, we must see. But this is now too interesting and valuable a world to abandon. There is too much potential here. You have demonstrated your courage and your resourcefulness. You know the danger and the true enemy. You know how to use the jewel. You are now our representatives here—and you will have to observe and report to us. You will be busy. The social scientists in particular will be coming in and out of here in droves after this report is filed, and they will need assistance."

Both of them gasped. "You're giving *us* jewels?"

"Not jewels—one. One shared between you. Asmodeus's former jewel, once we get this Eye broken up and retune its sensitivities from him to you. Once it is returned—in about a month or so, your time—one of us will be back to give it to you and instruct you in its fine points. It will be attuned so that only the two of you together can use it, neither of you separately. It is quite a responsibility. Do you accept it?"

Jill gripped Mac's hand tightly in hers and looked into his face. "Well? What do you say?"

He grinned at her. "What a team we're going to make!"

They turned back to face the nine, but the creatures were gone. There was only the warming sun, the gentle breeze, and the ruins of Reno.

Mac looked at the bar, which had, miraculously, remained standing through it all.

"I think I need a drink," he said lightly. "Shall we celebrate?"

Jill laughed and linked her arm into his. "Let's!

We've got a little time to get to know each other better!"

They had only a few more minor problems. One was that reality caught up with them in a little under three weeks, and another was that the University didn't get around to them for almost three months.

The demons never did have a proper concept of time.

Epilogue

Naked Couple Arrested on I-80

by Michael Walsh
Reno *Sun-Times* Correspondent

RENO, Oct. 4. Tourists and locals were startled early today when a nude man and woman appeared in the median strip of I-80 just off the Sparks exit. The couple "just seemed to appear out of nowhere," rush-hour eyewitnesses swore.

"They seemed as surprised as we were," averred Joe Mayhew, a former Catholic seminarian. "That's true enough," agreed Trooper L. Fred Ramsey, who was giving Mayhew a ticket at the time. "They just sort of appeared, *kerplop,* in the median and looked around, kinda dazed. Then they started laughing and hugging and kissing each other like mad. Needless to say, I got out there in a hurry. Damn near got run down. Traffic was tied up for miles."

At least seven fender-benders are attributed to the exhibitionist couple.

Neither of the two could explain why or how they were there, and both refused to identify themselves other than by their first names, Mac and Jill. "They were stinko on something," Trooper Ramsey told the *Sun-Times*.

Both the man and woman were described by everyone as stunning in appearance, almost like classical Greek sculptures of the gods by Michelangelo. This reporter can attest to that fact, having attended their preliminary hearing.

Chemical tests proved negative, and the pair are now being held for psychiatric evaluation. Several casino owners have offered them bail and a job, and they are said to be considering the offers.

About the Author

JACK L. CHALKER was born in Norfolk, Virginia on December 17, 1944, but was raised and has spent most of his life in Baltimore, Maryland. He learned to read almost from the moment of entering school, and by working odd jobs had amassed a large book collection by the time he was in junior high school, a collection now too large for containment in his present quarters. Science fiction, history, and geography all fascinated him early on, interests which continue.

Chalker joined the Washington Science Fiction Association in 1958 and began publishing an amateur SF journal, *Mirage*, in 1960. After high school he decided to be a trial lawyer, but money problems and the lack of a firm caused him to switch to teaching. He holds B.S. degrees in history and English, and an M.L.A. from the Johns Hopkins University. He taught history and geography in the Baltimore public schools between 1966 and 1978, and now makes his living as a freelance writer. Additionally, out of the amateur journals he founded a publishing house, The Mirage Press, Ltd., devoted to nonfiction and bibliographic works on science fiction and fantasy. This company has produced more than twenty books in the last nine years. His hobbies include esoteric audio, travel, working on science-fiction convention committees, and guest lecturing on SF to institutions like the Smithsonian. He is an active conservationist and National Parks supporter, and he has an intensive love of ferryboats, with the avowed goal of riding every ferry in the world. In fact, in 1978, he was married to Eva Whitley on an ancient ferryboat in midriver. The Chalkers live in the Catoctin Mountain region of western Maryland.

ANNE McCAFFREY

LEIGH
BRACKETT